The Violet Hour

Katherine Hill

PENGUIN BOOKS

PENGUIN BOOKS

UK | USA | Canada | Ireland | Australia
India | New Zealand | South Africa

Penguin Books is part of the Penguin Random House group of companies
whose addresses can be found at global.penguinrandomhouse.com.

First published in the United States of America by Simon & Schuster 2013
First published in Great Britain by Viking 2014
Published in Penguin Books 2015
001

Printed in Great Britain by Clays Ltd, St Ives plc

A CIP catalogue record for this book is available from the British Library

ISBN: 978–0–241–96413–2

for my parents

I Tiresias, though blind, throbbing between two lives,
Old man with wrinkled female breasts, can see
At the violet hour . . .

—T. S. Eliot, *The Waste Land*

The rarer action is
In virtue than in vengeance.

—William Shakespeare, *The Tempest*

The Violet Hour

Prologue

For a moment that afternoon, it was only woman and water, the bay in all its sickening glory squaring itself for a fight. The waves flexed before her, muscly and ultramarine. The wind taunted her, whapping strands of hair across her Vaselined lips, where they stuck, and stuck again, no matter how many times she brushed them free. Spray flew, the shoreline canted—the whole scene smacked of chaos—and above the sails, large plates of cloud shifted tectonically, exposing a lethal sun.

Cassandra was no seafarer. That was Abe, who'd loved the water since childhood. They'd bought this boat because he'd always wanted one, and because she felt compelled to make concessions. It was only her second time joining him, and though the first had passed without incident, she was still in the process of gaining her sea legs. For now they seemed to work best when they were idle. So with a gin and tonic sweating anxiously in her hand, and an invisible coating of sunblock thick as paint across her face, she reclined on the cushioned bench in the stern, her feet crossed, then uncrossed, then crossed again at the ankle.

She tried to suppress her nausea, even tried to enjoy the nodding of the boat on the water, the congratulatory slapping of waves on its back. When they passed beneath the Bay Bridge she looked up into its belly, where triangle trusses pointed toward land like floor lights on an airplane, illuminating the emergency exits. As long as they sailed during the day, with the shoreline always in sight, she knew she could be strong. The open sea was another story, wider and deeper than all of human civilization, with levels ever rising. There was a time when the mere proximity of the ocean had thrilled her, its color and moisture a fresh discovery, as though she were a pioneer at the end of a punishing journey overland. She used to love the way the water merged with the sky, blue asserting itself as the most dominant color in nature. It used to make her feel very powerful. Now it only made her feel frail.

Of course these days, she saw her weaknesses everywhere she went. They leapt out at her from newspaper stories of distant atrocities she'd done nothing to prevent, and from the dusty, neglected corners of her studio at home. And the truth was, she *was* frail. Not yet in body. Her body still worked quite well. But in judgment. How else to explain Vince Hersh: thirty-one and broad, if not quite handsome, a rambunctious clown in bed. She hadn't intended to sleep with him, at least not the first time. Yet through some weakness she'd given in, then through some other weakness gone back for more. Even breaking it off had been a weak decision, made in fear of getting caught. He owned a fashionable gallery in Oakland, a slick place where Cassandra never felt she really belonged. But he'd chosen one of her pieces, and then he'd chosen her. She gripped the rail now as they bounced through choppy water, amazed at how life had surprised her. She'd been an adulteress, a slave to sensation. With her husband she owned a sloop.

The affair was beyond her comprehension but she was trying her best to understand the boat. Abe's white, perpendicular pet, with all its funny parts: fairleads, halyards, jib, boom. On this late June afternoon, she wore mirrored sunglasses, a canvas hat, and a thick belted cardigan to keep her warm. In a brave attempt to relax, she left her shoes belowdecks.

"Elizabeth!" she called as they neared shore to drop anchor for a while. "Come take some more sunblock!" She set her glass in a cup holder and reached for the tube in her bag.

Her daughter climbed down from the prow in a bikini so red it was almost patriotic. As a child, she'd been fair like her mother, but now, at eighteen, she'd suddenly managed a buttery tan. Cassandra hardly recognized her. "I don't need any more," Elizabeth said, checking an arm. "Daddy's genes have finally reported for duty."

Cassandra looked at her husband, who was bronze, and always seemed to need less than she did—less sunblock, less affirmation, less risk. He had the wheel in one hand, his gin and tonic in the other, and a volume of Borges waiting on the bench. He liked his drink, and occasionally his dope, but really he was addicted to reading. He spent hours at it every night in bed, illumined by a slim, bending lamp, growing melancholy as he neared a book's end, as though some part of him were ending, too. He was now almost done with the fatly collected Borges, yet this time he appeared unfazed, as though he hadn't really been reading it, only giving each page some air. Something was bothering him, something he probably had to work out for himself. She'd learned years ago not to pester him when he fell into one of his moods.

"I'm not sure it works like that," Cassandra said to Elizabeth. "I think it probably has more to do with the ozone and the time of year you got your first exposure to the sun. You were in Mexico in March."

"Then here's my other theory. Beer. I've had more beer this year than any other. I think it might've altered my body's chemistry. Made me more susceptible to tanning." She couldn't suppress her laugh—rational, honest Elizabeth.

"That's ridiculous. It's the ozone."

"Mom. It was a joke." She shook her head and went off to assist with the approach.

Elizabeth knew a few sailors at her school, blond, beach-club types in polo shirts, their collars popped unnaturally toward the sky. She found them vaguely preposterous, and was likewise suspicious of sailing. It's not about who does it now, Abe had told her, it's about how it used to be: John Smith, Columbus, Odysseus, Noah! So what? she'd protested. Everyone in history sailed, from the famous to the forgotten. Exactly, Abe told her, his point.

Nevertheless, as first mate, she'd learned gamely, scrambling for the lines according to the wind, and lowering the anchor as she did now, according to her father's direction. Already she was a pro. The anchor secured, Elizabeth began to circle the deck, checking on various knots.

In the welcome calm, Cassandra allowed herself the pleasure of marveling at her daughter, as adept at sailing as she seemed to be at all things. How different she was—what complete faith she had in herself. Cassandra could hardly wear a bikini when she was her age, much less buy one, yet here was Elizabeth in magnificent tatters, apparently not even cold. She was going to college in the fall— Harvard. The word still gave Cassandra a little thrill every time she saw it printed on a piece of their mail. She'd done it. She'd given her vocationally trained parents a Harvard-bound grandchild, the icing atop their second-generation American cake.

Elizabeth's tan legs returned now and walked up the deck. They stepped onto the port gunwale, then up to the guardrail above it, balancing precariously as if on a tightrope, and an instant later, had sprung, splayed and fearless, into the freezing bay.

"Your sister's a regular circus artist," Cassandra whispered to Ferdinand, the Portuguese water dog, who had come to rest his brown head in her lap.

"An artist?" Abe asked from his bench.

Over the years Cassandra's art was one of the few things that had given him hope when doctoring turned gloomy. It was incredible, the things she could make for no other reason than she wanted to. Abe was a rheumatologist, and his patients, beset with lupus, osteoporosis, and debilitating strains of arthritis, were people in great pain. They came lumbering in with walkers wide as doors, fat ankles spilling out over their shoes like muffin tops. They had hunchbacks and butterfly-shaped rashes across their cheeks and bodies as brittle as glass. After two decades of approximate science—"How much does it hurt, on a scale of one to ten?"—inconclusive labs— "Your blood work shows no evidence of the rheumatoid factor, but of course twenty percent of patients never do"—and infinitesimal changes in dose yielding negligible changes in pain, he was encouraged that his wife saw a different future for their daughter. At least with art, it was possible to lose yourself in beauty, to forget for a moment that life was mostly brutal and unfair. At least with art, one did not have to look a thirty-three-year-old mother of four in the eye and tell her that thanks to some inexplicable, overzealous urge of the immune system—genetic, hormonal, he couldn't say why—she had suffered irreversible damage, the cartilage having almost completely worn away, the pain destined only to increase.

"I've just been thinking about Elizabeth," Cassandra told him, caressing Ferdinand's ears. "Everything keeps coming so naturally to her. She's a teenager; she ought to be tormented. But she's not. She's a regular magician."

"And that makes her an artist how?"

Cassandra looked out over the wrinkled water, which seemed as fruitless in its journey as they sometimes were in conversation. Abe awaited his wife's response, his finger calmly marking his page.

"*Circus* artist," she said, hearing this second time how stupid her comment had been.

"Ah. Because of the way she was standing on the rail . . ." His voice trailed off. "Remember that play she did in the hall? With Jessica? And those togas they had to keep gathering at their knees to keep from tripping? It was very witty."

Cassandra remembered the play for other reasons, but in many ways she preferred Abe's version of the past. "She was in middle school. Can you believe that's already five years ago?"

"Good God, what happened?" he asked. "How did we let her get away with this?"

She laughed, and in that moment of sweet understanding, she felt she ought to tell him about Vince, that he'd forgive her and pull her to his chest as he'd so often done when they were young. If there was one thing she'd loved about their marriage back then, it was the freedom they'd felt to be honest. She could tell him when he'd been hurtful, and he would hear her, and try to change. She could confess her own transgressions, and be forgiven and even understood. It would take more effort to be honest with him now, and Cassandra couldn't quite bring herself to do it. She shook the ice cubes in her glass as he stood to fuss with a line.

Most things about her husband now were firm: his reason, his resolve, his rules. Even, at forty-seven, his body, with its extraordinarily durable bones. He knew and sometimes overestimated his strength, imagining himself armored by his scrappy layered heritage—German Jewish, Italian, Scotch-Irish, African. Abe himself was inscrutably tan, which seemed to give him permission to disappear in any crowd. He watched the white sails ahead of them shrinking toward the bowing bridge and wondered how many outings it would take before Cassandra would be ready for the ocean. It still disappointed him that she, who'd never really lost someone, could be so frightened of the truest, greatest things.

Suddenly restless, Ferdinand lifted his head from Cassandra's lap and vigorously shook himself out. He circled a few times, then went straight for Abe's leg, which he thumped against with a sigh. Cassandra clucked her tongue and retrieved an apple from the snack cooler as Elizabeth reappeared on the boat. Funny the things that bugged her: Elizabeth's tan, Ferdinand's loyalty. She felt the onset of a dangerous feeling and, biting into the apple, tried to chew the feeling away.

"Hey, toss me a towel, will you?" Elizabeth stood, shivering, a weed coiled around her ankle, her bathing suit heavy and dark. She pulled the corners of her top down over her goose-bumped breasts.

Cassandra did, and Elizabeth cloaked herself, blotting her limbs and the seat of her suit. With a twist and a squeeze, water streamed from her hair to the deck.

"Daredevil." Cassandra held out Elizabeth's hooded sweatshirt. "How was it?"

"Cold!" She wrapped the towel around her waist and pulled the sweatshirt over her head, teeth chattering in confirmation, her shoulders hunched, her face now a lavender-gray. "Too cold for you, Mom. But not too cold for Dad!"

"It's probably too warm for Dad," Abe said, happy to extend the myth of his stoicism. Like Cassandra's effortless hair and Elizabeth's effortless grades, it was part of their sense of themselves as a family, another facet of their specialness. They would never be some great, big powerful clan—the Rosenbergs, the Kerrys, the Poznanski boys who all played football—but in some ways they were more special because they were just the three. A family rendered in its most essential, basic parts: mother, father, child.

Elizabeth pulled up the anchor and joined Cassandra on the bench. She was nearing the limit of her patience with parents. "When do you think we'll head back?" she asked, once they were under way again.

"An hour maybe," Abe said. "Too pleasant to turn in just yet."

Elizabeth sighed. "Not too much longer, okay? I want to meet up with some people tonight."

"What people?" Cassandra always wanted to know, to imagine the scene.

"The same ones who are always there . . . Rachel, Jessica, Brian . . . Henri."

"Henri? Do I know him?"

"He's just this diplomat kid. We've been hanging out a few months. He's friends with the guys."

"That's an old-fashioned kind of name." This was Abe, from the wheel.

"Whatever, so's Abraham."

"But I'm a boring, middle-aged dad. I'm supposed to be old-fashioned. How old is this poor Henri?"

"What does *that* matter?" Elizabeth asked, her cheeks a sudden pink.

Abe's eyes met Cassandra's. He hadn't expected this.

"Don't be running around with older boys, Lizzie," he said, trying to keep his tone light. "You don't want that kind of trouble."

"Dad!" She laughed. "I'm going to college! All the boys will be older in college."

"Hmm, might want to rethink that, too."

"Daddy!"

"Just be careful." He cleared his throat. "That's all I'm saying."

Elizabeth flushed again, irritated at her father's sudden seriousness. "Of course I'm careful. I'm not an idiot. I can handle myself with anyone. Doesn't matter if he's eighteen or twenty-three."

Cassandra winced. "Is that how old he is—twenty-three? Honey." She leaned forward to look her daughter in the eye. "Are you dating this boy?"

"No! . . . I mean, not necessarily . . ."

"Christ." Abe swung the boat sharply, getting in line with the wind.

"He's a really good person! His age doesn't matter!"

"Easy, Abe!" Cassandra clutched the handrail and her hat.

Elizabeth pulled her orange-and-white striped towel tighter around her hips. She hadn't intended for it to come out like this, if at all. But now that it had, she couldn't let them get all worked up, absurdly imagining him to be some kind of predator.

"He's actually about to start a Ph.D. in French colonial literature," she told them. "He knows people who have worked in clinics in Africa, and he knows a *lot* about wine. Like, maybe even more than you."

Abe gave a humorless laugh.

"Not so fast, Abe!" Cassandra's stomach dropped. "You're scaring me!"

"Oh, for God's sake, Cassandra, it's called *sailing*."

"You guys should meet him," Elizabeth said. They were all slantwise and speaking louder at their brisk new clip. "I'm not saying I'm going to marry him or anything, but I think you'd both really like him." She felt mature, idly talking to her parents about a man.

"Elizabeth," Abe said. "I'm not making any judgments about him. I just don't want you to have any illusions. Don't be thinking you're going to lose your virginity to some romantic Frenchman."

He had never mentioned her virginity before. The word on his lips was mortifying.

"Well," she said, as everything flapped, the sails above them full. "That's not going to happen."

It wasn't going to happen because it had already happened, at a party the previous fall. Zach Lando: white rapper, baggy shorts, large nipples. Flat on her back on a blanket in the woods, dead beetles crunching dirt underneath. Afterward, they'd smoked a joint, and she'd pretended nothing had hurt. "You'll hate me in a few days," he'd said. He was right.

"Good," Abe said, feeling even more unsettled than before.

Cassandra had grown silent. Her daughter was having sex. There was a moment in the recent past when it had begun, and somehow, in her selfishness, she'd looked away and missed it. She reached for Elizabeth's hand. "You're being safe, of course?"

"Mom!" Elizabeth cried. "Of course!"

Abe's brow grew moist and hot. His lip twitched, and he suddenly felt he couldn't control the muscles of his face. His glass was already empty, his throat constricted and dry. They were all crowded so close to one another, and he needed something to drink.

He left the wheel with Elizabeth and went below to the galley. Over the aluminum sink, he measured out a generous portion of gin, adding ice and only a splash of tonic. He sipped, allowing it to burn slowly down his throat. Through the porthole, he could see Elizabeth at the wheel: a sweatshirt with two legs, her towel having dropped to the deck. Cassandra stood beside her, an arm around their daughter's waist. She leaned in and whispered something in Elizabeth's ear. They laughed, like schoolgirls conspiring. His beautiful redheads. He remembered a time when he thought it dangerous to have a wife this beautiful. Like opening your wallet on the street, you were just asking for someone to rob you. In the old days, when he took her to bed at the end of a long day apart, he was reckless, sometimes tearing buttons from her shirts. If he wanted her so badly, he could only imagine how other men felt, who couldn't have her at all.

This was the last of the gin, and still, he needed more. He had not yet begun to feel light.

"Cass!" he called from the hatch. "Where's the—wine?" He shuddered, thinking again of Elizabeth's Frenchman.

"Just have some gin!"

"None left!"

"What?" Her voice was small and resonant as though she were speaking from inside a tunnel.

"None left!" He stepped up for her to hear.

"*None?* Abe, I was saving that!" She came toward him, tentatively, bracing herself on the rails.

"Then don't tell me to drink it." He held up the empty bottle for her to see.

"Where'd it go?" The wind rushed past her ears, whipping her hair into her mouth, forcing her to continue shouting, though she was now face-to-face with him at the hatch.

"I think we *drank it,*" he said, growing impatient with her refusal to comprehend.

"But it was half full. God, are you really such a *pig?*"

She was teasing, and didn't mean the word in anger. But her body, which had betrayed her before, betrayed her yet again. With the gin, and the wind, and the faintest hint of seasickness rising, Cassandra's mouth had been growing drier and phlegmier all day, and though she had not quite realized it before, it became apparent to them both in that moment, when, on the sharp, punchy syllable "pig," she accidentally spat in his face.

"Well," he said, wiping the bubbles of saliva from his cheek, even as they evaporated.

"Oh, Jesus." She touched his shoulder. "I'm sorry." Cassandra was expert at apologies. They often leapt off her tongue before she fully knew what she'd done wrong.

"Well," he said again, more acutely this time, suddenly aware of everything. "Why don't you just go fuck Vincent Hersh."

She was stunned. "Who?" she asked, instinctively, withdrawing her hand, hoping she'd somehow misheard.

The wind slowed and Abe found himself wanting to strangle her. She'd been sleeping with the kid. He'd known this, he realized, for weeks. The way he'd singled her out at the opening. How happy she'd been. He'd had all the clues, yet remained somehow stumped, like a foggy-brained Scrabble player unable to unscramble his letters. He'd kept himself in the fog, making nonwords, not wanting to believe her betrayal. But with the spit, it was as though the fog had lifted and the tiles finally clicked into place. He felt he could squeeze her throat until her face turned blue.

"Don't deny it," he said. "I know."

Her eyes watered; she was guilty. She couldn't have looked guiltier if he'd caught the two of them in bed. "Abe. I didn't—"

"Jesus Christ, Cassandra, I know you did!"

"Listen, Abe—"

"No, *you* listen," he roared. "Fuck. You. Really, Cassandra. *Fuck. You.*"

"Daddy!" Elizabeth reproved him, her voice breaking in panic.

A moment ago, she hadn't known a thing, and now she knew too much, as though she'd grown up in a matter of seconds. She wanted to rewind, to stuff all she'd learned back in its bottle and toss it overboard and never have to see it again. She wanted that, but she knew it was impossible. Her father had unleashed the *fuck*. For her family, saying *fuck* was less like opening a bottle than like turning on a broken faucet. The *fuck*s would continue to pour out, limitless, insensible to the damage they caused.

"No, fuck *you*!" Cassandra cried, suddenly enraged. "Fuck you for always making me feel like *shit*!"

Worse things were said, things that might have been funny in another situation, but in this moment meant the end of the world. Abe was dead inside; Cassandra was an unrepentant whore. They hated each other and pronounced it with glee. They flung their words violently, ungrammatically. They scrunched their faces like babies, tears spilling down their noses and cheeks, their voices oscillating wildly, covering every decibel of rage. Elizabeth stood clutching the wheel, watching her parents completely break down. They'd been known to shout, but this was worse than any shouting they'd ever done before. This was practically unrealistic. People wouldn't believe it had happened this way if she tried to tell the story later; they'd say she had forgotten something, left a crucial detail out. Perhaps they'd be right; perhaps she would; perhaps she was already erasing it as it occurred, saying no to a life of hysteria, turning their insanity away at the door.

Fuck fuck fuck fuck fuck fuck fuck. Was she even there? Could they even see her? Elizabeth steered deaf through the tempest, heading for the marina as if for safety, as if she believed their fury, like a fish, couldn't survive on land.

And then, suddenly, her mother was sitting, gripping the bench with her fingertips, and her father was standing, purposefully, on the very edge of the starboard gunwale. They were silent under the noise of the wind. And then her mother stood and started to say something, and her father turned his back and dove. His body was in the air for an instant over the water, and then, as if by some camera trick, there was nothing but water and air. They rushed to the sides, looking everywhere, until a moment later he surfaced, already behind them, his head bobbing up and down in the waves, his arms stretching in sequence, one after the other, pulling for the shore.

"Stop the boat!" her mother cried. "Turn it around!"

Elizabeth ran back to the wheel. The wind seemed to be coming from all directions; she didn't know which way to turn.

"I have to think!" she yelled. "I've never done this alone!" She looked at the horizon and at the other boats for help. Ferdinand was barking at the water on the side where her dad had jumped and her mother continued to shout at her, or maybe at her dad, though he wasn't responding in any case. He was swimming away from them, and making it look ordinary, growing smaller and smaller against the rumpled sheet of blue.

Which left her mother, barefoot and stricken on the deck, and herself, a sudden grown-up, in charge of getting them home.

A moment passed. Maybe a year. Maybe she'd already graduated from Harvard and these weren't her parents at all.

Remembering the motor, she turned it on, and the horizon steadied itself into recognizable layers of sky, land, and water. There: something to hold on to. She clung with every particle of her eye. In her ears was an awful empty sound where the wind had been. Even Ferdinand no longer barked.

"I'm sorry, sweetie," Cassandra said finally, having come to stand by her side.

"It's okay," Elizabeth told her, because it wasn't worth it to say much else. "Do you think Dad's going to swim the whole way?"

"He'll make it."

"Are you sure?"

"He's an excellent swimmer."

"Then I guess we ought to head back."

"Yes," Cassandra said. "Thank you. I love you."

"Sure, Mom. I love you, too."

IN THE BAY, Abe swam full on toward the trees. He wasn't far from the coast—a mile maybe, no more. There were small sharks in these waters. He'd seen them when they surfaced, but he didn't care. They could eat his legs if they wanted. In his rage, he'd outswim them anyway. With each stroke he felt he was shedding an atom of his accumulated anger, replacing it with an icy atom of the sea. He breathed in brine: it seeped through his pores. His eyes became silty pebbles; bay grass overtook the straining bands of muscle in his arms; his heart became the heart of a halibut: flattened, bottom-dwelling, varying its color in vibration with the earth.

When he washed up on the marshy shore ages later, Abe crawled, insensibly, to higher ground, and slept, his cheek in the mud, sludge filling his ear. A salt marsh harvest mouse and a pair of brown pelicans looked on, a tuft of glasswort in the mouse's paw, the pelicans' mouths open wide and empty. Endangered species too, they were no strangers to a sea change. They stood crouched on opposite sides of the shivering man, as if wondering what he was. Beads of water clung to his surface and the grass around him shifted while the pelicans regarded each other with elongated beaks. After a space of time they seemed to reach an agreement and scuttled off. The mouse remained a moment longer, chewing on the last of his glasswort. When he was done, he sniffed the man once more in case he harbored some morsel of food. Finding nothing, he made for the water. A third pelican was not far behind, taking flight in preparation for a dive.

Part I

1

Elizabeth's friend Lucie was getting married in Battery Park, at a venue she'd chosen for its geography: the tip-of-the-island panoramic views of New York Harbor, with the Statue of Liberty and Ellis Island looking on. "I mean, it's only a restaurant," Lucie had said when she'd settled on the spot, nearly a year before. "Nothing extravagant. But the food is legitimately excellent, plus it's all bright white and airy, and they'll do a great big tent on the terrace."

"I just hope I'm not on call," Elizabeth had told her, having no idea yet what her fourth year of medical school would be like.

The day had arrived, a muggy Saturday at the end of August, and Elizabeth was available, having arranged her schedule to give herself a little vacation the following week. She had friends who'd recently returned from Turks and Caicos, others from Paris and London. Several of her former Harvard classmates were doing significant things in Beijing and Rio and Mumbai. One poet—a poet!—was even on a Fulbright in Nepal. She herself had done a service trip to South Africa the summer after her first year of medical school, but no glamorous destination awaited her this week. This week, she was taking her boyfriend, Kyle, to Maryland for her grandfather's eightieth birthday party. Labor Day weekend they would take off for some cabin in Connecticut that Kyle had found online. Her plans couldn't have been tamer, but maybe this year tame would be okay.

Kyle showed up at her apartment that afternoon carrying a hiker's pack and a garment bag and smelling, almost magically through his sweat, of grassy, spring-scented soap. His face was angular, football handsome, and he looked so much like a dozen different celebrities that it seemed inevitable he'd be famous one day, too. An actor, he was constantly in plays, both in New York and on the road. For a long time, his biggest break had been playing a first-time home buyer in a national ad for life insurance, but in a few weeks, he'd be auditioning for a handful of guest roles, most of them cops, on a long-running network crime series. He'd been fired up about it for days.

"Ready for our little adventure?" he asked, dumping his things on the floor.

"Oh, let's see. I'm half-packed, unshowered, and I have no idea what I'm wearing."

"I thought you bought a new dress."

"I did, but the fabric's a little heavy and with the humidity I'm worried I'll be miserable."

"Let me see." He settled into the couch.

She brought it out, a dusky blue sheath with an embellished bust that shriveled into itself on the hanger. "You have to see it on," she explained, hurrying out of her shorts and T-shirt. The crisp, shimmery fabric stretched across her body, ruching at the waist and along her thighs. She'd gotten it at a sample sale and had since seen photos of a television actress who was attempting to transition into movies wearing it at a major premiere. It was amusing to think of herself in the same pool with people who lived in the public eye, and yet, why not? After Harvard and all its dead presidents, the center of the world didn't feel so out of reach. She swam through it every day in New York.

"You can walk in that?"

"That's the beauty of it, it stretches." She lunged at him to prove it.

He whistled, and launched into an Appalachian drawl. "Wull awl *be!*" Kyle was a constant actor, regularly answering her in character.

"Don't tell me: *Deliverance: The Musical.*"

"I wish! Someone is doing a musical of *Caligula,* though. That's one workshop I would've loved to have been in on."

He spoke with his usual male confidence—as though he'd just catch the next train that came along—and yet in her chest she experienced a little wing flap of despair. In his profession, the missed opportunities were so endless it was almost unbearable. What would work out, what wouldn't—you could never really tell. She pressed a hand to her breast; she would rather talk about anything else.

"See what I mean, though, about the fabric?" she said. "I don't think it's going to breathe. Stupid Lucie and her outdoor wedding."

All of a sudden, he stood. He'd alternated between wide receiver and free safety on his college team, and he tackled her now, in that performance-minded way that he had: expressive face, explosive body, a target always in mind. She howled and clutched at the dress.

"Lizzie," he said, after they'd landed on the couch. "You're crazy. You have to wear it. You look unbelievably hot."

He was strong, and he was so certain. He had told her, early on, that he'd always known he wouldn't play professional football, even before he'd chosen a liberal arts college in Minnesota with thoughtful seminars and Division III sports. It was too much work, and too much punishment for something that was only a game. She believed in him. Of course she did. But she also wondered what he thought acting was.

THE AIR-CONDITIONING wasn't working in their cab, a defect their driver didn't admit until they were already moving, when it would've been awkward and rude and a waste of time and money to get out. Resigned, they opened their windows, which brought some relief once they got going. Kyle loosened his collar and held his jacket in his lap. Elizabeth propped an elbow in the open window and stretched her other arm across the seat back, vainly hoping to keep her underarms dry. She got out of the cab readjusting her hair, already feeling a little deflated, her forehead gluey with powder and sweat.

In the entryway, they were greeted by a marble table of tented place cards, bivouacked around a heavy glass tower that erupted with flowers at the top.

"Show me the money," Kyle whispered.

"So much for not extravagant." She held up their card, letter-pressed in a convoluted script.

He pantomimed a squint. "I can't entirely make it out, but I think it's telling me to get a real job."

She patted his arm in solace, half ironic, half sincere. With the help of the staff standing guard, they meandered through empty dining rooms to the terrace, where the sailcloth tent Lucie had promised stood ready to embark on the evening. On an adjacent green, white folding chairs awaited the ceremony. Elizabeth's friends were standing around a section of seats in their sunglasses, making good use of the bottled water and paper fans someone had thought to provide. She'd seen almost all of them at the bar the night before, which was fortunate, because sober hugging in such weather was the last thing any of them wanted to do. Friendly but subdued greetings were exchanged all around. They were friends of the couple from Harvard, some married, most not, all of them looking forward to the moment when the drinking could begin.

Seeing the place card in Elizabeth's hand, Jane Donaughey, more Lucie's friend than Elizabeth's, waved her own and exclaimed, "Aren't they so elegant?" She'd played field hockey in college and had the relentlessly chipper affect of a woman who'd been getting manicures from an early age. Talking to her invariably wore Elizabeth out. "And the table names are really inspired."

"Oh, I hadn't even looked." Elizabeth opened her card. She tried not to wince as she read it: *Table 7, The Great Gatsby*.

"All their favorite novels," Jane explained. Lucie and Rob were getting doctorates—hers in education, his in comparative literature—

and were fond of recommending books. "Such a nice little touch. Of course, *we* know they love books, but I wouldn't have guessed *Infinite Jest*!" Jane held up her own card, grinning, and Elizabeth was momentarily relieved they weren't sitting at the same table. Jane was single. Conventionally pretty, good-humored and talented—yet single. She was rather publicly on the hunt for a husband, and as far as Elizabeth could tell, she never stopped being excited for her happily coupled friends. It distressed Elizabeth to listen to her praise a wedding's little touches—Jane, who advised multinational health care firms as a well-paid midtown consultant.

Jane turned to the next willing listener just as a small feminine hand clasped Elizabeth's. "Are you a Gatsby, too?" This was Becca, her closest friend after Lucie. Becca was also single, but proud of it. Bets had already been placed on which cousin she'd be taking home.

"I'm a Gatsby," Elizabeth said.

"Hooray. Why do you think she gave us that one?"

"Mmm, because our voices are full of money?" The one line she was proud to remember from the book.

Becca threw her head back. "Ha! Hardly." She wrote for a political magazine in DC, where her bosses regularly encouraged her to get a book deal rather than offering her a raise. "No, now that I think about it, it's her favorite. After *Invisible Man*, which probably wouldn't have been appropriate for a wedding."

"Oh, and Gatsby's appropriate? The desperate mansion-builder?"

"Well. Lucie's nothing if not self-aware."

Elizabeth tried to remember this about her friend as the women in headsets came around to ask them to take their seats. They sat, all two hundred of them, Elizabeth and Kyle on the coveted aisle. Silent cheers went up from their section as Chris, a Google programmer and the previous night's sloppiest drunk, scuttled in at the last possible moment, miming headache and taking a solo seat in the rear. Bystanders had gathered in the neighboring park, and soon the quartet began to play, pulling the wedding party out of the restaurant and down the aisle in turn. First, with the assistance of cousins, came her tiny, turtle grandparents, then his, astonishingly all still alive, a complete generation that Elizabeth's family tree had never known. Then the siblings, bridesmaids and groomsmen, the girls dressed tastefully—maybe too tastefully—in long black satin with cowls draping at their backs. Then Rob, escorted by his parents, who were divorced, but smiled amiably as they processed.

Finally, they all rose, the skin on Elizabeth's thighs pulling painfully from her seat, as the bride and her parents made their way toward the crowd of well-wishers and digital cameras. Lucie looked taller, and it wasn't from her shoes. She'd always known how to treat an occasion. The dress, which Elizabeth had seen at an early fitting, was structured at the bodice, flowing in the skirt, and not what she would have chosen, though she could see now in its fully tailored state how well it suited her long-torsoed friend.

The reception tent billowed expectantly in the hot breeze as the congregation turned to face the wedding party. Elizabeth's mind tended to wander whenever things got serious and ritualistic, but she tried her best to pay attention now. She clicked her heels together and stared straight ahead, while Kyle, the romantic, reached over to take her hand. In the harbor, a pair of bright white sails sidled up as if they'd been paid to complete the scene.

Though she hadn't said so to anyone, not even Kyle, Elizabeth was hurt not to be a more intimate part of her best friend's ceremony. Family bonds were strong, she knew, but the sight, from ten rows back, of Lucie's stately family and Rob's fractured but good-humored one coming together for this one event only made her feel even further away from the most important moments in life.

How could her own parents ever walk her down an aisle? It was unthinkable. They led entirely separate lives. Even from the other side of the country, she now knew things about them both that they, who still lived in the same metro area, couldn't possibly know about each other. How her mother had begun eating bananas instead of grapefruit in the morning because of the high-blood-pressure medication she was taking. How her father still kept Ferdinand's leash by the door, long after the dog had died. These were things a husband or a wife would know, but they hadn't been married for years.

The judge was taking advantage of the easy crowd to make everyone laugh, even as several people had begun to hold their programs over their heads to block out the pestilent sun. One of the grandmothers—Rob's—rose to read a poem. "From the beginning of my life I have been looking for your face, but *today* I have seen it," she pronounced. She had a long, bohemian braid, and as she read, she continued to hold the paper in both hands, which shook a little, either from nervousness or a tremor, or both, though her voice remained steady and triumphant, her figure like a flood marker before the retreating sea.

ELIZABETH HAD ONLY one set of grandparents, the pair on her father's side having died long before she was born. But even from a young age, she knew they weren't like other grandparents—that she called their home *the funeral home*, and not *Grandma and Grandpa's house*, was just one of many indicators that there was something uncommon going on. Something that centered itself in their basement. Something secret and exciting that she desperately wanted to see.

Her grandpa, it was clear, knew everything. His forehead was creased like an accordion and he gave off a spicy-oily musk that Elizabeth at first thought originated in the cushion of his chair, but soon came to understand was actually the smell of old man. His eyes, on the other hand, were young. Bright blue and sloshing, they looked like tiny portholes on the sea, and when she was brave enough to hold his gaze for more than an instant, Elizabeth often thought she could make out the shape of a little steamship on their waters, passing from one eye to the next, on its way to France, or perhaps Finland, that ancestral land she'd so often heard mentioned. Her grandfather wore a hat in all seasons and carried a ruler with him wherever he went, which was convenient, because Elizabeth frequently wanted to know the size of things.

Grandma, on the other hand, was a creature to be feared. She wore her red hair in historic-looking curls and was shorter than everyone who wasn't a child—which in those days was pretty much everyone who wasn't Elizabeth. It hardly mattered. She completely filled every doorway—and it seemed she was always standing in doorways, giving orders, issuing judgments, hurting feelings, and generally making it impossible to get by her into another room. The basement rooms especially.

LUCIE AND ROB kissed, married now, and they all rose up in a clamor. The quartet sprang to action. Elizabeth and Becca hooted and clapped. Kyle put his fingers to his lips, and pulled a sharp wet whistle from his mouth.

"Yikes." Elizabeth pointed at a man their age standing a few rows up, his shirt so thoroughly drenched with sweat that the pink of his skin showed through. "And I thought I was dying." Her sunglasses kept fogging and sliding down her nose.

"Amateur," Kyle said. "That's why you wear an undershirt."

Chris had joined them from his seat in the back. "They couldn't have had this thing inside? I saw the restaurant. It's *empty*."

"The rain plan was indoors," Becca said. "They have it just in case."

"Oh, why didn't it rain? Isn't it hurricane season?"

"Actually, there's a massive one heading toward the Gulf."

"Come on, they just got married," Elizabeth said. "Happy talk."

The crowd crawled toward the bar like scuba divers weighed down with their equipment. Elizabeth and Chris weaved in and out among splotchy shoulders and slouching backs, passing tuxedoed servers offering hors d'oeuvres.

"Hungover much?" she asked him as they waited in a clump by the bar. He was tan, a weekend surfer, but that evening he looked rather ashen.

"Actually, I think I'm still drunk." A silver tray of mojitos came through, bailing them out of line. Chris sipped his in relief. "That's better. You look smoking, by the way." He placed his free hand on her hip, a gesture she allowed herself to savor because she, along with just about all of their friends, was still pretty sure he was gay. They'd hooked up freshman year, just once. The entire time she couldn't shake the suspicion that he was doing it just to prove that he could.

Then, suddenly, there was Kyle, parting the partygoers with a lime-capped cocktail in each hand, having somehow made it to the bar. "I got you a gin and tonic." An older woman behind him turned appreciatively to watch him pass.

"I'm set." Elizabeth gave him a flirtatious head tilt, to reassure him, in case he needed it, that she was still very much his.

"I'll take it," Becca said, having reappeared beside them. "I have to admit, that was a ridiculously sweet ceremony. They looked so happy, didn't they?"

"I thought Rob might've had to pee, he was bouncing around so much." This was Hank, another med student, in from Houston.

The bride was approaching now, the glowing, tailored Lucie. They cheered her arrival. "Friends!" Lucie gave a little dip and hugged them each, Elizabeth extra fiercely. "Every single one of you has to have a wedding. Then you'll know just how amazing I feel right now." She glanced at Chris. "Or whatever, a huge party with everyone you love. It doesn't have to be a wedding." She was emanating heat, physically shaking with glee, and it was infectious. They were all laughing now, offering her drinks. "Oh God, no," she said, "but thank you."

"The vows were perfect," Becca was saying. "What you said about being stronger together because you're individuals first."

"And that grandma!" Hank said. "She's what my grandpa would call a pistol."

"I know, isn't she awesome?" Lucie was all teeth, seizing every bite of pleasure from her night.

"I kind of wanted to take her home with me," Elizabeth said.

A tray of hefty mushroom tartlets came by, and for a moment, everyone chewed.

"And that's saying a lot," Kyle said, once he'd swallowed, "because we're going to see her actual grandparents tomorrow."

"Oh, you are!" Lucie said, surprisingly happy to talk about something other than the wedding. "That's wonderful. In Maryland?"

"The old funeral home," Elizabeth said, and they all made murmurs of recollection.

"Personally, I'm excited," Kyle said. "I think it's going to be interesting."

For better or worse, Kyle was interested in everything. He always seemed to be lucking into behind-the-scenes tours of power plants and major-league ballparks, where he invariably asked dozens of vigorous, probing questions. He'd snorted lines with a pair of *Saturday Night Live* comedians, one of whom still occasionally left him voice messages pretending to be his Russian mail-order bride. He had bungee jumped. He had volunteered at a retirement home. He'd shot a deer in his native Wisconsin. All of it, he said, was experience, life experience, which was invaluable to him as an actor.

"Well," she said. "I hope you're bringing other things to do. It can get pretty lifeless in that house." Everyone groaned, and then another tray of hors d'oeuvres was before them.

"PLEASE, MOM? *Please* can I see the bodies?" she had finally begged on a holiday flight to Washington. She had turned seven and was due to receive a Lego hospital for Christmas. On the other side of the metal armrest, her mother had responded with the mildly alarmed expression she usually reserved for strangers on the phone.

"You don't want to see them," she said. "*I* don't even want to see them, and I'm a grown-up."

"But shouldn't I see them eventually? Doesn't everybody?"

"Oh, sweetie," her mother parried, pulling her across the armrest for comfort she didn't really need. "I hope you *never* have to see them."

Clearly, asking was not the best strategy. She was going to have to take a more direct approach. Later, after the Lego hospital and countless other presents had been unwrapped, Elizabeth marched into the room with the Christmas tree, where her mother and father were reading in matching chairs.

"If you don't let me see the basement, I'm never going to believe anything you ever say again."

Both her parents looked up from their books, then at each other, and then back at her for what felt like an abnormally long duration. Were they expecting her to say something else? It was maddening, the way they looked at each other, evidence that they had been talking about her, which was normally a good thing, but not if it meant they'd somehow colluded to tell her no again, after she'd gotten herself all worked up.

To her surprise, then, it worked. Gradually, her mother's expression melted from inscrutable ice to acquiescent water, the faintest rim of tears forming on the lower lids of her eyes. Her father was probably making an expression of his own, but her mother's was all Elizabeth could see.

Sensing victory, she added the coup de grâce. "I mean it. And I'll never talk to you again."

"Don't say that," her mother said. "That's a terrible thing to say. If it means that much to you, of course. All you had to do was ask."

Elizabeth flushed. Hadn't she asked already? Had her mother really forgotten so soon? Or perhaps she'd misunderstood the question. Maybe she thought Elizabeth only wanted to see the basement rooms, body-free. She needed to make sure they were talking about the same thing.

"I mean the bodies," she said. "That's what I want to see."

"We hear you." Her dad snapped his book shut. He leaned forward on his elbows, shifting his weight from one knee to the other. "You have to be sure, though. Once you see them, you can't take it back. You'll have the memory with you forever."

Her mother flung her arm out. "Why tell her that?"

"If I don't like it, we can just come back upstairs," Elizabeth said, eager to demonstrate that she'd considered every contingency.

"That's what I'm saying, sweetheart." He was crouching down in front of her now, trying to prevent her from looking anywhere but at his face. "You can stop looking, and you can leave the basement. But the brain holds on to things the eye sees—sometimes forever. You can't erase it. So you have to be sure you're prepared to handle whatever it is you've allowed yourself to see."

His eyebrows were thick with crisscrossing hairs, and one arched downward more severely than the other, an asymmetry she'd never noticed before. She looked down at her feet, then back at his eyebrows, which were, despite their misalignment, easier to settle on than his actual eyes. "How am I supposed to know what I can handle when I haven't even seen anything yet?"

He exhaled sharply, clearly not expecting her to protest. "How can you know," he muttered while he worked out a proper response.

"I'm looking at the Christmas tree right now. Are you saying I'm never going to forget *that*?"

"Please, Abe," Cassandra said. "Just take her."

Elizabeth turned to face her mother, who was sitting on the edge of her armchair, her legs angled under and bouncing, like she might spring from the room at any minute. She was so alive, she could rarely, if ever, sit still.

"No, Mommy," Elizabeth said. "I want *you* to take me."

INSIDE THE DINNER TENT, theatrical lengths of white fabric trapezed above them, heralding the great new life Lucie and Rob were to share. In lieu of favors, they had donated to an education charity, according to the cards at everyone's place. Though actually there were favors as well. Tiny chocolate truffles had been set in boxes shaped like cloth-bound books.

They slurped preset chilled soup and selected breads, receiving champagne and chardonnay. Elizabeth, still on her second cocktail, struggled to find a spot for it amid the full flight of stemware already at her place.

"I'm so sorry," she said, flagging down the nearest waiter. "Can you just take this extra glass? I'm afraid I'm going to knock them all over, and that would be extra stupid, since I don't even plan on drinking red." He smiled, a skinny boy with dark, longish hair he had to tuck behind his ears. He reminded Elizabeth of a greyhound, and she pictured him sitting on his haunches like a dog, awaiting permission to take off and run.

"Plans can change," he said. "You sure?"

"I mean look at this. Five glasses for one person. It's ridiculous."

"Excuse me," Kyle shouted, raising his arm. "Can I get another gin and tonic?"

"He's not our waiter." Elizabeth lowered her voice instructionally.

"It's all right," the waiter said. "We're all in this together."

"All hands on deck, right, buddy?" Kyle pointed at him as though they were old friends. Because he was also a waiter, he saw himself as being exceptionally cool to fellow tradesmen, tipping well and treating them with the respect and appreciation they so often failed to receive on the job. But Elizabeth thought he was actually more of a bully, forcing fraternity in a manner that bordered on condescension.

"What?" he said when he noticed her looking at him. "It's a wedding!" He shook her shoulder in mock desperation. "We're *having fun*!"

"Elizabeth!" She leapt to her feet at the sound of her name. Here was Lucie's psychiatrist mom, Joan, in a taffeta toga of mother-of-the-bride beige. She hugged Elizabeth, told her she looked smashing, and demanded to know where she was doing her residency. Across the table, Hank leaned in, his face slashed by a knife of evening light.

The volume under the tent had risen so raucously that Elizabeth felt compelled to answer in as few syllables as possible. "Here. Dermatology. I hope!"

Out of the corner of her eye, she saw Hank nodding sympathetically, as though she'd already failed to match. He knew as well as she did that dermatology was the golden stag of specialties, the most money, the best life, a long shot even for someone as well-credentialed as she was.

"I love New York!" she said, louder this time, hoping to crush his doubts, and her own. "I really don't want to leave!"

"Well, we don't want you to leave *either*!" Joan proclaimed, gripping her hands before another guest dragged her away.

Sitting again, Elizabeth put her hand on Kyle's leg. She'd been in New York three years, long enough to set herself to its standards and rhythms, to feel she was meant to stay. It was her city, not some wilderness she fell into randomly through her parents. California had always felt like that—an accidental place no one knew how to manage. But in New York she knew what things cost, where her perfect apartment would be. She knew too many people to ever grow bored. She even knew the people she didn't know, the ones she saw online or on the street. The bankers, whose French cuffs and pleated-front trousers masked alarming, shape-changing moles. The models suddenly crusted with psoriasis who feared for their careers. These were the people she wanted to treat, people who needed her, perhaps even desperately, though mostly just to lead nicer lives. It wasn't an ambition that would endear her to a selection committee—for that she had her grades and scores, her strategic research on pigmentation loss, and her Columbia mentors making calls behind the scenes—but it was her ambition nonetheless. As a premed she'd had nobler dreams. She saw herself traveling the world in rolled-up sleeves, administering shots to children in Africa, India, and Latin America. She wasn't quite sure where that old idealism had gone—perhaps it had been sucked up by some true activist who wanted and needed it more—but now she just wanted New York. She wanted to live as well as she could, looking closely at every kind of skin.

"Good thing you don't have acne," said Hank, who did.

A lull fell across the party as the entrees began to appear. The dagger of light crossing Hank's face thinned, and thinned again, as though some would-be murderer were slowly developing a conscience, until suddenly, all at once, it vanished, the sun having at last slipped below the horizon. A cheer went up from the now-reprieved eastern end of the tent, and in the new, dusky light Elizabeth looked around at all the well-washed hair and flowing table silks, the nubile peonies anchoring each table. Everything had regained its color with the shade, and in the drowsiness of drink, it looked like a movie, a lavish scene she'd watched so many times as a child that it was all she could do not to speak aloud the lines she knew were coming next.

WHEN THEY FINALLY made it down the pea-soup-carpeted stairs, across a hallway smelling strongly of rose-petal potpourri, and into the chapel where the funerals were held, the sight of the body in its open casket wasn't nearly as dramatic as Elizabeth had hoped. It was a middle-aged man's, slightly rubbery, with a patina of chalk around its face and a chest that seemed to collapse at the center, like a cake several minutes out of the oven. With its eyes closed, it looked sort of like a person taking a nap, but more than that like a costume of a person, to be zipped on for the next Halloween. She felt bad for this body that it had to be dead, but what could she do?

As she stepped down from the little stool her grandfather had provided, she couldn't help feeling that her parents had been wrong to worry. She hadn't seen anything she regretted, and she wanted to laugh at the idea of having bad dreams, or whatever it was they had feared, over the sight of this quiet rubber suit lying obediently in its box.

Even now, she remembered nothing about the original body's face—whether it was broad or pinched, big-nosed or small, freckled or tan, or marked by any kind of scar. The face she did remember, in that sober, wallpapered room, was her mother's, normally animated by some favorable charge that made her eyes and mouth seem larger than other people's, and her skin paler and more interesting to watch. That evening, after Elizabeth had released her hand to step up to the bier, her mother had receded into the rows of stackable chairs arranged for future mourners. When Elizabeth next glimpsed her, her face was in disarray. She seemed to have allowed her features to fall out of connection with one another, her mouth slack, her eyes wobbling in and out of focus. She looked, in that instant, utterly lost inside herself, as though her body were also a costume that had somehow slipped askew.

Now, at twenty-six, Elizabeth recognized the wisdom of her father's warning, though she was too young to recognize it then. There were some things you couldn't unsee. An anonymous body was just science. But a mother struggling to inhabit her eyes, to press herself back into place? What seven-year-old could forget the sight?

EVERYONE CROWDED into the restaurant to watch as Lucie and Rob, having taken lessons with a choreographer, performed their obnoxious first dance, mixing waltz steps with florid rump shakes to a mashup of crowd-pleasing tunes. Just when Elizabeth thought she could bear their specialness no longer, the band appeared with horns and backup singers at least ten musicians strong, and the rest of the evening was a whorl.

There were shots at the bar and a war zone of desiccated limes left behind. There were break-dancing kids, and a body-rolling boyfriend who kept hogging the center of the floor. Three pork-necked cousins played air guitar, and put their ties around their foreheads, and screamed every word of "Don't Stop Believin'." Chris tried to dip Becca, and fell, both of them lying on their backs, laughing soundlessly. Elizabeth's flailing arm broke somebody's glass. Someone else lifted a girl into a light fixture.

Then, for an excruciating interval, a screen came down and it all stopped, and they were forced to watch a slide show of photos from the night—the night that was theoretically still happening. There was Lucie with her eyes closed getting powdered in black and white. There were the rings in someone's hand in sparkling color. There was the ceremony they'd all just seen, already a perfect memory. Women throughout the crowded made fawning sounds; Jane appeared to be wiping away tears. Chris gripped Elizabeth's arm. "This is *killing* the party," he hissed. "Are they serious?" Off to the side Lucie and Rob stood embracing and pointing at themselves on the screen. Elizabeth went and ate a piece of cake, which she was pleased to find rather dry.

At last the screen withdrew and the band struck up another tune. The older guests began gathering themselves toward the exit, but enough young people were still huddled by the dance floor that the party was able to go on. Rob conferenced with the band leader, earning a last song seven more times. Jane was seen talking to a man twice her age who was later seen puking in the harbor. Kyle hugged Hank like a brother and everyone smoked cigars outside. Elizabeth swung Lucie's hand back and forth and said she couldn't be happier for her, and out there in the evening harbor air, which was finally beginning to cool, she knew she really meant it, just as she'd meant all the sad and bitter things she'd said and thought before. Funny how honesty worked, how divided she could be against herself.

They hung around long after the music had stopped, making their own on a convenient baby grand, drinking down the half-empty wine and scotch glasses they found scattered on tables inside. Lucie and Rob got into their limo, sailing off to their first married sex. The cabs started coming soon after, one by one in a safe yellow line. Jane gave her good-byes and got into one alone. To another, Becca hauled a tie-headed cousin and hastened them all in behind her. Elizabeth had nearly folded herself onto Kyle's lap when she heard, like a voice from the past, someone shouting her name.

"Elizabeth Green? Elizabeth Mirabelle Green?"

"Hold on, guys," she said to the packed car, sliding herself out to the curb.

Now standing, she saw that it was the greyhound waiter. In one hand, he held up her tiny black evening bag, in the other her driver's license. She stared. In the photo, her eyes were half-closed, and she was twenty-two. It would expire in less than a month.

"That's me," she said, remembering. She'd left the bag on her chair.

"Mirabelle." He said, as though she'd made a joke. "Should've been your first name."

She looked back at the cab, where Kyle was yelling something jovial at the driver and everyone was still struggling to fit. "Yeah, it's Elizabeth."

"Elizabeth is good," he agreed. "But Mirabelle is a song."

"Okay." He was weird, but he seemed familiar somehow, the line of his nose a line she knew intimately, like a rooftop seen daily from her window. All at once she remembered Henri, the French boy she'd met at a gallery opening for her mom, who'd gone down on her one night in the kitchen while her parents were still murmuring in their room. He was a waiter and his nose had been linear, too. She wondered where he was now, if he'd ever gotten his Ph.D. "What's your name?" she asked impulsively.

He answered as though she worked for the government. "Ferdinand Toby Steinberg."

She burst out laughing. "Shut up! Ferdinand was my dog. I don't think I've ever met a person named Ferdinand before. What were your parents thinking?"

He was laughing, too. "I think they were thinking about the discovery of America—you know, Ferdinand and Isabella. Or sailing around the world like Magellan. There's a Ferdinand in Shakespeare, too."

Those had been her father's reasons for naming the dog. She felt the sidewalk rock beneath her feet as she recalled her Ferdinand bracing himself against the waves. Try as she might, she could not escape that sailing trip, the great tempest of her life.

"Crazy," she said.

He held up his hands in mock defense. "Hey, that's my name you're talking about. I had nothing but nice things to say about yours."

It was true. What had he said—melodious?

"I go by Toby, though," he was saying now. "So you won't have to confuse me with your dog in the future."

The cab was calling for her, beckoning her still further into the night, to more freedom and more fun. She waved at the waiter and before long she was in, stretched on her back across Kyle's lap and the legs of her college friends, coasting uptown, away from the water, the monuments of New York rolling over her like sky, outdoing the constellations.

SHE AWOKE TO the chaos of a vibrating phone, spinning itself on her nightstand. There was morning light and Kyle's body incubating beside hers. All over the floor she saw their clothes.

"Hi, sweetheart! You must have had a late night!" Cassandra spoke in a caffeinated tone borrowed from infomercials, her cheer studied and well performed. She'd arrived in Maryland the day before, and she wanted to know what foods she should buy them, what train they'd be taking, if there was anything else she could do.

Since the sailing trip, Elizabeth's mother had changed. An initial period of conversation-stopping silences, mostly empty glasses of red wine left on bathroom vanities, and what must have been a record number of consecutive appearances by her ratty rose terry-cloth robe, soon gave way to a reformed, more positive Cassandra. She'd started seeing a therapist that summer, and started running, and by the time she and Elizabeth were in Cambridge, rounding up freshman dorm furnishings, it was as though she'd been cloned, fully Stepford-wived, so determined she was to smile and sublimate herself to the needs of others. Elizabeth had never known stackable plastic storage crates could stir a person so profoundly until her mother discovered them in an intra-aisle ziggurat at the bedroom superstore. "Sweetheart," she'd said, clutching one. "These are *so you*." It was alarming, even more so than the earlier bouts of bathrobe grief. Those, at least, Elizabeth recognized from romantic comedies.

She squeezed her temples and assured Cassandra that they'd be fine with anything she bought. They were aiming for an eleven o'clock train. She heard a rustle of activity in the background, the birthday preparations already under way. Grunting, Kyle dragged himself to the bathroom.

They said good-bye, and Elizabeth lay in bed awhile longer, watching her window curtain dance over the air conditioner and wondering what to do about her mom. Cassandra's bright affect had endured so long now that it had to be considered somewhat genuine. Even so, Elizabeth worried, knowing its roots were in regret. Whatever her mother's crimes, they no longer mattered. What's done was done; both her parents were to blame. Cassandra's penance was now the harder thing to take. She'd spent the past eight years showering Elizabeth with kindnesses she could never adequately return: handmade pop-up cards for no reason, winter care packages of California citrus, an indefatigable memory for the dates of interviews and exams. As a martyr, she was practically Victorian, a modern-day Tess of the D'Urbervilles, working the postal service the way Tess worked the starve-acre fields. She just couldn't forgive herself, no matter how much her daughter wanted her to.

Elizabeth exhaled, tasting compost breath and unbrushed teeth. She felt sheepish and unworthy, as she always did after a drunken night. What had they done? She hoped she hadn't said anything really stupid to Lucie's mom. Shuddering, she swung her legs to the floor and stepped over her suitcase to the closet, grateful they were skipping the brunch and getting out of town.

2

For his eightieth birthday, Howard Fabricant was building a sauna. His wife was throwing him a party, so it was only fair that he got to have something for himself. They'd all made such a fuss over him recently: Eunice, his daughters, even his son, the city councilman in the other Washington, who was usually about as demonstrative as a spreadsheet. It was as though none of them had expected him to live that long. Having sludged through Guam at nineteen, where bullets had missed him by millimeters, he hadn't quite expected it himself. Yet here he was, a day shy of eighty, surprisingly able and light on his feet.

The party was on his actual birthday, a Monday, the only concession he'd won. He didn't want people sacrificing their weekend for him, especially Lizzie, who according to Cassandra was always working or doing things with friends. His children had arrived already: sweet Mary with her twins, Howie, and Cassandra, who greeted him at the airport with a fresh, deep kiss on the cheek. Howie had always lived alone, but Cassandra was the loneliest, divorced several years and still no sign of a new man she might want to introduce to her parents. If his children wanted no part of the business he'd spent his life building, he at least wanted them happily settled, with someone to care for them when he was gone. He didn't think it was so much to ask.

This weekend, they seemed to believe they were caring for him, his house suddenly full again with all their voices, arguing over how many cups to buy and when to vacuum the rugs. He was surprised to discover he'd missed the racket of other people—*his* people, the way it ate up empty space. Their other-room murmurs insulated him, cushioning and warming whatever room he was in. His hands and feet had grown numb and tingly over the years, and most mornings he had to flex his fingers and toes for several minutes before he could walk to the bathroom, hold a toothbrush, and give himself a shave. But with his children in the house, he hardly noticed the tingling at all.

He dressed in his work clothes and came downstairs, where his wife was opening and closing kitchen drawers. They'd been married fifty-four years, an astonishing number when you considered her temper, her ungenerous judgments, and her penchant for holding a grudge. He knew there weren't many people short of sainthood who genuinely *liked* his wife. They'd had their troubles, to be sure, dark stretches he wasn't proud of when he preferred looking down a bottle to looking at her unrelenting face. But there were fewer agitations now that he was retired and all the kids were grown. And anyway, he was loyal. Once he committed to something, he committed; she was built the same. When she nagged and frowned at and embarrassed their children it was only because she knew, fiercely, as only a mother can know, how capable they were, how much more they could achieve if they tried. And what smart, singular kids they had. Eunice had raised them right; you had to give her that.

"Well, good morning," she said, as though he'd already made a mistake. She was dressed for church, a ritual he didn't often indulge her in any longer. "You wouldn't be coming with us, would you?"

He started the coffeemaker and leaned back against the counter while it did its business. "Us who?"

"Howie's joining me." She thrust her chin up, proud, wrinkling her nose the way she'd always done. It was a cute face, and she knew it. She never quit, his wife. She was different from most people in that respect.

"Nah, better get on with that sauna," he said. "But who knows. I might be moved to have a few words with God out there."

She frowned, her usual response to his ideas. "Well, I'm sure He'd love to hear from you." Howard didn't quite know what she believed in other than the importance of regular church attendance. If she spoke with God herself, he hadn't heard her—not that she'd be inclined to let him witness her in a position as vulnerable as prayer. Even naked, she was in charge: in the tub with her hair slicked back, her breasts announcing themselves to the water, the skin on her shoulders startled pink by her ceaseless, hard-scrubbing hands.

Howie came into the kitchen looking not quite full enough for his western shirt and slacks. "Do I have to wear a tie?" he asked his mother. He was fifty years old and over six feet tall, and still, he asked these questions.

"Come on, son," Howard said, teasing. "Don't they know how to dress out west?"

Howie's face was milky and opaque. He stooped as though he didn't trust the ceiling. "It's a little more informal. I can't remember the last time I wore a tie."

"How about the last time you went to work?"

"Not usually, no."

This was news to Howard. His son the elected official didn't wear a tie to work?

"You look fine," Eunice said to Howie. "Ties aren't required in church anymore either. Which you'd *know*, Howard, if you ever attended."

Before he retired, he hadn't gone a single day without putting on a tie. It was simply the way one dressed. He found it ludicrous that his wife was suddenly pretending to have developed a more casual view. There wasn't anything in the world she'd want more than for Howie to wear a damn tie. Preferably a dark one.

"If it's all right with everybody," Howie said, in a tone that suggested it didn't really matter what his parents wanted anymore, "I'll just stick with this."

"Good," they answered in unison, equally unsatisfied.

"Have fun, then," Howard said. He pressed his toes into the ground, feeling the pleasing return of sensation. It would be a good day for sauna building. "I'm framing out the roof this morning."

"The roof," Eunice repeated. "When are you going to hire someone who actually knows what he's doing?"

"Hard part's over," Howard said. "Plumbing, electrical. The carpentry's a piece of cake. You oughta know that."

"And you ought to know you're not as young as you used to be. You could stand to let someone help you."

Howard glanced at his son, who never offered his assistance anymore, not that he'd have been much use. The few times he'd helped in the workshop as a boy, Howard had felt fortunate they'd both made it out with all their fingers. Still, he could probably pass Howard rafters. A near-sighted grandchild could do that.

"All right, all right," Howard said, not even annoyed. "Get on with your worship."

Something in his tone amused Howie, who smiled with such sudden magic that Howard nearly abandoned his morning plans to share a pew with his bewitching only son. Perhaps if he spent some thoughtful time in his company, taking in the stained glass depictions of Christ's red-and-purple life while listening through the sermon for the hidden sounds of Howie's own particular silence—perhaps this might help him understand what made his son his son. But then Eunice shouted, "The coffee!" and the moment soured, and passed.

After they'd gone, Howard poured his mug and stood in the kitchen waiting for the caffeine to liven his senses. Was his son gay or merely shy? He couldn't bring himself to ask, not because he disapproved—the older he got, the less he cared about any of that—but because he didn't want to violate Howie's privacy. If only there were a way to say he loved him, would love him no matter whom he loved.

He knew men his own age who'd raged against their sons' romantic choices, feeling they'd somehow lost a son because he hadn't bedded a woman they might've liked to bed themselves. Ridiculous. His son was hardly lost. He was right there in town, visiting him for the week, the same mystery he'd always been.

If anyone was lost, it was Abe, his former son-in-law, whose handiness Howard had sniffed out the first time Cassandra brought him around, putting him to work on home repairs almost immediately, tasks for which the young medical student seemed actually grateful. Howard couldn't look at his oldest daughter now without mourning a little for her sturdy, provider husband who'd really made something special of his life. It had happened so suddenly. They were married—happily, he thought—and then they were not. As though Howard needed any further reminder that nothing in this life was permanent.

He looked at his watch: quarter of eight. His project awaited and the day, which he could feel emanating through the kitchen window, was going to be warm. He'd just set down his mug when Cassandra and Mary appeared in spandex, their hair ponytailed, their foreheads mirrored, back from a morning jog. They had never looked or talked alike—Cassandra low-voiced, pale and redheaded, like a person existing only in paintings; Mary blond, solid, and eternally flushed, a cheerful instruction in every breath—and yet they favored the same exercise attire. The same complicated athletic shoes, the same grafted racerback tanks. Looking at them, he felt that sometimes people's similarities were the greater truths, their differences merely distraction.

Mary was immediately in the bread box, humming and pulling out loaves for her kids' breakfast, while Cassandra hung back in the doorway, scratching her hip, deciding something. The oldest, she had been his first hope for the future, having taken a surprising interest in the preparations of decedents as a kid. What had she been—eight? She was the kind of child who couldn't keep her thoughts to herself. "It has a propeller on top, so it can go into space!" she would tell him, zestfully, as she drew him a flying house. She was not that way now, slinking through rooms like a tidy cat, hoping to go unnoticed. It saddened him, how interior she'd grown, how small she seemed to want to make herself, almost in spite of her success.

"You girls are up early," he greeted them.

Cassandra came forward now to kiss his cheek. "Morning, Pop."

"It's too hot to go any later in the day," Mary said. Ever suspicious of contamination, she was examining a loaf of raisin bread through its clear plastic sack. "We had a nice run, didn't we?"

"We did. I always forget how leafy it is out here."

"Find any new trees?" Howard asked. Cassandra had been consumed with work since her divorce, installing glimmering forest patterns into the bedroom, living room, and dining room walls of the West Coast elite: high-tech millionaires and venture capitalists, the owner of an NBA franchise he hadn't even known existed, an Oscar-winning actress he'd most often seen in campaigns for climate awareness. Her work on the actress's house had been featured in one of those celebrity magazines Howard sometimes browsed in the pharmacy line, just to see what it was that Americans were now supposed to want. To his eye, it didn't much differ from what they'd wanted in the past: a pool, nice hair, an audience real or imaginary.

"Actually," Cassandra said, pausing to blow air at her forehead, "I haven't done a tree in several years."

Howie didn't wear ties; Cassandra wasn't doing trees. Maybe he hadn't been asking the right questions. "What happened?"

She shrugged. "The fad lost steam. There are only so many of these super-rich people, and most of them know each other. At a certain point, you top out. They don't want to look like copycats. Truthfully, it's a good thing. I was losing steam. It was really just the same thing over and over again."

"Like funerals," he said.

Cassandra's hand rose halfway to her mouth. "I didn't mean it like that!"

"It's all right." Howard laughed. "Most things are the same thing over and over. Personally, I always liked the chance to perfect it. Do each time better than the last."

She considered this. "I wasn't close to perfection. I think I was just ready to be done serving the rich and their grand ideas of themselves." He appreciated her discomfort, was even proud of it a little. It seemed to him that her work was a varietal that grew especially well in California, where life was a movie, a constant visual metaphor that everyone mistook for real. He'd felt it when he'd gone out to visit her: those redwoods, those expensive juice bars that grew grass behind their counters. People there coveted natural splendor along with wealth, so that when they were finally rich enough to build their own dramatically situated homes, they had to hire her to bring the natural world inside. Merely seeing it through floor-to-ceiling windows wasn't enough.

He thought of his sauna, which would be a natural world in itself. Its volcanic temperatures, its heater stones, its simple northern woods. "Well, if it doesn't bore you too much, maybe one day you can make a tree for me," Howard said. "For the sauna. That might be nice." A simple tree carved into the wood, to remind him where everything came from. Perhaps he'd been too quick to judge her wealthy clients.

"And how *is* that sauna?" Mary asked. "Coming along?" She removed the lid from a jar of red jelly and sniffed.

He nodded. "I'm starting on the roof."

"What does that mean, the roof?" Cassandra asked.

"What does it mean? It means the top, the cover, the thing that keeps the rain out."

"You're a riot, Dad, but she's talking about your process," Mary said. "Where, exactly, in space are you going to be? On the ground, or balancing fifteen feet in the air on a two-by-four?"

He grinned. So serious, his Mary. She might've been a fine funeral director, too, but instead she taught middle school and was used to ferreting out liars. "The second one," he said. "More or less."

They looked at each other, as if silently discussing his case before deciding whether to let him proceed.

"You'd better be careful," Cassandra finally said.

"Everyone's always telling me to be careful. The way you girls and your mother talk, you'd think I'd never built anything in my life." He stretched, as if to remind them of all that his body had accomplished over the years—not just the reconstructed dead, but the carpentry work as well. The wooden picnic table, the slate patio beyond the sun porch, the lean-to shed where he kept his tools on their orderly pegboard wall.

"Well, get on then," Mary said. "The more calories you burn, the more cake you can eat tomorrow."

He'd always had a sweet tooth. "What kind?"

"That's for us to know and for you to find out."

He looked over at Cassandra, who folded her arms in solidarity with her sister. This week, if he had one boss, he had three. Truthfully, he rather liked the way his daughters ordered him around, taking after their mother, though they'd never admit it. There was concern in their toughness, which took him back to his military days, when guys screamed their heads off to keep you from getting killed. What was a harsh voice compared with a chest split by shrapnel, or holding your own brains in your hands?

TOBY STEINBERG TOOK his time in Union Station, not wanting to upset the cardboard box he carried, which contained a purple orchid. He was back in DC, and who should he see on the platform but Elizabeth Mirabelle Green, his wedding guest from the night before, laughing and holding the hand of her pushy boyfriend. They passed him in a draft of summer fabrics, too much in a hurry to notice him. It was just as well. Wedding guests were always spirited at the party: they grabbed his arm and joked, they applauded his arrival with food. If they somehow discovered he was a musician, they made exclamations and wished him well; sometimes they even made him dance. But once the champagne wore off and he met them out in the world they tended to regard him blankly, not remembering, or worse yet, with looks of pity he just didn't need.

He got off the Metro at Friendship Heights, emerging on a strip of luxury stores that seemed to have fallen off Fifth Avenue and landed, dismayed, in the unfashionable wilds of suburban Washington. He turned away from the main drag and walked the six tree-lined residential blocks to his mother's house. Letting himself in the front door, he set down his guitar case, then tiptoed into the kitchen, where he unpacked the flower on the granite-topped island. Potted with dirt and pebbles, the *Phalaenopsis,* as the grower had lustily called it, looked as elegant as the day he'd first seen it, in Gallery A of the Rockefeller Center orchid show nearly a month before. It stood out prominently on its table, the single purple flower amid blocks of pink and white. With its faintly ruffled petals and its black, sea-floor veins, it seemed to quiver in anticipation of moisture. He'd had to have it for his mother.

She and her husband, Ed, were gardening enthusiasts. At some point when Toby wasn't paying attention, they'd become people who couldn't talk about anything without being reminded of the new fertilizer they'd tested or an excellent tip for fending off pests. For several years now they'd grown the most assertive fruits and vegetables, distributed among a series of rectangular plots contained by railroad ties that Ed had salvaged from a local developer. Titanic eggplants and squash, perilously bursting tomatoes. Trellis after trellis of dainty beans and peas. There was even a mighty column of corn, all within their quarter-acre lot. The garden—and Ed—were evidently here to stay.

All of which aided in bringing about Toby's recent realization that his mother was a person with desires of her own. He'd been arrested by this idea late one night in his Harlem apartment, while eating a container of wasabi-covered peas and watching a disappointing installment of *Inside the Actor's Studio* with Renée Zellweger. As he beheld her puffy, evasive eyes, and her discomfort each time James Lipton asked her a question about her craft, it occurred to him that Renée Zellweger was a separate person from the roles she played, and that his mother—Ruth—was a separate person from her role in raising him. He'd nearly called her on the phone right then, stopping himself mid-dial when he realized it was well after one in the morning.

The next day he'd awakened wanting to give his mother a gift, to show her he understood. But she was happily married now; what could he give her that she didn't already have? He'd puzzled over the question for days until he came upon the orchid. Though Ruth was a master gardener, she focused exclusively on stuff you could eat; everything had to have a use. He, on the other hand, was a pure aesthete, worshipping jazz, shots of espresso, high cheekbones and high-fashion photography, the movements of European footballers, the poetry of Eliot and Pound. It was beauty he worshipped most of all. It drove him wild half the time, and whenever he tried to explain it, he found himself shrugging foolishly without the right words.

With the orchid, he hoped they could reconnect. He rubbed a petal between his forefinger and thumb, then ran his hand over the pebbly bed, grazing the top of a perfect round stone. He turned it over a few times in his hand, admiring its smoky blueness and parallel white stripes. The garage door opened; his mother and Ed were home. On reflex, he put the stone in the pocket of his pants.

"Toby!" Ruth cried, setting her reusable grocery bags on the floor. "You're home, you're home!" He let himself be hugged and thanked—"An orchid! Sweetheart, it's gorgeous!"—feeling at the same time that there was probably something wrong with him that he wasn't happier to see her smile.

In HER PARENTS' kitchen that afternoon, Cassandra filled a teakettle with water. Eunice, back from church, sat at the counter behind her, clipping coupons and watching her husband through the casement window. She saved every coupon she needed and plenty she didn't, just in case.

"Eighty years old," Eunice said, shaking her head. "It's foolish."

"He's had projects every year of his life," Cassandra said. "We're supposed to tell him he has to stop now that he's having a certain birthday?"

Eunice's scissors snipped angrily. "You could tell him. He doesn't listen to me."

Cassandra peered out the window at her father, whose head and chest were sprouting from the rafters of his gentle gable roof. Light gleamed through the remaining strands of his slicked-back, old-man hair.

"He's looking steady to me." She felt somewhat ashamed to have chided him earlier. Her mother's pernicious influence.

Eunice snorted. "I'm not the one with emphysema, I'll tell you that. *You're gonna break your neck, Howard! It's eighty-five degrees out there!*"

"Let him be," Cassandra said, igniting a gas burner under the kettle. "He'll finish much faster if we stop interrupting." She took her sketchbook from underneath Eunice's stack of unclipped coupons. "I'm going out front to watch for the kids."

"They should've been here already," Eunice said, on to the next disappointment.

Cassandra forced a smile, refusing to let her mother's spirit win out, though in this instance, they were pretty much in agreement. Elizabeth and Kyle were late, and part of her was starting to worry. "She's had a busy couple of days. Anyway, shout when the water's ready. I know you will."

The front porch of Fabricant Funerals looked out over a busy intersection, coursing with SUVs that hurtled like rhinos escaped from the National Zoo. A cluster of office buildings, hotels, and posh new condominiums encircled her, rising taller than they did in downtown Washington, where zoning restrictions kept just about everything short and squat, which was supposedly more European. Kitty-corner from the Fabricant home was a high-end hotel and public plaza, complete with large sculpted bushes, a regular rotation of street performers, and an elliptical fountain that was illuminated with pink and orange lights after dusk. At the front end of the plaza, just behind the fountain, a subway entrance spewed forth commuters, tourists who preferred sleeping in the suburbs, and teenagers in idle packs.

Abutting all this activity, the Fabricant porch was not the sort of place one sat for peace and quiet, but Cassandra took a stubborn comfort in watching the world expand while her parents heroically maintained their ground, clipping coupons and building saunas, as though their neighbors were still the butcher and the dentist, rather than the investment banker, the real estate attorney, and the uniformed concierge. She sketched a quick study of the hotel, a jagged early-eighties thing that was the opposite of a tree.

Her parents' time had been the sixties, when the surrounding area still had a farm or two. Back then, there were large, airy spaces between buildings, family-run restaurants and gas stations, and ample parking on every street. The Fabricant house was a reminder of that past. Built in the colonial revival style in 1922, its white columns and red brick façade made it a kind of architectural driftwood, bobbing perplexedly on a glittering sea of mirrored office windows and flashing modern lights. It had remained largely through Howard's perseverance, and because—such luck—its foundation cleared regulations when the Metro came to town. Washington and its suburbs had never felt old, but lingering among the sharp edges of new, her parents' home was a relic.

She was adding the Metro entrance to her scene when Elizabeth and Kyle appeared, as though conjured, two sweaty torsos rising from the underground, laden with bags and leaning on the escalator rail. Waving to them across traffic, Cassandra congratulated herself for having resisted the urge to call to check on their progress.

In the front hall, she relieved them of their things.

"You must be exhausted!" she cried, kissing her daughter fervently on the cheek. "Was your train late?"

"Right on time," Kyle said, receiving a hug of his own.

"Oh?" Cassandra looked at her watch. It was nearly four.

"We missed the early one because the subways were running local," Elizabeth explained, wiping the last beads of perspiration from her forehead.

"How annoying!"

"Lizzie was annoyed, all right," Kyle laughed. Elizabeth frowned. They'd been dating for almost two years.

"Well—you're here now," Cassandra stuttered. "Come in, come in. Come see Grandma and Grandpa."

Eunice met them halfway to the kitchen, scissors still in hand. "There's my granddaughter!"

"Hi, Grandma." Elizabeth stooped and wrapped her arms around her shoulders. Eunice squeezed back, stiffly, then turned to take in Kyle.

"And who's this?" She glared at him, as though no one had told her he was coming. He stood young and large, a full foot taller than she. The pinched corners of her mouth turned down.

"Mrs. Fabricant, I'm Kyle Christensen. It's wonderful to finally meet you." He took her hand between his two, dimpling and showing his teeth. "No need for the weapon. I assure you I've been a perfect gentleman when it comes to your granddaughter."

"Well, listen to this!" Eunice raised her eyebrows. Nothing pleased her more than a tall, flirtatious young man. "A gentleman! Come have something to drink. You want a soda? I'll get you a soda." With her little hand firmly on his wrist, she led Kyle into the kitchen. He looked back over his shoulder, shrugging and smiling as though he couldn't quite believe the force of his charm.

Elizabeth turned to her mother. "What did I say? She loves him."

"Of course she loves him. He's a man." Howie, the only boy, had always gotten the most praise, even before Cassandra fled home, married a man of dubious parentage, and disgraced herself in divorce. Even now, after all her worldly success. "I mean, really. What is the deal with that? Are boys just easier?"

"Not worth pondering, Mom. It'll only make you angry."

The kettle was whistling when they entered the kitchen, but

Elizabeth hardly heard it. Her eyes immediately found her grandfather. Framed perfectly in the window, he was floating ten feet off the ground in the middle of a wooden structure she'd never seen before.

"Mom!" she cried. "How can you let him do that?" Her whole life he'd been a tall man but now he looked tiny in the space between the rafters.

"Hasn't he made wonderful progress?" Cassandra asked. She poured the boiling water into a large glass pitcher loaded with tea bags. Steam rose in a column as she stirred, hovering around the strong kitchen lights. "He's nearly done with the exterior."

"Howard!" Eunice called out the door, much louder than was necessary. "Lizzie's here!"

"One minute!"

Using a pot holder, Cassandra set the pitcher on a trivet near the sink. "Don't touch this, anyone. It's very hot. But it'll be iced tea by dinnertime."

"You'll finish it later!" Eunice called to her husband. "Come see Lizzie now!"

"In a *minute*, Eunice!"

"Crazy old man," she muttered, her lips tightening. She took a can of Coke from the refrigerator for Kyle, who was sitting politely in the breakfast nook. "Hold on, I'll get you some ice." She reached over the steaming pitcher of tea to open the cupboard where she kept her knock-off Waterford tumblers. On the way back down, her arm brushed the pitcher's edge and, jolted, she dropped the drinking glass in the sink, where it broke with a violent crack.

"Are you all right?" Cassandra rushed over to have a look.

"*I'm* fine," Eunice crabbed. "But my tumbler! What are you doing leaving that pitcher there?"

"Christ, Mom, I *told* you it was hot." Cassandra lifted the largest piece of glass from the sink. The tumbler had broken right along the crest of one of the diamond cuts. Feeling the tickle of a tiny shard on her fingertip, she began pitching the chunks of glass into the garbage.

While her mother made a show of cleaning up the mess, and her grandmother stood by stubbornly, virtually blocking the trash, Elizabeth flashed Kyle a look of desperation, which he returned with a sympathetic grimace. The embarrassment had already begun, no more than ten minutes into their visit. "My tumbler," Eunice repeated into the garbage, this time in a more wounded tone.

"Well, you'll just have to buy another one," Cassandra said. "It's not the end of the world."

"There's no need to be hostile. You're the one who made me drop it."

"What now?" Howard appeared at the open back door. Leaning into the frame, he mopped his sweating forehead with a grime-stained handkerchief.

Before anyone could respond, Elizabeth was hugging him. "Been working hard out there, Grandpa?"

"Oh, I keep busy," he said, patting the back of her head. If Eunice preferred boys, Howard most certainly preferred his girls. And Elizabeth, who was everything a young girl ought to be—pretty, low-voiced, and clever—was far and away the best. When she first declared as premed, long after he'd given up on keeping the funeral home in the family, he liked to joke with her about going into business together. "Just keep me in mind when you're making referrals," he'd say, and she would laugh, not at all alarmed or offended, the way he knew some people would be.

"How come you never write?" he teased her now. "I don't mean e-mail. What ever happened to good old-fashioned letters?"

"She's too busy to write," Eunice said.

Shush, Mother, shush, Cassandra told herself, as she mopped the counter with a cloth. With her therapist, she'd come up with an arsenal of strategies that would keep her from speaking her mind in potentially ugly situations. Admonishing Eunice now would only embolden her more. Better to clean the counter and pretend she was cleaning her mother's attitude. *Shush, Mother, shush.* Her silent mantra for the week.

"Can't trust the mail these days." Here was Elizabeth to the rescue. "What if it got lost?"

"You'd be taking a risk all right," Howard agreed.

It was something he knew all about. He'd spent his youth somersaulting from one risk to another, first as an unpromising high-school graduate, stocking hardware shelves in St. Paul by day, getting smashed out of his mind by night. Then in the army, with the war and all its muck, both human and topographical. Surviving that, against such enormous odds, he joined his cousins in a trucking venture, ferrying bales of foodstuffs and equipment from Minnesota to California, from California to Arkansas. When he was driving, he'd test the limits of the truck, pushing her to eighty, ninety, even over a hundred in the blistering Nevada sands; when he rode shotgun, he liked to hang out the window for a thrill, feeling the dirt in his teeth, his tongue dry as one of the reptiles that were always skittering away from their wheels.

Marrying Eunice had been another kind of risk. By then, he'd been making more East Coast deliveries and had taken a liking to the studious bluster of Washington. It turned out to be packed with guys like him, guys from the middle with military service but no other background to speak of. Finding themselves alive at the end of a war, they'd come to realize they'd been pretty successful serving their country and might as well try to keep on. In Washington he felt like a member of their great big American club. He wore a gray felt fedora and went to restaurants and saw himself as a man with countless possibilities.

What he needed next was a woman. After losing his mind and a good portion of his lousy savings to a walking pinup named Rose, he decided he'd be better off with a no-fuss wife who would do her part. Have a few sensible ideas, maybe bust his chops a bit, force him to make something of himself. And no sooner did he come to this conclusion than he found himself at a church dance, walking across the floor to talk to Eunice, a plain but queenly woman who stood up straight and looked at him as though she were the best-looking person in the room. She had ideas all right, the loudest of which was that a business needed a product that was always in demand. And maybe she *was* good-looking. Certainly he found her attractive. Adhesive, even. She was the kind of woman who would stick to him until she fixed him, and it made him feel manly to matter so much in her life. Of course, this arrangement had its own hazards, but it was better than being alone.

And so, in 1951, he put his G.I. Bill benefits toward a mortician's course and a stately house in Bethesda. The embalming equipment cost him more than he'd estimated, so he also had to pawn their wedding silver and his wife's two heirloom brooches until he could make up the difference. When he finally moved Eunice and their baby, Cassandra, into the house, he still hadn't bought a single piece of family furniture. There were chairs and sofas for the main chapel and his hand-built bier at the front; upstairs they had nothing but a bureau, a secretary desk rescued from a Dumpster, and a foam-padded mattress on the floor. But Eunice had been right: there was money in funerals, and furniture soon came by the truckload, in the same used Buick that Howard had bought to convert into a hearse.

Elizabeth's voice pulled him out of his reverie. "Grandpa, I'd like you to meet—"

"Kyle Christensen, sir." A blond boy was standing before him: boulder shoulders, torso descending like a vee. Here was risk, if ever he saw it. Who was this boy to be touching his granddaughter?

Howard shook his hand warily. Kyle squeezed back, polite.

"It's a pleasure, sir." A flash of even teeth. "I really admire what you do here."

Howard shoved his free hand further into the pocket of his jeans. "Well, I hardly do it anymore. Alvin's the one who runs things. I just build pleasure houses for my wife out back."

"It's a *sauna*," Eunice blared. "And I don't know why you keep telling people it's for me." It shamed her each time she spoke the word. Didn't everyone know you were naked in a sauna?

"Well, come on," Cassandra broke in. "Let's get you upstairs."

"Where's Mary?" Elizabeth asked as they unfolded the sofa bed in the third-floor study. "And Howie?"

"They went to the store. Apparently Estella and Max need a particular brand of yogurt." Estella and Max were Mary's middle-school twins, pale and blond. Pretty kids, with gimlet eyes. They were fond of mystery games and wrestling, and they always laughed the loudest at cruel jokes. To most, they were charming and precocious; to Cassandra, unsettling achievers. They were born when Mary was in her late thirties, and even though the Cold War had ended, Cassandra couldn't help but think the KGB had missed a golden opportunity in her young nephew and niece. It was an unfair prejudice, she knew. Their father, Vladimir, had left the Soviet Union in the seventies, a professor of systems engineering and a legitimate defector. He had a broad, humble smile, and was both earnest and fervent in his belief in democracy. But his children were another breed. With their hooded eyes and jagged glacier cheeks, they seemed the children of a Russian mafioso—in spite of his warmth, in spite of butter-yellow Mary. Cassandra had colors for everyone, and Estella and Max were both ardently black.

"Okay." Cassandra sheathed and fluffed the last pillow and tossed it onto the bed. "Kyle's in here with Max, and Lizzie, you're with me in my old room—you didn't think they'd let you two sleep together, did you?"

"No," Elizabeth said, uncertainly. "But what about everyone else?"

"Mary and Estella in Mary's old room—until Vlad gets here anyway. Howie in his old room. Grandma and Grandpa in their bed as usual."

"Well, this is really great, Cassandra," Kyle said. "Thank you." He flopped onto the bed and stretched out his legs. Resting his head in the palms of his interlocked hands, he smiled, as though the arrangements didn't bother him a bit. "I was expecting a couch in the living room."

"You may prefer that after a night alone with the devil Max," Elizabeth laughed.

"Oh, don't worry about him," Cassandra said. "I have a feeling he'll like you. He's always been enamored of big strong men." She nudged the bed frame with her knee.

"Mother." Elizabeth's face clouded over.

If Mary was yellow and Estella and Max were black, then Cassandra's own Elizabeth was true to her name: a firm and pitiless green. Somehow, in the years since she'd left home, Elizabeth had become an intimidating creature, prone to flashes of disdain that were capable of momentarily, but regularly, breaking her mother's heart. Between Harvard and med school, she'd developed a sense of certainty that was as narrow as it was unforgiving, and it seemed that the more she achieved, the more Cassandra fell short. Without a doubt, Cassandra had fallen short—in many ways, on many occasions—but she had always been her own sternest critic. It was a painful new experience to find herself censured, even casually, by her daughter, whom she very much still wanted to advise.

"Is there anything else we can do?" Elizabeth finally asked, allowing the moment to pass.

"Oh, why don't you two just relax for a bit," Cassandra said, collecting herself. "Have some alone time. It may be a while before you get another chance."

An instant after Cassandra had shut the door, Elizabeth dove into Kyle's lap. Wrapping her legs around his waist, she pulled him up into a sitting position so that she could rest her chin on his shoulder.

"Whatcha doin', little monkey?" He was smiling; she could hear it in his voice. His baby talk knew no limits. It had surprised her in the beginning, such precious, twee words coming from the mouth of a jock, but she had grown to expect and even relish it, and found she enjoyed answering him in kind. It was liberating, the closest she could come to admitting she was afraid of being an adult.

"Hangin' on a big stupid tree."

"Pretty monkey. Will you take me to the crypt?"

She shook her head, pouting, and hid her head in his neck. She knew she was lucky to have this boy of hers—this large, affable boy who genuinely seemed to find her beautiful even when she looked like crap. He was the beautiful one, and he spoiled her.

"So they really live here," he said in his regular voice, his breath warming and dampening her neck.

"My mom's whole life. Totally traumatized her, I think." She'd told him all about it, but he was curious enough that she allowed herself to go on. "Alvin Dao, my grandfather's partner, runs it now."

"Right," Kyle said, kissing her neck, undoing the top button of her shirt.

Elizabeth ran her fingers through his hair, squeezing the back of his head with her palm. "My grandfather's basically retired, but I think he still does some mortuary work now and then."

"Just for kicks?" Kyle's voice softened. He had completely removed her shirt, eased Elizabeth onto her back, and was working his fingers down.

"Budgets and business strategy were never his forte. He's a man who likes to work with his hands." She raised her hips for Kyle's hands. Her underwear came off; his fingers pressed inward, hooking her and grabbing hold. "With Alvin here, he could withdraw . . . from management, focus on the work that needed . . . a human touch." She almost giggled, but did not.

"In another life," Kyle concluded, his tongue in her ear, "he might have been an artist."

This was the story she told about her grandfather, a lean, mysterious man named Howard Fabricant, who came from a different time, when people were more pragmatic, and true callings always consigned to "another life."

"He could probably use a hand out there," Elizabeth said, her spine arching up, aching toward Kyle. "We should offer to help."

"Would he want our help?"

"I don't know." Kyle's mouth was endless on her breast. She turned inside out; they might be caught at any moment.

"Probably not," he breathed.

She bit his shoulder. His mouth. His cheek.

Yes, she said.

HOWARD REPOSITIONED HIS ladder and climbed carefully, eager to finish the frame before dinner. He had studied sauna mechanics for months before selecting a design and mapping out his construction schedule. The plan was to start the serious building in September, after the swampy summer was behind him, but once he'd purchased and arranged all his materials, he found himself too excited to wait. So far, the heat had been a nuisance but not insufferable; if anything, it helped warm his fingers and toes.

The windows of his sauna would face west, perpendicular to the house. Several experts had counseled him on this point—saunas were best enjoyed at sunset—and in this regard, Howard considered the orientation of his yard to be a blessing. Though his property was now grotesquely dwarfed by towers of steel, glimpses of nature remained. One such glimpse, through a break in his trees and a gap in the buildings beyond, produced a perfect cut of the western horizon from the spot where he chose to build.

Howard pulled himself up to his walkway. He'd always been a sunset guy. The sky leaking into dark in the east. The ongoing riot in the west. The excruciating binge of bright just before the sun finally gave up. He loved how, paradoxically, the world became clearer in those moments after the drop, how much better he could see the things around him. The dailiness was reassuring, too. Here was something you could count on that wasn't tragedy; that wasn't accident, atrocity, or disease.

Positioning a nail, he began to join the last set of rafters.

After a moment, he looked up. A flash of movement had caught his eye. Standing in the northeast corner of his yard was a doughy young man dressed in an oversize white T-shirt and gray athletic shorts. It was Joseph, who lived with his mother in one of the affordable-housing complexes and attended Eunice's church.

Howard couldn't remember the name of the mental disorder the boy supposedly had, only that his was a sad case, requiring all kinds of drugs and therapies that put his mother in the red. He stood below Howard uncertainly, his round face bumpy as a squash, his arms dangling leafily at his sides. A real vegetable garden kind of kid. He gave off an oniony odor, even from that distance, though his clothes looked clean enough. Howard returned to his project; the boy would grow restless and move along. Best not to stare and upset him.

But the boy didn't move. "What are you building?" he asked, his voice reedy but steady in pitch. It was the first time Howard could remember actually hearing him speak.

"It's a sauna. Gets real hot."

Joseph nodded. "There's a sauna at the Y. I saw it once on a tour." He sounded lucid, like any other boy—perhaps more serious than most kids his age, but that was all.

"So you know all about this." Howard set his hammer down and smiled in what he hoped was a friendly manner.

"Well, they didn't let me take one. But I will one day. It's on my list."

"How 'bout that?" Howard's gut flooded with recognition. "I have a list, too."

"Everyone should. So you know you're doing—" He stopped abruptly. Perhaps he was shy.

Howard rapped his knuckle on a beam. "This is on my list."

Joseph quailed a little and stepped back, as though the beam had been his hand.

"It's okay," Howard said, immediately regretting the gesture. "Don't worry. So. What brings you to my yard?"

The boy itched his head in a slightly broken motion, moving it back and forth against his fingers. "I was taking a walk. I do that sometimes."

"Just around the neighborhood?"

Joseph began shifting his weight from one ponderous foot to the other.

"It's a nice neighborhood," Howard tried again.

"I like walking. There are always new things to see." Head scratch, foot shift. "New buildings. New stores."

"Are you nervous about something?" Howard asked.

"Yes."

"Don't be. You're okay here."

Joseph shifted backward now, then forward, then over to one side, then the other. He was nearly doing a box step.

"Don't be nervous," Howard repeated, trying again to sound calm.

"I'm always nervous," Joseph said, and made another box step.

"Why?" *Why talk to him?* a panicked voice inside him asked. But Howard shoved that voice out of mind. He felt he could help the boy. No one ever seemed to talk to him. Surely talking could help free him just a little from whatever was happening inside.

Joseph stopped swaying and came to a sudden stop. "They say don't get too close, but then you go the other way, and they say don't go too far."

Howard's chest fluttered at the ominous mention of *they*.

"Who's saying that?"

"They say stay away from the monster on the rock, and stay away from the water that swirls. Nowhere to go but down the middle. Straight down the middle the only where to go." Joseph's pimpled face looked as tangled as his grammar.

"Shh," Howard said, looking around, not wanting to attract any attention. "No they don't. No one's saying anything. You're safe."

"She will devour you, she will eat you whole, she will swallow you and spit you back up."

"Shh, shh, no she won't. She won't hurt you at all."

"She bashes like rocks, she burns like pox, she screams and sings like cocks. Iraq."

Howard had never heard anything crazier in his life. He ducked down under a rafter and came into a squat on the side nearest the boy.

"Where's your mother?" he asked, gripping the edge.

It appeared this was a good question to ask. Joseph had been standing rigidly with his fingers spread wide by his sides. But now he blinked several times and resumed his bizarre habit of scratching his head against his hand, which after the outburst looked almost like an act of tenderness from a pet. "She's at work," Joseph said.

"Will she be home soon?"

"Yeah, soon." A look of relief rolled over his face. "She doesn't like me taking walks. But I can't stay inside all day. The television watches me."

"Not to worry," Howard said, exhaling partially. "I won't tell."

"I gotta do my summer reading."

So he was still in school—that was something. "Sounds good," Howard said.

Joseph's face drained. "I'm sorry for what I said."

"Not to worry," Howard repeated, wanting to reassure him as much as he could.

"That was Scylla and Charybdis. They're just in the book."

"That's right," Howard said, only vaguely recognizing the names.

Joseph flapped his hand good-bye and Howard began to straighten himself back up. But as the boy made his way along the perimeter of the yard, his toe caught an invisible mound of earth, and he tottered a bit, reaching out to the nearest bush for support. With a great clatter of wings, several small gray birds flew out from its branches, gurgling, heading straight for the poor kid's face. He closed his eyes and didn't make a sound, but held up his arms in an X to protect himself. Diverted, the birds flew on.

Suddenly, they were in front of Howard, nearly blocking Joseph from his sight: pigeons beating their wings uselessly, trying to reach the safety of a wooden beam. Seeing Howard hunched there in his hothouse steeple frightened most of them back, and within a few moments all had returned to the bush save one. It was sick, or old, or otherwise unfit for pigeon life, its tongue bulging outward like a cyst. Howard swatted at it, but the bird surged forward again, grasping for a perch with its scaly, purple claws.

"Damn it!" Howard muttered. The desperate pigeon opened its mouth wider, emitting a throaty, ghoulish grunt. Cringing, he turned and swatted at it again, whacking his head on a rafter. The bird's wings made an even more ferocious ruckus than before and all of a sudden he felt himself losing his balance. With ringing ears, Howard pitched forward, saw luscious green grass below, and felt his head, shoulders, and chest pass over the edge of the frame. His stomach vanished and he closed his eyes, releasing himself to the inevitability of the fall. *How unlucky,* he thought, as he tumbled freely through space. *If I'd been just an inch farther back.*

The ground hit him with a snap, and a light warmth spread loosely through his body. *Not so bad,* he thought, *could have been worse.* He had flipped over somehow, and was now looking up backward at the sky. He could see that the old pigeon had indeed made it to his roof, though it was redder now and more elongated than it had been. The sound of pianos and strings filled his head, swelling like a wave about to break upon the rocks. The bird's head swiveled, seemed to explode, and Howard closed his eyes again. *Damn bird* he shouted over the music. *Goddamn, good-for-nothing bird.*

WHEN EUNICE SAW her husband stretched like a vine on the ground, she did not immediately think he was dead. His head was tilted back, as though he were watching the clouds roll by, and his legs and arms lay comfortably enough that she thought he may have fallen asleep mid-gaze. Howard had always been industrious, but Eunice liked to entertain the fantasy of a lazy husband. It seemed to justify her own vigorous work ethic, and it gave her a natural object of blame when events didn't turn out the way she expected. She took a mischievous pleasure in catching him asleep, and Howard, for his part, obliged her fun. "Damn it, woman!" he'd say, sitting up in his recliner. "Can't a man get any rest in his old age?"

She'd heard a commotion in the yard a few moments before, while she was rummaging in the pantry for her cake stand. These days, in their neighborhood, there was rarely any cause for alarm. But Eunice still liked to double-check.

"Wake up," she shouted as she approached his motionless body. "Wake up, you lazy old man. We've got company, remember?"

A pigeon flew down from behind her, coming to rest by her husband's leg.

"Shoo!" she cried, flapping her hands. "Damn bird!" The pigeon cocked its head, ruffled its wing, then took off as ordered for the trees.

It was only at this moment that she realized something was wrong. She took a few additional steps, more tentatively now, until her toes nearly brushed his head. Peering down, she saw that his eyes were closed, but that his neck was somewhat oddly bent, and a trickle of red was forming at the corner of his mouth.

"Howard?" she asked, more softly than she usually spoke, nudging his shoulder with her toe. "Howard, you're all right. Get up." She looked at the sauna frame and saw his hammer hooked on a beam, a box of nails nearby.

"Mom?" Cassandra's voice came from somewhere above. Eunice looked up to see her daughter's concerned face in a second-floor window. Her bedroom—no, no, the bathroom—three windows over from the left.

"Everything all right?"

"Well," Eunice replied, reaching her verdict. "Dad's dead." Her voice came out curt on the first word, but was audibly shaking by the last.

"I'll be right down." Cassandra took a towel from the rack as she left, thinking it might somehow help.

At the bottom of the stairs, she met Mary, Howie, Estella, and Max, each carrying a plastic shopping bag full of food. Estella was wearing a childish candy necklace, and was in the process of biting off a bright pink piece. They had, by chance, just walked in the door.

"It's Grandpa," Cassandra shouted, relieved to have people to tell.

They spilled into the yard en masse. Eunice was sitting on the ground by Howard's head, her hands gripping each other in her lap. Her shoulders shook like leaves on a branch. She was laughing.

Elizabeth appeared at the back door, her hair matted, nearly breathless. "What's going on?" she asked before running out to join her mother. "What happened?" But then she saw her grandfather lying on the ground, his skin unmarked, and understood. Had she been smarter, had she foreseen, she might have been there when he fell. She took another step forward and crouched down by his body. She touched his sleeve. All around him, like a soft crust, the grass was green.

Tears streamed down Eunice's face and she continued to laugh in vindication and disbelief. "I *told* him he was going to fall and break his neck!" she managed, nearly choking on the words. "I told him. And look what happened. He *did*."

3

Howard was dead; people had to be told. The party guests first and foremost. Fortunately, Mary found comfort in the phone. She grieved, not by crying or shouting or needing to be by herself, but by pressing the hard plastic to her ear and telling the story to friends and relatives—some as soon as an hour after he passed. She needed to be straightforward, to convince herself it was real. Her father was dead; he had died; party's off.

Once she'd gotten through her share of the most urgent calls, she sat down in Howard's leather office chair, covered her eyes with her hand, and envisioned a map of the United States. In her mind the country was dark, with tiny white lights marking the locations of her aunts, uncles, cousins, and friends: the modern Fabricant universe, fully graphed and illuminated. She'd called each of the brightest lights: New Jersey, St. Paul, Colorado Springs. She'd even called her mother's sister, Trudie, who lived in a retirement home near Phoenix and who thought that everyone who phoned was her dead daughter, Leigh.

Still, Mary wasn't satisfied. A large swath of the country remained grimly in the dark; a light was missing out west.

*   *   *

ON THE SUNDAY that Howard Fabricant died, Abe awoke in San Francisco fog, with a chafing itch in his throat.

He sailed now more than ever, and he looked like a seaman, his cheeks tawny and taut, his hands chapped as old leather gloves. His new boat was shorter, leaner, and lighter than the tarnished one, and under its sails he sought a more physical life. He wore wind-resistant pants and white T-shirts full of holes. He sang chantey songs on the waves and in the shower. When he walked onshore, it was as though he rolled, flowing to the office and ebbing back each day.

His old mentor Sam Upchurch sometimes came out with him, and in recent years, he'd made a few other friends at the yacht club. He'd even found an apprentice: his secretary's son, a goofy kid who'd somehow developed a thing for boats. He liked Asante because he reminded him of his own youthful fascination. Abe had seen the ocean for the first time on a trip to the Jersey Shore when he was five. He knew the water was dangerous, but he felt compelled to run in anyway. His parents had egged him on from the sand, flinging their hands overhead. They'd been brainy Philadelphians, eccentric; they wanted him to see the world. Later, in the surf, his mother squatted down and pointed at a white triangle perched defiantly on the faraway waves. "Hey, water boy," she'd said. "Wouldn't that be a fun thing to do?" He had his mission.

Twice a week now, the teenaged Asante came to sea with Abe, giggling across the deck, tying perfect knots, and trying to predict the changing winds. When the air was calm and they dropped anchor, Asante entertained himself by reading aloud. His favorite books were drippy spiritual fables, books like *Siddhartha* and *The Alchemist*, which he never tired of defending to Abe.

Some years back, sailing had been a useful escape. Offshore, there was no risk of encountering Cassandra or any of her arty friends. But

the sea was also a better way of life. It was indifferent and unclut-
tered, solitary, which had always suited him. If he'd had anger once,
he didn't now. The ocean had all but washed it away. That, and Proposition 215, which brought cannabis back into his life just as his marriage was drawing to an end. On the water, and under the influence of
self-prescribed, hand-rolled grass, he became more aware of himself
and the world. He'd thickened with age, expanded, but so had the
ocean, both of them growing more powerful as human civilization
declined. Eventually, of course, he'd die—he was as guilty as any
carbon-emitting life form—but not for many years. For now he still
had his strength.

Downstairs in the kitchen, he drank a full glass of water with his
pill and brewed his coffee as usual. By nine, the itch in his throat had
become a full-blown ache; twenty minutes later came the sneezes. He
blew his nose thoroughly, took several puffs of a searing nasal spray,
and fled for his regular Sunday sail.

On the water, everything cleared: the fog, his nose, his throat. By
the time he returned to the marina, all that remained was a dull, pin-
prick ache in his cheeks and along the ridge of his brow. He credited
the sea air, Asante's good spirits, and his own resilient cells. Back
home, he ate a lean dinner of salmon and greens and, deciding after
his eventful morning to forego his usual toke, he poured himself a
small but brimming glass of pinot noir. Later, on his deck, he read the
latest Philip Roth, and poured himself another. He had just finished a
chapter when the phone rang.

It was Cassandra's sister, Mary. She identified herself right away,
saving him the embarrassment of pretending as he groped for con-
text. The wine warmed the bridge of his nose and he found himself
conked back to where he could almost see her as a teenager, when she
wore headbands and sandals so tall she could barely walk. It had been
years since he'd spoken to her. He'd almost forgotten she existed.

Her adult voice was businesslike and arid, the voice of a person
with allergies. "I just wanted to let you know that our father died this
afternoon." Or a person who'd cried herself dry.

"I'm sorry to hear that," he said, reflexively, as though they spoke all the time. "Was he sick?"

"Just fell off a sauna he was building and died, around four o'clock East Coast time. I tried you earlier but you must've been out. Anyway, I thought you'd want to know. We're all a wreck here in Maryland."

She told him the details in a hurry: an aborted birthday party, a pigeon, a viewing at the house, the date still to be determined. She'd be in touch again when she knew for sure. "Thank you," he said, not knowing what else to say.

After he hung up, he stood thinking. His own parents had died in a highway crash when he was ten; then his grandmother Helen, who he'd gone to live with in Virginia, had succumbed to a heart attack just before he graduated from medical school. Both times, the losses fell upon him like sun spots, zapping out all other connections. In the end, he could hardly remember the deaths, or the life he'd led before them. All he knew was he'd been changed, emerging a new man both times.

He went into the bathroom. From the medicine cabinet, he retrieved a canning jar he'd bought at an upscale kitchen store downtown. He popped the metal clamp and considered the cannabis inside. Enough for at least two good joints. And to think he'd told himself he'd go without it today. He would write himself a refill in the morning.

Abe rolled a joint, bit down the edge, and took it to the bedroom. Dope-smoking had advanced over the years, but Abe still preferred the mellow, old-fashioned doobie. He didn't need to be out of his mind. He liked his mind, and he liked the pleasure of rolling his own joints. He sat cross-legged in the middle of the bed and inhaled deeply through his nose. When it became apparent that the room was too quiet, he turned on his clock radio, which brought him a pleasurable and entirely inconsequential argument about the moral character of Barry Bonds.

It occurred to Abe as he smoked and looked at the clock that his sinuses had cleared around the same time that Howard had died.

An eerie, discomfiting coincidence. The thing with the pigeon was another. Just loafing about the scene. Eight years earlier, when Abe had almost drowned, the last thing he'd glimpsed before he'd lost consciousness was a pelican with wings patterned like a stretch of desert viewed from the crest of a hill. He considered the nature of birds: their cloudy eyes and hard beaks, their tragic inattention. Human machines were always in their flightpath, their deaths so often our fault. Of course they'd seek out retribution any way they could.

IT TOOK SOME TIME to get Eunice to leave the yard. She remained sitting in the grass by Howard, smoothing his eyebrows and tucking in his ear whiskers, careful not to nudge his angled head. Alvin Dao stood by with a gurney. "The coroner's coming," Cassandra told her, but Eunice wouldn't move until he'd arrived. Even then, her children had to pull her to her feet and walk her inside.

The family spent the evening huddled in the master bedroom, drinking iced tea. Newly widowed, Eunice rested on top of the covers, her short legs stretched out in front of her, her shoulders propped up by mauve ruffled pillows along the wooden headboard.

"I should call the church," she said. "He hasn't been in months."

"We'll call them in the morning, Mom," said Howie.

Howie was fifty, with a perennially adolescent appearance. His face was virtually without wrinkles, his chin round and sparsely haired. Though bank tellers and waitresses still spoke to him in condescending tones, Howie's youthful appearance had actually spurred his greatest success. In five consecutive elections, the people of Bainbridge Island, Washington, where he'd moved in his thirties for the climate and outdoor activities, had made him a city councilman, finding him earnest, sweet, and considerably less phony than his opponents. It amazed Cassandra every November that a voting district so recently acquainted with her brother could understand him so well—

perhaps better than her family ever had. He sat now by his mother's side, patting her tiny cold wrist.

"Is Alvin all right?" she asked.

"He's taking care of Dad," Mary said. "Don't worry about that now." Mary was an organizer. Besides making calls and serving as the liaison to Alvin, she'd also organized her children into a row for comfort. Estella, Mary, and Max sat one in back of the other on Eunice's chaise lounge, hugging like bobsledders.

"We'll have to tell everyone there's no party," Eunice said. "And talk to Wendy about the flowers."

"It's under control, Mom," Mary persisted. Estella made a snuffling sound and bit off a lurid blue ring from her candy necklace.

"Don't forget the cemetery people. Your father had a deal with Frank for a plot on the west side, but I don't know where those papers have gone."

"Really, Mom." Howie patted her hand again. "It's Sunday. We'll do everything tomorrow."

"He wouldn't have wanted us to drag our feet," Eunice snapped.

"Well, he wouldn't have wanted to break his goddamn neck either!" Cassandra cried out from the bottom of the bed, where she lay curled around her mother's feet like a spaniel. "But he did! So he'll just have to be patient while we grieve."

"Shh, shh," Mary said.

"I'm fine," Cassandra said. "It's fine."

"Oh, Grandpa!" Estella cried, before burying her face in Mary's chest.

"Are you okay, Howie?" Cassandra looked up at her brother. His shoulders were shaking, and his face was wet.

"No," he said.

"Me neither."

"Me neither," said Max, who appeared fine.

"I can't stop thinking about the timing," Cassandra said. "The day before his birthday. With all of us here. It's just plain eerie." Howie reached down to squeeze her hand.

Elizabeth sat on the floor, her knees pitched, her back against the wall. Kyle was on her left, and now and then, she rested her head on his shoulder. This was her family. It really was a wonder he'd been alone when he died. How was it that half of them were at the store, and the rest no better than deaf? How, she wondered, had she not heard?

"I should have been out there," she said.

"Oh, Lizzie, no!"

"What could you have done?"

"Don't blame yourself!"

The chorus of protest was instinctive and sure—the voices of people who knew the ritual of death, but had not yet mastered the feeling.

AFTER DINNER, Toby went upstairs to his room. He no longer felt right in DC, where his mother lived so blissfully with her husband. Toby and Ruth had been extraordinarily close when he was growing up—just the two of them—but she'd changed with the ascendance of Ed. The things Ruth said no longer interested Toby; he felt increasingly that she'd turned out to be a member of another species, predestined to miss the point.

He sat now on a low stool with his guitar in his lap, his shoulders erect and calm. A blank notebook and pen lay within reach on the bed, though he didn't really need them. This wasn't practice, but something else, more central to his health. He played gently, his body hardly moving as his gaze shifted from the wall to the windowsill to the tips of his curling fingers.

When something caused Toby pain, he often found himself holding the guitar, passing hours in focused stillness. He thought through the instrument, made decisions in progressions of chords, and when he emerged he knew how he felt, knew what he needed to do. The music he made during these trances was never much good, but then, it wasn't that kind of music, not meant for an audience to hear.

In time, there came a knock. He turned to see his mother cracking the door.

"I don't want to interrupt," she said.

"It's fine. I was only thinking."

She moved halfway into the room, hands clasped behind her as though hiding a present. "I love my orchid," she said at last. "And I'm touched that you thought to buy me a plant."

"That's great, Mom. I'm glad you like it," he said, wishing he could slip back into solitude. Maternal fawning was no substitute for real conversation.

"No, really," she said. "This is important. I don't think most men your age are as aware of their mothers' interests as you."

He shuddered at the word *men*: a stretch. "Well, it was the best I could find."

"It'll be a new challenge for me, caring for it."

He looked at the blank page in his notebook. "I'm sure you'll succeed."

She came in further, studying his bookshelf; she wasn't getting the message. "My mysterious son," she said to the rows of his high-school paperbacks. "College graduate. What are you up to these days?" At dinner, he'd told her about an exhibit he'd seen at a gallery downtown. He thought that would have been enough.

"I've been studying some new jazz recordings. Maybe I'll tell you about them tomorrow."

"You haven't mentioned anything about your girl." Now that she'd found Ed, it was clear she wanted him to find someone, too. Before, she'd probably have been content to stay a widow forever, as long as Toby was around.

"She isn't mine," he said, thinking of Ramona with the short blunt hair, the most recent in his string of casual heartbreaks. He wasn't actually sure which girl his mother meant, but it didn't matter; nobody was his. He stood and set his guitar on the bed. "I'm meeting up with John tonight. I don't want to be late."

Her smile vanished and she bobbed her head, suddenly embarrassed. "We have all week." She backed into the hallway to let him pass, forcing a tiny laugh. "I only hope I won't have killed the orchid by then!"

"No," Toby said, "don't."

He wasn't actually meeting up with John, a friend from high school whom he hadn't seen in years, but he'd had to give some reason to leave the house. He backed his mother's teal Subaru out of the driveway, and at the strip of luxury stores turned left, away from downtown.

Driving provided another kind of trance. He held the wheel and turned this way, that way, letting the suburbs surprise him. Even the suburbs were sometimes capable of this. In the late evening light, he cruised down the avenue, admiring trees and stone houses, turning onto a side street now and then for a closer look at a painted door or a line of gingerbread trim. Before long, he'd wound his way to Bethesda, an affluent hub that had expanded even since he'd last been home. He parked in a garage and strolled along a sidewalk freshly poured that spring, according to a date someone had scrawled when it was wet. Two teenagers approached with their arms flopping around each other's waist. He crossed the street to avoid them and found himself in front of a multi-level bookstore. Inside, he browsed the tables until he came to one showcasing paperback fiction, finally deciding on a Western-themed novel that had been a finalist for a significant prize.

Having paid, he went down the street to the Starbucks. He'd heard all the arguments against corporate coffee, but was never persuaded to give it up. He felt that Starbucks was good, felt its dominance proved this, and considered himself more honest than the snobs for embracing it. Wiser in many ways, too; you gained back your own perspective when you entered the ubiquitous thing. He ordered a decaf espresso, tipped the bar staff, and found a plush corner chair in which to sit with his book.

He read two chapters straight through, pausing only a few times to contemplate a woman fidgeting with her sandal in the opposite chair, and a man in line who was disappointed to learn he'd ordered a drink that didn't exist. It was Sunday evening, quiet, when most in the suburbs were at home. He fingered the stone in his pocket and decided he'd come again the next day, and every day that week, until DC felt like any other place, for which he harbored no expectations.

4

Eunice was up early Monday, occupying the kitchen. With a damp cloth, she gently cleaned a set of turquoise salt and pepper silos, followed by a set that looked like a peasant boy and girl, and one that resembled two chicken eggs lightly flattened at the base. She'd chosen each set herself, all of them perfect pairs, delightful little objects that felt sturdy in her hand. By the time she opened the dishwasher, she was deep in the domestic zone. There, in the top rack, crouched four of her eleven diamond-cut tumblers—because, she suddenly remembered, she had only eleven of them now. Was that even enough for them all? She counted hurriedly on her hand, beginning with her thumb—Howie, Cassandra, Mary, Elizabeth, Max—then refreshed her fingers and began again—Estella, Eunice. That was it. How could she forget! Kyle. And eventually—ring finger—Vlad. Even so they were only nine, her pinky still drooping on her palm. She stared at it a moment: a shriveled thing with a tattered white cuticle and a tough old nail that was foggy as a horse's hoof. She closed her fist and hid it behind her then looked back at the glasses in the rack. It may have been the day after the worst day of her life, but she still had a house to keep straight.

Half an hour later, Cassandra paused in front of the round window on the second-floor landing. A teenage boy was standing on the footpath in the front yard, his head bowed as if in prayer. So the world already knew. Cassandra peered closer. His stance seemed to require a hat, held demurely behind his back. Fragmented by the window's soldered panes, the image of the boy reminded her of a modern movie set sometime in the iconic past. Who stood that way anymore? Her parents' house had always attracted the oddest visitors.

Eunice was distributing forks and spoons among the silverware drawer's dividers when Cassandra entered the kitchen. It was not yet 7:30.

"There's a boy in the front yard," Cassandra said, starting the coffeemaker.

"People will be coming by all day."

"But this early?"

"Death doesn't keep an ordinary calendar, Cassandra." Grief axioms never failed Eunice—even when the grief was her own.

The doorbell rang at eight. "That will be the first of the flowers," Eunice said.

"I'm sure it's not. We haven't even ordered them yet."

"I mean the flowers from other people. Trust me." Eunice went for the door.

But it was not flowers. It was Dorothy Chamberlain, Eunice's best friend, and also her most officious. A transplant from the South, she was a tall woman who dyed her short hair blond and wore dramatic eye makeup and heels even in the kitchen. She and her husband, Jules, had left Dallas fifty years before when he came to work for the Defense Department, and she spent the next five decades telling everyone she'd never forgive him. But Jules had died of a heart attack, several years had passed, and still Dorothy was not making any effort to return to Texas.

The moment Eunice opened the door, Dorothy was talking. "I told myself I'd wait until morning," she said. "The family needs that time at first to themselves. And I knew you were all here together—dare I say it: a blessing—and so I thought, 'Best leave them to themselves.

Eunice is a big girl. She can take care of herself.' But oh my Lord you poor thing: look at you, just look at you."

She pressed Eunice's head to her padded life raft of a shoulder.

"When my Julie died, I sat on the floor and cried for *weeks*. Wasn't it weeks?" She released Eunice. "But look at you, you're standin' and carryin' on just like you always do. My Lord, how *terrible*. To fall from a *roof*!"

Eunice smiled grimly. "I always say you have to carry on the best you can."

"Well, enough of that! I'm here to help. You'll do no more carryin' on today. Did you know there's a boy in your front yard?"

When the doorbell rang again that hour, it was a deliveryman, bearing the first of the condolence flowers. *Our deepest sympathies*, read the card, from an undertaker in DC.

"You see," Eunice said to Cassandra. "I know how these things work."

Cassandra experienced the rest of the morning as a steady stream of flower deliveries, phone calls from distant relatives who'd received Mary's message, and visits from neighbors and business associates with food. The family awoke one by one and began moving about the house like automatons, drinking something, eating something, sitting in one chair, sitting in another. Elizabeth had been the next person up after Cassandra, and yet they'd found little time together. Too many other voices and bodies, and Kyle was always nearby.

Dorothy ran the kitchen, baking casseroles and organizing the delivered food on trivets all around the house. She was a proud widow; the first to come and the last to leave whenever another woman's husband went under.

Meanwhile, Alvin Dao had arrived. It was supposed to have been a day off for him, and he had a family, but he was nothing if not a dedicated worker.

"Alvin," Cassandra cried when he came through the front door. They were alone in the hall; the voices of the rest of the household crackled in other rooms. "Thank God you're here." She nearly hugged him.

"I wouldn't usually come into the family home," he said, blinking rapidly through small round spectacles. "But I wanted to pay my respects in the proper fashion." He was a consummate undertaker, almost a parody of the profession: careful with the living, stiff as their dead. "Your father," he continued, "would have wanted it this way."

Cassandra nodded, her eyes watering, suddenly overcome with affection for the dour man who'd shared her father's business interests for so many years. She looked at Alvin, tacitly begging him for information. His eyes blinked several more times, and in an uncharacteristic gesture, he clasped her hand in both of his. Then, after a curt nod, he released her and hurried into the kitchen like a messenger with urgent news to share. Several rooms away, Cassandra heard Eunice's voice rise almost happily to receive his condolences, followed by a flattered mumble from Alvin himself. Cassandra had come to suspect that Alvin liked her parents more than he liked his own family. She thought of his solid, tidy wife and backpack-wearing school-aged boy, and felt sad.

The rest of the day, the Fabricants moved spastically through emotions and rooms. Eunice had always maintained that there was a hierarchy to grief: widow first, young grandchildren second. The children and older grandchildren who knew how to cope were last, expected to help with the planning and management of grief. It was a pecking order that Eunice, the Grande Dame of Grief Decorum, had developed assiduously over the years, promulgating it at every funeral she staged. This time—this one time—the hierarchy would focus on her.

Cassandra, Howie, and Mary were prevailed upon to decide where things should go, which calls should be answered, and who else should be notified of events. The most emotional of the three, Cassandra was the least equipped for such work. But she didn't want to disappoint her more stoic siblings, who were counting on her assistance. Between accepting hugs from near-strangers, she answered questions, took the phone, and tried to keep her mind focused on minutiae. Her eye sockets buzzed like lightbulbs, her body flew through space, numb and indefatigable. She had the sense that nothing could kill a person in grief.

In breaths, she found herself missing her daughter. "Where's Elizabeth?" she asked the nearest person whenever it occurred to her. She got a different answer every time.

"Did you see that strange boy outside?" she heard someone ask.

Another puzzle Cassandra felt compelled to solve. But only after the phone stopped ringing and the well-wishers stopped dropping by.

LATER THAT NIGHT, she sat on the large upholstered ottoman in her parents' bedroom, an empty bottle of beer at her feet. She'd come out of some compulsion, some childish hope that she and her mother might talk, only to find Eunice already asleep and snoring, which was really just as well. Other people evolved, went through phases, changed, but Eunice had always been Eunice: uncompromising, profit-driven, short on tenderness, loud. Cassandra had had fifty-three years to accept it, yet for some reason she could not. She felt resistant to her mother's personality, as though it were a medicine she'd taken too often as a kid. They simply didn't fit together, they didn't *get* each other. Even now, mourning the same man, they were probably better off apart.

The fact of her father's death ambushed her once again. She closed her eyes and steadied herself, chanting her new mantra, *Daddy is dead, Daddy is dead*, until she felt she'd been convinced. *Daddy is dead. Howard Fabricant is dead.* She pictured his face, still and rigid, lids lowered over sightless eyes. Alvin had a colleague working on him already; he'd be a wax person, embalmed, a glowing memory picture by tomorrow afternoon. *Daddy is dead. Howard Fabricant is dead.* The words would make her believe it.

His name, though, was too much alive, and in repeating it, she couldn't help herself; she began to feel she was somehow resuscitating him. It was as though they were still planning his party, and someone was keeping him away while she readied the cake and champagne. For a moment, she became convinced the body sprawled on the grass had been nothing but a shell, discarded for a ready-made replacement. He was still out there somewhere, suiting up: zipping his fresh skin into place, snapping a new spine to his core, getting dressed and excited for his party. She looked back at the bedroom door. *I know what you're thinking, woman,* he'd say to Eunice as she led him into the hushed and crowded room, *but your nagging will do you no good.*

Cassandra heard the sound of footsteps approaching in the hall. She waited, her eyes still fixed on the door. After a moment, the knob turned and it opened. She held her breath as Elizabeth came in, holding two bottles of beer. Cassandra looked away, mortified. She'd actually been expecting her father. She'd been waiting for him ever since she'd looked out the bathroom window and seen him lying there at her mother's feet. She had to stop forgetting and then remembering, forgetting and remembering. The pattern was too cruel, the surprise too genuine each time. It wasn't fair that grief had to work this way. That her father couldn't die just once and be done.

"Is she okay?" Elizabeth asked, joining her mother on the ottoman.

Eunice's snore had developed into a prowling purr that tripped every now and then on some invisible wire in her breath.

"Probably better than the rest of us." Cassandra took a swallow of the new beer.

Elizabeth moved closer and leaned on her mother's shoulder. "I'm going to help however I can. Anything you need, I'm going to do it."

Cassandra, still unaccustomed to her daughter's adulthood, said, "Thank you," and tried to think of something that needed to be done.

* * *

HER FATHER WOULD'VE known what to do. Or her mother, had she been awake. Her parents had never been uncertain, wielding an authority that had maddened her for most of her life, but would've been welcome now.

Neither of them had gone to college, so they were determined that Cassandra would go. "If you do well here," her mother had told her, sitting her down at her kindergarten desk, "you'll go on to first grade, then second grade, then all the way through to college." Even at age five, college sounded to Cassandra like the most glamorous place in the world—a place halfway between this world and the next where you lived on your own in brick buildings and all the girls wore dresses that swished when they walked through the constant grass. In reality, college was just half an hour up the Beltway, the University of Maryland at College Park, with its row of white-columned fraternities that reminded her a little too much of her own house, where the dead came in cars to be displayed.

"You'll help us in the office over Christmas," Eunice told her in the fall of her freshman year, and Cassandra did, returning home after every semester to balance the accounts for the glut of funerals the Fabricants staged every holiday and summer season. People died in those months more than any other, as though they were all just waiting for Cassandra to go on break from school, so that she could help her mother bill for services from the office downstairs.

Cassandra had made it through the first few years of childhood not thinking much about the people in her family: her mother, her father, then her brother and sister when they arrived. They were each just facts of life, like stop signs or the solar system. But then came a moment in the second grade when her teacher passed out a stack of blank index cards and instructed each student to write down the name of a hero, or a person most admired, suggesting the boys might say their fathers and girls their mothers if they had no one famous in mind. Cassandra sat in her pigtails and jumper with her pencil poised over her card, thinking about her mother for perhaps the first time. She was redheaded, with a nose and mouth Cassandra suddenly couldn't quite visualize. Who was this woman? She never wore shorts. She never failed to give instructions. This was her mother? Or had she been living with a shape-changer all this time, a creature who'd fooled her into thinking she was her mother, that a mother was even something a girl was supposed to have? She looked around the room at the other girls, trying to decide if all of them had mothers. It was possible they didn't; she hadn't been to everyone's house. She sat there until the teacher came around, at which point she hastily wrote "Judy Garland" before her mind could run away from her again. By the time she started junior high, she'd come to realize she didn't enjoy spending time with her mother, that there was actually something a little disconcerting about stepping off the school bus and seeing Eunice's face in the kitchen window, expecting her.

She was not homely, like some mothers, nor did she administer spankings. She was simply fond of saying no. She *was* the word. A ringing and resounding No to almost everything Cassandra wanted or tried to do. No eating with your hands. No growing your hair long. No jumping rope after school.

"You're not being nice," Cassandra had retorted once, when she was six or seven and feeling exceptionally brave.

But Eunice didn't care; she hardly missed a beat. "I'm your mother. It's not my job to be nice. It's my job to make sure you don't end up on the street!" In Eunice's vision, the street was a hellish place crawling with atomic garbage and unsavory trolls who basically ate children for breakfast. It was often invoked as an alternate way of living to keep her kids in line. "You think they have bathrooms on the street?" she'd ask them. "No! You think anyone on the street cares if your blanket itches you at night?"

It was strange that this walking No wore such smooth, slender shoes, and had a knack for finding books Cassandra liked. For all her threats, there was clearly a reason she was in charge.

In the business realm alone, she deferred to her husband. Eunice was a certified funeral director, but Howard had the mortician's license. Cassandra had read the words on that wall-framed document over and over, only vaguely understanding what they meant. Before she was old enough to help her parents with the business, she'd sometimes done her homework on the blotter at the big wooden desk, pretending to answer the phone and schedule appointments, as she'd seen her mother and movie actresses do. Both her parents spent great amounts of time downstairs—in that office, and behind other, even more grown-up doors off the long carpeted hall where she and Howie had several times set up soda cans and bowled.

She was nine when she saw her first body, sometime in the summer before she started fourth grade. The day was damp and Eunice had been staring at the kitchen calendar, murmuring to herself as she often did when someone had failed to show up on time. By then Cassandra knew better than to call attention to herself, so she sat in the nook eating Cheerios, looking neither at her mother nor at her siblings, who slurped across from her, but at the cluster of little O's that came up floating in her milky spoon. *Don't eat me!* she imagined them crying as they clumped together, the Cheerio mothers and fathers trying in vain to save their Cheerio daughters from her mouth. After she'd finished, Cassandra had taken Howie's and Mary's bowls along with hers to the sink, where she rinsed and loaded them all into the brand-new GE dishwasher, as was her daily responsibility. Water whooshed from the tap, filling her ears with sound. When she looked back at the breakfast nook, her brother and sister were gone, and her mother was standing in the adjacent doorway, holding out her commanding hand.

"Come with me," she barked.

"What'd I do?" Cassandra asked. "I'm sorry."

"You're not in trouble. Just come."

Uncomforted, but feeling she had no choice, Cassandra followed her mother downstairs to the basement and into one of the rooms where she'd never been before. The room was significantly cooler than the hallway, with many white cabinets, and in the center a blanketed shape loomed on a high table that came level with Cassandra's eyes.

Eunice stood in front of the table, hands clasped, as though the shape were something she could just hide behind her back. "Now," she said, "do you remember asking me where Daddy goes when he works?"

Cassandra nodded, though she hadn't asked in some time. The closed doors had become their own explanation; she didn't need a tour.

"Good." Eunice gestured around at the cabinets and counters, where several metal tools lay in a serious row. "Do you know what Daddy *does* when he works?"

Cassandra sucked her lips and looked down. "You know. He . . ." She lifted her head again. Eunice was looking at her, waiting. It was just like getting off the school bus at the end of the day. She wanted to go back to school.

"He makes the bodies," Cassandra finally said, without conviction. The bodies she'd only heard about in conversations between adults. The times she'd been in the chapel where they had the funerals, the bier had been empty, an excellent base for a game of tag. She'd clung to it with her fingers as Mary shrieked and Howie came lunging by, reaching for her sleeve, but she'd never seen a body.

Eunice was nodding and moving her hands with sudden decision. "You're a big girl now," she said. "It's time."

Cassandra felt a rush of panic. But before she could protest, Eunice had pulled the blanket back to reveal a monstrous, blanched forehead with two arms and two legs dressed in a plain gray shift. The eyelids below the forehead were bruised and sunken, as though someone had come in before them, raised the blanket, and punched them several times. Cassandra stood still, focusing her eyes on the cloth of the shift. Her mother rested her hand on the table by one of the arms, and began to speak. She explained that in every town, someone has to take care of the people who pass and that it was a very honorable and kind thing they were doing for the families in their community. She then explained that they'd been running this business since Cassandra was a baby and that her father was an expert who everyone wanted to consult and that there was now another room just like this one across the hall, which let them help more than one family at a time. "Never forget that we help people," Eunice said. "We do the thing that's the hardest thing in the world to do, and we thank heaven every day it's not us up there on the table." Cassandra looked down at her pink jelly sandals and tried to think of a question to please her mother. Something about the metal tools on the counter would be good, or what happened to the man to make him pass, but the question she simply couldn't help but ask was the most babyish one of all.

"Is he asleep?"

The whole thing left Cassandra feeling lofty and insubstantial like she sometimes did just before she came down with a cold. When the time came for lunch she couldn't eat, and for once, her mother didn't scold her, merely cleared away the plate with her sandwich, and put it in the fridge for later. When, that afternoon, it began to rain in dense, grapelike drops that splattered against the front windows, and a restless Howie, who clearly had no idea what she'd seen that morning, suggested they play some tag in the chapel, Cassandra demurred, finding sudden interest in a volume of Nancy Drew her mother had brought home from the library. Dinner passed without event, Eunice serving up pot roast, Howard chewing in his special seat, where no one could sit but him. Cassandra ate most of her dinner, but didn't taste it, the meat and potatoes dissolving into nothing on her tongue. The next day she took her book to a hideaway she'd made with pillows behind the living room's swirly gold-patterned couch. There, with her knees tucked up in front of her, she followed Nancy down a hidden passageway between two mansions to free her kidnapped father. The story grounded her again. It was nice to know that other people had worse problems, and that even these could be solved if one was only Titian-haired, eighteen, and determined. She wished her parents had had the sense to name her something cute, like Nancy. She couldn't wait to be eighteen.

Like most strange feelings, Cassandra's light-headedness soon wore away, and within days she was onto a new game of stitching fabric into people shapes with her mother's sewing kit. She worked her way through the Nancy Drew series and when she thought again of her father's two preparation rooms and all the people who called to consult him about their loved ones, she began to feel curious rather than frightened and resolved to be the big girl her mother had instructed her to be. Cassandra Fabricant, girl detective, would solve the case of the mysterious body. Without any schoolwork to do, she began to hang around the basement office again, hoping to give her father clues that she was interested in more than just bowling.

"Whatcha doing there, Cass?" he asked her, as she swung herself back and forth in the doorframe, feeling the exhilaration of the almost-fall and the neat competence of her fingers at the catch. He was wearing his glasses and making some sort of calculation. He hadn't even looked up when he spoke.

"Nothing," she told him, pulling herself upright, suddenly embarrassed. Her father was the fun one, but he was also serious about his work. Through his glasses, he went *into* it, which meant that he could sometimes be very far away even when he was sitting right in front of her. She was not sure how she was supposed to behave in the presence of such professionalism.

After a moment, he set down his pencil and looked up at her, giving her a wink so quick it might not even have happened. "Well, what were you doing before you started doing nothing?"

He repeated her word jauntily, which seemed to give her permission to keep being a kid. She swung herself forward and back again, trying to decide what to tell him. "Making people," she finally said, thinking of what he did down the hall.

"Oh, yeah, what kind of people?"

She couldn't explain it. Who could explain the weird little dolls she had created with her mother's remnants and half a jar of dried beans? She ran upstairs and collected them so that she could show them to him instead. She'd made four, a series of wiggly bean bag people each topped off with a small but heavy head from a sack of Howie's marbles. They were held together with thread and different combinations of patterned fabrics leftover from aprons, handkerchiefs, and curtains. When she laid them out on her father's desk, their arms and legs flopped wide.

Howard picked up the pink plaid-and-paisley one and gently turned it over in his hand, rubbing its belly with the tip of his thumb. "You made these by yourself?" he asked.

"Yep. I mean, yes."

"Yep's fine by me. Just don't tell your mother. She'd have our heads." He made a motion with his finger at the doll's bunched-up fabric neck. "Did you have a kit or instructions or anything like that?"

"No, I told you. I just made them."

"You're telling me the idea just came into your head and off you went?"

"I guess so." His questions were all exactly the same and yet somehow each one was more difficult to answer than the last. "I don't *know*," she wailed.

Then her father did something very strange. He saluted her and placed the bean person in his shirt pocket, where it hung forward like someone knocked unconscious by a villain in Nancy Drew. "Can I keep this one?" he asked. His eyes looked watery.

"I have boy colors, too," she said, hastily holding up a boring blue-and-gray striped doll.

He patted his pocket and placed his other hand on top of her head. "This is the one I want. Come on. Let's go find your brother and sister and see about getting some ice cream."

Elated, she left her dolls lying there on his blotter, and followed him up the stairs to the hallway, where she waited for him to gather everyone else. At Howie's request, they took the hearse, and because Howie and Mary had been squabbling over crayons, Eunice sat between them in the back, which meant that Cassandra got to ride up front with her dad. He put on his hat before he got in, and lit up a cigarette at the first stoplight. As he drove he tapped the ash out the window as though making a trail to follow back home.

At the ice cream parlor, Cassandra ordered a double chocolate malt and her father danced the doll along the marble countertop. "You see what my little girl did?" he said to the owner, a shiny-headed man with whom he'd always been friendly. "She made this. With her own hands. You know what kind of kid does a thing like that? An *artist*." He slapped his hand down on the counter as though it were a catapult, making the bean doll jump. "That's what kind! My little girl's a born artist." He kicked the doll's leg out then clicked its heels in the air like Gene Kelly. The bald man laughed and congratulated them all, giving her an extra cherry. She sucked at the red-striped straw and twirled it between her fingers. It was like a propeller, she thought, thinking like an artist. She could save the straw and cut it open when she got home. Everything made so much sense now that her father had said it. Even her mother was smiling and putting a warm hand on her back, her mother who had never once suggested she could be anything of her own devising. Teacher or nurse, she'd always said—never artist. For all Cassandra knew, artists lived on the street.

In the weeks that followed, she continued to hang around the downstairs office, making new dolls: out of cotton swabs and her mother's torn stockings, out of carefully scissored brown paper bags. Finally, one day at the very end of the summer, it was somehow arranged that she would watch her father put the final cosmetic touches on an old woman's body while her mother took Howie and Mary to buy new shoes for school. Cassandra could hardly speak, she was so twitchy with competing feelings—first excitement, then terror, then determination to suppress her terror. This was important, she told herself. This was a secret most kids her age wouldn't know. She was beginning to sense the limits of her knowledge already—the paper-bag doll failing to stand on its own, the stocking doll lacking features on its face—and here was a chance, in her very own house, to know something that would set her apart. Was she an artist or not? Was she a big girl or not? On the eve of fourth grade, the time had come to prove it. At breakfast that morning she considered telling Howie, whose ears turned such a satisfying red when he got jealous, but ultimately decided against it. It felt better to keep this challenge to herself.

Cassandra read in her room until the appointed hour, hearing the sounds of whining in the hallway, followed by a door slam as her mother and siblings headed out, and still more whining—muffled now—from the driveway below. The car drove off and she read on, digesting none of the words as she waited. Lost, she went back to the beginning of the paragraph and started afresh, only to be interrupted by her father, whose knock on the wall outside her open door was so soft she never would have heard it had she actually been reading her book. His face was solemn, but bright, as though he couldn't be seen smiling, but wanted her to know just how happy he felt. "Well," he said, and waved her over with his strong, reliable hand. She closed her book and followed him down the two flights of stairs.

In the embalming room, he slipped enormous adult-size latex gloves over her hands and knotted them tight at her wrists to keep them from falling off. She wiggled her fingers underneath, feeling the talc clot against her skin. The deceased was a Mrs. Ida Hanover, whose ancient puffy face was about to receive the last brush of color that it would ever know. Her heart racing, Cassandra stepped onto the little stool her father had set up and prepared to do as she was told. She looked down. Ida was clad in a silk frock of royal blue.

"Her dress is pretty," Cassandra said, trying to be casual, as though she assessed burial clothes every day.

"It is," Howard said, snapping on his own properly sized gloves. "Her daughter chose it because it brought out her eyes. Silly, right?" He gestured at her closed lids. "But you can't argue with people." He looked at her with swift concern. "Ready?"

"Yes," she said, not because she was, but because she wanted to be.

"Then we're off." He dipped his latex-covered fingertips into a tub of cream and transferred half the volume to his other hand, then set about massaging the cream into Mrs. Hanover's cheeks and along the bridge of her nose, up to her eyelids and forehead and down again along the jawline to her chin.

"Always make sure the skin is nice and soft," he said. "Never do any makeup without moisturizing first."

He moved his fingertips in tiny circles across her skin, some-times adding pressure from the thumbs. As his fingers worked their way down, the skin he left behind seemed brighter, warmer even, as though considering coming back to life. Cassandra watched closely, but Mrs. Hanover never moved—not even when Howard dipped his finger in the vat of cream again and returned with a final dollop that he smoothed one-handed into the top, bottom, and insides of her lips.

Next, he held out three vials of skin-toned liquid and asked Cassandra which one looked the most like Mrs. Hanover. He pointed to a color photograph he'd pinned to a small bulletin board. "Always choose a shade that's subtle. Never dramatic." In the picture, Mrs. Hanover was standing in her blue dress with her hands clasped in front of her next to a low stone wall in the country. The collar that now lay flat against her chest lifted slightly in an invisible wind and her skin was pale but pinkish, her features clearly, in that moment, alive. Cassandra looked back at the liquids and strained to see the differences among them. *Always subtle, never dramatic*. She decided finally on the palest of the three shades. Howard agreed and set about dabbing a small amount across Mrs. Hanover's face, more heavily in the darkened spots on her nose and upper right cheek, before dusting her amply with powder. He then applied a light blue eye shadow and two faint streaks of powdered rouge across her cheeks, pretending to doff Cassandra's nose with the brush when he was done. The muddy smell of makeup and the thousands of powder particles now shim-mering in the air near her nose tickled her throat, making her feel for a moment as though she couldn't breathe. She turned away and sneezed into her latex-covered hands, and when she turned back, her father was holding out a handful of uncapped lipsticks and asking her once again to choose.

She'd seen her mother apply lipstick in front of the bathroom mir-ror, and she'd seen the red paper rainbows in drugstores advertising the variety of choices, but she had never before seen so many shades of pink and red open to the air all at once. She wanted to sweep their luscious, extended tips across her cheek and have every color upon her face at once. But this wasn't playtime; it was business. And the business at hand was not her own face, but Mrs. Ida Hanover's lips. What color were they? She looked back at the sunny photograph. "Your mother will want her to look like a lady," Howard said. Cassandra agreed and thought hard before finally selecting a dull, sturdy pink that best matched the lips by the wall in the country.

Howard painted Mrs. Hanover's mouth in six deft strokes, a short and two long for each lip, then stood back, capping the stick, so that Cassandra could admire the finished face. It looked, if not alive, then at least yearning for life. "This is what the families want," Howard said, standing on the floor behind his daughter. "They want to see their loved ones one last time."

She sucked in her breath. Her father was in the business of imitating life. Suddenly the room seemed incredibly small and bright, like the hospital elevator she'd ridden with him and her brother on the day when Mary was born. It had paused for several seconds before opening its doors and Cassandra had wondered in that time if they might have to live in there forever. The possibility of such a sudden and drastic change had made her feel as though her stomach were somehow being sucked out her back. Now, in her father's workroom, the sensation returned. Only this time, it excited her. The things she was learning from her father today meant she would never again be the person she'd been before. She'd be smarter than her classmates, a person who knew great secrets. She placed a hand on his arm in gratitude.

"That's a brave girl," he said, removing her gloves. "Now," he said, turning her to face him. "Don't tell your mother."

He held up a round hand-held mirror with little ripples circling the edge, as well as a fresh trio of lipsticks still in their cellophane. She had never seen anything she wanted more. He let her stay there while he moved Mrs. Hanover to another room, so she sat down on the stool and practiced her stroke, a short and two long on each lip as he'd shown her, covering her mouth with layers of China Rose, Scarlet, and Bardot Beige. How magical they were! Now she knew what people meant when they said a shade really brought out someone's lips. In the mirror, hers floated freely from her face, taking on a life of their own. They were practically old enough to be in high school, these lips—and she was only nine!

When she was done playing, she huddled the mirror and the three shades together on the counter for her father to hide, then took care to wash her hands and face thoroughly over the little aluminum sink. The talc from the gloves was initially stubborn between her fingers, and the lipstick left her mouth looking slightly blurred, but the water was cool, and the soap smelled piney and dark, like Christmas. When she was done, she crept back upstairs to her room, where she picked up her book once again. She reread the same paragraph in which she'd been mired that morning, but got no further before her mother came home.

"I hope you had a good morning," Eunice said. She stood formally at the edge of the bed in one of her nicest dresses, a white flower pattern over a French blue background that was lighter but somehow more vivid than the blue on Mrs. Hanover downstairs.

Cassandra sat upright and pressed her lips together, in case any evidence remained. "Oh, yes. I learned a lot."

Her mother's eyebrows rose, with her chin following close behind—a look of expectation suggesting there was still more she ought to say.

"Thank you," Cassandra said, hurriedly, hoping she'd guessed right.

Eunice smiled, and Cassandra relaxed. Her mother had a pretty smile, shiny and almost extravagant when compared with the severity of her resting expression. It colored her cheeks and rushed her face to life. "Well, you're welcome," she said. "If you're good you might get to help your father again."

She wasn't so bad, Cassandra thought. She only wanted what was best; she just wanted it badly. Cassandra could see it in the way she held on to that shiny smile, tucking it up high into her cheeks, as though waiting for someone to take her picture. A picture of success.

Already in her young life, Cassandra had wanted many things she was still waiting for, so she knew something about impatience and how panicked it could make you feel. Maybe her mother was just a little bit panicked, too.

When the bullying heat of late summer finally capitulated and gave itself up to the fall, Cassandra returned with her siblings to school. A new attitude began to take hold of her. A more grown-up, fourth-grade attitude. Her mother wanted what was best, so maybe it was best if she didn't always know what was going on. Cassandra didn't confirm this reasoning with her father, not directly, but something in the way he tilted his head when she appeared at his office door after school suggested he felt the same.

"Your mother hopes you'll take over the business one day," Howard told Cassandra one afternoon, as she sat in the embalming room, copying out her weekly spelling list. Which was the most he ever said about what it was, exactly, that Cassandra was doing down there.

That fall she was simply in awe of her father's workrooms, finding them almost sacred in their capacity to transform. When he let her join him, she brought her dolls, which she sometimes stashed among the tools and vials, making the preparation space just a little bit her own. She brushed her hair and removed the strands that remained in the bristles, tossing most of them in the trash, but sometimes saving one or two to hide in her father's jars when he wasn't paying attention. She made more dolls and put on her lipstick in the corner, and when she got restless, she practiced dancing on the cold cement floor. She posed for her father, kicking her heel up like a girl onstage. "See, Daddy," she said, swiveling around the room as though underwater. "I'm Esther Williams. I'm the Million Dollar Mermaid!" He applauded and she pretended to have turquoise flippers, and flecks of glitter all over her cheeks. It was their secret place, where people could be reborn, if only for a few hours, and not quite as they were before.

One afternoon, she looked up from her worksheet map of the counties of Maryland to see her father straightening his back as the body before him approached completion. It was an old man's body, long and gaunt with knuckles twice as wide as his fingers. Her father looked from the man to the photo on his corkboard, a finger to his lips in contemplation. She inhaled, smelling something slightly foul she hadn't noticed before. Hardly realizing that she was holding her breath, she watched her father, captivated, as he reached some important conclusion.

"Looks like I'm going to need one of your colors this time," he said at last, reaching for the cupboard where he stored her private collection. "Good old Bardot Beige." Before she could respond, he had uncapped the stick and was applying it to the man's sunken mouth.

"You can try this one if you want," Howard said, handing her a shiny silver tube. "Never used."

The new stick was a ripe pink no different from the color of her tongue. Using the mirror, she poised it over her lower lip and would have rolled it on as she'd always done had it not been for a thought that suddenly flicked across her mind like a flea, gone before she even knew where exactly she'd been bitten. Spooked, she realized she was about to do to her lips what her father was at that very moment doing to dead lips, and though she'd done it thoughtlessly before and had just as often seen her father hard at work, this precise new way of looking at things overwhelmed her and made her wonder what she'd been thinking all this time. He'd bought this color for the lips of a dead man. *Dead* lips! It was horrifying.

She made an involuntary squawk, which caught and gargled in her throat, a sound that spooked her further and broke her into tears. When he rushed over and shook her shoulders, told her to quiet down and just stay calm, she only cried louder, helplessly, tears coursing down her face with abandon, though she knew it meant getting her kind father, her greatest ally, into trouble. She couldn't bear the thought of her mother discovering their secret, but even more than that, she couldn't bear the thought of spending any more time in that unnaturally chilly, horrid-smelling room or doing anything to her face that her father did to the faces of people who'd died.

"No!" she shouted, tearing herself from his grip. She stumbled into the hallway. Back in the room he stood dumbfounded. It was awful; it was worse than if she'd seen him naked. "I can't!" she cried, willfully now. "I can't I'm sorry I *can't!*"

After that it wasn't long before Eunice was screeching at him like a jay, demanding to know how he could have thought to give their daughter makeup—she was only nine years old! Not to be outdone, Howard bellowed back—loud, clear words about being a man and knowing harm from fun and really it was all her fault for scaring everyone so much. The house was flooded with noise as it always was when they fought. Her mother panted and screamed as she would at a murderer. Her father practically choked on his words. "Why don't you have a drink and lighten up?" he said, bitterly, pouring a sloshing one for himself.

It didn't stop until he gave up and retreated, stalking past her and out of the house after dark, a vapor of cigarette smoke filling the space behind him. He was going out, he shouted from the hall, to be alone, to be with reasonable people who said reasonable things, and though he appeared again at breakfast the next morning, showered, dressed, and smiling as though nothing had happened, the echo of those words stirred uncomfortably between father and daughter as they sat eating their Cheerios and milk. She had let him down. She had been unreasonable and she had betrayed him to the most unreasonable person of all.

UNABLE TO MAKE a decision of any kind, Cassandra remained on the ottoman with Elizabeth, which was where Mary found them a short while later. She looked tired, but no less efficient than usual. "The bakery delivered Daddy's cake," she said. "Plus a couple extra gratis. We can put one out for the wake, save the other two for Thursday."

"Cake for a funeral?" Cassandra asked. "Isn't that a bit inappropriate?"

Mary furrowed her brow in condescension. "Cassandra," she said, "it happens all the time. You know that."

In fact, Cassandra didn't know. Or if she'd once known, her adult life, far away from funerals and their rituals, had allowed her to forget. What surprised her was Mary's authority, as though she hadn't been off living an adult life of her own, teaching seventh-grade history in Pittsburgh, attending intellectual dinner parties with her academic husband, and hurrying her twins through their gauntlet of college-preparatory activities. As though she'd stayed home to run the family business and planned funerals here every day.

Mary twitched her head slightly. Her fine blond mane, which had poured down her back as a child, now sat up neat and short around her face.

Seeing her opportunity to leave her mother in someone else's care, Elizabeth stood and kissed Cassandra on the cheek. "I'm going to bed."

"Make sure Kyle's out by the time I come in," Cassandra said.

"I *will*." Elizabeth slouched out, like a teenager, the hem of her T-shirt barely skimming the waistband of her jeans. She closed the door behind her.

Alone with their mother, the sisters were silent. Mary stood aside, watching Cassandra, who watched Eunice, still slumbering. Cassandra could tell Mary had something to say, something she wouldn't want to hear.

"I called Abe," Mary said finally. "Last night."

Cassandra snapped her head up, though in truth, she'd expected her sister to interfere. Mary stood with her arms folded across her chest, her hair accusing Cassandra of some negligence. When Cassandra didn't answer, she sucked in her cheeks; for a moment, her features aligned in a familiar scowl. Mary was even more like their mother than she was, Cassandra realized with some relief. Which sparked no new sympathy for Eunice, but somehow made her love her sister more.

"I didn't ask your permission because I knew you wouldn't let me," Mary said.

"Damn right I wouldn't."

"Well, it's about time you talked to him. That's all."

"I talk to him enough."

"Bullshit. When?"

"All the time! You can't not talk to your ex-husband in this day and age, can you? We have to talk about Elizabeth, and her future, and how well we're doing without each other."

Mary gave this her full consideration. "I didn't know," she finally said.

"It doesn't matter."

"It *does* matter." She sat down eagerly next to her sister. "All this time I thought you were being an idiot."

"No."

"What a relief."

She waited for Cassandra to respond, getting nothing.

"Now that Vlad's here," Mary went on. "Estella has to sleep on a couch. I made Max go with her so she's not alone."

"Mm."

"So if you're talking, why didn't *you* call him? Why did I have to do it?"

"Jesus, Mary, I don't *enjoy* talking to him. I don't like him. The last thing I needed today was the sound of his voice. I'm sure I would've called him tomorrow."

The little sister held up her hands, *mea culpa*. "Fair enough. I jumped the gun."

"So there you go."

Mary patted Cassandra's knee. Eunice gargled and seemed to sing.

"Can we be sad about Dad now, please?" Cassandra asked. "I'd just really like to cry about *this* right now."

"Cry, then. No one's stopping you."

"No one's stopping you either."

Their childhood had forged in them a certain bluntness. Only outsiders were allowed to be surprised by death—people who had not spent their formative years glimpsing body bags rolling into and out of the basement service entrance, who had not been called upon as teenagers to fill seats at embarrassingly underattended wakes.

Cassandra threw her arms around her sister's shoulders, a clumsy sideways embrace. "Fuck," she said. "All day long I've been waiting for him to come back."

Mary freed an arm and curled it around Cassandra's back. "I think that's normal."

"It's pathetic," Cassandra said, settling in to rest her head on Mary's shoulder.

"Well, yeah, of course it's pathetic. But that's just the way it goes."

SHE'D LIED TO Mary about Abe. She hadn't meant to. But the way the day was going, it seemed the easiest course to take.

The truth was simply too strange. The truth was that Cassandra had not actually spoken to Abe since they set their terms of divorce. Abe had left the lawyer's office first; Cassandra waited for the second elevator. And then it had been eight years. It startled her every time she remembered. Had she been asked, in another life, if it were possible to quarrel with a man after twenty-some years and never speak to him again, much less a man she'd once loved ferociously, she would have answered that it was impossible, however doomed the relationship had become. But here it had happened, and to her.

To her surprise, it had been easy, like losing a baby tooth. Wrenching at first, when the roots twisted and snapped, a pad of blood rising in the gap that remained. But you lived, you went on. You put the severed tooth under your pillow, pearly and grooved like a stone from the beach, something inanimate and hardly yours, and you said goodbye to it—forever.

Yet when she'd stepped onto the boat that day, she hadn't wanted to end her marriage, nor did she really believe she could. Even when she and Elizabeth arrived back at the house that evening, and she put a yearning Linda Ronstadt album on the stereo before readying ingredients for a midsummer risotto—even then, Cassandra hadn't believed it would end. The fight was already beginning to recede from her mind. She felt vaguely embarrassed and not herself, and her hand shook enough that she had to steady her knife for a good moment before cutting into the onion. But as the minutes pulsed by, she remembered less and less of what had happened, and rued it less still. Before long she felt safe in her assumption that Abe would walk in the door after a few hours, stirred to his senses by his swim in the bay. They'd acknowledge each other and tacitly make up. A few minutes later they'd be talking about dinner, or a patient of his. Later on that night, she'd find a way to apologize and make it clear that her affair was over, and he would nod and wave the explanation away.

But when Abe did arrive, beleaguered and dripping across the white kitchen tiles, it became apparent that none of this could be. Another reality had already taken hold. Down the hall he went, past her almost uttered apology, shaking his head, never looking back, a line of water droplets curving in his wake.

By then she knew it was too late. As she stared down the hallway after him, watching his wet trail glisten in the fading evening light, she realized how wrong she'd been to hope. She'd let him swim; she hadn't chased him. She had, after all, gotten just what she'd deserved. Shaking, she covered the uneaten risotto, no longer daring to wish for forgiveness.

Since then, she'd made many more risottos. She still lived in the Berkeley house, excessive though it was; she hardly needed all that space. "Your client will keep the house," his lawyer had proposed, and Abe had looked down murderously at his interlocked hands. Rather than sell it or kick her out into the street, which would've been the sensible thing to do, he seemed to want her to live with what she'd done, to see the ghost of him in every room. In her timid worthlessness, she acquiesced. She had, after all, destroyed something rare and precious; her life should bear the punishment, as inescapable as death.

* * *

TIRED OF WATCHING Eunice sleep, Cassandra said good night to Mary and went down the hall to her room. Pausing outside the closed door, she placed her hand on the wall, as if to detect the presence of Kyle inside. She heard movement in the room, and then a whisper that was Elizabeth's voice, tinny and echoing, like a radio program picked up from several counties away.

"Don't touch me."

Cassandra held her breath. She put her ear to the door, hearing nothing but silence and then a rush of motion that made her jump back.

A moment later, Kyle was in the hall. Seeing Cassandra, he let out a sudden taut laugh. "Jesus, what a day."

"Is she all right?" Cassandra asked.

The skin on Kyle's face was gray and thin. She felt she could have reached up and peeled it right off, leaving him with nothing but a sadly smiling skull.

"Of course she's not all right," Cassandra babbled, answering her own question.

"I'm sorry." Kyle was grim. "I don't know what to say. She's having a tough time."

Mustering her maternal comfort, she squeezed his arm. "You're a sweet boy. I know you'll be there for her."

Kyle ducked his head and walked heavily up the stairs to his room.

"Oh," Cassandra said. He stopped, one leg poised to take the next step, and turned his head like a warrior on a mission he knows will be his last. "Estella and Max are on couches tonight. So you've got that bed to yourself."

Kyle nodded nobly. "Good night."

"Good night, Kyle."

She went into the bathroom and squeezed a smear of toothpaste onto her electric brush, then stood back and watched it buzz across her teeth in the mirror. Her face was webbed with tiny blood vessels, the hollows beneath her eyes shaded as if with a pencil. She didn't look well. Or rather, she looked about as well as she could expect under the circumstances. What surprised her was that she also looked mean, her pupils hard, her jawline unnaturally clenched. Mean, like a mom who needs to tell her kids how to be, who enjoys stopping other people from having fun. Not at all the good listener and sympathetic hugger, the easygoing, laughing mom who really gets it—the mom she'd always been. Or thought she'd been, anyway. Wanted to be. She rinsed her toothbrush and put it back on its little charging stand, then flicked the light switch and went across the hall to her bedroom, opening the door a crack.

She might have let him sleep with her daughter. With Howard dead, it didn't seem anyone would care. But Elizabeth's whispered rebuke had made her feel protective. *Don't touch me.* If that was, in fact, what she'd said. Whatever had occurred between them, she knew her daughter. She was a fragile creature, her Elizabeth, and Kyle was perhaps too clumsy to be much comfort. A lion's paw could easily crush a kitten, even if it meant to be kind.

The room was dark but she could see in the blade of light from the hallway that Elizabeth was curled up on her side under a blanket, facing away from the door. She didn't move when Cassandra came in, but Cassandra couldn't tell if that was because she was already sleeping soundly—Elizabeth did have a knack for it, falling right off on airplanes, and even, as a teenager, at her desk, with a lamp still blazing in her face—or just pretending because she didn't want to talk.

Well, Cassandra would let her pretend. The world would be a much more pleasant place if everyone were allowed to pretend a bit more. She undressed in the dark and when she finally slid under the blanket, Elizabeth shifted slightly, as though consciously or unconsciously making room for her mother in the bed. Cassandra turned to face the back of her daughter's head, and as her eyes adjusted, the redness of Elizabeth's ponytail emerged from the dark, triumphant and familiar as ever.

5

As a kid, Elizabeth had always had projects. A Saturday in autumn and she was creating a play. One of her friends was over, a waifish brunette named Jessica who spoke in complete, overly enunciated sentences that just weren't normal in a twelve-year-old girl. She had a bubble head and large, ferocious brown eyes, and was famous for her endless straight A's. A dark version of Elizabeth, as much her rival as she was her friend.

"*Frenemy*," Mary had once told her on the phone. "You never had one? I had lots." After that conversation, Cassandra tried out the word, whispering it under her breath as she wiped down the bathroom vanity. It was too cute for what it seemed to mean. She couldn't say it without wrinkling her nose.

Even the girl's name, Jessica—never Jessie or Jess—suggested a precocity that made Cassandra uncomfortable. As though she were the child and Jessica the adult. The girls had spent the better part of the afternoon in Elizabeth's room, singing and thumping around. Trying to stay out of the way, Cassandra retreated to her attic studio to work on a series of bowls for the PTA auction, so that Elizabeth and Jessica and all their classmates could partake in the traditional seventh-grade camping trip at the Angelo Coast Range Reserve. Jessica's parents were scientists at Cal, so she, she could not help mentioning, had already been there once.

But now the girls were before her in the studio. Elizabeth tilted her head and made a screwy face, like a character in an after-school sitcom. She was such a ham, a perfect mimic. A perfect everything as a matter of fact.

"Cool bowls, Mom," Elizabeth said.

"Thanks, Liz. What do you want?"

"No, really. Aren't they, Jessica?"

Jessica regarded Cassandra's workstation neutrally. "They're great."

The bowls were round and blue-glazed, with streaks of earthy tan and white. Just the sort of thing the school's mothers went mad to serve ice cream in. Cassandra had seen similar bowls in numerous East Bay shops, which was how she got the idea. She could've sold these in those shops, and maybe she'd think about it after the auction, if she could bear the boring week it would take to toss off several more sets.

"Well, they're coming together."

Elizabeth traced a wave pattern with her toe along the floor. "Don't you think you might need something to pack them in? Some Styrofoam or something?"

"I have a whole roll of foam sheeting in the closet."

"Oh." Elizabeth looked back at her toe. Jessica was staring at the corkboard Cassandra had hanging by the door. It was covered with postcards, photos, and magazine cutouts. Inspiration for future work. Elizabeth looked up suddenly, bright with a new idea. "Well, what about fabric? Maybe to wrap around the bowls somehow, to present them?" Jessica snapped her head over and nodded.

Cassandra laughed. "Lizzie, I'm not covering my bowls. I want people to bid on them!"

"All right, Mom." Elizabeth crossed her arms under her chest. She had only recently acquired her first set of bras, earlier than was probably necessary but apparently later than everybody else. The lavender strap of one of her most padded ones slipped out from under her tank top, bowing coyly along her downy arm. With a huff, she yanked it back. "Here's the deal. *We* need fabric, and I thought if you were going to the store we could come with you."

"Hmm. What do you need the fabric for?"

"For our costumes, okay? We're making togas. That's all I'm telling."

"Togas! Now I really can't wait to see this play."

"We can do it for you tomorrow," Elizabeth said. "Which is why we need fabric today."

"Not to interject, but we have to have at least one dress rehearsal," Jessica said. Not to *interject*?

"You can't use sheets? Most people nowadays make togas out of sheets."

"But we want to cut them."

"Look," Jessica barged in. "We made sketches. We've planned." Out of nowhere she produced a sketch pad and feathered its pages for Cassandra like a flip book. Elongated girls with giant, Disney eyes sailed by in various colored-pencil getups. She saw headbands and tendrils and what appeared to be a lyre. Jessica's work, no doubt.

Cassandra reached out to stop the flying pages. "Let me see."

But Elizabeth threw herself between them, forcing Jessica to hug the sketch pad to her chest. "After, okay? It'll spoil it!" Her voice was manic, even jealous. Cassandra almost regretted showing any interest at all. Her daughter's face was still the face of childhood: moony, cheeky, every expression whirling open like clay on a moving wheel. Yet an early rim of adulthood had already formed. It hovered there in the corners of her large, expressive mouth, which probably would not get any larger, a guideline for the rest of her, still spinning into place.

"Come on, please?" she begged, bouncing on one foot.

THE FABRIC STORE was on San Pablo, well past the yacht club, where Abe often sailed, and sometimes drove her just to look, threatening in his teasing way to actually buy a boat. She was happy enough on land, on her own well-balanced feet, or in her car, even, trundling down San Pablo with the girls. Elizabeth fanned out across the front seat, her bare feet up on the dash in the free-and-easy mode Cassandra had always relished in her daughter, while Jessica sat primly in the back, gazing out the window at the palm trees and traffic gliding by.

They parked on the corner across from an empty, weedy lot on one side, and a strip mall on the other. A whole crowd of people stood around the bus stop out front. "Well, well," one of them said as Cassandra guided the girls toward the store, and not for the first time Cassandra couldn't be sure if this person was approving of her figure or the figures of her daughter and her daughter's friend.

Inside, the girls were off, not quite running, but not quite walking either, making a great show of holding themselves to a measure of decorum as they veered toward the aisle Cassandra knew they had in mind. Elizabeth's favorite: the satin aisle, where roll after roll of delicious liquid color lay ready to pour itself by the ream into hungry preadolescent hands. Cassandra hurried to catch up to them. When she finally turned the corner, she found them already flinging themselves about, their eyes darting high and low, crying, "Blue!" and "Pretty!" and "I want to be silver. No, gold!" It was Elizabeth who made this last declaration, and as she spoke, nuzzling up to the roll in question, her cheek actually seemed to catch the hue, as though gold were not just her desire, but also some chemical need. This, Cassandra thought, was a child who knew how much she was loved.

"I don't know, guys, satin's pretty tricky to cut." She said it for show only, because she'd already decided she was going to let them have any fabric they wanted.

They went to the counter with their colors in their arms: sunny gold for Elizabeth and cobalt blue for Jessica, with clover green, and cranberry red, and a plummy shade of purple as well. The woman at the counter was petite and snub-nosed with the liberated air of a retired schoolteacher. "What are you making?" she asked them.

"*Actually*," Jessica said. "We're writing a play." Cassandra winced at her pedantry. As though merely making something weren't enough. "These are for the costumes we designed." Mercifully, she didn't bring out the sketch pad.

The clerk gave a veteran smile and asked no further questions. "Break a leg," she said as she slid their plastic bags across the counter.

On the drive home, Cassandra popped a tape into the deck and they all sang along to Joni Mitchell, contending to nail every syllable, pause, and modulation. To her surprise, the girls actually seemed to enjoy the competition. Elizabeth swiveled her head to smile at Jessica, and Jessica beamed back, even as her lips kept moving, straining not to miss a beat. Cassandra wondered if maybe competition was healthy after all, if it did, in fact, as every PE teacher had insisted since the dawn of PE, make you stronger. She saw Jessica blush in the rearview mirror as she wheezed over a line she didn't have the breath to complete. She gulped for air, her nose crinkling with a hint of self-deprecation, and then came back bravely, openmouthed and joyful, her large eyes closing for an instant as she felt a high note click into place.

She was only a girl, after all, only a girl trying to find her place in the world. And if she needed to enunciate her advanced vocabulary to secure that place, as a smart girl and a good citizen with a bright future still forming ahead, so let her. She was not her daughter's enemy. She was just like her daughter, her compatriot and friend.

JESSICA'S PARENTS TURNED OUT to have plans the next day, so the whole production was put off another week. In the interim, Elizabeth went to school wearing her bras and enormous backpack, having long stopped letting Cassandra walk her to the bus. Evenings, the fabric came out, still uncut, still full of possibilities. Elizabeth wound it around herself in constricting, mummifying bandages that made it impossible for her to walk down the stairs.

Meanwhile, Cassandra and Abe made their appearance at the PTA's Saturday night fund-raiser, a semiformal dubbed the Night of a Thousand Stars. Everyone was encouraged to be "wacky" and "creative" in their attire, so Abe wore a beret and red velvet blazer and Cassandra wore a black flapper dress with fringe from a Halloween costume many years prior. The straps, made of satin, were her private tribute to Elizabeth's latest scheme.

They carpooled with their back-door neighbors, Steve and Gail, whose older son, Andy, was a year below Elizabeth, and whose taste in garden vines and patio music had been simpatico with theirs for years. Steve had volunteered to drive so that Cassandra, Abe, and Gail could all enjoy themselves more thoroughly. Gail had, by chance, gone to the University of Maryland, like Cassandra, and though they'd never crossed paths in the year they overlapped, in mixed company they often liked to pretend that they were best friends from college, rewriting years of pre-California history in a single jovial lie.

"Abe's looking fit," Gail murmured, once they were all out of the car. "Has he been hitting the gym?" Gail looked like Grace Kelly and talked like Barbra Streisand. Her mint-green strapless tulle that evening was one hundred percent Grace.

"He just sails," Cassandra said, watching the men kick at imaginary pebbles on the asphalt. "Good genes. It isn't fair." A chilly breeze set the fringe on her dress swinging. She felt momentarily hollowed out, like she hadn't had enough to eat.

The cafeteria had been made over, as it was every year, into a more inviting space for adults. Lanterns hung from the rafters and the overhead fluorescents were dark, with rented standing lampposts providing most of the ambient light. Someone handed Cassandra a leaflet itemizing the goods up for grabs, and though she'd scanned a draft of it earlier that week when she dropped off her bowls, she thumbed through the final list now, looking for her entry. There it was, in the midrange bracket. A set of six ceramic bowls by Cassandra Green. Value: $90. Starting bid: $45. Above her entry was a glass pendant necklace on a recycled fiber cord by one of the jewelry-making moms. Below it a hand-knit replica of a mouse dissection by one of the crazy moms whose work Cassandra had seen in those very same

Berkeley shops in which she was considering displaying her bowls. Was this really a market she was prepared to enter? She shuddered and turned the page. Here were the big-ticket items: helicopter ride, dinner at Chez Panisse, handmade guitar, year of weekly homemade desserts. What poor woman had offered that? Someone who was whipping up cupcakes and cookies every week anyway and finally wanted someone to appreciate it? Actually, Cassandra understood the impulse, more than she wanted to.

Gail and Steve had wandered off somewhere, but Abe was by her side with wine.

"Anything good?" he asked.

"Oh, I guess. We should probably set limits. For instance, I'm not bidding on anything unless I actually want it. No more feeling sorry for people." She remembered the private magic show she'd almost walked away with the previous year, because the magician—the weird boyfriend of one of the math teachers—was working so hard to drum up bids. There was something embarrassing about the way he thunked around the stage, shoulders hunched, hair glistening and vampiric, looking one parent in the eye and then shifting his kooky gaze to another, that Cassandra could see the crowd growing uncomfortable, all of them wishing they were someplace else or invisible, or at the very least not in any way responsible for the childish delusions this man still held about himself. For a painful moment, no one said a word, until, unable to bear the sight of a performance ignored, she shouted, "Fifty!" The encouraging smile of the emcee and the endless, flat silence that followed were almost as excruciating as the silence that had made her speak up in the first place. *What have I done?* she thought wildly. Fortunately, just before her thoughts had a chance to grow darker, a few other parents, those with younger children who might actually like a magic show, piped up, settling on a modest $300, and she never had to bid on him again.

"How about a dollar limit?" Abe said now, sipping his wine. "Isn't that more practical?" And he was right. It was about how much they were willing to donate to the school. For Elizabeth. But she could never think in those terms at an auction. She thought only of the individual transactions. Of having the things that she wanted and avoiding the things she did not.

"Cassandra, hello!" Here from somewhere below was Sheryl, Jessica's mother, whose diminutive features and height—she couldn't have been more than five feet tall—surprised Cassandra every time she encountered her. Sheryl was a geographer stationed at Cal, involved in mapping various changes in the San Francisco Bay estuary, and with her short, boyish hair, slender shoulders, and ample, athletic hips, she looked good in her magenta cocktail dress, if not entirely comfortable, or fully grown. She wore sharp black heels to give her a few extra inches, but so did everyone else, and she swayed in them now, unnaturally, like someone experiencing a minor earthquake.

"Good to see you," Cassandra said, stooping to kiss Sheryl's cheek. "Big weekend."

"I guess it is, yes!" Sheryl looked around at the other parents with an expression of bright curiosity, as though they were a species she was tracking for her work. "I had no idea it was such a production. This is the first year we've been able to make it. Usually, you know, I've got work, but tonight I got to leave a graduate student in charge. Hello, Abe!"

"Sheryl." Abe raised his glass while Cassandra sipped from hers. Sheryl was never not cheerful, but she regularly spoke in the self-aggrandizing mode of university people, gently undermining even the most innocent of small talk. Cassandra suspected it had something to do with her childish appearance, and with some deep academic insecurity—her husband was a full professor while she was apparently only temporarily on the faculty—but it irritated her nonetheless.

"And then, of course, we have the theater tomorrow," Cassandra went on, grinning mischievously, determined not to feel defensive. Gail and Steve had rejoined them, each with a glass of wine. Abe was elbowing Steve in the ribs like an old teammate, and Steve was dancing back and waving his hand. "Hey, Doc," he said, "I can have one or two, can't I? We'll be here all night."

"What are you seeing?" Gail asked.

"Yes," Sheryl chimed in. "What?"

Cassandra looked at Sheryl. "I was kidding. The girls are doing their play for us." She turned to Gail. "It's this whole big thing."

"Oh, of course!" Sheryl said. "When you said theater, I thought you meant, you know, theater. But the girls. Right." She pressed a thatch of hair that was already obediently in place. "Well, you've seen the rehearsals—they've been doing all this at their house," she said to Gail before turning back to Cassandra, "—any idea what it's going to be like?"

"All I know is they're wearing togas. I took them to Discount Fabric last weekend."

"These girls," Sheryl said, beaming and shaking her head. "Where do they come up with this stuff? I swear it's not from me."

"Oh no," Cassandra said. "They've got minds of their own."

Sheryl's husband, Jeff, a biologist who did something with microbes, appeared, balancing two more glasses. There was nothing wacky or creative about his attire, a tweedy blazer and khakis he no doubt wore to class, but then, there was nothing wacky or creative about Jeff, either. He smiled deferentially, seemed to want to speak, but didn't.

"Shall we get some food?" Sheryl finally said, and they all made for the buffet.

As they ate they browsed the silent auction. Cassandra watched Gail and Steve giggling—like kids, really, sometimes they were just like kids—and pretended not to notice the cluster of women gathered around her bowls.

By this point, the band had taken up their instruments, a group of graying long-haired slouchy dads and their equally slouchy teenage sons. The female singer now adjusting the microphone taught chorus at the high school. "We'd like to thank the PTA for having us," she said in a faint bluegrass drawl. "And we'd like to thank you all for giving a bunch of washed-up musicians a chance to shine on this fine evening." She herself couldn't have been much older than thirty but Cassandra knew what she meant. There was, in some ways, no place more washed up, more rinsed out and hung up to dry than a PTA auction on a Saturday night. Everyone in the room had been young and revolutionary once. They'd been human and animal rights activists, actresses and writers and hippies and lovers. People who read big books and had big ideas. They'd looked ravishing on two hours' sleep and even better with a joint between two fingers. But now they had faces lined like old paint and costumes that disguised nothing, that were the same as their ordinary clothes. They had children who were eleven, twelve, and thirteen years old, and more hopes for them now than they realistically had for themselves.

But the band was good, covering various classics, and before long, Cassandra had drained her second wine.

"I see we're headed for a real party," Abe said, collecting it.

"Don't judge."

"Who am I to judge?" He held up his own empty glass. "Be right back."

She watched him go off with the deliberate stride of the long-successful, his butt twitching boyishly to the music, and felt a little sad. Not because he was disappointing in any way, but because he was so damn good. When Elizabeth was younger, he read to her every night before bed. He'd do it now, too, if she'd let him.

Cassandra was still standing there when a dad with puffy gray mutton chops and a red-and-white striped Vaudeville jacket appeared onstage to start the live auction. The Chez Panisse dinner was up first, an instant hit, though there was no one in the room who hadn't been.

Next was two months of free housekeeping. Cassandra had quit using a maid a few years prior and was beginning to feel musty once again. All those corners she couldn't quite reach.

"One hundred," she called, offering the first bid.

"Good choice." This was Steve, who was suddenly at her elbow.

"Oh no, Steve, will you be fighting me for this?" She was feeling saucy all of a sudden, imagining all the lost earrings and socks her new maid would recover.

"Nah, we're set. Between our weekly service and Andy. You know he's become a neat freak? Sometimes I catch him at the bookshelf, lining up all the spines. He's meticulous about it."

"Lucky you! Elizabeth does nothing but make messes." Which wasn't strictly true. "And every day she loves us less." Why had she said *that*?

Fortunately, Steve was lost in his own problems. "He insists on separate plates for his food, too. The string beans can't touch the chicken." He divided the air with his hands.

At eleven? This didn't sound right. She tried not to look alarmed. The bidding was already up to $200.

"But," Steve said, "at least he doesn't insist on wearing a cape anymore. He made us call him Batman." Steve worked at Cal, too. Something to do with data systems and information technology.

"Two fifty!" she shouted, thinking, for some reason, of Steve coming into her house with the maids, straightening her books like his son.

Abe returned with more wine, and she won the prize at $500. "Cheers," he said. "To cleanliness." When the band started up again, they danced. Cassandra let Abe lead her as she knew he liked to do. He spun her this way and that, pushing her waist with his hand. She looked down at the fringe that swung over her breasts and hips like layers of silky black hair. She had always been a good dancer. Still was. Amid all the grown-up smells—the spiky perfume, the wine-splashed silk, the vaguely sweet, pickled sweat of people slipping past their prime—she caught a whiff of milk carton, that fresh, sterile fragrance of dairy on paperboard that greeted their children every day. She couldn't understand why she'd felt so out of sorts before. She felt young now in the school cafeteria.

Then the emcee was back, auctioning off more luxuries to an ever more enthusiastic crowd. A bidding war erupted over the helicopter ride, the band drum-rolling along in encouragement, the emcee offering a wheezing push-up for each improbable new bid.

Cassandra felt light. She shouted like a football fan for the fiftieth push-up, everyone shouting right along with her, for they all had a stake in the school. They loved their children. Though sometimes their children were unlovable, they loved them so much it hurt. Or maybe that was why it hurt. Their voices lifted and mixed together amid the lanterns, closer in air than they ever could be on the ground, even within the intimacy of marriage and friendship, even brushing up against one another's shoulders as they did now, in their community, with their people, their crowd.

She leaned into the shoulder she thought was Abe's, but it was not. It was lower down and solid like a gymnast's. It was Steve's. Somehow Abe had slipped away. She looked around for him, but her vision was slightly blurred, and all she saw were middle-aged heads and shoulders facing toward the stage. And Steve. She looked at him tenderly. They were just the same height. Brave Steve, father of Batman. His eyes widened like, *Oh, Christ, what the hell,* and all at once she smelled his aftershave.

"Don't tease me," he mumbled.

"What?" She turned to glance at nothing. And suddenly there it was, that old familiar feeling at the back of her neck, where she imagined Steve was looking. That warm, tingly feeling, as though the outermost cells of her skin there, the ones that were by all accounts nearly dead, had suddenly raged back to life, wanting more. It was the feeling of being noticed by someone. Of having powers without even trying. It was the feeling of being herself.

"You're too amazing," Steve said. "It isn't fair."

She didn't know what she said after that. She fell into him. She nearly kissed him.

She didn't, though. She didn't kiss him. That part was important. There were so many things a person *might* do when drunk, when among other people, when in costume, when lost in any powerful feeling or thought. But it was what you *did* that actually mattered. And she had promised Abe that there would never be another slipup. She'd promised him in such formal, unambiguous words—"I will never, ever do it again"—that she swore she could still hear them knocking around inside her head, resonating in the dry roof of her throat, meaning exactly the same thing all these tired years later.

Did he know that, though? Would he trust her? No sooner had she felt the rise of Steve's gymnast chest against hers, and pulled back to see the tremulous hesitation in his face, did she see Abe crossing toward her bearing a plate of dessert in each hand.

THE NEXT MORNING, Cassandra took the dog for a walk, something Abe usually liked to do, but he had gone to the store to collect fixings for an East Coast breakfast: bagels, cream cheese, capers, lox. He'd woken with a craving, he said. A college-morning taste in his mouth after their college-style night. He gave her a wink, as though he'd been the wild one. Ferdinand trotted a few feet ahead of her, turning his head every now and then to make sure she was still with him. "I'm here," she told him, crabbily. The cool morning sky spread above them, cavernous and blue with a reef of blotchy white clouds that tacked it to the highest recesses of its dome. An East Coast sky. A sky that promised a change of seasons.

She still wasn't sure what Abe had seen. She'd been drunk, and her first instinct had been to act even drunker, save her ass. She sat down extra heavily at one of the tables and made a show of digging through her purse for a pen to make her closing bid. When she finally found one, she stood and made her way to the silent auction table, where she took great care in printing an extravagant number next to the tidy, unequivocal letters of her name. *Cassandra Green.* She was going for the mouse dissection she'd suddenly realized was brilliant, and was exactly the kind of crazy thing Elizabeth would want to have. When Gail appeared, she hugged her. "I love you," she said, breathlessly, resting her chin on Gail's shoulder. "Thank God you're here." Which she meant. She thought it all the time. What the hell did Steve think he was doing? He had the Princess of Monaco right there.

When they got home she made an effort to wobble out of her shoes, and when Abe shushed her, she shushed him back, giggling, with a finger to her lips. It was easy playing drunk, especially when she already kind of was. The headlights of Gail and Steve's car flashed like a camera as they drove on around the block, and she must have looked nice in the light, because out of nowhere, Abe swooped toward her, semideranged, and hoisted her up over his shoulder. The gray-knit mouse, with its red-knit heart, hung by his butt in her hand.

He managed to get all the way up the stairs and into their room before he set her down again, on her back on the bed, her arms and legs stretched comically wide as though she herself were ready for dissection.

"Scalpel!" she'd whisper-cried, as she often did when they were young. Doctor wasn't a game they played much anymore now that they were older and had Elizabeth, and Abe was a doctor everywhere he went.

But for whatever reason, he'd complied, drawing an incision line with his finger from her throat all the way down to her clit.

Ferdinand tugged sharply on the leash, yanking her into a run. The frothy tail of a squirrel was flying up a tree. "No, Ferdinand," she barked, planting her feet and pulling his head back. "Heel! You hear me? I want you to heel!" The dog just glanced at her, not even ashamed, then surged forward against the leash once more. She gave up. She let go. Ferdinand took off down the street, feeling the air in his coat, the mounting seconds of motion. She didn't even panic. She knew this dog. He only wanted a taste of freedom, the thrill of chasing a squirrel. As soon as the squirrel was out of reach, and he found himself alone, he'd come padding back, the loops of his collar jangling against themselves, as though he'd never been anywhere else.

"This is your one strike," Abe had said when she screwed up the first time, his face so expressionless she thought she might die. She still saw that face in her mind. She'd do anything she could to avoid seeing it again in real life. "You can never, ever do this again." He spoke like it wasn't his choice, just the way things had to be.

He hadn't seen. Couldn't possibly. But how close she'd come. How *close*.

She sat down on the curb and folded her arms across her knees. The concrete was hard but the grass behind it was blanketed in morning wetness. She rocked back and let the edge of her butt get pleasantly dewy while she awaited Ferdinand's return.

JEFF DROPPED OFF Jessica while they were still eating breakfast. Elizabeth leapt from her seat to get the door, leaving behind a dogleg of bagel slathered with cream cheese and a plate full of sesame seeds.

"We'll be back at one," Jeff called from the car, holding his arm out the window in a sheepish attempt at solidarity.

"Makeup!" Elizabeth shouted in a grand-dame accent, as Jessica chased her up the stairs.

By the time Jeff and Sheryl arrived for good, dressed as though they might actually be going to the theater, the girls had arranged four chairs in the sitting room and tied an afghan blanket to the wooden balusters on the little balcony overhead. They were hiding upstairs, leaving Cassandra to answer the door.

Nobody harbored illusions that this visit was about anything other than the kids, but Cassandra played hostess nonetheless, ushering Jessica's parents into the kitchen for nuts and crackers and cheese.

"Thanks, no, I'm still stuffed from last night," Sheryl declared. She'd said thanks, though somehow it felt as though she hadn't. "That's the trouble with tapas and sushi. It's all so small, you think you can just go on forever. But you can't, can you? The body has limits!"

"Or how about something to drink?" Abe was there, suddenly, shaking Jeff's hand. "Iced tea? Perrier? Something stiffer?"

"Whatever you're having," Jeff said to Abe.

"I'm just having water, if anything."

"Oh, well, then do you have an orange soda?" Jeff asked.

"*Orange* soda?" Cassandra repeated. "Let me think."

"It's fine if you don't."

What was it about these people that made her so determined to please them? Who had orange soda just lying around? She recalled standing uncomfortably with them in their front hall one afternoon when she'd come to pick up Elizabeth. It was an overcast weekday, and they were both home, their stacks of papers and academic journals standing in dreary pedestals around the living room.

"I've got some root beers in here," Abe said from the fridge. "That do?"

"No, really, I'm fine with water," Sheryl said before turning to Cassandra breathlessly. "It's so nice to see you again! That was fun last night, wasn't it?"

"It was fun."

"We won a case of wine, did Jeff tell you?"

Cassandra glanced back at Jeff, who was accepting a root beer from Abe, and looking rather unhappy about it. "No, that's great."

"And we wanted to bid on your bowls, but we didn't. You were so nice to donate them. I don't have anything anyone would want."

Cassandra gave a curious smile. Why would you tell someone you wanted to bid on their bowls if you didn't? Really, why mention it at all?

"Aren't you glad you came, though?" Cassandra asked, passing Sheryl a glass of water. "I always leave feeling so good about the school."

Sheryl looked into her glass, as though hoping to find something interesting at the bottom of it. "Who was that couple you introduced us to? I know I must've met them before." She seemed to be combing her enormous brain, pushing past species and salinity levels, to remember this basic detail.

"Who—Gail and Steve?"

"I think so. Maybe." As though Gail and Steve were side characters and not some of her closest friends! Didn't Sheryl understand that *she* was the side character, the one who never came to school events?

"They're dear friends of ours," Cassandra said, hearing herself. She sounded prissy and loud. Filling her own water glass, she made an effort to modulate her tone. "We had you both for dinner a few years back. We made fish on the grill?" It had been a quiet night, despite Gail's constant storytelling, despite Abe's magnificent tumble down the porch steps with six short-stemmed aperitif glasses in his hands. Remarkably, not one of them broke; he landed on his knee with his arms in the air, like a Christian athlete in the end zone. Cassandra, Gail, and Steve had laughed hysterically, and Jeff, to his credit, had cracked a smile, but Sheryl just sat there.

"Oh, yes, of course," Sheryl said, uncertainly. "Steve seemed fun! I saw you dancing at one point. He actually seemed to know what he was doing!"

Cassandra's neck grew warm. "Last night? I don't think I danced with Steve."

"No?" Sheryl fingered her pearls—such an odd choice, pearls. On a Sunday afternoon. In Berkeley. "I'm pretty sure you did."

Cassandra suddenly felt passionate about the facts. "Really, I didn't. We talked, of course, but no dancing."

Sheryl frowned. "Is there another woman who looks like you?"

"I don't know." Her tone was measured.

"Well, I hope so. Otherwise I'm going to have to start worrying about my memory, and God knows, I'm too young for that!"

Cassandra looked at Abe, who mistakenly took this as a signal. He loped over in his easygoing way and placed a hand on her shoulder. She hoped he couldn't feel the flush of her skin underneath.

"We were just talking about memory loss," Sheryl said to Abe.

"*Ladies* and gentleman." Here, at last, they were interrupted. Elizabeth stood in the kitchen doorway cloaked in one of her father's white coats. "The performance is about to begin." She spoke in her theater voice, projecting: half British Isles, half deaf.

Relieved, the parents took their root beers and waters to their seats.

Then came silence. Then the sound of bare preadolescent feet. Then, all at once, music: synthesizers and a clap beat from a boom box upstairs, a song by Paula Abdul. The afghan curtain rushed up and there was Jessica; above her, on the second floor, Elizabeth popped out from behind a wall. Their arms flew out and clasped their elbows above their heads. They rolled their hips, not unseductively, but also a bit like electric mixers grinding dough. They were wearing their togas, of course, and they seemed to have assembled them well. Each girl had a flap of fabric over one shoulder that she'd pinned to her bra strap, while the other shoulder stood bare and free, the bra strap somehow tucked under. When Cassandra squinted, her daughter was almost a woman.

The choreographed dance complete, the parents applauded, but their daughters were only just getting started. Now it was on to the featured presentation.

Jessica returned to center stage, this time dressed as a boy. She was wearing a plastic breastplate over her toga, and carrying a plastic sword. "Let Rome in Tiber melt," she proclaimed, "and the wide arch of the rang'd empire fall! Here is my space."

"So you say." Elizabeth appeared behind her, her arms folded crankily across her chest. "But you, Antony, are married to another. Tell me you love me and not Octavia!"

As a family, they'd seen a production of *Antony and Cleopatra* a few years prior. Cleopatra had had long, thick dreadlocks and Antony was often shirtless and heaving. At the time Cassandra had worried it was all too erotic for Elizabeth, but Elizabeth was more disturbed by the deaths. She sat quietly through much of the performance, and as it neared its conclusion, and the lovers were defeated at Actium, she began to grip her armrests like a nervous passenger on a plane. When the climax finally arrived, she stared, mouth agape as the berobed Cleopatra put a lifelike snake to her breast.

"But *why*?" she asked on the car ride home, her dress bunched between her legs.

"They'd lost the war," Cassandra explained. "And Cleopatra would rather die than become Caesar's slave."

"Why couldn't they have run away? Maybe Caesar would've let her go."

"But that's the nature of tragedy, sweetheart," Abe said. "An opportunity is missed, and a great life ends. You are supposed to feel sadness and regret. You are supposed to wish it hadn't happened."

Elizabeth considered this. In the rearview mirror, Cassandra watched her look out at the light-filled hills of the city as they headed back across the bay.

"But, but," she said, finally. "The snake! She did it to herself."

The play had stuck with her. It had to have been her idea.

"You care about Rome more than you care about me!" she cried now in her toga. "You don't love me. You never have!"

Where had she learned to shout like this?

She swung at Jessica, who clapped her hands as she spun offstage. A trick Elizabeth had learned in theater camp and practiced on her dad. There was no mistaking it for an actual slap, but Sheryl gasped anyway.

"O, never was there queen so mightily betray'd!" Elizabeth wailed. She lay down and put her hand to her forehead. She panted and writhed on the floor. "What I wouldn't give for my salad days, when I ate nothing but vegetables, and they tasted so good."

Here again was Jessica, sans breastplate, sans sword. "Madame? You called?" She seemed to be trying to sound like a twit.

"Yes, Charmian, come hither!"

Jessica minced over and arranged herself elegantly by Cleopatra's side.

"Tell me," Elizabeth went on, "why do I need Antony?"

"Honestly, Madame, you don't. You're the most famous woman in the world!"

"Exactly!" She got to her feet, gesticulating. "I'm Queen of Egypt. My word is law. My way or the highway. I think, therefore I am. And you know what I think, Charmian?" Here she crouched and stage-whispered to Jessica, cupping her mouth with her upstage hand. "I think a girl's gotta have her fun. Let's hit the town. Meet some boys."

"Ooh," Jessica squealed. "Boys!"

The performance went on from there, but Cassandra could not follow it as closely as she had before. Watching Elizabeth play a man-eater in their living room was like watching herself cry out to be caught. She was aware of Abe in the chair beside her, and the regular rhythm of his breath keeping pace. Calmly, she tried to synch her breath with his, tried not to fall behind. But it was only a matter of time, wasn't it? Before they fell out of step once again. And what then? Would she fall straight into someone else? She didn't think so; it had been so long. But Steve had been her warning. That stirring on the back of her neck. The way he'd spoken to her out of the blue. Even if he hadn't really meant it—and for Gail's sake she hoped he did not. Regardless, it was possible. And then what would Abe do? Throw her out, as he had threatened? Blame himself, try to win her back?

She didn't know which was better.

For now at least, she was safe. She continued to breathe with Abe, and every time she glanced his way, she felt a little less agitated. He leaned back with his arms folded confidently across his chest, taking in the performance.

The play concluded with Antony prostrating himself before Cleopatra and Cleopatra taking him back. Perhaps in some other universe, they continued to rule the world, dancing an encore, as the girls did, to the inevitable "Walk Like an Egyptian."

After Jessica and her parents had gone, Cassandra and Abe gave Elizabeth the mouse dissection. Cassandra had wrapped it in a drape of satin she'd found in her bag of remnants. "This is so gross!" Elizabeth said excitedly, poking the thread of its exed-out eyes. "I cannot *wait* for high school."

She was going to be a doctor, Cassandra could already tell. Despite the play, despite her mom.

"They were awful, weren't they?" she said to Abe once they were under the covers that night. "I hope we don't have to see them again for a while."

"Who, Jeff and Sheryl?" As though she might've meant someone else.

"Yes."

He looked up from his book. "I don't know, they're not so bad. Jeff had some pretty interesting things to say about laboratory protocols."

He'd been known to do this. Often, when she needed to be catty, he'd undermine her, casually refusing to be on her side. As though he wasn't aware that there were sides to begin with. Still, she was surprised. He'd flayed her on this very bed the night before, consumed her. Why the indifference now?

She supposed it was partly her fault. One of her biggest problems was that she was constantly surprised by people. How different they could be from her, how inconsistent. She was nearly forty. She might've grown used to inconsistency by now. But she'd known Abe for more than fifteen years and every month or so it seemed she needed to be reintroduced.

She watched his chest rise and fall against his book. She made her chest do the same, kept pace. She concentrated on the feeling of it, the movement deep inside her, the stirring of cells where the air warmed the surface of her skin.

6

By the second full day of mourning, Elizabeth was finding herself surprisingly capable of ordinary human behavior. She ate, went to the bathroom, went for a run, and otherwise did as she was told. She'd even watched, and chuckled at, a movie on TV. But observing her family and Kyle, she found their behaviors strange. Her grandmother spoke at length to people she'd always claimed she didn't like; her mother looked drunk, even when she wasn't. Was it natural to be so quiet, as Kyle was? He stayed near her, like a bodyguard, but his hugs were somehow less firm, as though she had a contagious virus he didn't want to catch. He hadn't done a voice in days; he'd barely cracked a joke. He was never this somber when they were alone, never this traditionally respectful. Why the act now, of all times?

For a while on Tuesday, Eunice introduced her to everyone who came through the front door. Policemen and butchers and librarians—but mostly wives and mothers. A few of them tried to talk to her about a hurricane in New Orleans, as if to—what? Make her feel that her loss was small? "He would've volunteered his services," one of them told her. "If he were with us, he'd be there right now." She wasn't sure about that, actually, but she smiled at them all and tried to think the best of everyone, until Eunice, perhaps sensing her fatigue, finally sent her upstairs to sort through photographs for display at the next morning's wake.

"Bring me all the best ones," she said, "and I'll choose."

In the third-floor study, Elizabeth settled herself on the floor, legs extended, a cardboard box balanced on her lap. Kyle sat on the edge of the folded-up sofa, leaning forward and bouncing his knees.

"You sure you don't want ice cream?" he asked.

"I can still barely eat." She tossed another snapshot of her grandfather in a black suit onto the pile of possibilities.

"What about a beer?"

"No. Thank you."

"You've gotta want something."

"I want you to stop bouncing your knees."

He was still, his voice pathetic. "Sorry."

"No, I'm sorry," she said, reflexively. "I didn't mean it."

But she did mean it. Why did he irritate her so much? He'd done nothing but touch her and look at her and talk to her on her terms for two years. From the moment she'd picked him up in Rob's friend's smoky kitchen, he'd been ready to follow her map. "Take the Brooklyn Bridge," she'd told the cabdriver, en route to Kyle's apartment, where she'd never been. "I won't argue with a woman!" Kyle had said. "Me neither, man!" the cabbie said. "They always right!" Elizabeth had been drunk, but she still remembered Kyle's teeth winking in the dark, how proud she was to have conquered the cutest boy at the party.

"It's all right," he said, trying a different approach. "Did you see Dorothy's shirt? She looked like Liberace." He held his kneecaps down with his palms.

"Maybe I do want ice cream. Will you go?" She had to get him out of the room. Even at a distance of five feet, he was sitting far too close.

Vindicated, he stood up. "What flavor? What kind?"

"Surprise me," she said, out of character. She always knew what she wanted.

Alone, Elizabeth continued to peel through photographs. Her teenage mother holding a 4-H ribbon in front of a table of frosted layer cakes. Her uncle Howie on a pony with a cowboy hat on his head. How nice to live only the life shown in photographs—a life of prizes, parties, and fun.

Before long, the room was invaded again, this time by the twins.

"I *hate* it down there," Estella said, slamming the door behind her. "So loud."

"Yes, it's much quieter up here," Elizabeth said sharply.

Max scowled by the window, the backyard below him: a pile of tools, an unfinished sauna.

"Your boyfriend left." Estella knelt down next to Elizabeth. "He looks like Matt Damon. What are you *doing*?"

"I'm looking through pictures for Grandma."

"Not Matt Damon, moron," Max said.

"He does," Estella insisted.

"You mean Mark Wahlberg."

"*Mark Wahlberg*?" Estella was disgusted. "No."

Kyle always reminded people of a movie star—any movie star, it hardly seemed to matter which one. Women became bolder when they spoke to him, or shier, depending on their feelings about celebrities and themselves. Older men wanted to be his advisor, younger men his friend. He was always connecting with people, or otherwise being discovered, which was probably a useful quality for an aspiring performer to have.

"Are you going to marry him?" Estella taunted.

Elizabeth pictured Kyle in his suit, bowed over the bar at Lucie's wedding. "Maybe. I don't know."

"Guess I'll have to be your flower girl."

"Ha. You might be a little old for that by the time we get around to it."

"So you *are* going to marry him! Has he proposed?" Estella crouched forward on her knees, pressing her fists into her cheeks.

"I thought you were supposed to be a tomboy. You're as bad as Grandma!"

Estella flinched. "No, I'm not," she said, already sensing you didn't want to be like Eunice, even a little bit.

"He hasn't proposed, and that's the last I'm going to say about it. Now, help me choose some photos for Grandpa."

"Okay," Estella said. Max nodded. Both twins had cried the first night, but were now much less affected. They plopped down on either side of her, their slim memories of their grandfather having already begun to fade.

Together, they flipped through another stack of unsorted photos: 1969, 1981, 1932, date unknown. The twins listened as Elizabeth recounted some memory she had of a photograph—this one was in her mother's leather album at home, this one was enlarged and framed on the downstairs mantel. But most featured people she didn't know, in places she'd never been. The images of their mother always attracted the twins' interest, and at every blonde sighting, they stopped Elizabeth's hand. "Is that Mom? Is that her?"

After about fifteen minutes, Elizabeth had had enough. Her back was stiff from sitting on the ground, the photographs had made her sad, and the twins had resumed their saucy bickering. Life was going on just as it had. No one seemed focused on the catastrophe at hand.

She looked out the window at the sky above the backyard—the last thing her grandpa had seen before he died. Or had he turned his gaze to the side to see his wife rushing toward him, her face rigid with alarm? She thought about Kyle, out in some gleaming frozen-foods aisle piling a basket full of Klondike bars and pints of Ben & Jerry's, paying for it all in crumpled restaurant cash. Would he make it as an actor? His opportunities only seemed to grow, if slowly. A number of his castmates and mentors had taken her aside at one loud bar or another to scream into her ear that he was special, that he never held anything back. They knew better than she did, and yet she couldn't escape the feeling, when she watched him onstage, that he was some-how trying too hard, that he might do well to hold *something* back—though what, exactly, she didn't know. It was still possible that he would succeed. But she wondered. If he was really so special, then why did it so often embarrass her to watch him when he performed?

There was a knock at the door.

"Elizabeth?" It was her mother, her voice tentative and sympa-thetic.

"Come in!"

"Elizabeth, honey, are you in there?"

"I said come in!" Elizabeth shouted, more harshly than she meant to sound, though probably no harsher than she felt. There was a pause, but no indication that Cassandra had heard. They all waited for a moment, still as the faces in the photos that looked up all around them, until at last, Elizabeth stood and flung open the door. Cassan-dra was leaning against the frame, her eyes squeezed shut, her finger-tips pressing her temples. On seeing Elizabeth, her expression opened up and she reached for her daughter's cold hand.

"You can handle another shock, can't you, sweetheart?"

"I think I'm going to be sick."

"Not that bad! Not another death." Cassandra steered Elizabeth down the stairs to the second floor. "We'll face this one together, okay?"

"For God's sake, Mom, what is it?"

A wave of some emotion crested over Cassandra's face, break-ing in the form of an embarrassingly loud laugh. "It's really an odd thing, and there's no way to adequately prepare you—other than to say your father's here. He just arrived, he's spoken to Mary, and now he's standing downstairs in the hall."

Elizabeth peeked around the corner and over the railing. Abe stood squarely in front of the door, straddling a lumpy duffel, his tanned arms freckled and folded across his chest. He was wearing his Giants cap, and his face had the mildly curious expression of a person waiting for an escort he's never met. She'd last seen him in San Francisco in May. He'd taken her to a seafood restaurant, and over plates of glossy, blue-mouthed mussels, she'd told him she was applying for residencies in dermatology. He'd seemed distracted then, and when he asked her, not even judgmentally, "What happened to Africa?" she nonetheless found herself flailing to ward off the sting of his disapproval. "There are still opportunities to contribute," she'd sputtered. "You can treat skin disease anywhere."

Never in a million years would she have guessed he'd turn up here. Her parents didn't see each other; they didn't even speak. Her father, who had seemed so normal and upright—so thoroughly boring—had, out of nowhere one day, stood and flung himself from their boat, but not before barking in a truly terrifying manner like some kind of police dog ordered to attack. The word *fuck* was used a lot, another shock. It wasn't so much the sound of the word, which she'd heard him use on numerous occasions, but rather its connotation that shocked her. This time it meant something vile and specific, something her mother had done.

Elizabeth had sat on the boat in her musty hooded sweatshirt and understood all at once that every petulant resentment, every claustrophobic moment, every sneaking teenage suspicion she'd ever had that her parents were wacko, unbalanced, or just plain not normal had turned out after all to have been right. Cassandra had taken a lover, and while she flashed with hatred for her mother at this sickening but all too imaginable thought, she hated her father even more for forcing her to know it and then immediately clearing out. "You know, Dad, the brain holds on to things it sees," she had wanted to tell him later that week when he started loading cardboard boxes and junky desk lamps not to mention Ferdinand—her pet—into his car. "I'll have this memory with me forever!" The memory of her father and her dog, driving away together down the road.

But one thing about her parents was that she'd never been able to stay mad at them, even about that day. They exerted such a sustaining force on her that even when she'd wanted to shut one or both of them out, even for the briefest of spells, she couldn't. She felt light-headed, empty, and vaguely panicked when she tried to imagine her life without them. So, after a few days of clumsy uncertainty, in which she kept setting a dinner plate for her father that her mother never filled, and in which the way things were had not yet become the way they'd always be, she eventually adapted to living alone with her mother, and then, once her dad had secreted himself into an anonymous condo building in San Francisco, to throwing her bag into the car and driving over the bridge for a few nights with him and Ferdinand. For the rest of the summer, neither mentioned the other, not even to acknowledge the place from which she'd just come. It was as though they believed they were each her sole parent and that she only materialized from time to time, having been off doing whatever it was that teenagers liked to do. "You always have plans," her mother would say. "There you are," went her dad, as though they were trying to respect her privacy instead of intensely safeguarding their own.

When it came time for college, she harbored a grim hope that everything would blow over while she was away, that all would be back to normal by the time she next came home. But college was basically the same: a call to one of them one night, to the other one the next. And it was the same when she returned. On those early breaks—Thanksgiving with Abe, Christmas with Cassandra—she occasionally waited, as one waits for the lights to come back on after a power outage, for one of them to ask how the other one was doing. But the power never did return, and she soon became accustomed to living two lives, both slightly in the dark. It wasn't the best situation, but it wasn't the worst, and the truth was, she was flexible as long as she had some kind of routine. With enough time and reinforcement, she felt she could get used to anything.

Yet here, again, was a disruption. A disturbance in her routine. A reminder that the way things are is not necessarily the way they'll always be. And once again, her father was the source of the disturbance. What spell had come over him, he who never strayed from his course, who never admitted a fault?

She ducked back behind the wall. "So this is it, then? You're breaking your vow of silence?"

Cassandra cringed. "He's downstairs, isn't he? What choice do I have?"

"You could refuse to see him, like you've always done."

"I never refused. It just never happened. There's a difference—a world of difference."

Elizabeth looked away. Cassandra felt wild, fearing she was about to lose her biggest ally: the one person who'd never leave her. "Are you okay with this, Lizzie?" she asked. "I have to know that you're okay."

"*I'm* fine. Let's just get it over with," she said, and strode to the top of the steps.

"Hi, Dad," she called.

Abe looked up to see his wife and daughter leaning over the rail, like passengers on a ship from which he'd jumped. And wasn't that fitting? Wasn't that probably just how they looked that day, had he bothered to glance back and see them? He was jet-lagged; his eyes watered; the world swiveled and sharpened in its frame. There they are, still on the boat, he thought for a maudlin moment, before he remembered that Cassandra was his *ex*-wife, no longer his wife at all.

"Hi, Lizzie. Hi, Cassandra." He spoke their names slowly and smiled.

"Hello," they said, not quite in unison.

The skin along her jaw was smooth, but somewhat loose. Her upper lip was thin. She'd aged. *No surprise,* he thought. *People do.*

Part II

7

He saw her for the first time in December. He was a medical student, dropping by a local free clinic to offer himself as a volunteer. She was the office assistant—competent and full of herself, clearly too big for the job. He fell, not right away, but nearly enough that when he told the story later, he'd say he loved her from the moment she first spoke, when she chided him for being wet.

It was raining that day, and as he stood in the tiled vestibule, shaking water from his sleeve and hair, he became aware of a mildewed smell rising from his wet wool coat. He looked up to see the office assistant staring at him over the front desk, crinkling her nose as though she could smell it, too, even from across the room. He smiled at her and she, in response, tilted her immoderate red head. She seemed ready to school him in some way, as though she were the reigning world champion and he an unknown upstart she didn't think she should even have to fight.

Once he had discharged himself of enough water to feel satisfied he wouldn't make puddles all across the floor, he approached her desk. "Hi," he said, in what he believed to be a friendly manner. "I'm a medical student at UCSF. I was hoping to talk to someone about volunteering."

She was about his age, give or take a year, with a rather long white neck rendered whiter by the contrast of her hair, which was kept out of her face by only the flimsiest of metal bobby pins. No, she was certainly younger. He could see that now. Still, she was the one in charge. She pursed her lips, assessing him once more. He stood up straighter. He realized it would've been smart to have brought a transcript, or some sort of letter of reference—something other than his hospital ID. "It's been raining all day," she finally said. "Do you really not have an umbrella?"

The truth was he hadn't listened to the forecast, had hardly glanced out his window. He'd just returned home from his final overnight shift for many months and was so elated with the work he'd done in helping to repair a severed toe, so not-tired and so ready to take on another challenge, that he'd simply run a comb through his hair and put on civilian clothes and gone back out again, determined finally, at long last, to volunteer at the little corner clinic he passed regularly on his commute. By the time the sky opened and let him have it, pouring water straight into his collar and thoroughly soaking his shoes, he was already so many blocks away that it wouldn't have been worth it to double back.

The assistant was still awaiting his answer, her eyes bright with color, if not interest. Blue, like a deep pool he'd dropped a coin in, thrilling him with the likelihood that he would never get it back. He straightened his shoulders affably and held out his empty hands. He was, after all, offering to do a difficult thing for free. She seemed a little surprised at this response, or perhaps at her own tone of voice, echoing back at her now in her head. She relented and waved her hand at the room full of sick people slouched in rows of hard plastic chairs.

"Of course," he said, understanding. "I'll wait."

He settled himself in an orange chair between two yellows, holding his elbows close in his lap. Because it was a crowded Tuesday (or was it Monday?—no, he'd spent Monday night on call) there was only the one empty seat. On one side of him sat a huffing, overweight man whose arm pressed into his shoulder; on the other was a little girl, probably Mexican, who stared up at him like a cat. He'd brought nothing to read, which was just as well. He wouldn't have been able to comfortably hold a book in that chair, and anyway he was much more interested in watching the redheaded assistant.

She picked up her patient list and called a name, which belonged to a teenage girl with an eye patch and a splash of scaly burns across her cheek. The girl stood abruptly and made her way to the desk, where the assistant received her forms and made a show of reading them over to ensure they were complete. As she read, her forehead wrinkled, almost sorrowfully, but every time she looked up it was to reassure the girl with a smile. The same sorrowful look returned when she bent her head to make a few additional marks on the form, as though there were nothing more poignant than the date and time of this poor girl's intake. She stapled an additional sheet to the form, which she then handed to another assistant, who stood ready to take the girl down the hall.

The scene repeated itself many times, each with a different patient—first a sweating, oscillating junkie with spots of missing hair, then the large, increasingly wheezy man to his left. As each of them went down the corridor to be seen, another patient came along to take the now-empty chair. People coughed and cleared their phlegmy throats. Babies in laps began to cry. Soon there were no empty chairs at all, and Abe found himself standing in the corner near a blighted fern so that all the patients could have seats. All around him, people held cheap plastic pens and concentrated on their forms; at the desk, the redheaded assistant answered the phone and spoke brusquely, though not without warmth, seemingly oblivious to his gaze.

It was possible he was being tested. Could he be patient and respectful in a place so packed with need? He shoved his hands in his pockets and tried to keep from nodding off, his post-call euphoria at last beginning to wane. Only the beautiful assistant—yes, he could admit it now, she was beautiful—kept his eyes open. Several times she stood up—she was not short—and walked to the back of the reception area to confer with one of the doctors or to move a stack of forms into a bin. In his pockets, he dug at the cuticles of his thumbs. He could leave and come back another time, not that he wanted to leave. He was beginning to feel like the fool she obviously took him for.

At long last she caught his eye. "You can go on back," she said from across the room. Several heads turned to see who she was addressing, their indifferent faces wavering slightly when they saw he was not one of them. He nodded and moved swiftly past her desk, hearing the crunch of typewriters in the office space beyond.

The chief doctor met him in the corridor and ushered him into his office. Young and jittery, with dark curly hair encircling his head like a massive wreath, he spoke at an urgent volume and wore a pink T-shirt under his white coat and stethoscope. He clicked on a desk lamp and told Abe he could really use his help, having been understaffed since the summer opening, as he was sure that Abe could tell. He produced a waiver from a drawer, and while he waited for Abe to read and sign it, he bounced among the piles of paper and medical supplies that cluttered his windowless office, telling him they treated the people no one else would treat. "Druggies, immigrants, the poor—you name it!" His voice nearly cracked. Leaning against the wall was a framed diploma in Latin. On his desk was the largest mug of coffee that Abe had ever seen.

After a quick tour of the facility, Abe returned to the waiting room. Through the storefront window he could see the brightness of sudden, late afternoon sun, a definite absence of rain. He stopped by the desk where the assistant sat collating papers, licking the tip of her index finger to make sure she'd separated each sheet. He felt good standing near her, knowing he'd be back again the next day to work.

"I'm not asking you to dinner," he murmured, though he hadn't planned to say anything at all. The background noise of typewriters, coughing, and chairs scraping linoleum seemed momentarily suppressed. She looked up, eyes blank, and he nearly panicked—what had he done? it was so *unlike* him to speak without thinking—but then a smile crept across her face, as she took in the full implications of his line.

"And I'm not giving you an answer."

They had a game now, a bit of suspense. For the next two weeks, whenever he showed up to work, he knew that Cassandra would wonder. (For that was her name—Cassandra—even better than he could've hoped.) Would this be the day he would ask her? And he would wonder, too, because he had no idea when he'd finally buckle and blurt it out, nor could he be fully certain what she'd say in reply. They hardly looked at each other, ducking their heads as they politely shuffled past each other in the corridor, or handed over forms in triplicate.

And yet, the slightest fraction of a glimpse of her flipped his stomach. Even when she was completely out of sight, he often felt he could see her hair, warming the edges of his peripheral vision. On the rare occasions when she did look him in the eye, it was with an almost asphyxiating force. That blue—he was drowning! Once, he swore he saw her blush, a moment he replayed in his mind over and over on the walk home and again that night while he boiled rice, allowing himself to hope that she was falling for him, too.

But the next day, when he attempted to stand close beside her chair for a longer and weightier stretch than he'd permitted himself in the past, she abruptly stood and moved to the back of the office, where she busied herself with a set of files. He didn't think he had ever known disappointment until that day, when he saw the back of her head more times than on any other day he could recall. It had become his enemy, that beautiful head, the way it kept turning and hiding her face.

By a quirk of his schedule, three more days had to pass before he was able to work again. Determined to wait it out, he filled his mornings, afternoons, and evenings with tedious laboratory trials and his nights with bourbon in the company of friends. When he finally came in for his clinic shift, his eyeballs were buzzing, his palms made of mush. He hadn't slept. He'd barely combed his hair, and his was clumpy, the kind that needed to be combed. He was ready to surrender, whatever she said.

"I want to take you out Saturday night." He was standing across the desk from her. It was just like the first time they met, only this time, he was dry.

She looked at him the way she did. Blue eyes. She really was like a painting, one of those idyllic scenes of a woman with a pitcher in a room. Or a sea nymph on a half shell, disorder spiraling the waters beneath. That flaming hair, that icy skin. She looked like no one looked anymore. The world couldn't sustain such people. Such people could hardly sustain themselves.

"Okay," she said. "What time?"

8

They stood in the front hall—Elizabeth and her mother at the top of the stairs, her father on the carpet down below—and for an excruciating moment no one spoke. Did they expect her to mediate—she, who'd been speaking to them both with undramatic normalcy all these intervening years? She, it occurred to her now, the only real adult in the room? Her mother sucked in the corners of her mouth, faintly pouting, so that she looked at once defiantly adolescent and withered with sudden middle age. Her father pressed his feet into the floor, his shins tensing visibly, like slats on a blind drawn closed. She looked from one to the other, relishing their awkwardness, feeling that their discomfort was somewhat deserved. Let them wait, she told herself. Let them wonder just how the hell this is going to go.

When the moment passed and still no one spoke, Elizabeth became aware of an unusual current passing between her parents, a tacit agreement of some kind. She experienced with surprise a feeling she was used to having with Lucie and Rob, but that she'd forgotten could extend to her parents, a feeling of intruding on their privacy, of being somehow in the way. They'd had no qualms about dissolving their union right in front of her, but this negotiation—this they seemed to want to conduct between the two of them alone. They weren't each waiting for the other one to speak. They were both waiting for her to leave.

Well, if that was what they wanted, they could have it. She felt suffocated enough as it was, in close proximity to so many kindred genes, white-haired visitors dribbling constantly through the house—and the funeral not until Thursday! What she needed most just then was an escape. She grazed her mother's hand, darted down the stairs, and kissed her dad on the cheek. "I'll talk to you later," she whispered, having no idea if he'd heard, and burst out of the past into the day.

CASSANDRA HAD ALWAYS assumed she'd see Abe again. She spent the first year after their divorce haunted by the possibility of stumbling upon him unprepared. She took to scanning crowded rooms and movie theaters, on the lookout for his distinct posture, his eggish, overeducated head. On the freeway she tried to avoid ever coming directly in line with the car in the next lane, on the off-chance it was driven by Abe; at lights, she checked her rearview mirror. On sidewalks and in supermarket aisles, she took her corners wide, to protect herself from a sudden collision, the most painful of all ways she could imagine running into him—violently, with bags of onions in her cart. For a long time, even as she took these neurotic precautions, she felt trapped, as though she were steeling herself against the inevitable.

And yet the inevitable never occurred. She saw him, or a man very like him, only twice—once in the first year at a play in Berkeley and once more recently at the Ferry Plaza farmers market. In both instances, the crowd kept them comfortably apart. As the years passed, each one an incredible new record—four years without seeing her ex-husband, *five* years, *six!*—she began to wonder if she'd unconsciously made it over a definitive hump, something akin to the hurdle addicts have to clear to ensure they won't relapse. The longer life went on, the more certain it seemed that the danger had truly passed.

These days, she rarely lost her breath at the sight of tall men with tanned skin, mossy hair, and well-proportioned shoulders, because she'd discovered, through innumerable losses of breath in the past, that there were many men in the world like Abe, and especially in San Francisco. These days, she could hardly remember his face.

Until, out of nowhere, he reappeared, in her very own childhood home. She looked down at him, grateful to have been peeing in the second-floor bathroom when he arrived, feeling her upstairs vantage somehow gave her the upper hand in whatever negotiation was to come.

She considered his body before speaking. In his baseball cap, he seemed to be the same man she'd forgotten, if older, and perhaps more freckled, too. It surprised her how easy it was to look at him again. There was his face: the warrior nose cascading into a plateau of iron cheek; the darkly arched brows shading the piercing whites of the eyes; the waxen, perpetually unshaven jaw sprouting dozens of tiny black hairs—all of it familiar. So much time had passed that nothing seemed to have changed. There were just two days in her entire life: the day they'd separated, and today.

The moment was so extraordinary, and so emotionally uncertain, she could do little more than confirm the facts. "You're here," she said.

He took off his cap and ruffled his flattened hair with his palm. "Mary told me."

"She told you to come?"

"No, she told me what happened. Coming here seemed like the right thing to do."

The blazing afternoon sun had shifted from behind an obstruction of some kind, casting sudden light over Abe's head and making it difficult for Cassandra to read his expression in the glare. She leaned forward to duck the beams, resting her forearms on the banister. Not that he'd ever been easy to read. He stood now with his arms folded across his chest, right hand still bunching his cap.

"The wake's tomorrow."

"I know," he said, solemnly, before his eyes drifted away from hers, coming to rest on the multicolored Chinese vase that sat on the narrow entryway table beside him.

"I've always liked that thing," she said. "Even though it's just a cheap replica. It's the one piece in the house I'd take with me if I had the choice."

"Yes," Abe said. "I think you've told me that before."

Cassandra started at this mention of *before,* an embarrassing era she suddenly realized she'd been lucky to escape. It was like being reminded that she'd been a teenager once, and had done all the same careless, fun-crazed things that made her balk when she heard about Gail's youngest son doing them now. She gripped the banister with both hands. Below her, Abe was looking at the vase, his profile inscrutable as he studied the central tableau of little people gathered for a wedding in colorful robes.

"So what's your plan?" she asked him, her tone neutral but direct.

He turned back. "I don't know," he said. "I've got a hotel."

She couldn't believe how not-angry they were, how unmoved by their reunion. Standing there, at the bottom of the stairs, was a man Cassandra had loved, then hated, and to whom she now had nothing to say. There was a damning line that described this situation. Who had said it? The opposite of love is not hate; the opposite of love is indifference. Had he flown all the way across the country simply to give her his dispassionate condolences and be gone?

"My father—" she began.

His chin jerked and he began nodding soberly, as though remembering the reason he'd come. "I'm so sorry."

"I know," she said, her eyes filling with tears. He could've gone on, but out of some mercy, he didn't. Instead he looked up at her, expectantly.

"It's strange," she said. "I'm not as upset as I should be."

And then he did something odd. He sighed, and scrunched his shoulders, and said, "Me neither." It took her a moment to understand that he was talking about something else entirely—about them and their tragedy, which wasn't the point of this day at all. "I haven't been angry with you in a long time."

She felt stung; she hadn't been expecting criticism.

"Well," she said, pulling her body backward with great effort, even now not angry, just resigned. "Maybe we'll have more to say to each other when we are."

He gave a nod as though he hadn't quite parsed her meaning, but expected to at any minute, and watched as she bravely made her way down the stairs, one hand on the banister for support, the other swinging erratically by her side. She passed within a charged arm's length of his body, and proceeded on to the kitchen, where she could hear someone—she hoped her sister—making room for further well-meaning platters in the fridge. She was proud of herself for not retreating to her bedroom, which still bore all the time-oiled books and pink-glazed furnishings of her childhood, and where she would've immediately felt imprisoned, unable to know when Abe had gone and the coast was clear.

The kitchen, at least, was exactly as she had foreseen. It smelled of roasted onions and earnest deli meats. Mary's butt, clad perkily in berry-red vacation shorts, mooned from the open refrigerator, which was filled to the light fixture with a smorgasbord of foil-wrapped offerings.

"Well," Cassandra said, drawing Mary out of the land of casseroles.

"How'd it go?" Beneath her party-line cheer, Mary's voice was penitent. When she'd phoned Abe, she was basically pressuring him to fly out. It was just what you did when your wife lost a parent, whether you were still married to her or not. Fortified with the righteousness of her own grief, and convinced that her sister and ex-brother-in-law needed a kick in the pants to start treating each other properly again, she saw nothing questionable in her call.

It was only when she answered the door and saw him standing there, looking tanned, certain, and at the same time entirely unresolved, and then, moments later, the scrim of horror that crossed

Cassandra's face when she told her who was there, that she recognized the truly combustible nature of the situation she'd helped create. She had forgotten what a disaster her sister's marriage had become, and how poor some people were at hauling themselves up from the wreckage and getting back onto land. Mary was a fixer, a teacher for whom no task was too large that it couldn't be accomplished in discrete, rational stages. But some people, when they encountered their own messes, just sank further, were better off cutting losses and moving shop than trying to salvage and piece back together whatever random parts they found lying around. Perhaps, she thought grimly, her sister was one of those.

"Is it too early for a drink?" Cassandra asked. She was no longer in the mood to beat around the bush. It was only now, in the fragrant whir of an overstuffed suburban kitchen, that she realized how strenuously she'd been holding herself back, taking care to say much less than she felt, while suggesting much, much more. Her few minutes with Abe had exhausted her.

"It's afternoon, isn't it?" Mary disapproved of almost everything, but would never deny an adult her alcohol. She reached into the packed fridge. "Fancy some screw-top chardonnay?"

"How'd you guess?" Cassandra collapsed in the breakfast nook, happy to keep trading questions that required no answer.

Mary set a glass on the table and filled it, the pale gold wine hissing icily against the bowl. "I think Estella has a crush on Kyle," she said, sitting down across from her sister.

Cassandra's first sip went straight to her head. Somehow she'd failed to eat lunch. "What makes you say that?"

"Mother's intuition. I keep catching her staring at him. This morning I winked at her," she said, winking, "and she blushed."

"Maybe she's just interested in theater." Cassandra winked back and took another sip. She was starting to feel, if not good, then at least a little bit better.

"Don't you like him? For Elizabeth, I mean. Or whatever." Another wink.

"Of course! He's serious for an actor. And I think he's serious about her, too. I don't know if they'll get *married*, necessarily, but they might."

Mary considered this. "I guess it couldn't hurt her to wait until she's a little older. Make sure she really knows what she wants." Her voice wavered with a dreamy authority, as though she were recalling being twenty-six, reliable and fun, with a lifetime of sensible choices ahead of her. Mary herself had been an over-thirty bride.

"But the hurricane damage looks as bad as everyone feared," she said now, abruptly. They'd hardly gotten going on Elizabeth; Cassandra hadn't expected to change subjects so soon. "They're calling it apocalyptic."

"Katrina?" Cassandra was disoriented but decided to go along. She was pleased to have remembered the name. It was something from the world, something outside herself.

"Huge sections of New Orleans underwater. Can you imagine?"

Cassandra shook her head. She could not, though of course it was not her job to imagine. It was someone else's job, someone in Louisiana or just down the road in Washington, probably a whole belted, boot-wearing brigade of someones with hard hats and master's degrees in engineering and the trust of the people at their backs. This time, though, they had failed. She went under for another, longer sip and came up feeling more disoriented than before.

Mary went on as if reading her mind. "You know, most of it was below sea level from the start, the poor neighborhoods especially. So there's going to be a lot of finger pointing. We had no excuse not to be ready for this." She was growing indignant, convincing herself as she spoke. "*No* excuse at all."

She was right, of course. And she was doing her best to distract her sister from the subject of marriage, which she knew left a bad taste in her mouth. But in introducing a new flavor made mostly of guilt and blame, she brought Cassandra straight back to the episode minutes prior that she was still trying to escape. Her disaster was personal, not at all the same order of magnitude as the devastation in the Gulf, but the comparison only heightened her pain and made it impossible to appreciate the massive human tragedy she knew was mushrooming just out of sight.

The fact was, she had no excuse either. Abe had turned up at her parents' house and she'd received him neutrally, though she'd been preparing for the moment for years. She'd always known they'd speak again. But today—God, today—today she was drained from grief. He'd come upon her at her saddest moment, when she ought to have been thinking of her father and no one else; he'd come in and he'd taken her unaware. There were many better ways to respond than the way she'd responded just then. She ought to have been able to tell him precisely how he'd hurt her, in words even he couldn't refuse to understand. Or at the very least, she ought to have been able to tell him generally how she'd felt when he left: that he'd broken a vow more sacred than the one she'd broken, that you just don't leave a person in silence, no matter how unfaithful they've been. But at the crucial juncture, she hadn't been able to muster any of it. She'd failed to find words either specific or general that would do herself the justice she felt she deserved. He'd given her eight years to rehearse. Had she needed nine? Then would she have gotten it right?

"Cassandra." Dorothy Chamberlain's voice snapped her out of herself. She was standing like a baroness in a ruffled blouse, her hand on the back of an equally assertive-looking senior citizen in a tennis visor and whites. "Joanne Hickory just wanted you to know what a gem you have for a daughter." She nodded at Mary, who joined the two older women in smiling significantly at Cassandra. "She met her just now on the porch and she—well, I'll let Jo tell it."

"Elizabeth?" Cassandra said. At that moment she wanted, more than ever, to have her daughter near.

"She's just lovely," Joanne said. "Polite. Smart as a whip. I know mothers always want to hear nice things about their daughters . . . My deepest condolences, by the way. Howard was a wonderful man."

"Thank you," Cassandra said, at once impatient and ashamed to be impatient with this smiling, genuine stranger, who was starting to look a bit rattled.

"Go on, Jo," Dorothy said.

"Well, I had lost an earring, a diamond stud Lou—that's my husband—had given me, and I noticed it just as I reached the door out there. Of course, I could have lost it in the car or back at home somewhere, but you know what it's like when an earring goes missing. You immediately start looking all around you. So then who comes up but your daughter, and even though she was clearly in a bit of a hurry, she sees my distress and immediately crouches down to help. 'What are we looking for?' she asks, so calm, as though she'd been sent especially to assist me. She found it in a matter of seconds, under the rim of a planter, where I just know my eyes never would have seen it."

"Do you know where she went?" Cassandra asked.

"No, I . . . no, she didn't mention it."

"I'm sorry." Cassandra stood suddenly. "Do you mind?" She pressed past them in the doorway, catching a mighty whiff of old-lady powder and sunscreen. Under her visor, Joanne's face caved in embarrassment and she began making meek little clucks of apology.

"No, *I'm* sorry," Cassandra said, squeezing her hand, remembering her bereavement decorum. "Thank you very much for sharing that story with me. I'm a lucky mother."

She stepped out onto the front porch, where her father had liked to stand before a funeral, so that his dignified, comforting form would be the first thing the mourners saw when they arrived. Elizabeth was nowhere in sight, all the cars still safely in the driveway. Perhaps she and Kyle—she hadn't thought until now of Kyle—had he gone with her? Surely Joanne would've mentioned him if he'd been there; he was not a person who went unnoticed. Perhaps she was heading out to meet him, the two of them together on a walk. She supposed that could be fortifying. Anything could be fortifying after so many hours in this creepy house.

She glanced around, taking in the passersby, most in sleeveless shirts and sandals, some still in suffocating suits, and wondered which way they'd gone. Her eyes came to rest on a figure at the end of the walk—blobby, large and pale, as though it were still gestating, still coming into form. It was the strange boy. He was back, standing frozen like some kind of ghost. The second time in two days, and right on the heels of her ghostly ex-husband. How peculiar. Had he come to pay his respects?

"Come in!" Cassandra called. "You can come in if you like."

The boy shook his head, as though all he'd wanted was to be noticed, and having achieved this, was ready to head home. Arms hanging rhythmlessly, he went off down the sidewalk toward the subway, pausing at the corner to look back. "I'm sorry for your loss!" he shouted, through cupped hands, and crossed the street when the pedestrian sign flashed WALK.

Bewildered, she returned to the kitchen. Finding it empty and her wine right where she'd left it, she took the glass and bottle to the screened-in sunporch, one of the few places in the house where she could still hide as a fully grown adult. She poured another glass and settled into the rattan sofa, stuffing extra, vaguely mildewed cushions behind her back for support. The backyard, where no one had ventured much since Sunday, stretched raw and abandoned before her, the sky the color of a dirty dishrag. On the front porch, she might've watched the town go about its business, but watching other people meant being watched. It meant opening herself to whatever Dorothy Chamberlain wanted to say to her, to conversing with whomever was brave enough to give her a few words of encouragement.

She did not want to talk to, or listen to, or be seen by anyone. She wanted the shelter of a backyard and a flat suburban sky: real, American privacy. It still existed in her infinite country. A nation that offered doors to close, and rooms with no one else in them. A nation that needed space, and always found it.

*   *   *

ELIZABETH STORMED DOWN the sidewalk until she came to a large intersection dominated by a multiplex theater. A free tabloid newspaper rested on the curb, its ad-filled pages idly flipping in the hot breeze. Beyond it, the marquee announced ten films in tall black letters. The last time she'd been to the movies, Kyle had canceled at the last minute, when she was already on line; his rehearsal was going to run all night. Hurt, she'd bought a ticket anyway—plus popcorn, which she spilled fantastically just as the opening credits began. She'd made a further ruckus trying to scoop up the kernels at her feet, drawing a chorus of indignant shushes from all sides. Eventually, though, she'd settled in, found she rather liked being there by herself. The warm bath of the movie soothed her thin skin, and dampened her irritation with Kyle.

Today again she needed something to distract her, something that would spirit her away from the painful drama of being her parents' child. In a movie, she'd be unreachable for at least two hours. But then they might start looking for her, combing the streets, while she sat calming herself in the dark, chewing her way through a box of Swedish Fish. She scanned the marquee. None of the movies interested her, anyway. She picked up the newspaper, the lone piece of litter on the otherwise spotless street, and deposited it in the nearest trash can.

In New York, she calmed herself by wandering. She enjoyed ducking into shops, even ones in which she knew she'd never make a purchase. In between, she'd take in the life of the street—the stoop-sitters, the stroller mothers, the skateboarders in backpacks and Chucks. She'd wonder where these people lived, what histories they contained—not only where their ancestors were born but also what operations they'd had, what medical quirks ran in their families. Aside from sleeping, it was the thing she most liked to do when she had a few hours off. More than running. More than talking to her parents or any of her friends, more than talking to anyone at all.

New York. Her stomach fluttered at the thought that she might soon have to leave. All of her top-choice residency programs were in the five boroughs, yet even so, there were no guarantees. Her record was excellent, but so was everyone's, and in the end, she'd have to go where the system placed her—or, in the romantic parlance of her field, where she matched. Lately, every chance she got to make a dumb, superstitious wish—fountains full of pennies, fallen eye-lashes—she wished she would match in New York.

She came now to a sign staked in the grassy strip in front of a row of plush furniture and carpet showrooms. OPEN HOUSE, it said in large capitals, a bundle of red and white helium balloons waving flirtatiously in the gusts from passing traffic. An arrow affixed to the bottom of the sign pointed her off the main drag, down a residential side street. Small but sufficient lawns came marching up to smooth sidewalks; in the dense leaf cover beyond were porches and gables and crisp college flags.

The open house was beige with white trim, and it completely filled its narrow lot. Flanked on two sides by matching bungalows, it was an obviously new stone-and-siding construction with windows of vari-ous shapes and dimensions. She felt a little embarrassed for it, the way it had used every trick in the book to appear as storied and venerable as its more modest neighbors. It sat up high over its green garage, which gave anyone who entered the front door the opportunity to process grandly up a flight of steps that bent at an angle, like the stony elbow of some comfortably middling medieval castle. Still, it wasn't awful, and through the large picture window in the front, she could see a dark-haired woman in a suit—the agent, she assumed—look-ing right at her through the blemishless glass. The woman smiled at Elizabeth in a way that could only be construed as friendly and beck-oned her inside.

She had no business at an open house, much less an open house in a town where she didn't live and where she had never and would never dream of moving. But she could see beyond the agent a cavern-ous, near-empty room painted a neutral tone that glowed a little, like skin, so that you knew it was alive, and on the street around her not a person in sight to suggest that anyone else would bother her if she went inside for a look.

She climbed, holding the iron handrail and counting the steps as she went. At the top—fourteen—she was met by the agent, who already had the paneled green door open for her to enter.

"Welcome," she said brightly. Her cheeks were high and cupped, like nutshells, and she wore a bracelet that had been a popular style at some point, made of large, silvery links, either from Tiffany's or a perfect knock-off. Elizabeth was reminded of countless girls she'd known in college, starting with silly, decorous Jane Donaughey, and she realized how little thought she had given to this diversion. Now she would have to talk to this person. She would have to tell at least a half-dozen lies. She stood with her careless hands behind her back as though trying to hide the bag she hadn't brought. She hadn't brought anything, not even keys.

The agent, though, was unsuspicious, and, despite their closeness in age and background—she couldn't have been much older than thirty—she appeared uninterested in chat. "Feel free to have a look around," she said. "The fact sheet is on the bookshelf." She returned to her station in front of the picture window, where she had a little armchair and a celebrity magazine.

Gratefully, Elizabeth took one of the sheets from under a domed glass paperweight. The number at the top was nearly a million. She folded the sheet in half and took it with her like a ticket.

The rooms opened one after another, each with no more than a few pieces of furniture to suggest habitation. Wood floors ran beneath her feet throughout, lighting the way from one room to the next. Upstairs, she found the bedrooms. They had windows with plantation shutters and closets that rolled open on tracks. She could park cars in these rooms. She could nest inside them whole apartments from Manhattan. The largest was at the back of the house, and in the center, under an angled skylight, was a white sheeted queen-size bed, topped with two plump white pillows and a folded beige coverlet, just like in any chain hotel.

It looked awfully comfortable. On her way to the window, she placed her palm on the coverlet, testing the firmness of the mattress. Her detour here was not a total lie. She might buy a house one day—she might buy anything one day—and surely she couldn't be expected to buy a house without first imagining how it would feel to live in it.

She'd share the house, of course. It was too much for one person, even a person who liked to be alone. So there would have to be a husband, and possibly a few children, though the latter were still difficult to envision. A husband was easier: tall, respected, assured. A vigorous athlete who knew things about the world but never made her feel stupid. She sat in the window seat and looked at the little patch of grass out back, a patch she imagined he'd know how to mow. Would he be white? Probably. Most of the people in her life were white. Even her dad was, basically. Few people looked at him and thought otherwise.

She looked back at the pristine bed. Would her husband make it regularly, or would that be their constant quarrel, that because she cared more about well-tucked sheets, she had to be the one who tucked them? She tried to imagine waking up here. Would her husband be an early riser, already brewing coffee in the dark downstairs, or would he be more like Kyle, up late on the other side of darkness, glowing, gaining strength and momentum as everyone else dropped off?

Kyle.

It was the first she'd thought of him. She looked around. She couldn't imagine him here. She couldn't imagine herself here, not really, but she couldn't imagine him at all. At the moment, she was having trouble even picturing his face. Elizabeth the future doctor; Kyle the future—what? Was he really going to get that TV show, suddenly make it at twenty-nine? All of a sudden she felt certain they were headed nowhere together, a pair of mismatched carousel animals spinning around and around. She the standard, purposeful horse, he the extravagant lion. It wasn't the first time she'd had doubts. She recalled, early on, watching him play a soldier in *Coriolanus*, a role that showcased his wide stance, his muscles on a machine gun, and little else. As he jogged onstage with theatrical importance, she was struck by the searing notion that he was trying to be an artist and she was trying to be a doctor, just like her parents. Her mouth grew dry at the obvious parallel and she found herself rushing to the lobby at intermission, determined to beat the crowd to the water fountain. Of course, everyone else wanted the bathroom or the bar, so she was able to take her time, glugging swallow after swallow as the cool water plastered her lips, and a tiny distortion of herself regarded her from the base of the brushed metal head. Since then, she'd found ways of dismissing the fear. She was much more forgiving than her dad, and Kyle was much less needy than her mom. They certainly hadn't married in a rush. It was important to her not to be traumatized by her parents' separation, not to have hang-ups or types she just wouldn't date. But it was also important not to make their same dumb mistakes.

So what could you do? You had to test things out. You had to tour the house, try the life.

And really, she wondered as she moved away from the window, why not? She still had no idea what kind of person she would be. She slipped off her sandals and reclined on the bed. It felt normal, as normal as trying on a cocktail dress before buying it. She imagined Kyle beside her, breathing heavily. Above her, the skylight framed a blank sheet of atmosphere that she could color however she liked. Downstairs, she heard the ring of a cell phone followed by the agent's upbeat voice. She was a nurturing person, this agent; she was reassuring someone of something. Elizabeth freed her hair from under her shoulders and gently closed her eyes.

Soon she began to feel light, buoyed by an unseen force. A quiet raged as it rages underwater, thick and active and endless in her ears. She was at sea. Her hair stretched outward to infinity, lashed by currents in the water's surface while her body rocked gently beneath. She felt a warmth on her shoulder where a handsome male was pressed. They had to get out of there, he told her, but when she failed to do or say anything in response, he raised an arm and paddled off. She wished for a moment that he would come back, but it was a halfhearted wish at best. His back shrank into the waves, leaving her alone and feeling magnificent, far away from even herself.

Voices crackled somewhere. She looked toward land, where the people calling to her were no bigger than periods, punctuating the shore. There was grass on the shore, a slather of green on top of beige. A grass-and-sand sandwich on two generous slices of blue.

The voices again. She turned and kicked, pushing toward land. Now she was deeper in the bay, looking up at an approaching ship. Now she had made it to the grass, looking up at a house's wood frame.

"Master bedroom," said one of the voices.

Three faces peered down quizzically. She blinked, not understanding where she was. She was her grandpa, flat on his back in the grass. Neck snapped, paralyzed; the irrevocable ribbon of blood.

"I can't move my legs," she said, panicked.

"What?" This was the agent, the nurturing woman with the patrician face. She was pressing her lips into blades. Next to her was a middle-aged couple, he in wire-rimmed glasses fencing a field of doctorly gray, she in highlights and bangles, a brown leather notepad under her arm. They looked torn between concern and accusation, like parents in a hospital room.

Elizabeth sprang from the bed. "I'm sorry!" she blurted. "I must really need some coffee!"

"Oh, don't worry," the agent said in her hospitable way.

"That skylight!" Elizabeth gushed, to make up for it. She was hopping on one foot, pulling her sandal back over her heel. "Thank you for letting me look around. It's such a lovely space." The couple was conferring in the corner, not even waiting for her to clear out. Already they were counting outlets, deciding which walls to knock down. She fled the room, hating them, hating herself.

"Thanks for stopping in!" the agent called as Elizabeth clambered down the stairs, one sandal still half unstrapped.

Back on the sidewalk, she hefted her foot onto a nearby bumper just long enough to secure the buckle, then took off again, dodging the remnants of her dream. She tumbled from the shady block into near-blindness on the main thoroughfare, whitewashed and steamy in heavy afternoon sun. She took a hasty survey as her eyes adjusted: there were the carpet stores, the glassy banks, and at the next corner a familiar disk that soon revealed itself to be green. Starbucks.

A middle-aged dad in board shorts and Birkenstocks stood by the concrete planter at the entrance, his tanned arms lassoing the shoulders of a boy and a girl doing noisy, openmouthed battle with their rapidly slumping soft-serve cones. She stared at him, trying to understand why she'd been so embarrassed on the bed. She was never going to see that agent or that conniving couple again. So what? she asked herself. So what so what so what? The dad caught her eye and grinned as if to suggest she might want to chill out. Fuming, she flounced past him.

In the short line inside, she swayed back and forth, looking over the baristas at the menu on the wall. She knew its offerings by heart, but she didn't know what she wanted. Soon she was alone at the counter opposite the cashier, a blond girl with braids who was waiting for her to speak. She ordered an iced coffee.

"Two fifty-four," the girl said.

Elizabeth touched her pocket. "I'm sorry," she said. "I don't have my wallet."

"Oh no," the girl said reflexively. She continued to look at her, waiting.

"I mean I just don't have it."

The girl stared stupidly and Elizabeth's cheeks grew warm. Forgetting her wallet suddenly felt like a colossal error, definitive proof of her genetic inability to function in a normal world. She caught a couple her age escaping out the side door, the girl lividly sucking her frozen drink, the guy, in aviator sunglasses and a plain white tee, casually palming his own beverage like a celebrity trying to be photographed playing football on the beach. It seemed to have been decided: dudes were happy-go-lucky, girls just couldn't relax. But really, how the hell was she supposed to relax? She'd been so careful with her life, donning all the recommended protective garb, avoiding detonative personalities, counting each step toward perfection. And still people were ripped away from her, or showed up where they didn't belong.

Just when she thought she couldn't stand there a moment longer with her failure, a voice behind her spoke up. "Don't worry. This one's on me."

She turned to see a vaguely familiar face under the brim of a newsboy hat.

"This seems to be a habit of yours," it said. She stared blankly. Her brain was not thinking fast enough.

"Elizabeth?" He was a boy and his voice was growing unsteady.

"Yes."

"It's Toby. I worked the Battery wedding on Saturday?"

"Oh my god!" Her memory lurched into place. "My bag!"

"Yeah," he said, visibly relieved. His eyes were gray. "You never seem to take it with you."

"Do you want the coffee or not?" the cashier asked.

"She'll take it," Toby answered, hastily sliding some bills across the counter. "Are you okay?" he asked Elizabeth, as though he'd pulled her to her feet from a fall.

"I'm fine," she said, darting her eyes around the room. She didn't understand where he'd come from. "Did you pay for my coffee?"

He pressed the ice-filled cup into her hand and led her away from the counter. "Don't worry about it."

"I'm sorry. I'm just a little confused."

"It's okay."

"What are you doing here?" she asked him.

He said something about visiting his mother, held up a paperback book. "I just needed to be somewhere new. Listen—" He tried to catch her eye. "Are you lost? Do you need a ride somewhere?"

"My grandfather died," she said.

All the energy escaped from his face. "Oh, man. Was he really sick?" He seemed genuinely concerned. Tears surged forward in her ducts.

"He fell. On Sunday."

"Jesus! Are you sure you don't need a ride? I have a car."

She shook her head. She couldn't bear his pity. "I walked. I have to be getting back."

"I'll walk with you."

She shook her head again, more firmly this time, as if shaking off her vulnerability. "No, really." She held up a hand. All she wanted was for him to leave. "I'm fine. Thank you for the coffee."

Still jittery, she left the Starbucks with her cup and stumbled back toward her grandparents' house. The coffee was oversweetened, and it rattled the roots of her teeth. She sucked half of it through the long green straw, then tossed the rest into a trash bin in disgust.

She ought to have prevented it. This was the thought breaking over her now, dipping and rising up and crashing down on top of her, like a traffic jam after miles of steady motion. She was practically a doctor, for Christ's sake. First, do no harm—and yet her own grandfather had died not thirty yards from where she lay, shamelessly fucking her famous-looking boyfriend. She might not have done any harm, but she sure as hell hadn't done any good. Would she ever? Was she even interested anymore in doing good?

Back at the house, she slammed the door behind her.

"There you are!" Estella emerged from the kitchen holding a spoon.

"I need Kyle," Elizabeth shouted, stomping up the stairs, aware that she was on the verge of throwing a terrific tantrum, but unable to help herself.

"He's up there!" Estella called after her. "He brought four different kinds of ice cream!"

Elizabeth found Kyle holding a book in the study. She slammed this door too and rushed at him, wrapping her arms around his waist. His book fell open to the floor.

"Where the hell have you been?" he asked. "I go get you ice cream and then I come back and you're gone."

"Just shut up!" she cried. She pushed at him with all her strength. It wasn't enough to knock him over, but she caught him off guard, and he stumbled backward. He stared at her, blankly questioning, waiting for her cue.

"Don't give me that right now," she said.

"Oh, baby. I'm sorry. Come here. You're beautiful." He pulled her to his chest.

"Ugh. I'm sick of that, too!"

"But you are," he insisted. "You *are*." He wrapped his arms around her body and squeezed her so tightly she suddenly felt she couldn't breathe. He was strangling her with his big stupid kindness. She felt her head might pop off its stem. She imagined it rolling in the corner, eyes bugging, gathering dust from the floor in its ear. He inhaled, trying to guide her to serenity, but when his chest rose hard into her face, she knew she couldn't bear him any longer. She opened her mouth and bit down through his shirt.

"*Fuck!*" he shouted, flinging her back. "What the hell was that?"

Her elbow knocked against a bookshelf, which only wound her up further. She came at him again, gripping into his arms with her nails this time, sucking at his neck through her teeth. *Beautiful*, he'd said. Please. It didn't matter how she looked. Those were surface cells, nothing more. She had to make him see beneath them, the pile of damage she'd constructed all by herself inside.

"Get off me!" he said, shaking her away. She saw his face twist with rage, saw his hand swing down across her face.

It was like falling off a roof, and knowing you would break your neck. She pitched backward toward the folded-up couch, and when she landed on its sticky leather, she curled her knees up and made herself small, her chest heaving airlessly, her head thundering with sobs. The delicious, flayed sound of her pain poured out of her body and into the room. She felt sublime, better than she'd felt in a long time. It was like catching a glimpse of herself, not in a water fountain where everything was out of focus, but in a perfect mirror, in the middle of some chaotic, dressy affair, and having thought, up until that moment, that she had been a girl, when it fact she was not a girl, she was a woman with painted lips and a shifting recess between her clavicles. It was sublime but also terrifying; it meant that everything would change.

Toby Steinberg drove the neighborhoods of south Bethesda, trying to calm himself down.

When she'd walked through that door, panting and fragrant, he'd nearly lost his head. This was the kind of sign he yearned for. Returning a pretty girl's wallet was one thing. But seeing the pretty girl again, lost, in another city and state, and finding she'd misplaced her wallet *again*—well, these coincidences did not occur without reason.

She was not just pretty: she was intoxicating. Red hair, white skin, mobile blue-green eyes. A profile smoother than marble. So radiant, he imagined most people couldn't even see her. She was a secret perfect prize, real to him alone. His chest flashed electric at the privilege. *Elizabeth. Mirabelle.* No doubt she couldn't even fathom her own beauty; she just hummed and moved around inside it, never knowing how intensely it governed her life.

Toby made figure eights throughout Maryland and the District, weaving around neighborhoods and parking lots, waving to children playing in sprinklers and parents fanning themselves on porch chairs. Everyone's clothes sagged, soggy with the heat. Toby Steinberg did not care that his thighs pooled with sweat against the Subaru's neoprene seat. He knew the secret to happiness.

When Elizabeth finally looked up from the couch, she saw Kyle sitting against the desk on the opposite wall, a hollow look in his eye. He'd picked up the book he'd been holding when she came in and was gripping it now in both hands.

"Before you get any ideas, I'm going to remind you that you started it," he said. He articulated each word, as though he'd been rehearsing the line for days. "You bit me really hard." He lifted his shirt to reveal a dotted, mouth-shaped welt just above his soft left nipple. It was already the deep purple-brown of rotten fruit, and the cratered marks of her teeth were still visible. He prodded the welt delicately with his fingertips, as though fearing he might smear the evidence.

"But," he continued, lowering his shirt, "I should never have hit you."

She wiped a stream of moisture from her chin. "I hate you," she said.

"We've gotten rough before, right?" He seemed to be pleading with her. "It's *hot* when we get rough. Even when you bite."

She closed her eyes and remembered.

"But this was different," he said finally.

"It was."

THE NEXT THING Cassandra knew, someone was standing in front of the screen door, large and penitent, a suitcase at his feet. It was dark, the sun had set, leaving rosy-fingered streaks across the tops of the backyard trees. She blinked until her eyes adjusted, but even before then she knew it was Kyle. Zippers dangled everywhere: on the suitcase, on the wrinkled pockets of his cargo shorts, on the hem of his lightweight jacket.

"Aren't you hot?" Cassandra said. "Why are you wearing that?"

"I'm going home," he said, carefully. "I couldn't fit it in my suitcase—don't tell Lizzie."

"What do you mean, don't tell her?"

He repeated his line in the same maddening tone. "That I'm going home."

"I heard you the first time. Kyle, she'll know."

"I mean don't tell her you saw me leave. She'll want to know why you didn't stop me, which you wouldn't have been able to do anyway. This way's better for everyone."

"Kyle." She felt the need to say his name again. "Her grandfather just died."

A wrinkle of pain registered on his face. "I realize this makes me look bad. But trust me, she doesn't want me here. I don't know if she ever did. Anyway, she's got her dad now, and you. I think it's for the best if I just leave her alone for a while."

"Why are you telling me this? Did you stop here on purpose?"

He shrugged. "I was going to sneak out the back but then I saw you sleeping here. I guess I wanted to make sure you were okay. And I guess I didn't think I could leave without telling *some*one. That just seemed like it would've been cruel."

So Kyle was still a cut above Abe, and barely half his age. It figured. "Yes," Cassandra said. "It would've been."

He frowned. "Do you need water or anything?"

She really must've looked ghastly. "I probably do, but don't worry about it. I'll find some after you're gone."

"I left her a note, if that helps."

"I'll see that she gets it."

"No, she'll find it. Remember, you didn't see me."

"Right. So get out of here, then, before she hears us talking." She closed her eyes, and when she reopened them, he'd disappeared.

Immediately, she felt burdened. She leapt up and flicked on the outdoor light, illuminating a yard empty of anything save the sauna, still half-built, still expecting someone to return to give it walls.

THE LOBBY OF Abe's hotel was virtually empty when he arrived. Just some sectional lounge furniture, a statue of a samurai, and an ultra-young desk clerk holding a fresh paperback edition of *Persuasion*. She had large eyes and appeared to be reading the introduction. Abe felt vaguely salacious asking her for a room.

"I have you down for two nights, Dr. Green," she said, looking into her hidden computer monitor. "How would you like to pay?" Her voice was like a cricket's.

He handed her his credit card. "I should warn you, I may need more than two nights."

"Plans up in the air?"

"You could say that."

She struck more keys than seemed necessary. "Fortunately, we do have vacancies. But you should try to let us know at your earliest convenience if you plan to extend your stay."

"Will do. Is that for school?"

"Excuse me?"

"*Persuasion*. Are you reading it for school?"

"Well, it's summer. And I'm twenty-seven." She placed her hand on the book, over the pallid Regency face on the cover. "But I did read it in school. Now I'm reading it again."

"Liked it that much?"

He knew his questions seemed strange, but he didn't care. He needed to talk to someone. The clerk looked mildly puzzled, but for the sake of her job, perhaps, she humored him.

"I always said it was one of my favorites," she said. "But then the other day, someone asked me what happens in the book and I couldn't remember. I kept getting it confused with all the other Jane Austen books. I couldn't even remember the man's name. I thought it was something with an R or a J."

"And was it?"

"Nope. Captain Wentworth." She flashed him the back cover, where, presumably, it said something about the characters. "Ever read it?"

"Strangely enough, I have. They didn't make boys read much Austen in my day. Now I talk to these medical interns and every one of them, male, female, has read Austen, and every one of them has a blog. It was a good story, though." He bit the side of his tongue, aware that he was sounding older and more conservative than he felt.

"I guess times change," she said, smiling. She didn't look remotely offended. He wondered what kind of boyfriend she went home to at night. An aggressive law student, or perhaps a restaurant manager with frosted tips. Either way, he was pretty sure the guy didn't read Austen, even in these enlightened times.

She passed him his key card. "Just refurbished," she said.

The room was nicer than he expected, but it was still a hotel room: rectangular, carpeted, uniformly made beds. He kicked off his sneakers and stretched out on the bed closest to the bathroom, flicking on the television with the remote. A smiling blonde on the hotel channel greeted him, and for a moment he thought it was the clerk from downstairs, checking up on him, though on further reflection, he remembered that her hair had been brown. He flipped past news coverage of Katrina, landing at last on ESPN in the midst of its nightly rundown of baseball highlights, a regular comfort. Finding a hole in the big toe of his sock, he pulled it off, then pulled off the other sock and threw them in a wad at the trash. Standing, he touched his toes and thought about Cassandra's father, then thought about Cassandra, then thought about his toenails, which were yellowish and gnarly and in need of trimming, not that anyone would care.

If he were a different kind of guy, he'd invite the clerk up for a drink of something strong he'd bought on arrival. He'd have a girl-friend her age back home who wouldn't know, and an airplane-ready bottle of acrid European cologne. There had been girlfriends once, in the years right after his divorce. A string of sweet, vaguely damaged women who thought him damaged, and fancied themselves his rescu-ers. But no one lately. Lately it was easier to be alone.

He hoisted his suitcase onto the other bed and opened it, reach-ing down past a few layers of shirts and shorts, groping for the thing that would get him through the night. When his hand closed upon the object he was looking for—a slim bottle of drugstore-brand sun-block—he closed his eyes and exhaled. Another safe landing.

He uncapped the bottle and sniffed it; its contents smelled, as they should, of coconut, grease, and the beach, a reminder of his recent solo sailing missions, and of countless vacations when Elizabeth was small.

Over the bathroom sink, he reached into the bottle with his index finger. Feeling the tip of a plastic bag, he trapped it against the side of the bottle and slowly dragged it out. The baggie was rolled up like a tiny carpet, airtight and covered with hypoallergenic cream. There were papers and enough herb inside for one joint, maybe two, if he was prudent. Either way, it would have to last him until Thursday, when his package arrived at the house.

For years, Abe had smoked casually: on the weekend, or at the end of an unusually challenging day. It was easy now, so why not? Only recently had the habit become more regular. Since around the same time he'd stopped seeing Amy, the real estate agent and cyclist who'd suddenly craved children, the last woman he'd seriously dated. Since Elizabeth had graduated from college and all of a sudden stopped coming home. Since Ferdinand had died. Somewhere in there. On the bathroom counter, he prepared his joint, careful not to lose the smallest trace of herb. Then, with the joint in his mouth, he set up his towels, flipped the air conditioner fan speed to high, and lit up in front of the TV.

He paced a few more times and picked up the room service menu, which looked adequate if not appetizing. He and Cassandra had eaten room service on their honeymoon, at an inn overlooking the Chesapeake. He was so elated then, watching the boats slice through the water from their little balcony, that he didn't even regret not sailing them. He picked up the phone now to order, but he must've blanked for a moment, because the next thing he knew the dial tone had vanished and the girl clerk's voice was chirping in his ear. Startled, he hung up, and the whole freshly hatched idea went sour, as hotel living so often can. He thought about the warming covers that decked room service carts like glistening silver crowns, and how once they were lifted, the magic evaporated, as everything hurried on its way to being cold and picked over; how a hotel bed was a gift, a gift he'd messed up the moment he'd laid down; how hotel rooms were both the happiest and the most depressing places in the world.

He remembered the room he'd slept in the Sunday after that sail. It was a Holiday Inn downtown, and after hitching a ride home to pick up his car, he'd driven right up to the door. A flabby-necked truck driver had picked him up near the shore where he'd collapsed and had gotten him as far as the marina. He'd wanted to check to make sure Cassandra and Elizabeth had made it back safely with the boat, and sure enough, it was there, moored to its dock as though it had never been out. Slackened with wet clothes, Abe tried to press a few sodden bills into his samaritan's hand, but the man refused, embarrassed. Grimly, Abe waved him away and stood staring at the boat, once his baby, now his battlefield. It stared back, like a cat, placid, unconcerned. He knew he might have slept there, in the small cabin underneath the deck, but it felt wrong to revisit the scene so soon, so he hitched another ride to his house, which he entered only to retrieve his keys, feeling a hotel room was now the only place to go. He'd come back the next day for Ferdinand.

In his present room he turned off the light and pressed his forehead against the window. It was important that no one see him smoking. Marijuana was still illegal in Maryland; in this hotel even cigarettes weren't allowed. There was asphalt below him, a parking lot with numbered spaces and people in shorts cutting through on their way to someplace else. It was good, he decided, that there was always someplace else, even if it was just another hotel room. His country had seen to that. Beyond the parking lot, he saw the towers of the new Bethesda, a squadron of soft red condominiums, anchored by chic, family-friendly restaurants. Earlier that evening, people had parked their cars somewhere out of sight, then converged on the sapling-lined pedestrian promenades, beaming and clinging to each other's arms, as though they'd been waiting their entire lives to pretend to walk to dinner. Abe knew this town. There were dozens more like it in California. His younger self would have scoffed at their lack of imagination, but time and circumstance had driven him around on that. His heart soared now every time he saw the steel skeleton of a new building go up—a place not yet ruined for life.

Once, when he and Cassandra were newly married, they were driving somewhere in Virginia. They crossed a small river and came upon a redbrick house that had been destroyed on the side of the road. Its back wall was largely still intact, as were pieces of the sides, but the front had been removed, like a life-size dollhouse, leaving the empty rooms inside to rot. The second floor hung on in chunks, jutting out of the remaining walls, and moss covered every naked edge like cartilage at the end of a bone. Cassandra begged him to stop. "We have to," she said, already digging in her knapsack for her camera. He'd grown up in Virginia; ruined houses were nothing new to him. But she was insistent, so he pulled over a few hundred feet ahead. Together they walked down the shoulder, stepped over the guardrail, and went right up to the edge of the gutted house. The grass came up to their knees in some places, and the trees around the site were blaringly green and strangled with kudzu. Cassandra finished off a roll of film, then reloaded. She said she would use the photos to kick-start a project; she didn't know yet what it would be.

"Don't go inside," he'd said. "I don't think the floorboards will hold."

They'd walked around the back, where they found a rusted wheelbarrow facedown beside the wall. She photographed that, too, then turned it over and photographed the worms that swiveled in the dirt underneath. They continued on around to the front again and speculated on what had happened: a fire, a hurricane, a slow death to abandonment and rain.

"This is just like America," he said.

"I don't know," she said. "Don't you think America is California? What happens after this. It's whatever the people who lived here did next. Their children."

"But it's the ruin, too. The Indian villages, the Old South, the rusted factory towns up north. The ghost towns where miners used to live out west."

She thought about that for a moment, then reached out and squeezed a piece of exposed wood from the staircase. It was wet and her hand left a print that slowly evaporated as she wiped the dampness away on her jeans.

"Well," she said, her eyes open wide like her lens, "why do you think I'm taking these pictures?" It was clear from the way she said it that she continued to disagree.

"Give it here," he said.

"What?"

"The camera." He took it from her and snapped a shot, before she could protest or fix her hair, which was flatter on the side where her head had been resting in the car.

They continued on, eventually, to Richmond, where they were headed. Cassandra continued to snap photos, but more quietly: of the towering statues of Robert E. Lee and Stonewall Jackson that lined Monument Avenue, of white and black men passing one another on the street, of falling fences and rusting cars at a highway gas pump. He remembered her photographing his grandmother's grave, which made him happy, even if he had to look away and pretend he hadn't noticed her do it.

The photos came out well, flooded with color and depth—pretty much all of them but the one he'd impulsively taken of her. Her face there was pale, fuzzy, and out of focus, because he'd never learned to use a camera as well as his photogenic wife. It wasn't fair, he thought, as he looked through the prints at the pharmacy counter, that a rotting house in Cassandra's hands was vibrant and beautiful, while the breathtaking Cassandra in his hands was smothered out with white.

He closed the curtains and lay down. On the floor by the desk he could see where his socks had missed the trash. His chest ached with the thought of Cassandra's hair and the carapace of that house, glowing and bacterially alive. She'd had the pictures tacked to the walls of her workroom for months, like culture slides in a laboratory. It was so lurid in his memory now that he could hardly breathe. He had to think of something else. He inhaled again, letting his lungs burn, and looked at the TV, which had somehow drifted back to the hurricane. A male reporter in a bright red slicker was crying in a flooded street. Abe stared. The man's hair was soft as money and still it rained. He stared harder, trying to find some hope in this paradox, some evidence that there'd been no disaster, that it was all just a terrible joke.

In the end, though, he gave in. He picked up the phone and asked for the club sandwich with fries. It was not the girl who took his order, but someone else—a man, which was just as well.

9

The obituary ran in *The Washington Post* the next day.

> Howard Johannes Fabricant, beloved father, husband, grand-
> father, and funeral director, died Sunday at his Bethesda home.
> He was 79 years old.
>
> Mr. Fabricant was born August 29, 1925, in St. Paul,
> Minnesota, the son of Finnish and German immigrants. In 1943,
> he enlisted in the Navy, serving in the South Pacific theater of
> World War II. He moved to the Washington area after the war,
> and in 1952, he opened the Fabricant Funeral Home in Bethesda,
> where he also lived with his family.
>
> A member of the Bethesda Lions Club and a parishioner of
> St. Eccles Episcopal Church, Mr. Fabricant enjoyed military his-
> tory and carpentry. He had been building a sauna when he died.
>
> Survivors include his widow, Eunice Fabricant; three grown
> children: Cassandra Fabricant Green of Berkeley, California,
> Howard John Fabricant of Bainbridge Island, Washington, and
> Mary Fabricant Shubin of Pittsburgh; and three grandchildren.
>
> A funeral service will be held at St. Eccles on Thursday at
> 11 a.m. In lieu of flowers, donations can be made to the Ameri-
> can Red Cross.

Toby read the notice at his mother's breakfast table while eating a toasted bagel with a thick layer of cream cheese and lox. For two days now, he'd been reading about the awful hurricane in New Orleans— the way the city was like a soup bowl just waiting to be filled with liquid, the way people had to stand stranded on their roofs in ninety-degree temperatures as corpses floated in a procession down the street. He thought about all the jazz musicians there, the legends about them, and how he'd always hoped he'd play there one day himself. He felt a pressure on his lungs, as though some of the water from the Gulf had spilled over into him, a sensation that embarrassed him and made him push the front page aside. He turned instead to the local section, and there was the notice about Howard Fabricant, calling out to him from the bottom of page ten.

"What are you reading, sweetie?" Ruth asked, tidying up the counters around him. "More New Orleans?"

He shook his head and swallowed. "I've moved on to the Obituaries." He gave a bitter laugh.

"Oh God, don't do that. Where are the Comics? Or Sports." She rustled through the sections on the table.

Toby paused before taking another bite and looked down at Howard Fabricant's angular but rather bemused face. "It's okay. I kind of like the stories. Homemaker, retired intelligence officer, amateur photographer. You know. Lived in the same house for forty-six years."

"A whole life in AP style. Yes, there is beauty in that." As an editor for the State Department, she appreciated sentences the way jewelers appreciate gems: for their color, for their clarity, for their cut.

"And actually, there's someone I know today," Toby said. "Well, the grandfather of someone I know."

"Who's that?" Ruth came over to look at the page with a stack of catalogs under one arm.

"Howard Fabricant. I'm pretty sure that's my friend Elizabeth's grandfather." The obituary held all the clues. The grown child who lived in California had the last name Green, same as Elizabeth's. The date of the death made sense. And the family home was just a few blocks from the Starbucks where Toby had seen Elizabeth the day before. Surely this was her grandfather.

"How sad," Ruth said, reading through zebra-striped glasses. "The day before his birthday. He was building a sauna. And a funeral director! Such irony. How do you know his granddaughter? From school?"

"From New York. I met her through Laura, Keith's girlfriend. She's a musician, too." He allowed the lies to pile up like laundry. He didn't know why he was telling them, but it didn't really matter. His mother would probably never meet Elizabeth, unless he somehow managed to marry her, in which case he'd be so insanely happy that he couldn't imagine caring about anything that had happened before.

"Did you know her grandparents lived in Bethesda?"

"No."

"That's funny that she wouldn't have mentioned it once she knew where you were from."

"Oh, well, she *did* mention it," Toby said quickly. "But you know, everyone in New York has relatives in Bethesda and Silver Spring; it's become so common I almost expect it. I'd actually forgotten about Elizabeth's grandparents until I saw this."

Ruth eased the catalogs into a brown paper grocery bag for recycling, then returned to the island counter to sort the rest of her mail. "God, what a week. What a world. Do you think you'll go to the funeral?"

Sometimes she had brilliant suggestions. "Yes," Toby said. "I think I will."

"Ed can lend you a suit."

Toby swallowed the last of his bagel. "Thank God for Ed." He wished he didn't have to sound so mean. Ed wasn't a bad man. He was openly in love with Ruth, and kind to her; he even asked Toby questions about himself, which showed a legitimate generosity of spirit. But somehow, Ed's good traits only made Toby more petulant. He needed to hate this man; it was in the nature of things that he should.

Ruth paced to the end of the counter and back. "My therapist says you'll get over this eventually. But I have to tell you, sweetheart, I'm beginning to wonder."

Toby stared straight ahead, sullenly, unwilling for the moment to give in to her. "Guess we'll just have to give it time."

Ruth bit her lip and added a stack of junk mail to the recycling bag. "This Elizabeth. Is she a friend, or is she more than a friend?"

"She's a friend! Just a friend! Can't I have female friends without everyone assuming there's something romantic going on?"

In fact, there almost never was. Lately, nearly every girl or woman he'd fallen for had been seeing another guy or was otherwise only half-interested in him sexually, happy to sit on his lap and tug at his shirttails but ultimately preferring to be "just friends." He'd endured that killing phrase more times than anyone should ever have to, and much to his chagrin, he knew the reason. Toby was thin—not just lean, but boyish. His elbows and knees were pointy, his body hair like the soft coating of down that makes a fourteen-year-old feel manly, but a twenty-two-year-old feel cruelly left behind. And it was cruel, for there had been hope when he was younger. Girls had liked his skinny hips and hanging pants in high school; he'd had two serious girlfriends and plenty of sex before the age of eighteen. Since then: a basic drought. Teenage girls still looked at him in shopping malls, giggling together behind their hands. The real women, the ones his own age and older, spoke to him as though to a friend's preco-cious younger brother, flirting as a means of teaching him about the world. He knew about the world! He knew that the bookish, shrug-ging women who might once have appreciated him now wanted rich, superficially manly men. Men like that unpleasant boyfriend of Elizabeth's: aggressively pally, often intoxicated, hormone-fed cuts of beef.

For a time, Toby tried to combat this injustice. His senior year at NYU, he invested in cartons of power bars and giant canisters of whey protein that lined the shelves above his bed. He carried a bar and thermos with him wherever he went. It was like eating a chocolate dessert at every meal, but with an odd, chalky aftertaste. Before long, he grew to love the flavors, craving them in the morning when he awoke and saw the friendly white canisters circling like guardians above him, their embarrassing macho labels discarded in a weak attempt to hide his vanity.

His efforts were at first modestly rewarded. Toby thickened, if only slightly, and the muscles in his arms and legs appeared to grow more defined. But after a few months of monitoring, he failed to notice any further progress, and his daily weigh-ins suggested that he might even be *losing* weight, the pounds trickling away in twos and threes each month. Thankful not to have any roommates, he often stood naked before his full-length mirror. He examined his shoulder blades protruding like sawed-off wings, his concave chest, his stubbornly sylphlike waist. Turning sideways, he felt himself disappear. And yet he was a man. He had the cock and balls of a man, heavy and proud and as powerful as any he'd seen in porn.

He met Ramona in his protein days. Though he wasn't fond of exercise, his cursory internet research had suggested that protein alone wouldn't build a body, so he occasionally lifted dumbbells in his room, and on nice afternoons, ran along the Hudson. Ramona was a runner, too, the kind with black eyeliner and a penchant for skipping meals. Her tiny legs moved in short, quick steps, which created the impression that she was running faster than she actually was. He'd seen her before in the student union, a sullenly beautiful china doll with a tattoo on her upper back like a labyrinth, beckoning him inside. His chance finally came one afternoon when she ran up to the water fountain where he was stretching out his calves. He stepped aside to offer her a drink and she touched her lips down to the stream. After a moment, she righted herself, gratuitously licking her lip. "You're at NYU," she said, panting gently.

Ramona was a sophomore and nineteen, perhaps the last possible age a woman could be and still find him attractive. Another year and she would've plunged into the abyss of burly men and six-figure salaries. Soon they were seeing movies together and she was laughing pleasurably at his scathing critiques. She was linking her arm through his when they walked down the street. She was getting drunk on vodka and Crystal Light and kissing him sleepily, her hot, anorexic breath sucking him in lip by lip. All of this happened in the space of a few weeks. And then, just as quickly, it ended.

He should've known it would. The women who approached him in college were always a little insane. Perhaps they were attracted to his smallness because they wanted someone to push around. A quick conquest: easily won, easily abandoned. In which case they were cruel, unworthy of his love. Or so he tried to tell himself. But moral superiority couldn't exactly mend a broken heart, nor could it prevent further injury, not if he kept falling for the same kind of off-kilter girls—the ones who talked to him first.

The one thing he learned was never again to tell his mother. He'd made a premature call about Ramona. "Mom, I like this girl." Pathetic. It was the last time he'd let himself be jinxed.

"All right, I'm sorry," Ruth said now, backing off, palms out in surrender. "It's fine for you to have friends who are girls, just fine. Look at me; I have lots of male friends. I only ask because I know how hard it can be to find someone in the city . . . "

He had two options now. He could cut her off, tell her he didn't want to have this conversation, which really was too embarrassing to be sustained, or he could turn mute, find something else on which to focus to drown out the sound of her poor, misguided voice. He chose the latter, pushing aside the Metro section and returning to the front page, which was so loaded with color pictures of water it was practically leaking blue.

"Okay, Toby, I see." She'd cut herself off, and was speaking to him now in a deliberately wounded voice. He finished his paragraph—let her squirm a moment longer—before responding with an innocent "What?"

"It's just that I was *talking*—"

"What, Mom? I'm sorry. I guess I wanted to read more about this hurricane after all." It was the article that compared New Orleans to a soup bowl, the one he'd stopped reading before. Chemicals, the article said. Rodents, poison, lizards and snakes, all mixed up together. Toby imagined waters spiced with toxins and serpent bodies, lizards clinging to bayou branches in the rain. Surely the lizards would survive. They seemed that kind of animal: capable of regenerating severed tails, of changing color to match their surroundings.

He wished he had that skill. Three months out of college, he still felt lost, unable to adapt. He lived in a grim studio with six guitars and a yellowish refrigerator that smelled of foods he'd never kept. Nights he didn't work, he sometimes stayed up late, strumming and getting inspired. He had notebook upon notebook of ideas, enough for a lifetime of work, and he kept at it, because that's what everyone said to do. Yet so far, he hadn't managed to find anyone to listen. All of his actions were met with silence, as though his life and music were merely illusions. As though as far as the world was concerned, he wasn't really there.

He ran his fingers through his hair, which was long and starting to curl in new directions. His mother was talking to him now about the hurricane—"Katrina," she kept saying, as though the storm were just another girl who'd trashed his unready heart.

ELIZABETH HAD GONE to bed on the foldout couch where Kyle was supposed to sleep. After their fight she'd gone to the room she was sharing with her mother, and when she returned she'd found his note. He'd left it for her there, on top of his fluffed-up pillow, where he knew she'd find it right away. *Lizzie, I think it's best for me to go . . .* She read the sentences in random order, already knowing what each of them would say, and the meaning they conveyed all together. Then she did the only thing she could, which was to fold the note along its creases, slip it under the pillow, and drop her head down on top, hiding the truth from herself. She slept there in her blouse and bunched-up shorts, on top of all the blankets.

The next morning, she found her contact lenses still in her eyes, and the sounds of relatives in rooms all around her. Her mother somewhere. Her grandma. Maybe even her father, too. Already, she was annoyed with them, for all the things they probably thought about her, and all the ways they'd never change. She was no longer accustomed to family life and it felt unnatural to her now: a brand-new nation-state slapped together out of some idea of a common past. She much preferred the freedom of being her own citizen in New York.

She reached for her phone, still waiting on the floor where she'd left it. There was a text message from Kyle, which she ignored. She thought about calling Lucie, before remembering she was on her honeymoon in Greece. That left Becca. "My grandfather died," Elizabeth blurted when Becca picked up, "and Kyle went back to New York."

There was a delay of perhaps half a beat, and for a moment, Elizabeth feared the connection had been lost. But in the next instant Becca was there, an expert comforter. Her words were so right, they were virtually without meaning, like the random winds and droplets of a tranquil sleep machine. Elizabeth cried a little, apologized, then cried some more, while Becca chirped and whooshed her despair into abeyance. "Oh, Lizzie," she said. "Of course it's okay to cry." Which seemed to give her permission to stop.

"When's the funeral? Do you need me to come? I have a meeting at ten but I can hop on the Metro right after."

She really had chosen wisely in Becca—a friend who would go out of her way. She didn't need her to come, but she loved her for asking.

"No," Elizabeth said, feeling calmer already. "But thanks, really. It's better for me to spend this time with my mom. And my dad, I guess. My dad's here."

"Whoa." Becca's voice acknowledged everything. "How's *that*?"

"It's unusual."

A knock came at the door. "Elizabeth. Are you awake?"

Elizabeth squeezed the phone tighter against her ear and lowered her voice. "It's my mother," she told Becca. "I think I have to go."

She closed her phone and dug herself a tunnel under the bedcovers, feeling for Kyle's note. The knit cotton blanket came over her head like a shroud, turning her skin dark and the rest of the world pink. She felt calmer immediately, and tried to ignore the nagging notion that she'd just made herself a womb. "Come in!" she called.

Her mother opened the door just wide enough to lean against the jamb. Elizabeth watched through the many tiny holes in her blanket as Cassandra tucked a strand of hair behind her ear.

"I see you," Cassandra said.

"I'm not hiding."

"Everyone else has been up for hours."

"Everyone? Even Dad?" The blanket brushed her lip, giving her a taste of 1960.

"Abe stayed at a hotel. I'm sure you know his plans better than I do. The twins are up. Alvin's here. We've got the viewing all afternoon." She was trying her best to sound fresh and sympathetic, but she couldn't entirely keep her voice from curdling with disdain.

"Is it going to be like this every day?" Elizabeth asked.

"I don't know what you mean."

"I don't either." She rolled over and gripped the big toe of her right foot, which suddenly felt missing. "I get the idea that people used to care a lot less. Grandpa's Vikings would've sent him out to sea yesterday. They would've already sung their songs and pulled their hair out and now they'd be back to building boats."

"Or plotting revenge. Forget plotting. The Vikings would've killed someone in retribution by now."

"There's no one to kill," Elizabeth said, almost mournfully, as though this were the real tragedy. It felt good to speak so brutally.

"There was the bird. Grandma said a pigeon was sitting by him when she found him. I would've killed that bird."

"Right. With what?"

Cassandra clenched her fists around an imaginary pigeon. "With my bare hands."

Elizabeth sat up and pulled the blanket off her head, meeting her mother's bloodshot eyes. The left one seemed to be gliding slightly to the side, like a stray grape in a holiday Jell-O. For a moment, she appeared almost insane.

"Mom, for Christ's sake, don't say things like that."

"Oh, come on. I'm speaking figuratively. I'm saying what I *feel*, not what I'd actually *do*. Give me a break, will you?" Her lower lip puffed out, and for a moment she was a grown child, a metamorphosis Elizabeth found grotesque.

She frowned. She couldn't help herself. "Well, I guess my feelings aren't that colorful. I'm sorry."

Cassandra was used to fearing her daughter—her seriousness, the sharpness with which she sometimes gave her opinion. As a child, she'd been almost censorious on learning that Santa Claus didn't exist. "But why did you lie to me?" she'd wanted to know. "Why are all the adults lying to all the kids?" Conventional wisdom had trained Cassandra to believe that the teenage years would be worse. Door-slamming, rule-breaking, shrill and erratic retorts. But as it turned out, the worst was not so bad. Elizabeth did well in school. She never got arrested or caught with drugs; even her driving record was flawless.

It was the current decade that was rough. How unforgiving her daughter had become, of herself, of everyone else. Cassandra wanted to ask about Kyle, wanted to signal with her eyes that she knew. But Elizabeth was refusing to communicate. She had no sympathy today; her mind was somewhere else.

THEY HELD A SMALL viewing service in the chapel, a prelude to the main event the next day. Howard lay with his hands folded over his abdomen, looking elegant and inevitable; in the corner, Alvin stood by, trim in pinstripes and nearly beaming. He had entrusted his boss to the best of their local colleagues, a glossy, new, almost scientific operation that ran out of Silver Spring, and the results were as lifelike as could be. Even in the heat, the line of Howard's jaw had the nimble heft of a man on the brink of responding to a question. His forehead furrowed as if in thought. An ice cream truck passed, emitting its tinkly melody, while old person after old person stooped by the casket to pay respects. Howard received them patiently, as usual doing his best to make everyone feel better about death.

Hurricane news trickled through the house all day. Televisions were on in several rooms, and then off, and then on again when someone needed another fix. They watched the aerials of the watery grid and heaps of people crying outside the Superdome. They forgot, for a moment. They became spectators, people who could lament the terrible things in the wider world instead of the terrible things in their own.

They were all there, even Abe, dressed in a collared shirt and slacks. Cassandra was aware of him in the house, talking cordially with Eunice, sitting to the side during the service, bringing plates of food from the kitchen and leaving them near her, in case she wanted something to eat. Was this penance? Was it showing off? His ease was palpable, and thoroughly maddening. How could anyone be comfortable in this world, in this country, in this situation? She stared on at the floodwaters, refusing to look at him. Yet even that couldn't prevent the torment she experienced when Abe, still out of sight but suddenly now always in the room, reached into his pocket and absently jangled his keys.

10

The evening Abe Green was to pick her up, she arranged her hair in the bathroom mirror thinking she'd achieved a new summit. Was there anything in the world more powerful than a twenty-two-year-old woman in San Francisco? With the corner of her fingernail, she flicked an eyelash from her cheek. She'd seen the way he looked at her, in barely concealed disarray. He was like a winner who'd just discovered that his race had been fixed, that everything he'd believed in until then had been a lie. She thrilled at the idea of dashing his illusions, of being the one to escort him around the corner of his world to show him the real world behind it.

She'd only just discovered it herself. That summer, not long after her college graduation, she'd moved out west on a lark, surprising everyone back home, her parents most of all.

"What are you going to do in California?" Eunice had demanded, seizing the lid of Cassandra's unzipped suitcase the day before her plane would depart. "No one knows you there. Why should anyone give you a job?" Her voice took its usual nasty tone but belying it were her eyes, shining frantically, and for the first time she seemed not terrifying but almost unbearably weak. Cassandra had to look away.

"I'll be fine," she said. From the pile on her bed, she matched and rolled another pair of cotton socks.

"You'll be nothing!"

She felt a little sorry to be leaving her father, who drove her to the airport in the hearse while Eunice stayed behind, ironing righteously—but not any more than a little. He had almost never defended her against her mother's tirades, always finding some excuse to leave the room or to have never been in the room in the first place. He'd made his choice long ago, and now so would Cassandra, though she let him hug her a little longer than was their custom at the gate.

The choice, of course, was right. In San Francisco, people got her. Everyone wanted to be her friend—her roommates at the boarding-house, her classmates at the art center. It was as though coming here had automatically made her more interesting, more noticeable among the crowds. She had a past now, a thing she'd run from, and though she often found it fun to change it around—to tell men in bars she was from Florida instead of Maryland, that her name was Jeanne instead of Cassandra—the very fact of having had a life before this life in San Francisco seemed enough to give her depth, an impression of being layered and worthy of excavation, that she'd never experienced back home. She was starting over here, finally, as an artist—she rarely lied about that—a vocation that seemed best pursued in a far-off place, in which her mother couldn't easily turn up.

In San Francisco, men wore their hair long and liked to be naked with her for hours, regardless of who she claimed to be. Sex was various and unembarrassed and not, as it had largely been back home, the awkward enjambment of clavicles and hidden underparts in the backseat of some wide-bodied car. Back home everything was furtive, lights-off, and not even terribly satisfying, as though being with a boy were a shower, or a multivitamin to swallow, just another secret to staying alive.

Which was sad, really, because *this* was life. Her old friends and parents—especially her parents—knew so little of the world. To them it had but one direction, which was all about church and business and what other people thought. All you had to do was look at things out here to see how narrow that view was, to see how little local opinions mattered. To the west of San Francisco the great cold ocean stung the air with saline. Enormous, almost infinite, it gnawed at the edge of civilization, and there was at all times the possibility that one day the earth might change just enough to send it swelling up and crashing down upon them. She hated that possibility, and she loved it; it made her life more important than ever, her journey west the bravest thing she'd ever done. She wished she could sit back over the Pacific and look inland at everything—every bay, every feathery redwood branch, every painted house, every layer of fog and mountain—rising at full size in one view. But it was impossible; the human eye couldn't take in everything at once. Instead, she looked at everything she could see; she took it in piece by piece. She went around the city with her eyes wide open, even in the middle of the night.

"That man is looking for a wife," her fellow assistant Diane said after Abe had left with a scrap of paper bearing Cassandra's rooming house address. "And if it's not you, let me know. I'll take him." Diane was only a year older than Cassandra, but already considered herself an old maid, destined to be overlooked. She mentioned her singleness often, and cheerfully, as though it were the funniest thing in the world.

Cassandra tapped a pile of papers into line. "I'm sure he's just looking for a lay." But privately, she knew Diane was right. Earlier that week she had watched Abe treat a meaty gash on a construction worker's cheek, his movements swift and calm as he laid eleven stitches in a perfect railroad track. Such focused men were always moving toward marriage. She pitied him that he had to desire her— Cassandra, who was no wife.

"You'll see," Diane said. "He wants to pack you in his suitcase. You were two seconds away from being kidnapped."

Cassandra grinned and flung her foot at Diane's leg, flattered but unconcerned. For all the delight she took in San Francisco men, she had yet to feel much for any of them. She enjoyed them as she might enjoy a good meal, smelling, tasting and savoring each bite but putting her fork down before she found herself too full. None had made her fall in love. In those days, the person she was actually falling in love with was herself.

Abe arrived at the appointed hour in a shirt that was unbuttoned at the collar. They went to an Italian restaurant in North Beach, a place that covered its walls with the signed portraits of celebrities and pseudo-celebrities. They were seated opposite each other at a small table under a window, and while Abe asked the waiter's advice on wine, Cassandra scanned the walls, picking out the faces she recognized as though each were a dear, old friend.

"So," Abe said, after the wine had been poured. "I know your name and I know what you do. What else do I need to know?"

It was true he already knew quite a lot, which meant that Cassandra would have to stick to specific lies if she were to think of lying at all.

"Well," she said, falling back on an old standard. "I have a twin sister."

"That so?" He sipped his wine, looking her in the eye over the rim, as though to let her know he wasn't fooled. His dark hair looked soft and dense, like moss, in the restaurant's dim, greenish light. He put his glass down and leaned forward slightly on his elbows. From neck to shoulders to arms to waist, he had all the right proportions; she was attracted, she realized, by the math of him.

"No," she said, laughing. "It's just something I like to tell people."

"You like to tell people lies?"

"All the time." She reached for the bread basket and tore off the heel.

He asked her what other lies she'd told, and because he seemed neither judgmental nor dismissive, only interested—perhaps even more so than people usually were—she told him more than she would've expected herself to tell.

"I mostly lie to strangers. Sorry. I guess that includes you." She touched his hand impulsively, fleetingly, then was back to her wineglass. He hadn't flinched. He was remarkably easy to be with. "But it's harmless stuff. I'll give myself a different name, a different hometown. The biggest is my job. Every week I call my parents and tell them about my research for an anthropologist who's writing an encyclopedia of San Francisco."

Abe smiled conspiratorially. "Volunteer thing? Because they think you're planning on graduate school?"

"No, as far as they know, it's my nine-to-five. I've never told them about the clinic."

Here his eyebrows arched in faint surprise and a series of thoughts crossed his face, too quickly for her to interpret. He took a piece of bread, buttered it with broad, careless strokes, and let the silence sit with them a moment. "Wouldn't they be proud?" he finally asked. She couldn't decide if he was disappointed or merely curious.

"It isn't that . . ." She felt silly. She sipped her wine, thinking perhaps he wasn't so easy after all. Perhaps he was actually rather difficult.

"What is it, then?" he pressed. "I'm interested. Truly."

How to say that she lied, not because the truth was sordid or disgraceful, but because, for the first time in her life, she felt she was making her own decisions? How to say that the less her parents knew, the less they could do to interfere? They'd be just as satisfied to know she was working in the clinic, processing people, many of them children, who couldn't afford basic care. Eunice, in particular, would've been impressed with anything involving children, the only category of people she deemed worthy of charity. But Cassandra's lies made her feel powerful, and nothing—not even parental approval—could replace the exhilaration of that.

She shrugged, unable to tell him so much so soon, if ever. "I just want to feel that my life is mine. Not theirs." And then, before he could challenge her further, she rushed on. "I also like to invent trivia." *Invent* was good. It sounded so much better than *lie*. "Like for instance, did you know that four percent of all cats in Texas have six toes on one of their paws?"

Abe leaned back in his chair, nodding seriously. "The most common cause of accidental death in California is shark attack."

"Exactly!" she said, poking the air with her finger. "Animals and states are great sources of material."

"At top speed, a bumblebee can fly faster than a cheetah can run."

"That one could be true. In Texas it's against the law to watch television through a window."

"You have a thing for Texas."

"It just seems like the craziest place."

"I'm from Texas."

"No you're not. You're from Richmond and Philadelphia. You told me that already." Another thing she liked about him. They came from neighboring states.

He smiled. "Got me. I'm not kidding about the shark attacks though. One hundred percent true as a fact."

"Really?"

"Yes." He stared directly at her.

"You're lying."

He laughed. "You're right. I'm glad you can tell the difference."

For some reason, this made her blush.

"But I am one-eighth black."

Looking at his face, she knew it was the truth, and she was pleased with herself for not caring. Her parents would care, she realized, but that only pleased her more. "Nice segue," she said. "Not scared."

The food came, filling the table with soft pastas and tender meats doused in creamy tomato sauces. They ate, moving onto other truths. She told him about the funeral home and her sculpture class, and he told her about medical school and the car accident that had killed his parents when he was ten. His mother's mother had raised him thereafter, a cautious white woman from Virginia, who told him it was better to say he was Jewish, and only if people asked.

"Someday, when I'm drunk, I'll tell you about the accident," he said. He sipped his wine, then set it down again, bringing his hand back to rest by his plate. "I hate talking about it, but I know I should."

"You aren't drunk now?" she asked, slipping her hand toward his a second time. She was drunk, a little. Everything was rising, shifting a half-step up. Under her fingers, his knuckle bones were rounded and substantial, a row of tiny, well-constructed domes, protecting whatever was inside. She felt he must have much to protect. He had rolled up his shirtsleeves when she wasn't looking and now she could look nowhere but at the hair, skin, bones, and veins that made up the geography of his arm.

"I've gotta hold something back," he said. "Don't I? If I ever want to see you again."

"That's a sad game to play." The hair on his forearm was dark and moderately dense, like a forest of leafless trees on a stretch of sandy soil. His cheeks and jaw, were they not freshly shaven, would probably look much the same.

"Ah, but it's working," he said, his knuckles rising slightly under her hand.

She watched his dark eyes swell and brighten as the headlights of a passing car crossed his face. It was as though something had plunged into his pupil, sending a ripple through the tawny water of his eyes. This was more than a change of light; something was happening inside his head. "You *are* drunk!" she exclaimed. "Or getting there."

"Maybe so."

"Well, what if I told you you'll definitely see me again? If you didn't have to worry about that. Would you tell me then? I'm *interested*."

He pulled his hand back and folded his arms across his chest. "But how can I trust you?" he asked slyly. "I know how you love to lie."

She pursed her lips and stamped her foot under the table. "Oh, you're cruel," she said, her hands suddenly cold without his touch.

"Yes, *I'm* cruel." His smile enfolded the edges of his eyes. "You're the one who's prying. You're morbidly curious."

Her cheeks grew warm, and then her ears the instant she was

aware of her cheeks, and then her forehead the instant she was aware of her ears. She'd always been an extravagant, chain-reaction blusher, even when the discomfort she was experiencing inside was rather mild, which this was not.

"I promise you I'm not," she blurted, in spite of the splotches cascading across her chest, in spite of the dangerously scrambled thoughts she was about to put into words. "I have absolutely no interest in death." She flung a hand at the window as if showing him something outside. "My dad's an undertaker, remember? I grew up in a funeral home. And if you knew me better, you'd know I'd never make up something like that. It's creepy and awful."

He was laughing. "Calm down, funeral girl. I'm kidding. I brought it up, remember? I'm going to tell you eventually."

She felt a little faint hearing him address her so intimately as *you*. On the table once more his hands looked unusually strong, almost too big for his body. It was clear that she had underestimated him. Back at the clinic where he'd looked bedraggled and smitten, a onetime hero who had swum up on the wrong shore and, in his confusion, believed her to be some kind of nymph, she ought to have recognized that he was still, underneath that confusion, the hero, still very much in command. She saw now that he was serious and purposeful—not just about stitches, but about life, and about love. He knew what it meant to have something and lose it, which made him careful having anything at all.

"Look," he said, when she said nothing. "There's no one in the world I'd rather tell." He said this, and then his face went gently blank. It was a blank she'd seen before, in some form or other, on all the mourning faces that had passed through her house growing up. She looked at his ungainly hands resting there on the table and was moved. To think of all that had slipped through those fingers—fingers that could otherwise fix any wound.

"That's good," she said, softly, afraid of disappointing him by saying too much. But then her words just hung there, inadequate, so she hurried on to add, "I'm glad."

Whatever he heard in her answer, it was good enough for him. The blank look evaporated and he withdrew his hands, settling into himself once more. "Not tonight, though," he said. "Tonight is about bad jokes."

"Like the guy walks into a bar?"

"Well, steal my thunder, why don't you!"

Relieved, she laughed, and the sudden sound of it surprised and somewhat embarrassed her, which made her laugh even more foolishly, at which point she couldn't do anything to make herself stop.

"That wasn't it, you know." He joined in, his own laugh jolly and percussive. "That wasn't actually a joke."

They lingered over amaretto cookies and coffee until they were the last patrons at the restaurant and the waiters had started stripping the other tables of their linens and flipping the chairs over on top. Abe paid the bill while Cassandra was in the bathroom. At some point toward the end of their meal it had begun to rain, and now it was coming down in fat, indulgent droplets that broke against the restaurant windows. She'd forgotten her umbrella, but this time—he jangled his keys—he had one in the car, so she stood in the recessed doorway while he ran, holding his jacket like a glider over his head, to where they'd parked his grayish Buick halfway down the block. He opened the passenger door and bent in, his dark back all but vanished in the rain. For a moment she thought he'd be better off if he just crawled on through to the driver's side and went on his way without her. For a moment she wished he would, that this would be the last she'd see of him, that she'd have no opportunity to cause him further pain. She worried she wasn't kind enough for this man; she knew she had grown somewhat cruel.

But he was running back now, under the umbrella, a tall black stork of a thing with an old-fashioned wooden handle, and when he handed it to her, his head still under its cover, the raindrops on his forehead and cheek were like sweat from the labor he'd performed for her.

She took his arm and her place in his car, and they rolled over hilltops to her rooming house, the city lights rising up through the rain to meet them with each descent, like the waves of the ocean behind them. He parked the car with its flashers on in front of a hydrant, and walked her to the door, which she fumbled to unlock as she did whenever it was dark and she'd had a few drinks.

His arm pulled her around to face him, and tucked her tight into his chest. There was a kiss so deep and forgetful that she had to reorient herself when she reopened her eyes. I'm in San Francisco. This is my house. This is the man I'm with; his name is Abe.

"I don't ever go to bed on the first date," she said. Across the street, the car flashed out a yellow rhythm for her breath.

"Ahhh." His sound was moist and strangely familiar on her cheek. "So whatever happens," he said, "we'll have to say it all started with a lie."

AT WORK THE following Monday, they were both there, and she was aware of his every movement. Even when he wasn't looking at her, he somehow was. His shoulder would be near her head, his footsteps telling her stories as they receded down the hall. Each minute that passed put her a minute closer to the possibility of seeing him alone. It was mid-December, one of the shortest days of the year. Outside the storefront windows the light took off early, the pavement growing violet in the dusk.

"Somebody's happy," Diane teased. "That's quite a grin."

Cassandra caught herself; she couldn't believe she'd been smiling. "I don't know," she said, trying to sound casual as she moved some papers around on the desk. "There might be something there."

AFTER THEIR NEXT dinner, Chinese food, they went back to his place, a tiny ground-floor efficiency near the university. He had a framed sketch of a nineteenth-century sailboat, a wooden bowl filled with citrus fruit, and hunter-green flannel sheets. The entire place smelled of shower soap with an undertone of rust.

Abe undressed her with confidence, and she put herself in his charge; her one contribution was to unhook her bra.

"I have a tattoo of a cross on my ass," she said, turning to show him she didn't.

He sat down on the bed to inspect. "So you do," he said, palming her with his hands. "Is it always a cross?"

It was more titillating, somehow, to play doctor with a medical student; it was as though she'd become part of his training, doing something of great consequence for the world. She pushed back into his hands until she was sitting in his lap, lightly rocking. "No. Sometimes it's a big purple elephant."

He held her hips, then her breasts. "I think you should get a sailboat on the back of your neck." He kissed the spot he had in mind. "Like that one up there."

She looked at the framed sketch again, imagining its lines sewn into her skin, imagining it sailing there always, even under the cover of her hair. Every man she'd ever known was obsessed with something in the world she'd barely noticed. This man—this man who was now flipping her onto her back—liked boats. He liked boats and he wasn't afraid to hold her arms down when the desire to do so possessed him. She strained back against him, wishing he would tighten his hold, then gasped in surprise when he did, as though he'd read her mind. She felt her arm muscles burn in his grip, smelled soap and rust in their fresh sweat. The next thing she knew, she was kneeling over him and holding him down in return. With his head against the flannel he looked as if he could barely breathe, and that alone was enough to make her come.

Afterward, they smoked grass together, just the right amount. In her life until then there had been secret sex and there had been open sex, but this was something else altogether; it was both and it was more.

*　　*　　*

AT HER MOTHER'S INSISTENCE, she spent Christmas in Maryland, but was hardly present, her mind and all her capacity for sensation remaining in California with Abe. She answered when spoken to, helped her mother and sister peel potatoes by the pound, watched as her brother walked ahead of her up the stairs, and understood that he was gay. *Poor Howie,* she thought. *What a tough road he has ahead.* And yet nothing could truly upset her; she saw her life moving onward, like a train. What was the use of being upset about something that was happening back at the station? Howie would find his way. He was resourceful.

She returned to San Francisco before the new year, which she toasted with Abe at a party in a rambling Victorian. The house was filled with medical students, journalists, and activist law students; one of the hosts worked for a local congressman. There were plenty of reasons to be distressed about the state of the world—Cassandra followed the news as much as the next person—but no one that night could do anything but sprawl across futons, toss hair from their eyes, and smile. They were the people who would be in charge one day, and they saw things differently than anyone who had ever come before. In the living room, someone had draped a blue scarf over the shade of a swing-arm lamp. Cassandra kissed Abe in its dim, lunar light and saw in his face how delightful she was, how very important it was to give herself over to the serious fun of being in love.

Then, trouble. Just a few days later, she grew furious with him when he failed to pick her up from work. Back in his apartment, she yelled at him for the first time, then calmed herself to tears, then calmed herself again to explain how small it had made her feel, and though he stiffened at first, somewhat shut himself down, he stood there through it all and eventually nodded, and told her he was sorry and that she was right.

Three months later, he gave her his mother's engagement ring while they lay naked together in bed. In his large hand, the tiny diamond shone like the tip of a laser. She'd never before seen anything so small emit such a sharp and powerful light. Her own mother's ring was dark, almost black, a sapphire, as though her parents had wanted to signal from the start that their commitment to marriage was also a commitment to funerals.

"Well, put it on," he said, laughing. "I'll give you a hint: it goes on your *finger*."

She covered it with her hand, then uncovered it. Each time, it shocked her to see it there. She looked at Abe, his fuzzy curls, his thinking eyes, and felt wiser than she'd ever felt when she'd earned a high mark on an exam or discovered, without instruction, a new technique on the pottery wheel. All of that just seemed like training for the real test, which was this. Against all odds, they had found each other and made each other giddy. Now it seemed to Cassandra that marriage meant securing their improbable feat, not just taking the plunge but making the plunge her life, a constant act of diving forward, into the better and better days ahead.

By the end of the year her last name was Green and they had moved to a larger apartment. She had never expected herself to marry so young—she was all of twenty-three, the same age her mother had been when she had Cassandra—but now she took to it with an evangelical zeal. "My husband," she said, whenever she could: to the bank teller, to friends who had known him before as Abe. She liked the succinct way it communicated so much. Just a few short syllables and people knew what you were about.

She rode the high straight into 1976. "I don't understand how you can stay out there," her mother wailed on the phone. "So far away from your own parents, as though we didn't even exist. Now your brother's talking about the West Coast. All of a sudden he cares about the forests and working to conserve the land—land he's never even seen! You're setting a bad example."

Even a year earlier, Cassandra's blood would've boiled at this accusation. Now it merely passed her by, like a garish billboard she'd seen many times from her car. She cradled the receiver against her shoulder and flipped through an art supplies catalog at the kitchen table. "Ever wonder if it's your footsteps he's following, and not mine?"

Eunice was born and raised in Colorado Springs, where she'd been a champion public speaker. As a young woman, she'd gone to Washington, DC, for one of the thousands of secretarial jobs that were exploding throughout the cabinet departments after the war. Hers was in Interior, and she'd maintained files on all the tracts of land that had been set aside as preserves in Colorado, Wyoming, Idaho, Montana, and the Dakotas.

"Don't be cute," Eunice said. "He knows I don't want him so far away. Why can't Abe get a job at one of the hospitals here? Your father can call around."

"Oh, well," Cassandra said. "You know my husband. He wants to get the best possible training. And UCSF really is one of the most prestigious hospitals."

On the other end of the line Eunice fell silent. Cassandra joyfully flipped through her catalog, letting each page make its little snapping sound as it turned. "What are you doing?" Eunice finally asked. "Are you lifting something?" Cassandra imagined her mother, her blouse ironed and her hair tightly styled in that way she'd always had of making herself look much older than she really was. It was afternoon in Bethesda, and the light this time of year—January—would be the grayish kind that meant it was already too late to do anything with the day. But Cassandra still had her morning. Three time zones and now a marriage. It was all just enough to make a world of her own, a world her mother finally couldn't penetrate.

"No," Cassandra said, flipping another page. "I'm loading the dishwasher."

"Well, don't overdo it on the detergent. If you use too much you'll end up with a residue on all your plates and glasses."

After they hung up, she dialed her brother's dorm. The phone rang and rang, as dorm phones often did. She hoped Howie was out enjoying himself, doing whatever it was he did for fun. But then the sound of her mother's voice came back to her, the way it had risen when she complained about Howie, as though she'd wanted him to hear.

Cassandra dialed the house again. "Is Howie there?" she asked when her mother picked up.

"As a matter of fact, he is." Eunice allowed her children to live in the college dorms only if they promised to return home for dinner twice a week. Howie, unlike his sisters, seemed to be home more often than required.

"Well, will you put him on?"

Eunice's suspicions flared. "What's this all about?"

"It's nothing. There's just something I've been meaning to ask him."

Reluctantly, Eunice called for her son. For what couldn't have been longer than a minute or two, but felt like a whole fast lifetime, Cassandra waited in suspension on the line. The faraway sounds of her childhood home—the creak of old wood floors under soft carpet runners, the mournful chime of the antique clock in the hall—ticked and shifted in her ear like the wrappers and receipts at the bottom of her purse, the remains of some past week or month that continued to ride around with her, no longer of any use and fated to be thrown away, just as soon as she got around to doing it.

"Hello?" Howie said at last, as though he didn't know he was speaking to his sister.

"Where's Mom? Is she in the room? Answer vaguely so she doesn't know what I'm asking."

"Yes," he said. "She's—yes."

"Listen, she told me about your plan to come west, and I think it's a good one. I think you have to get the hell out of there as fast as you can and make your own life away from all that gloom and doom."

"Okay."

"And tell Mary I said so, too."

"I will."

"Of course, I'll also tell her myself."

"Okay."

"But if Mom asks you, I didn't encourage you. If anything, you tell her I told you to stay near home, so you're defying me, too. It would be worse for everyone if she thinks we're all just ganging up against her."

"I agree." She pictured him wavering in the kitchen doorway, absently swinging his long, large flipper of a hand, while Eunice monitored him from across the room. He was the only one of the three of them who didn't seem to mind being watched. It was as though his inner self were deep enough that he could just turn in and reside there, leaving him with very little connection to the polite surface figure other people saw.

"Now make sure you have a specific story ready to tell her the second you get off the phone," Cassandra said. "About what I told you just now. Because you know she's going to ask."

"Well, that's a great idea," Howie said. "I'm also going to see a production of *King Lear* downtown. I'm sure it will help with my paper."

His quick reaction impressed her. "Oh, wow, are you really doing that? That's great."

"Of course," he said, so brightly toneless that she had no idea if he was continuing to fake a conversation or giving her genuine information about his life. "The professor really recommends it. Here's Mom again. Bye."

"You hear that," Eunice said, before he could've possibly gotten out of earshot. "At least he's taking his education seriously. A whole class on Shakespeare. He seemed excited, didn't he?"

Cassandra had always known Howie to be an even-tempered person, appearing to take the world as it came to him, rarely protesting or otherwise making a fuss, even as he quietly forged his own trail. He had almost never seemed excited about anything, certainly not in front of their mother, to whom he always solicitously deferred. She tried to picture him again and couldn't. All she got was a figure of a boy, with arms and legs and a head and hair. It seemed as though she hadn't seen him in years, though in reality it had been just weeks since she and Abe had made their Christmas rounds, stopping both in Maryland and in Virginia over the course of a long, ragged week. Her wedding, in which Howie was the stoic best man, had been just two months prior to that. For a moment she felt she had missed some opportunity with her brother, to take that outstretched hand and hold it, and in doing so, somehow convey all that she couldn't otherwise say.

But this was what it meant to grow up and marry. It meant that her old family had become less familiar as her new one took its place.

And, really, how her life had changed! Never before had her family been so small, or so satisfying. Abe came home each day with fresh news. This senior physician had praised his paper. That residency program had rated his application at the top of their list. Each compliment she took personally, as again and again the world seemed to confirm her instincts in love.

When he was awarded a residency at UCSF—his top choice—she felt as though *she* had been awarded a residency. As though a team of orderly, bespectacled intellects in long white coats had come into the studio where she sat throwing pots and announced over the whir of the wheels before her entire weekly class that she was the only one in the room who understood what truly mattered. The only one in the world, actually, other than Abe. They drank a bottle of champagne that night, just the two of them. He walked his fingers up her leg and gnawed upon her neck, striking spots she hadn't known until that moment were somehow connected to her toes.

SHE KNEW SHE had to be careful, being so happy. Other people were still searching for what she had. Her sister, her friends. Diane, with whom she'd grown close over the months spent working side-by-side, was wishy-washy about every man she met, and Cassandra soon found that this was not an easy way to live.

"He's so nice, but he's an awful dancer," she'd say of a new man. It had never occurred to Cassandra to seek out specific abilities or characteristics. That was why she and Abe worked, she wanted to say, but you could never tell people that kind of thing.

Diane often came over after work. Abe would return home, sometimes with a classmate, but most often alone, to find his wife and her friend flung across the two sofas in their living room, the air fragrant with the grass they were still or had just finished smoking. However far apart from herself she felt, Cassandra never failed to leap at him when he came in the door, her husband, her happiness, the center of all the goodness of her life. He had grown a beard, a full manly pelt that hid his face for her to find. Intimacy wanted a face. It demanded it, and so she never stopped seeking his out. His eyes would invariably water when she pressed her forehead into his, feeling the bones there. It was the smoke, she thought, the dense leafy air hitting him the moment he entered the house. It was her. It was everything.

"Hi, Abe," Diane would say from her sofa.

"Hi, Diane," Abe would say with his wife at his chest. He loved her friends as much as she did, and she loved to show him off. See, she was saying to Diane, there are good men. You just have to wait around long enough for one of them to walk in the door.

And then Abe would have a few hits if there were hits to have, and they would all go out for Indian food or pizza loaded with eggplant, zucchini, and other vegetables that were never found on pizzas back east.

Spring was approaching and Howie may have been planning to move west, but it was Mary who actually paid them a visit. The university's spring break fell in April, Easter week, and while Howie would be researching his senior thesis in the library, Mary, a freshman, wanted nothing more than to see the other side of the country where her sister and brother-in-law had lived all this time. Even Eunice hadn't been out to visit, declaring, almost in protest, that it was impossible to leave the funeral home at this critical time of year. All times were critical to Eunice, who saw the future not as something that was dawning and reaching wide, but as the next day and the day after that and the day after that. So much the better, thought Cassandra, who had no interest in hosting her parents.

Mary, though, was another story. She had grown into a real person since Cassandra had moved out: nineteen, fish-lipped, dramatic. She appeared in the arrivals hall underdressed for the weather in sunglasses the size of small plates and white shorts so infinitesimal her long blond hair almost covered them. She was dragging a wobbly pale blue suitcase by a strap and had to stop every few seconds to right it.

"They let you out like that?" Cassandra asked, pressing her sister's head into her shoulder.

"Of course not. Why do you think I had to come here? A whole week with them again? I couldn't stand it." Mary straightened with an awkward, balance-checking swoop, and Cassandra understood that her sister was using this trip as an opportunity to practice being someone new, perhaps even newer than the person she was in college.

They went out into the sunny afternoon between the terminal and the parking garage. Mary stopped on the sidewalk, not, as Cassandra first thought, to adjust her careening luggage, but to gape at the air and the light that were for the first time hitting her skin.

"Is it *always* like this?" Mary breathed, forgetting her new self. Her suitcase, still coasting on its momentum, plowed into the backs of her legs, an impact she hardly seemed to register.

Cassandra laughed. "Not always. But pretty much." She had been in California too long. She'd forgotten how it felt—how the mild weather could be like a mattress after years of sleeping on a plank. Even in a space as narrow and uninviting as an airport parking garage.

"I see why you don't come back!" Mary looked appalled, as though she sensed there was something not quite right about living in such weather, something vaguely dangerous about the whole sparkling, splendid thing. She pushed her suitcase back and regarded a giant potted palm with suspicion. It was still too soon to tell if Mary would undergo Cassandra's conversion, and this uncertainty alleviated a pressure Cassandra had been experiencing: a hard little bead of guilt she'd been carrying in her chest that she might be responsible for everyone leaving her parents. The bead shifted a little and resettled, in a place where it bothered her less and she might soon forget it was there.

On the road, Cassandra cracked the windows to offset the heat of the sun. The air that blitzed into the car was bright and cool. In the passenger seat, Mary pressed her legs straight against the floorboard and looked ahead at the road that wound them toward the city.

"I still can't believe Mom let you come," Cassandra said. "Some part of her must be counting on you to hate it. What does she know that I don't?"

"Nothing." Mary shrugged. "I mean, seriously, she knows nothing. I feel bad for her sometimes."

Cassandra made her standard calculation; it was nearly seven o'clock, dinnertime there. She pictured their mother laying out three full place settings, for Howard, Howie, and herself, in an effort to not think about her absent daughters, daughters who were even now talking about her across the country. "I know what you mean. But, come on, she knows more than we give her credit for. She went through a lot at a young age. Seeing her father humiliated like that." It was the one thing they had to cling to, the thing that could account for their mother's hard-heartedness, her relentless striving. That her father, a Colorado farmer, had once owed money and been beaten bloody in his own yard while a young Eunice watched from the window. It wasn't really an excuse, but it sure explained a lot.

"It's actually the opposite," Mary said in a pedantic tone Cassandra recognized from childhood, when Mary would share something new she'd learned in school, as though it truly were new knowledge, instead of something the rest of them had already been taught. "We used to give her credit for all kinds of things she was completely ignorant about." As the youngest, Mary had things the easiest, and had, as if in return for her freedom, usually been the quickest to defend Eunice's rules. Cassandra felt her chest tightening again.

"Anyway," Mary said. "I promised I'd call her when we get to your apartment. So she knows I didn't end up on the street."

"God forbid!" Cassandra wailed.

Mary laughed; the joke never got old. "Will Abe be there?"

"In a few hours. We can all go out for dinner to celebrate your arrival." She could feel Mary looking at her, as though she were trying to decide whether or not to say something. "What?"

"I just want you to know you guys don't have to hide your stuff from me while I'm here," she finally said.

"Well, thank you. What stuff exactly?"

"Your grass. I'm in college now. It's not gonna shock me."

"What makes you think—"

"Please," Mary snorted. "I heard you talking at Christmas." She stretched her legs farther, so that they began to look more like legs made of rubber than of flesh. "All I'm saying is I'm cool with it. And I won't even be offended if you want to offer me some. Maybe I'll even try it."

Cassandra thought for a moment. "You minx."

Mary grinned triumphantly.

Had she smoked grass at Mary's age? She must've but she couldn't remember. It was ages ago that she was in college, another life. She hardly wore any of the same clothes.

"Well, you won't be the first person to come to California for the grass," she finally said, still unsure what she was going to let her sister do.

Mary hugged herself, shivering. "Maybe what I really need is a California boy."

Cassandra laughed. "They're pretty nice, all right."

"But you picked one from Virginia." Her voice had formed an edge. She sounded jealous, which was ridiculous. Anyone could see that Mary had the long blond hair and erupting chest that attracted men on any coast.

"Who says he can't be both? That's why people come here."

"I thought it was for the grass."

Cassandra shook her head, and they lapsed into silence, cresting along in their pack of vehicles, sometimes gliding ahead of the others, sometimes drifting back. Cassandra felt herself sitting at a great distance from her sister, as though the passenger compartment had stretched, shifting Mary several lanes to the right and depositing her in another car altogether. But the distance gave her clarity. She glanced at Mary out of the corner of her eye and saw that she was puckering her lips, so used to watching others that she always expected she was being watched as well.

Cassandra took off several days that week to slink around town with her sister. The first day, they walked over the Golden Gate Bridge and back, then climbed down to the base, then looked back at it from a point farther down the coastal trail. Up close it was a machine goliath, far away a braided piece of string. On the trail, Mary looked pale, like a photograph of herself on a trip. The next day, feet and thighs aching, they went to a sunny diner and spent a fulsome hour bent over a newspaper crossword another patron had left behind. Cassandra thought about the way, as a child, Mary used to let her dress her in silly handmade costumes, holding her breath as Cassandra tightened a glittery vest over her shoulder, her eyes full and serious, as though afraid to disturb her in her work. She thought it was fitting that Mary should be the first member of her old family to visit her new one here.

That evening, Abe came home bearing bags of fruit and vegetables from the farmers market. Mary held a pitted half of an avocado as though it were made of gold. She looked at her sister with a wondrous envy Cassandra immediately wanted to erase. "Jeez, Mary, it's just an avocado," she said.

Diane came over, Diane who Cassandra often sketched and was more like Mary than Cassandra had previously realized, both of them patient enough to sit for her while she played her creative games.

"Isn't Cassandra's hair just indecent?" Abe roared. They were sitting around, the four of them and Abe's friend John, stoned. Cassandra had given in to Mary, and the moment she did, she realized her sister smoked grass all the time. She required no instruction on how to inhale, lighting the packed pipe herself without hesitation.

"Indecent how?" Diane asked.

"It's all on display," Abe said, crawling along the couch to reach his arms around Cassandra's waist. "Something that powerful ought to be contained."

"Abe!" Cassandra said in fake protest as his head fell into her lap. John got up to change the record. He was a sweet-tempered, unobnoxious person who had plans to be a surgeon. He was from Iowa. He liked glam rock. She was privately hoping he'd marry Diane.

"You're saying she ought to cover it up?" Diane was saying now. "Like some kind of Orthodox Jew?" Cassandra winced. Abe's father had been Jewish and Diane often said things that weren't really racist, but could sound racist if you were only half-listening.

Abe spoke into her thigh. "No, I'm saying I love it. My natural beauty. You know she doesn't wear makeup." He rolled over to look up at her, fingering the ends of her hair.

"Shh," Cassandra said, embarrassed.

"It was a good thing when we were growing up," Mary was saying. "I was blond, so no one ever assumed we were sisters."

"Yeah, who would ever want to be related to her?" Diane said.

"I didn't," Mary said. They laughed.

They were kidding, weren't they? She looked down at Abe, who was like a child in her lap. He pouted at her and continued to touch her hair. Across the room, her friend and sister were far away, flopping their heads on their necks. Mary was clutching a blanket around her shoulders. "It's way colder here than everybody says."

"Hello, Cassandra," Abe said. His voice was an imaginary line, hooking her back in among her people, a line that wasn't really there, but in which it was better to believe if she could.

*   *   *

THE NEXT NIGHT, the sisters were at a concert, a screeching affair in a checker-tiled room so soaked with beer and urine that its scuffed black walls seemed to radiate a pale yellow glow. They sucked lurid drinks through cocktail stirrers and spoke directly in each other's ear.

"I'll never meet anyone in College Park!" Mary shouted, after surveying the room.

"I felt the exact same way."

"You always met people," Mary insisted. "You just didn't like them as much as they liked you."

"Isn't that what we're talking about?"

Mary cleared her throat in exasperation. "I feel like I'm in the wrong club," she said. "The jock guys who keep asking me out. They aren't *my* guys, you know?" She tossed her hair out of her eye, flirtatiously. Don't waste it on me, Cassandra wanted to say, but didn't. The truth was it couldn't be wasted. Mary was nineteen and on vacation. Her allure was in limitless supply.

Another drink in, Mary lost her footing and Cassandra had to catch her by the soft, nubile arm. She loved the ugliness of the place, the way it made everyone inside it look beautiful, her little sister most of all. Then the screeching stopped and the main act—the act that John had sent them to hear—came on and filled the room with a thundering heartache of guitar, drums, and bass. The lead singer was a scrawny man who looked like a woman and held his high notes forever. Cassandra and Mary bumped against each other in excitement, and strangers bumped against them, too. A sweaty, older man with long hair bumped Mary a few too many times, finally abandoning the ruse and directly pressing himself into her, his stomach smushing where it made contact with her back. Even in the dark, Cassandra could see her shoulders stiffen at the unseen presence behind her, then stiffen more after she managed to glimpse his toothy face. She looped her arm around Mary's waist and spun her until she was in front of her, then pressed her own body against Mary's in defense. They remained that way for a moment, bucking to the music like one sister instead of two, closer than they'd been even on the nights they'd shared a bed as girls. The man moved on, miming a hat-tip and making them laugh, and before they knew it, they were separate again and dancing, and another man, this one much younger and much handsomer, in an angled, almost military way, was advancing on Mary from the side.

The floor was humming in Cassandra's knees, the music banging pinball-like from her chest to her neck to her knuckles, and she didn't know what Mary would want her to do this time. She watched her sister bob her head. Her hair, blond even in the dark, fell like a glare across her face as the man bent down from his great male height and spoke into her ear. Her sister's spine arched as she looked up to respond; her face turned away from Cassandra's. It looked very much like a situation in which Cassandra was not supposed to intervene. She stood there a moment on the scummy checkered tile, and then, finding she still had liquid in her cup, downed her last swallow of beer.

She reached for her sister, whose shapely body still swiveled just inches from her own. She pulled her toward her, away from the tall soldier and back into her frame of vision. She closed her eyes and kept her there, nodding to the crescendo that had since given way to a piercing, palpitating guitar. When she opened her eyes again Mary was there, smiling at her, swooping toward her for an embrace.

Cassandra held her sister and told her she was glad she'd guessed right. But Mary just shook her head and smiled, then shouted something explosive in Cassandra's ear.

"What?" Cassandra screamed back. "I can't hear you!"

"I can't hear you!" Mary mouthed in response.

AS THEY CAME back into the apartment, Cassandra's ears were ringing so violently she thought she heard the phone ringing, too. It wasn't until Abe, who'd been sitting with a book in his armchair, stood up that she realized it really was the phone.

Mary had already rushed on to the bathroom, so Cassandra stood for a moment in the entryway absorbing the glow of Abe's reading lamp, which softened the darkened room, drew it inward, and made it hers. When he came back from the kitchen, she didn't immediately recognize the expression on his face. She tilted her head at him, cutely, inviting him to tackle her. But instead he stood in the dining alcove and waited. In the next moment, she understood everything. Still she didn't move. She wanted to hold the moment one beat longer, the final moment before his tragedy became their tragedy, before everything could still be postponed because it hadn't yet been spoken.

It was his grandmother Helen, of course. A heart attack in her kitchen. One minute squeezing her can opener, the next minute gone. Sudden, like Abe's parents before her. "She was just using a can opener," he repeated, always one to focus on details. Cassandra led him to the couch as though introducing the act of sitting, and let him slump with his hand in hers, his head on her shoulder, not even at a comfortable angle, though he didn't seem to care.

It occurred to her then that Abe had never really described to her how he'd felt when his parents died. Of course, she knew he had to have been a wreck, that it had changed his life forever and continued to affect him even today. But how, precisely? Had he temporarily lost his appetite, his ability to sleep? Did he obsess over the event privately or did he put it out of mind, so that it seemed like something that had happened to someone else, something he'd heard about, maybe, on the news? These suddenly seemed like important things to know about the person she'd committed to for life, and she felt embarrassed and even foolish not to have tracked down the answers before.

Perhaps he had been waiting for her to ask him again, and in her happiness, she had forgotten. Perhaps he had tried to bring it up, but she had clumsily and inadvertently rebuffed him when he did. It was impossible to say. She looked at his forehead where it rested on her shoulder, so furrowed and porous, lightly perspiring with emotion. She couldn't ask him now, or even anytime soon. She'd just have to make a mental note, and remember.

When Mary finally opened the bathroom door—how long had she been hiding in there, sensing something was wrong?—her face was almost professional in its expression of concern. She hung back at just the right distance, so that her presence and support were felt but not broadcast. She was like an actress in a play in which Abe's grandmother had died, so finely was she performing the etiquette of grief. Much more finely than Cassandra, who felt feckless and ill-equipped to even sit on her own stupid couch. Mary was only nineteen, and her shorts were far too short, but it was clear she'd paid attention to the things her family had to teach.

Cassandra caught her sister's eye and motioned her over. Mary came around to join them, drawing her legs up beneath her like a pet. On her other side, Abe breathed in a rhythm that suggested nothing, and after a while, she stopped waiting for him to speak. She thought of Helen, who'd lived in a rural county all her life, but moved to Richmond when Abe fell to her care, to give him the best education. The framed picture of her late, darker-skinned husband she kept hidden in her bedside drawer. The eyebrows she drew in with pencil, the thick stockings she wore every day. The way she'd once admitted she was too fond of pigs to eat them, but bought and cooked bacon for Abe when he visited, because she hated to deny her boy his treats. Cassandra's foot, bent at what was now a clearly unsustainable angle, began to tingle, but she refused to move it. For a little while longer, she'd be still. She'd be like Helen and overcome her own discomfort. She'd give him whatever he wanted.

MARY'S RETURN TICKET couldn't be changed, so she stayed on with Diane while Abe and Cassandra went to Richmond. In the departures hall, Abe wore a jacket that made him look like a pilot, and for a moment Cassandra worried someone might show up and ask him to fly a plane. Mary and Diane had come to see them off, but in her distraction Cassandra could hardly give them anything. She told Mary about a soap shop near Diane's if she wanted to get a gift for Eunice, but it must have come out wrong, because Mary only pressed her lips together and leaned in for a hug. Over her sister's shoulder, Cassandra watched Abe intently as though he might wander away.

The funeral was the first she'd attended outside her parents' house, but it was a funeral all the same: unfashionable fabrics in a range of grim hues, voices laboring to sing in unison, the nagging feeling that none of this was really helping anyone, least of all the stricken family in the front. At the lectern, a newly shaven Abe eulogized his grandmother's tenacity as well as her slowness to appreciate jokes. He told a story about how he often liked to fake injuries as a child, just to see what she would do, and how she always came running, even after she ought to have known he was only messing with her. Cassandra looked at the congregation of old ladies, all of whom seemed to have heard the story before, and liked it. She'd never heard it. "And thank God for that," Abe said, hamming for the ladies, who nodded their hats at the memory. "Because when I really did fall and break my ankle, she didn't just leave me there on the ground!" Everyone laughed, including Cassandra, grateful to have the chance.

Back in Helen's bungalow, scented with cinnamon candles and vacuum exhaust, Abe accepted condolences and advice. He nodded and said, "Yes, ma'am." Cassandra took note of this, that in grief he was even more polite than he was in ordinary life.

In bed that night, he lay hard and almost unbreathing beside her, as though the mattress concealed a hundred knives, which the slightest movement would send plunging through his ribs. She drifted off easily, but when she awoke again in the middle of the night, she was troubled to find him gone, not in bed and not even in the room. With her eyes half-shut, she hauled herself out of bed and down the little staircase to Helen's living room, where Abe sat in his boxer shorts and threadbare undershirt with a fat hardcover book on the couch.

"What're you reading?" she asked, her voice raspy with sleep.

"Sherlock Holmes."

She came to sit beside him. "Really?"

"It's my old edition. A favorite."

She lifted the back pages to catch a glimpse of text. "I don't think I've ever read Sherlock Holmes," she said through a yawn. "I was more into Nancy Drew."

He closed the book over his finger and smiled at her, fuzzily, so that the parts of his face that had once seemed most vital were, for a moment, blurred out. She found herself missing his beard. "You can go back to bed," he said. "I'm fine."

"What do you mean?"

"I mean you're very sweet but you don't have to worry about me. Get some sleep." He looked her directly in the eye, and even in her groggy state, she could see that he wasn't just being generous; he was telling her what to do.

"Okay," she said.

"Look. Sometimes there's such a thing as too much talking. It can be toxic."

"But—we haven't talked at all."

"You know what I mean."

She didn't. "Well," she said at last, counting her syllables, "if you're sure."

"I'm sure."

"Just come to bed soon," she said, unable to help herself. "You need your sleep, too."

"I will." He said it kindly, though it was clear he had no intention of following through. She went upstairs and climbed back into bed, and she couldn't pretend it didn't hurt. She felt a warm tear land on the corner of her mouth and tasted her own salt as it soaked into her lip. It had never occurred to her he would ever not want her love, especially at a time like this.

In the light of day, she reasoned with herself. It's his death; he gets to decide how he mourns. Who was she to make him flail and cry? She stood in the living room doorway and watched him busy himself with a cardboard box of his grandmother's files. So as not to hover, she went for a drive through the historic downtown, where the grand, National Register houses looked mostly like frosted layer cakes, though every now and then there was an unrefurbished nightmare, sticking out like a rotten tooth. She couldn't decide which moved her more, the perfect ones or the ruins. She sat at a stop sign for a long time thinking about this, until someone honked and she lurched forward, leaving the thought behind.

When she returned to the house, Abe was still paging through the box, but now at least he'd thought of something for her to do. He asked her, in the even, professional tone she knew from the clinic, to pass along the flowers they kept receiving at the house. Happily, she stuffed Helen's Cadillac with sprays of gladioli and delphinium and drove it at low speed, like a parade float, to the nursing home down the road.

At dinner that night, he smiled at her while he chewed the pork chop she'd prepared, as though he tasted some part of her in the food. Perhaps he loved her for her funeral upbringing, because he knew the private pain of death, and thought she knew it, too. She sucked on the tines of her empty fork, tasting not him but metal. It was the opposite, actually, if that mattered. People in mourning had always been inaccessible to her, standing around her parents' house in their sad, exclusive club. She had no idea what they were going through, and she didn't really want to find out.

So when he slunk out of bed again that night, she told herself she was doing him a favor in pretending to be asleep. The truth was she was relieved. By the time they got back to San Francisco, she didn't even have to pretend, never knowing when she came in to breakfast to find him munching corn flakes and reading the paper if he'd merely risen a little before her, or if she'd slept the entire night alone.

Maybe it was for the best. A marriage needed mysteries, even at breakfast. One morning, as the percolator filled her mug with its bright, portentous brew, she realized she couldn't ever ask him how it felt to lose his parents, no matter what he'd promised her before. Love, she was learning, meant many things, and one of them was making room for solitude. They were separate. He needed his head space, just as she needed hers.

Their last day in Richmond, they had driven the city together, and he'd let her get up close to a ruined house on the outskirts of town. It was so covered in lichen and vines it looked like a traveling carnival that had finally abandoned its tour. She took pictures of every beam and shutter, just the way she saw them. If they were not separate she couldn't have done that. If they were not separate he couldn't have pinned her that night, nearly starving, after only a few sexless days.

Part III

Part II

11

Just after dawn on the day of Howard's funeral, the air temperature dropped and stilled, as though the summer had paused to respect the passing of Bethesda's oldest undertaker. Cassandra, who usually slept on her back in the heat, turned onto her side and tucked her hands up to her chest. Down the hall, Eunice dreamed of catching fireflies, one by one in a glass jar. She had counted up to an incredible number, yet every time she felt she was approaching the last, a new brood sprang up, farther out in the darkness. When she went after them, she found Howard in a doorway admonishing her, shaking his head and telling her she'd come too far. She shook him off and flipped scenes, coming to a large library where everything was in its place, rows of books in alphabetical order and on the center table, a pyramid of crisp green apples of equal size and sheen. Cassandra had less control over her dreams. They simply came at her and she endured them until her body had had enough. Deep in a well of color and indecipherable emotion, she pulled her blanket up more snugly around her shoulders, covering Elizabeth's as well.

Then the coolness passed, and everyone awoke in a deep summer sweat.

Cassandra and Elizabeth stood together before the upstairs mirror, soaking the night grease from their faces with astringent-dipped cotton balls. They had survived yesterday's wake. Only one more day of ritual awaited.

Cassandra turned and looked deeply into her daughter's ear. "How are you?" It was important to keep checking now that it was clear Kyle was gone.

"Same as yesterday."

"And how is that?"

"Sad!" Elizabeth's voice ricocheted off the vanity lights that lined the top of the mirror, ping ping ping like a series of misfired rounds. It was like that whenever she gave voice to her distress; a battlefield in her mother's ear.

Cassandra opened her travel case. "I think you should take a Xanax today, before the service." She held out a small white oval.

"Jesus, Mom, where did you get that?"

"It's only for emergencies. Look, I'm taking one, and I bet Mary is, too. It'll be easier, trust me, talking to all those people."

"What about Grandma?"

Cassandra waved her hand, still pinching the pill. "She's never even taken an aspirin, if you believe her. Anyway, she knows how to behave at a funeral. We're not like her." Xanax was the only thing that had gotten her through those first few miserable weeks after Abe had driven off with Ferdinand. She'd felt like an empty suitcase, as though when he'd left, he'd packed up all her insides, all the viscera and emotions that made her feel like herself, and taken them with him in a cardboard box. Except they weren't even with him anymore, because he'd dumped them somewhere, somewhere cold and dying, like the fossil ground at the bottom of the bay. That summer, it was all she could do to drag herself to the kitchen each day and pour herself a glass of wine, a Sisyphean attempt to refill herself. Her father's death brought back an ugly shadow of that old feeling and she could only assume Elizabeth felt worse. The Xanax would do her good.

"Well, when you put it that way . . ." Elizabeth took the pill between her index finger and thumb. "You're not supposed to drink with this, you know. That might be a problem."

"It's one day, Lizzie. Just one day. Don't tell me you've never made that calculation before."

Elizabeth examined the pill. Medicines had always worked too well on her body. Antihistamines scorched out her sinuses and put her deep into a well of Technicolor sleep. Xanax might completely erase her mind. If she needed it, she reasoned, it would've looked friendlier, a promise of relief. She would've been taken with its beauty or tasted its sugar already on her lips. Instead, it was alien, threatening, irresponsible. It rolled dully to the center of her hand, leaving a chalky wake, a reminder of all the ways the mind and body can crumble.

"We're so vulnerable!" she cried.

"I know, sweetie. I know. Sometimes, we just need a little help." Cassandra squeezed her daughter's shoulder. "Take it before the service. It works quickly, and it'll wear off right around the time people expect you to have had enough. Then you can crawl into bed or go out for a drink—or do whatever you want for the rest of the day."

"I hate people."

Cassandra's chest swelled. "I know. I hate them, too."

"Either they won't leave you alone or they leave you."

"That's why it's better to leave them first."

Elizabeth's eyes filled. Instantly, Cassandra wished she could take it back. What an insanely insensitive thing to have said! Elizabeth was torn in two: her eyes crying, her nose and mouth twisted in shame. "Well," she managed to say as Cassandra hugged her to avoid looking at her anguished face. "Next time, I guess."

It was half past nine when Toby entered the parlor, and already the room was buzzing. Elizabeth was standing in front of the open casket where her grandfather lay, receiving condolences. She was wearing a sleeveless black-and-white patterned dress and an attractive middle-aged woman was standing next to her—no doubt her mother, an older version of the same long-limbed, pale-skinned, redheaded girl. People milled around, eating nuts out of scattered bowls.

The last funeral he'd attended had been his own father's, when he was just six. He remembered holding his mother's hand tightly. He remembered being even more scared than he'd been of thunderstorms. What scared him most was the way the grown-ups were crying and talking to one another, moving more slowly than he'd ever seen them move. His father had died suddenly, a quiet brain seizure at his basement desk while he and his mother were upstairs in the kitchen. All he remembered from that day was his mother pouring steaming pasta into a colander and the perfect red Duplo tower he'd made at the table. The next thing he knew, his mother was hugging him, heavily, and then his grandmother was there, making him pancakes and holding his head to her chest, which smelled, as it always had, like breakfast and a closet full of coats. Then his mother was sitting with him on his bed looking tired and explaining that Daddy was gone and never coming back, and then he was drinking a milkshake and crying, and then he was at the funeral, wearing itchy socks and holding his breath. "You have to stop that," his aunt Carol had told him, crouching down to look him in the eye. "Your mommy wants you to try your hardest to breathe normally. She wants you to know that everything's going to be okay." Carol had a thin streak of dark ink under her eye, but her hair was soft and black, like a princess's. She was so pretty that he took her at her word. He knew he wasn't going to have a daddy anymore, and he knew this made his mother sad, but apparently none of that mattered in the end, because everything was going to be okay. He breathed for Carol and believed her.

In his memory, everyone at his father's funeral had worn black. But looking around now at the maroon dresses and navy ties interspersed with charcoal jackets and shawls, he realized that he must've been mistaking cinema for life. Even the widow, a short, unflinching woman who, he understood from the obituary, had lived in the funeral home for more than fifty years, was wearing a lavender scarf over her plain black dress.

Beside her, Elizabeth seemed to be barely holding it together. Her eyes were pink and she kept looking past him at the doorway, failing to recognize him. Toby looked around, uncertain how to proceed. He could join the receiving line, but he didn't want to talk to anyone but her. Deep in his pants pocket, he ran his finger over the pebble from his mother's orchid bed. He wished he'd brought flowers, or wine— anything—to make up for his miserable appearance. He had relented and was wearing Ed's sport coat, a fairly exquisite jacket made of a supple green wool somewhere on its way to becoming black. It fit him surprisingly well across the shoulders—he had no idea he and Ed wore the same size—and he had to admit when he looked in his bed-room mirror that he cut a fine figure, even sideways at his skinniest. But now, wearing it out in the world, the jacket just depressed him. Layered over his black waiter shirt and pants, which he'd previously thought rather smart, in a corporate, uniformed sort of way, it made the rest of his clothes look cheap and drab. Only his Lenox Lounge silkscreened T-shirt was worthy of the jacket, but it was buried, rel-egated to the role of undershirt.

Elizabeth continued to look past him at the open doorway, her posture rigid and unwelcoming. It would be easy to leave unnoticed. But he hadn't showered and come all this way just to see her across a room and go home. She was grieving and could use his sympa-thy, and after all, he knew what it was like. He fell into line, and in a matter of seconds, found himself before her. Her lips parted; she remembered him.

"Toby . . . ?" she said. The waiter from Lucie's wedding, and from the line at Starbucks down the road. His hair looked almost wet, slicked back with gel and tucked in behind his ears. He came forward swiftly and took her in his arms. "I'm so sorry for your loss," he whis-pered into her hair.

She had no idea what was going on. The wedding waiter—really?

She struggled for a moment to grip the rug with her feet, but he was too determined to comfort her. His shampoo smelled coconutty, like a woman's, and before she knew it, she'd surrendered to his weird embrace.

"Thank you," she replied, trying not to cause a scene. Her pelvis pressed awkwardly into his hip; her arms and legs sort of dangled in space. He was bony, but surprisingly strong.

Eventually, he released her, and they parted; Elizabeth took an extra step back.

"I saw the obituary," he said. "And after seeing you so upset, I knew I had to come." He held her gaze and appeared to be holding his breath even as he spoke.

He liked her, she realized. At that moment, the truth was so palpable that she almost said it out loud.

"That's so nice of you," she said instead. "I think you're the only person who came here just for me."

"You don't have any other friends in the area?" he asked. His voice was low and vaguely excited, and he seemed unaware of all the people waiting to be received behind him.

"I didn't really tell anyone," she lied, suddenly wishing she'd asked Becca to come.

"Well. You have me. We'll talk."

She frowned. He spoke to her the way you spoke to someone you'd known your whole life. "What would we talk about?"

He blinked. "Anything. The world. Have you read about the hurricane? We can talk about that."

"I haven't really been keeping up with the news."

"But this is something you have to know about. It's like that tsunami in Thailand last year, but it's in America, in New Orleans. Half the city's underwater. You've never seen anything like it."

An older woman reached forward to clasp Elizabeth's hand, forcing Toby to move aside. On the other side of the room, Elizabeth saw her father standing by the bookshelf, which gave her some relief. A part of her had been afraid he'd gotten on a plane and gone back to

California, without even saying good-bye. She wouldn't have put it past him.

"If you want, I'll bring you the paper this afternoon," Toby said, several people having already come between them.

She looked back at her father. He was wearing New Balance sneakers with his suit and he seemed to be waiting for her to answer a question she hadn't heard him pose. He'd always worn New Balances. She gave him a look to let him know she'd noticed the shoes, but the look wasn't transparent enough; he wrinkled his forehead and looked around, failing to understand. She allowed her hand to be clasped and her cheek kissed a few more times, tucking back her bra straps in between. Then, after all the mourners had said what they needed to say, she excused herself and went to the bathroom, where she'd left her mother's little white pill.

"Who was that boy?" Abe asked her later, after they'd filed into the church pew for the service.

"I really don't know." She wiped her sweaty palms on her dress and held her hands in her lap. Her grandfather's casket was wrapped in the flag up front, and the choir was singing the opening hymn. She leaned back against the hard wood and waited for the service to start.

Soon enough, the minister came forward in glasses and a bright white robe. Abe took her hand and squeezed it, and though her palms had begun sweating again, she squeezed back, shuffling her feet up next to her mom's. She was between them, contained, as though nothing bad had ever happened. Cassandra felt Elizabeth's feet and smiled, her nostrils faintly fluttering. Her mother had a nice face, and she'd been nice to give her the pill. Elizabeth leaned sideways, which should have been uncomfortable, and lodged her head in the nook between her mother's shoulder and neck. Abe continued to hold her hand over his knee, and she imagined they must look like a picture she'd like to have. She exhaled when the minister asked them to stand. They stood, all together, all at once. It was almost like being a family.

* * *

TOBY WATCHED IN a pew to the side. Elizabeth slouched through much of the service, though now and then, she abruptly straightened her back, as though she had just that instant recalled the formality of the event. Slouching or straight, she was a marvelous magnet, the central actor who carried the otherwise unoriginal show. He watched her cross and uncross her legs, watched her scratch the back of her long woodland neck. No woman had ever scratched a neck before this. He bit his lip in ecstasy.

The widow read a brief statement thanking the community for their support and proclaiming her departed husband a kind man, the most dependable she'd ever known. She loved him, always had, a confession that elicited an audible sob from a person several rows back. Elizabeth's uncle held himself together long enough to tell a story about his father's love of materials and the wood he'd helped sand as a kid. A song was sung and another story told, and finally, the minister stood to speak of the good life, its meaning and mystery. Throughout his sermon, Elizabeth's father looked up at the ceiling, as though reading along in the paint.

It was a funeral, like any he would have imagined, performed flaw-lessly by professionals in the field. It was surely just like his father's and the countless more he'd have to attend before his own. Jewish, Christian, it didn't really matter in the end. Yet here was his Elizabeth at the center, and instead of conforming, she stood out. Her curving back gave the ritual meaning, her uncertain profile its pathos. This is why we mourn, he realized. Because when grandfathers die, red-haired statues are left behind. Because if grandfathers die, red-haired statues must die one day as well. He was six years old again, clutching his mother's hand, wondering when he'd have to get into his own long box, and how it would feel to lie like that forever. Near the end, when no one was saying anything particularly poignant, Toby found himself dabbing a Kleenex at the corner of his eye.

Later, at the cemetery, while the casket was being lowered into the ground, Elizabeth tucked a folded note into the open dirt. Nei-ther her mother nor her father noticed; she was discreet and took care they shouldn't see. Only Toby, who watched her every movement, appreciated what she had done. *She's a poet!* The thought echoed in his pounding veins. She righted herself and flipped her hair over her shoulder, looking out into the heady sky. Toby had followed her to the grave, lights flashing in the sober line, a placard that read FUNERAL affixed to his mirror, connecting him to her. She ducked back into the limo she came in, clay trailing from her heel. Through the windshield of the Subaru, he watched her vehicle start and pull away, then turned the key in his own ignition and dutifully followed her home.

BACK IN EUNICE'S KITCHEN, Cassandra and Elizabeth scraped grave-side mud from their shoes into a garbage bag. Dorothy Chamberlain distributed plates of cold cuts to tables and buffets around the house.

"I'm not babysitting your father," Cassandra said. She dropped her shoes out the back door and stood barefoot on the kitchen tile.

"You don't have to."

"I don't know. If I don't, he might just leave without a word."

"That's ridiculous," Elizabeth said, though she'd had the same thought herself.

"Elizabeth, come here!" Eunice called from the rear parlor.

"Go on, go on." Cassandra shooed her down the hall.

Eunice was engulfed in an oversize leather chair with armrests wide enough to sit on. A few of the older women clustered around her on ottomans and chairs. "This is my oldest granddaughter," she said, smiling broadly, her face unnaturally shiny. "She's in medical school. She's studying to be a doctor."

"How nice!" "Smart girl!" Elizabeth nodded and let herself be admired.

"And you know, I always knew she would be. When she was a little girl, maybe seven or eight—she came to my house for a week with her mom. And she was so helpful in the kitchen, mixing batter for cookies and unloading the dishwasher when I told her to."

Elizabeth smiled uncomfortably. She remembered other things

about her childhood visits. The brusqueness with which her grand-mother had given her advice—"You should cut your hair. Girls look cute with their hair short"—and the frightening manner in which Cassandra had risen to her defense.

"And one day," Eunice continued, "I was taking the groceries in when I accidentally closed these two fingers in the car door. Oh, did it hurt! I thought my old bones were broken! But little Lizzie was right there beside me. She yanked the door open, and she took my fingers in her hand, and she said, 'Come on, Grandma, I'll get you some ice. It will be okay.' Can you believe it? A seven-year-old girl?"

The ladies made murmurs of admiration. "You did that?" one of them asked.

"Well, it had happened to me before, so I sort of knew what to do."

"She'll save lives," Eunice said. "And oh! You should see her boy-friend. Where is Kyle? I want him to meet my friends."

"Oh, he's around," Elizabeth said. She didn't want to explain.

"Go find him and bring him in."

"Later, Grandma. Okay?"

"Yes, why don't you bring him later," Eunice repeated, as though it had been her idea.

Elizabeth circled back into the hallway, pausing in front of the mirror to catch a glimpse of her tired face. People passed back and forth behind her with plates of food, jostling her closer to the mirror each time. Her head looked huge and out of proportion with her body, giving her a little thrill. She knew that everything she was feeling came from the Xanax, which for some reason thrilled her even more. Kyle would be proud of her for having this experience, for allowing it to alter her mind.

She knew there were three possible courses for Kyle. He could return. He could head to New York, where she would see him again in a few days. Or he could vanish from her life forever, maybe take off for LA. He wasn't very specific in his note. All contingencies would have to be considered. Doctoring had taught her this, and also how to be less hopeful. She monitored the symptoms of everything now, including her relationship with Kyle. She knew the risk factors going in and all the potential complications that might develop down the road; she gathered data, performed tests. He was a good actor, but was he good enough? If he failed, would his disappointments drag her down? For most of the past two years, she seemed to have been living diagnostically, trying to predict at every turn just how the relationship would die.

She remembered his text, still waiting on her phone, unread. Should she call him? It didn't seem prudent. They needed some time; they could use it to make up their minds. In the meantime, she had to do something; she couldn't just look in the mirror and thrill at the size of her head. So she went around collecting empty cups. She carried two stacks into the kitchen, where she pitched the plastic ones into the garbage bin and left the glasses in the sink, before circling back through the house once again. She passed through the dining room, walking a straight path along the worn runners that Eunice had lain to keep her fancy rugs clean. On the table were platters stinking of deli meat and tuna salad. More than a few used plates loitered on the sideboard, but surprisingly, there wasn't a human being in sight. She savored the solo moment, wished she had a glass of juice to sip—a real glass—to savor along with it. Suddenly, the kitchen door swung outward and Toby Steinberg stood before her, holding a plastic cup filled with pale green and orange melon balls.

"Hello," he said, as though he had never spoken to another person in his life. He had a strange voice: deep, sonorous, but vaguely encumbered by a lisp. It reminded her of high-school drama class. Wisps of thick, dark sideburns stood out from his face. She wanted to take a pair of scissors and trim them to a uniform length.

"I brought you this." He held out the fruit cup.

"I couldn't eat right now. But thank you."

"Okay." His forehead wrinkled. He was baffled, not knowing what to do with the fruit. He scanned the room for a flat surface on which to place it, finally settling on a corner of the sideboard, behind a pair of burnished metal candlesticks.

"So what's your story?" she asked, curling her fingers around the arc of a dining chair.

He stared. The dotted pattern on her dress was dizzying; black-and-gray-and-black-and-gray, rolling down her hip. It was like a scrap of infinity. "My story?"

"Who are you, why are you here. Et cetera." She smiled, to encourage him.

"Well, I'm a waiter and I'm a musician. I'm in town this week to visit my mother. And I'm here because I read your grandfather's obituary."

"Okay."

"And what about you? Are you a musician, too?"

"A musician?" she laughed. "No. I'm a med student. At Columbia."

He contemplated this new piece of information. "You're going to be a doctor."

"That's the idea." She leaned into the chair and traced her index finger along the fluting on its back.

"I wouldn't have guessed it."

"I'll take that as a compliment."

"What kind of doctor are you going to be?"

"I'm applying for residencies now. I actually did pretty well on the Boards, so I'm going for dermatology."

"Skin," he said.

"You got it. I'm as unserious and superficial as they come."

"Don't be so hard on yourself. Skin cancer's serious."

"That's what I keep telling myself."

"So do something else. Be a surgeon or something. Or not a doctor." He blinked as though it were an easy fix, like changing her order at a restaurant.

"Yeah, well, I've come this far. And anyway, I also kind of want to do derm. So there's that."

He shrugged. "I just graduated from college. I'm twenty-two."

This surprised her and caused her to adjust her perception of him.

His features became fresher, newly adult, his narrow waist the mark of recent youth.

"You know," he continued. "I saw your father in the other room."

"Yeah?"

"He was just standing by the fireplace, leaning on the mantel. He reminded me of a naval captain."

She laughed at his perfect description—he couldn't have known how perfect. "My dad does love to sail." Then, unthinkingly, she told him about her parents' separation. "Until this week, they hadn't seen each other since."

"My father died when I was six," Toby said. "I hardly remember him."

"I'm sorry."

"Growing up, it was just me and my mom. I can't even remember her going on dates. But then when I was a sophomore, she met Ed, and married him. They live together now in our old house."

"That must be nice."

"Well, actually, I hate him."

Elizabeth was impressed by the ease with which this odd conversation had unfolded. Toby Steinberg flattered and aroused her, but it couldn't be denied that he was stalking her as well. He reached for her hand. She let him hold it and press her palm with his thumb. In every nerve ending, she absorbed his attraction. His eyes were the color of gunmetal and they bored directly into hers.

"I have a boyfriend," she said.

"I know. I remember him from the wedding. But I notice he isn't here now."

She saw what was happening. Thanks to the Xanax it was suddenly clear as can be, as though time had stopped, allowing her to step outside its frame and examine the equation that had created the chemical moment in which she currently existed. In a single week, she'd lost her grandfather and Kyle, but had been given Toby and her dad. It was a trade. The energy on one side balancing out the energy on the other. Life was a constant trade, wasn't it? At any given moment you had something, and something else was taken away. Toby was simply the latest element, the person standing before her right now.

She sucked her upper lip and tasted the brine of dried perspiration. She stepped closer to his face. He was taller than she had initially estimated. Five-ten, five-eleven maybe. She willed him to tilt his head toward her until their foreheads touched.

"I need something sweet," she said, withdrawing. "I think there are some cookies in the kitchen." She disappeared behind the white swinging door.

He wandered into the living room, which was full of people, and when she returned to him, she was flushed and holding a glass of juice. She stood very near him.

"I can't figure you out," she said, one hand tense and aloft with her drink, the other languid at her side.

He reached for the languid arm, touching the fleshy underside of her wrist. His fingers rolled lightly over her veins, which popped out, blue and hungry. "I don't fully understand myself either."

"But you chose to come here today," she said. "You tracked me down. For all I know, you made up that stuff about living in the area. For all I know, you've been following me since Saturday night."

"No, I wouldn't lie to you. I might lie to other people, but not you."

"Not to be trite, but why me?"

"Because why not? Because we're all just passengers on this train." He looked around at all the old people accumulating like dust bunnies in comfort. "We loop around and around on the same fucking tracks every day of our lives. We've got nowhere to be, not really. So most of us never get off. We just sit back in our seats and endure the ride, watching the same fucking fields and rear ends of towns roll by."

"Shh," she said. People, even the deaf ones, were starting to look their way. Out of the corner of her eye she saw Joanne Hickory, her grandmother's friend who still had her husband, and her diamond earring, too.

"We take the guarantees," Toby went on, undaunted. "We take the money. We take the security of living by the book. But it's fear; it's complacency. And I say it's bullshit. When you see something from the window that's beautiful and good and rare and right, you have to get off the train. You have to put your feet down on the ground and you have to seize it."

"And that's me?" She felt faint. Who spoke this way?

"That's you." His hand now encircled her wrist. "I'm seizing you."

She forgot about their audience. Something inside her swelled, and it was glorious. She felt the intoxication of fame. She had a disciple; she was immortal; she could do anything in the world that she wished.

Rolling her wrist out of his hold, she seized his hand in hers. "Come with me," she said.

"Where are we going?" he breathed.

"We're getting out of here." She grabbed her purse from the closet and started stuffing it with mints from the dish on the telephone table. It had been years since she'd felt this dominant, this powerful, this good.

They burst out of the house into the blazing afternoon light, just as a gust of hot wind licked and lifted everything that wasn't nailed down to the street. Flags waved from a cluster of poles at the Metro stop and lunch bags got away from people eating sandwiches in the plaza. Elizabeth's jersey dress clung to her legs, her stomach, her breasts. She swished her hips as they walked, and gave in. She was female. She was sex walking out of a funeral home and into the still living day.

12

Upstairs, in Cassandra's room, Abe cut through the taped sides of his package with a pair of kitchen scissors. He'd rushed back from the church service, skipping the burial, which was really only for close family anyway, to wait for his delivery.

Since grass had become a constant in his life, he'd traveled as little as possible, for fear of being sniffed out for arrest by an airport security dog. When he simply had to leave California, for a conference, or an emergency, as in a way this was, he went to great lengths to deliver the drug to himself by the safest and least conspicuous means. He'd learned the sunblock trick from Upchurch, of all people, his old mentor at UCSF, who'd once brought grass back from Mexico in the fifties. But the brown parcel in his hands now was his own semigenius invention. Addressed to Dr. Abraham Green, it contained packing peanuts and a gift-wrapped box with a typed card that read, "Dear Dr. Green, Thank you for offering to visit my mother in the hospital on your trip. I would be so grateful if you could pass this gift along to her. I look forward to seeing you for my regular appointment next month—you'll be glad to hear my arthritis pain has lessened since I last saw you. Yours truly, Susan Johnston." It was a generic, and perhaps overly wordy note, not to mention 99 percent unnecessary, but it gave him an excuse. *It isn't mine. It's my patient's, and given the confidential nature of our relationship, I'm afraid I can't disclose what's inside.* He imagined himself standing up, shoulders back, indignant in response to whatever authority had questioned him. He hoped that if it ever came to it, he'd have the courage to behave as he'd imagined.

He set the card on the bedspread next to a disposable plate he'd snagged from the dining room buffet, and, after checking to see that the door was still shut, he gently slid his finger under the present's taped-down flap, so as not to tear the wrapping. In his rational mind, he knew he was home free, but it calmed him to preserve the paper, to make him feel he had one last defense. In the event a squadron of SWAT guys in short sleeves and hard black bulletproof vests burst through the front door to the Fabricant home, cursing and spitting and shouldering up to walls, he could rewrap the box as though nothing had happened, preserving his freedom and reputation. He ran his finger under the last piece of tape and, exhaling, removed the box from its paper. He held it up, and sniffed it, as he'd done when he packed it two days prior. It still smelled like cardboard.

Less paranoid now, he began to work more quickly, opening the box and removing the object that lay bedded in additional peanuts inside. It was a candy dispenser, shaped like a giant green M&M in the garb and posture of the Statue of Liberty. She wore a look of bemused pride on her face, and her minty robes, which hung from either her ear or her tiny shoulder or both, fell open scandalously at the chest, revealing a trademark blazing white *m*. Abe shook her a few times, smiling at the familiar thud inside. He then removed her crown and reached into her head, fishing out a chunk of hardened chocolate with streaks of color in the mix. "Oh, shoot," he said, playing along with his own moronic game. "They must have melted in the mail." He placed the paper plate on the floor and knelt down over it, holding the amorphous hunk of chocolate in both hands. With a decisive tap, he cracked it open, and the thing he needed most of all emerged: a clear plastic baggie, packed tight with papers and grass.

He peeled away the rest of the chocolate casing and returned it to Lady Liberty's belly, to be saved for an after-toke treat. The baggie went into his leather cigar case, which in turn went into his pants pocket, where he could feel it, secure on his thigh.

The whole thing made him feel like a cocky, irritable teenager. He was proud of his ingenuity, but resented having to exercise it at all. Abe himself had been a responsible kid, working a variety of part-time jobs to help his grandmother pay for college. In Richmond, he was called an egghead and sometimes even worse, but by high school he was mostly left alone, unbullied and uninvited, with plenty of time to read. Even in college, back in Philly, when someone finally offered him a joint, he sucked it mindfully, finely calibrating his high so that he would know how much he could handle should it ever come his way again. Before California, he never would've contrived to ship himself grass in the mail; he never would've kept it, let alone known how to buy it. He knew he was at a disadvantage now, having missed out on the lawlessness of youth. It would've been good training for a freer middle age; it would've taught him self-righteousness and how to dodge suspicion, how to be careful without always being afraid.

With the cigar case still in his pocket, Abe flattened the mailing box and wrapping, and took them down the stairs, past the mourners in various rooms, and out back to the place where the family stacked cardboard for recycling. That done, he drifted deeper into the yard, intending to slip out through the opening in the hedge that led to the side street beyond. He'd done his part, basically. He'd been the good guy who'd shown up when it counted. Now he figured he was entitled to wander, just a casual guy on his way to the neighborhood park, where he hoped to find a picnic table set off on its own, or some other private corner for his smoke.

Howard's unfinished sauna still stood naked in the middle of the yard, blocking Abe's path to the opening in the hedge. He glanced in through the uprights and was surprised to see Cassandra sitting on a small stool inside. She held her hands in her lap, cradling the right hand in the left as though she'd somehow sliced her palm and was waiting for someone to bring her a bandage.

She looked up now, and caught him staring. Her eyes were deep and dull, and for a frightening instant, she seemed not to recognize him. But then her face levitated into an expression of regret, and she released her unwounded hand.

"Were you going to say something?" she asked. "Or were you just going to stand there and wait for me to see you?"

"I thought you heard me," he lied.

She shrugged. "I'm coming down off Xanax."

He bit his lip at her matter-of-fact tone. One of his early weaknesses with his wife was that he used to think everything she said was adorable. She knew it and went out of her way to speak even more fetchingly than she might've otherwise done. In the old days, she wouldn't have simply said, "Xanax." She would've drawn it out, practically whined it, like a little girl talking about her kitty cat. And he would've fallen for it. How clever she was, poking fun at women who love their antidepressants the way children love their pets! He would've grabbed her and held her to his chest and she would've laughed, because she knew she was clever, too. But now, here she was, saying simply, "Xanax," like it was nothing but a drug people took when terrible things happened in their lives. Here she was, a woman who loved it without irony.

She stared at him. "Stop judging me."

"Who am I to judge?"

"That's right."

"Do you take it regularly?" he asked.

"What?"

"Xanax."

"Only every time my father dies. So, you know, once a week, on average."

"Well, which is it?"

"Abe. I'm not one of your patients."

"Mmm." He considered the opening in the hedge. He could walk away now if he wanted. She wouldn't dare call after him; she wanted to keep things civil. Her whole family was this way. It had something to do with funerals. You could get away with anything with these people at a funeral.

"What are you doing out here?" she asked.

He heard himself laugh. "Truthfully?"

"No." She smiled cruelly. "Lie to me."

Not an activity I'm familiar with. Maybe you could give me some pointers? The retort buzzed through him like a wasp, startling him, and leaving him in a state of suspicious tension, alert, poised to swat it in case it returned. Only once he was satisfied he'd say something civil did he venture to open his mouth.

"I was going to the park to have a joint." The truth after all. "Don't judge *me*."

She perked up. "What, just for fun?"

He saw a weighty explanation coming at him and tried his best to made it sound light. "It's something I do every now and then." He patted his pocket.

She continued to smile, waiting for his real answer.

He shrugged. "Anyway."

"Ohhh," she said at last. "You're addicted."

He didn't feel like explaining that grass is not addictive. "And you're not."

"It's a funeral, for Christ's sake. They recommend Xanax to people in mourning. I'm supposed to feel weak because I need a little help getting through it? Give me a break."

Abe stared at her blazing red hair; she must've taken to dyeing it. She noticed him looking and sighed. Her hands fell between her knees and she slumped a little on her stool.

"I'm so embarrassed," she said, finally. "I'm embarrassed of what we've become."

"We're divorced people," he said experimentally. It didn't sound half as bad leaving his lips as he'd expected.

"We're divorced people," she agreed. "So what? Half of all marriages end in divorce." It seemed to satisfy her to have a statistic.

"Frankly, it feels like everyone. Everyone but Gail and Steve."

She gave an assenting grunt.

"Have you seen them lately?" he asked. "How are they doing?"

"The same. Extraordinary."

"They know the secret, I guess. Probably should've observed them more carefully. We could've learned something."

She waved her hand dismissively. "It probably would have happened anyway."

He didn't quite know what she meant by "it," and he didn't ask. They had wandered too far into dangerous territory already. He didn't want to push his luck.

"How are you doing?" he finally asked, falling back on easy sympathy.

"You know," she said, "it's better if I don't talk about it. I've felt better these past few minutes than I have in days."

He raised his eyebrows. "I'm that good?"

She narrowed her eyes and made a squishing sound with her lips. "You're that annoying. It's a distraction. I need distraction." Her eyes drifted to his pants pocket, where his fingers still clutched his cigar case, waiting for her to release him. She pointed. "How about that joint, actually?"

THEY WENT OFF down the side street together, past redbrick homes that had been converted into apartments. Mirrored office windows flashed through the trees overhead and the sound of traffic dwindled the farther out they walked. If he'd felt like a teenager before, he felt even more like one now, sneaking off to smoke dope with a girl. Her face was pink from the heat and she kept stooping to scratch a fresh mosquito bite on her ankle. He started to remind himself that they were adults, then thought better of it. They had hurt each other as adults; they might have a better chance as kids. He thought of a colleague he'd once caught speaking to his wife in a goofy voice in their kitchen, where he'd thought that no one could hear. There was something impulsive and puppyish and downright kidlike in what he and Cassandra were doing now. Maybe that was the secret, the thing they'd been missing.

He looked at her, stooped to scratch her bug bite again, and then looked down at his own feet, which seemed to have trouble taking straight, normal strides. He veered toward her as she righted herself. Reflexively, she extended a hand, protecting her personal space.

"Watch it," she said.

They'd forgotten how to avoid collisions. It was something you learned living with a person every day, and they'd been eight years out of practice. He planted his foot and regained his balance. She resumed walking, wearily.

Watching her pull ahead, he realized it wasn't just the dope. There was something youthful in the way she wore her hair, too. She hadn't cut it like most women her age, and when he'd seen her the day before, he'd noticed that she hadn't given up the ponytail either, nor was she afraid to let her ends flip outward like a cheerleader's. Even today's sober, funereal updo seemed tentative, as though she were just a little girl playing dress-up, ready to shake out her bun at any minute to try out a different look. He barely stifled a temptation to pull her hair free himself.

She came to a stop ahead of him. The road had ended at a wood; a rusted guardrail parted to reveal a path between the trees. They went down it single file, the world momentarily dimmer and cooler as the pluming branches on either side formed a nave high over their heads. Then just as quickly, the trees fell away and they were outdoors again: a green playing field, a blue sky halfway vacuumed of clouds.

"Well, here we are," he said. The grass before them sloped up toward a large stone building with a severe white banner proclaiming it the Holy Redeemer Academy. "I guess it's a Catholic school."

"All roads in Maryland lead to Catholic schools."

Four rust-red tennis courts crouched by the school, each set of two encased in a chain-link fence. Floating halfway up the near wall of the first enclosure was the lumpy phrase SENIORS 06 which, on closer inspection, was formed out of dozens of wads of newspaper that had been stuffed strategically in the fence's holes. A spirited teenage pointillism.

They walked up to the fence. Abe plucked a ball of paper from the bottom of the first *S* and uncrumpled it: a page from the Metro section of *The Washington Post*, dated sometime last week. He balled the paper back up and returned it to its position. He took out another wad. This one was from a recent news section: "Katrina Pummels Southeastern Fla. with Heavy Rain." He held the page up.

"Tragic, isn't it? This hurricane."

Cassandra was running her fingers along the links and peering into the tennis courts as though awaiting the start of a match. "Hurricane?"

"New Orleans."

"Oh, God." She turned. "Of course. I don't know what I thought you meant."

They looked at each other, guilt-stricken. Simultaneously, they turned to the fence and began tearing out the wads of paper, uncrumpling them in search of news.

"The last *S* is all comics," Cassandra said, dropping wad after wad to the ground.

"News from last week," Abe said, jumping to reach the paper near the top.

"Travel and Style, this week's Business. Oh!" She waved her hand in his face. "This says something about . . . never mind."

They continued to open the pages, often tearing them in their haste. They were like pranksters from a rival school, undoing the spirit of Holy Redeemer. They were like revolutionaries, refusing to let false propaganda stand on public walls. Fueled by these fantasies, Abe moved more quickly, tossing crime pages and Beltway gossip, baseball box scores and crossword puzzles, updates on Iraq and the president's stand-off in Texas with a dead soldier's antiwar mom. Opinions, investigations, and analysis piled up around them. A mass of half-crumpled newsprint blanketed the grass at their feet, and still they'd found no breaking news.

"I guess it's been here for a few days already," Cassandra said at last.

Abe looked up at the fence and the ravaged word, now gaping with holes and sawed-off edges. He felt a sudden pang for the kids who'd worked so hard to make it—girls, mostly, he assumed. It was the kind of thing Elizabeth and her friends might have done.

"They must have used a ladder," he said. "I don't think we'll able to put it all back. Jesus, look at this mess."

She turned and walked away from him.

"Where are you going?" he asked.

"I'm getting us a paper," she called over her shoulder. She was moving quickly, already a thin mark of charcoal against the undulating green.

CASSANDRA CROSSED the school grounds and emerged on the street opposite the side they'd come in. Perky bungalows and repainted porches radiated out on either side of her, and she hesitated for a moment before deciding which way to walk. There wouldn't be any newspaper dispensers in this residential neighborhood, not that she had any change. On the other hand, it was the last week of summer, and people with the means to afford such charming first homes would probably have done whatever they could to escape the heat in town. She peered down the street, overhung with old branches and telephone wires. A sprinkler tapped out a rhythm and a kid was practicing skateboard tricks on the sidewalk, the friction of his board against the cement making a sound like ripping paper. The boy's blond hair hung in his face and he was looking at his feet. She turned the other way, and finding it clear, approached the nearest house without a car in the drive. Sure enough, several blue-bagged newspapers were scattered around the base of the stoop. Assuming they were regular readers, the people who lived in this house had been gone at least three days. Cassandra looked back at the skateboarding boy, now several hundred feet away, skimming a curb, his spine bent like a question mark. Satisfied he wasn't watching, she turned back to the empty house and walked casually up the path to the stoop.

She crouched down and peered inside the nearest bag. As luck would have it, it was that morning's paper. Pleased, she picked it up like a sack, twisting it a few times in the air. By the time she'd turned back around, the kid had glided up to the edge of the lawn.

"Where're you taking that?" He flipped the board up and stood it on its end. He was about fifteen and meaner than he'd appeared from a distance.

"None of your business." It wasn't wrong if she refused to admit it.

"The Hardings have been gone since Saturday," he said. "I was supposed to gather their newspapers and mail for them, to make sure no one else took them."

"Then why haven't you done it?" she asked.

"I was going to, today."

"You're lying."

He shrugged. "Say what you want." He reminded her of every student she'd ever taught, back when she led introductory classes at a number of middling Bay Area art schools. Her natural inclination was to feel tenderly toward student-aged people. She wanted to inspire them, to heal injuries they didn't even know they had. She loved making them laugh and seeing them understand something they hadn't quite understood before. It was why she'd become a teacher. But over the years she'd found that most student-aged people didn't want inspiration, or healing, or the knowledge she had of the wider world. What they wanted was to win, even in art. The classroom was a war, teacher versus student, and dignity was at stake. All the whines and the cons. I have too much work, my grandfather died, my friend's brother died. She knew people died—oh, she knew—but surely not as often as graded projects were due.

Now *her* father had died—actually died!—and maybe hundreds more people in New Orleans. Yet here was this wispy boy, just gliding through a neighborhood of first homes, thinking nothing. He'd probably conned every teacher who'd ever stood in his way, and come fall, he'd try to con a couple more. *There's a world out there,* she wanted to shout at him, *a world of actual pain! And it doesn't care about you or your fun.*

His face broke into a smile. "I'm just playin'," he said. "What do I care about these people's papers?"

"The Hardings," she said.

"Made it up."

She narrowed her eyes at him: a total jackass kid, a future ugly drunk or ruthless, know-it-all boss. She stopped herself. She couldn't know him from one encounter. Though certainly he needed schooling. If nothing else, kids like him reminded her that she was an adult, a person who knew things and had the authority to say them.

"I used to lie, too," she said. "You ought to watch it—it didn't work out that well for me."

"You get caught?"

"I got *divorced*," she said, succeeding in widening his eyes. "And everyone hated me for it." She thrilled at the harsh sentence leaving her lips. Sometimes it felt good to acknowledge her misery. Even better to rub people's faces in it.

"Man," the boy said, taking a step back. Not knowing what else to say, he threw his board down and wheeled himself down the block.

By the time she returned to the school grounds, Abe had replaced most of the newsprint. "Took you long enough," he said.

"I got into a confrontation with a neighborhood punk. Scared him off good."

"Scared him? What did you do?"

"I told him how hard life was going to get, and that no one was immune. Told him how asinine he'd feel when he realized he'd sneered at people's pain while he was young and not yet in need of their sympathy."

Abe blinked in disbelief. "You *told* him that?"

"Well, not in so many words. Anyway." She held up the blue plastic sack. "I have the paper. We can read all we want about New Orleans now."

They settled themselves at a picnic table at the edge of the soccer field. Cassandra spread the paper across the table, separating all the sections that ran Katrina stories from the sections that did not. On the opposite bench, Abe pulled his cigar case from his pocket and calmly prepared a joint.

His competence with the drug alarmed her, which was in turn mortifying, a reminder that she'd grown judgmental and old. She tugged at her blouse to cool her chest and asked him if he used a dispensary or if he grew his own, though she didn't really care either way. He told her, and she immediately forgot, bobbing her head and scanning the newspaper, reading headlines, leads, and pieces of captions all at once. He'd gone on to talk about something else—was it chocolate? She watched his eyes, waiting for them to grow dull, the first sign of a speech winding down.

Most of their conversations had been like this, after a while.

He lit the joint, took a drag, and passed it to her. She did the same and passed it back. This, at least, was a rhythm she hadn't forgotten. Belonging once depended on taking just the right kind of breath, the right squint and position of the fingers. As a teenager, she'd practiced her posture in front of the mirror, and as she fell asleep at night, she'd practiced the breath, like some forbidden form of yoga. In those early years, she never had any idea if she'd done it right; she suspected she hadn't. But it *looked* right, and she'd always gotten high, and she figured that was all that really mattered.

"I can't read this anymore," she said, suddenly. She was staring at a full-color timeline that made the cessation of ordinary life—the mail delivery, the bus routes—not to mention the leveling of neighborhoods and the deaths of hundreds, into yet another digestible chunk of information. "It makes me too upset. When did it become okay for the government to just completely betray its own citizens? I mean we're supposed to be a model democracy."

"But it's always been like this," Abe said. "You shouldn't be surprised. Remember Vietnam?" He spoke mildly, as though he hadn't noticed her tone, which had the pleasant effect of calming her down.

"Mmm, Vietnam," she agreed, for some reason unable to say anything about it.

"Or the Red Scare. McCarthyism."

"Terrible," she finally managed.

"Internment, the Trail of Tears—and don't forget *slavery*." He was getting really energized now.

Cassandra unbuttoned her blouse and pulled at it briskly. "Terrible, terrible, terrible," she answered, almost enjoying the sound of the word.

"And now what have we got: Don't Ask, Don't Tell. Iraq. That goddamned Patriot Act?"

"Don't forget Gitmo," she offered.

He practically collapsed on the table. "Terrible."

She smiled ruefully, feeling the shy knock of a rare sensation she hadn't entertained in ages. She cracked the door and there it was, convivial and bearing gorgeous drugs. It was communion, that rushing, happy collision of understanding with being understood. Had she really gone so long without it? Had she gotten it from no one else? Suddenly heady, she lay back on her bench and looked at the flat, bleached-out blue above her. She squeezed her eyes shut and tried to fashion a worthy state in her mind—a body politic, a golden dome, a palace of marble and justice!—but it was difficult to maintain her focus on something so grand and abstract. Her own body was right there, demanding attention. Trickles of sweat were forming under her arms and running, winding their way toward the center of the earth. She turned her head to the side, and when she opened her eyes again, she was facing Abe, who was reclining on his bench as well.

Rather than look at him, she looked at the scattered lumps of pink and white chewing gum and the ragged cobwebs that clung to the underside of the table. They were noticeably imperfect, the cobwebs. She didn't even have to study them closely to see the extrawide channels between the threads or the corners that snagged too sharply on the wood. The threads themselves looked inelastic and frail, and she considered the possibility that they were old cobwebs, abandoned to disintegration by an impatient spider in search of a better corner, with an ampler harvest of flies. She liked the idea so much that she wished she had her sketch pad: the sagging, abandoned cobweb, which so often grows in abandoned places. It was terribly pathetic, the ultimate symbol of forfeiture. Not just humans throwing in the towel, but spiders giving up, too.

Abe was looking at her. She saw his brown eye through the web.

"You laughed," he said.

"I thought of something funny."

"Well, what?"

She didn't know how to explain it. "I don't know. These cobwebs. I wanted to draw them."

He nodded. "I was thinking about those photos you took of that house in Virginia. Remember, the abandoned house by the side of the road?"

She did remember. The lichen was the most electrifying color she'd ever seen. She'd been desperate to use it, but the photos just lingered on the walls of her studio. Her beautiful ruins, becoming nothing. She'd been working freelance for a small graphic press at the time, designing high-end paper products for educated wives. "In retrospect," she said, "I probably should have tried to use those photos for a calendar or something, instead of hoarding them for myself."

"That's a funny thing to say when you're doing so well. Malibu mansions aren't enough for you?"

"I guess word spreads." She was happy he knew about her success. That meant he had to have thought about her, too. She relaxed further; she could let go of her deepest fear. He hadn't completely erased her from his mind.

"I saw the write-up in the *Chronicle*," he said. "Impressive stuff. You really took that tree motif and ran with it."

She was surprised at his admiring tone. Her first tree didn't have the best associations.

"Well," she said, carefully. "I think I'm done with it for now. On to the next thing."

"Which is?"

She exhaled like a gauge releasing steam. "Who knows. Maybe I'll go back to that Virginia house."

"Oh yeah?" He sounded encouraged.

"Probably not, but maybe." Cassandra looked back at the sky, flat as her flattest forest mural, a sitting room piece with redwoods she'd created for a Hollywood producer. She'd tried to convince him that her installations worked best when they played with three dimensions, but he would have none of it. He wanted two dimensions or none at all. With those standards, she remembered thinking, he'd have been better off buying wallpaper.

"That was Helen's funeral, remember?" Cassandra said now. Abe relit the joint and offered it to her again. She accepted, keeping her eyes trained away from his face.

He made a chugging sound, as though searching his mental Rolodex. "I think it was after she died. You took pictures of her grave."

"Right, because we were in town for her funeral."

"Mmm. That's not how I remember it."

Cassandra shrugged. "Suit yourself." She took another hit, letting the smoke burn her lungs a little longer this time. When she exhaled, she sighed audibly. She wanted him to hear her. She wanted him to recognize all that he'd suppressed. That he'd been so devastated when his grandmother died that he'd pushed her own comfort away. Her breath cooled the sweat on her upper lip, and she began to cough.

"You okay?" he asked.

She lay there and had it out, a string of coughs in twos and threes, each new series breaking as the last one ebbed. She held out the joint for him to take. "Fine," she finally managed. She collected herself. "Maybe I will dig out those photos. Maybe Mel still needs a calendar." She pictured the trollish, impossible-to-please owner of Hampton Papers, who hated almost all her ideas.

A breeze rolled over the playground and rustled a burger wrapper some careless person had left behind. She watched it swivel toward them.

"Were you sleeping with him?" Abe asked out of nowhere.

She sat up on her elbows, only to realize by the time she got there that she wasn't even offended. "With Mel? God, no. You remember him. He was disgusting. That gut and those scrawny arms? He was always spitting when he talked." She shuddered and lay back down.

"I just remember things went sour quickly," he said. "One day you were making the best invitations anyone had ever seen and the next day you were in art school."

"They weren't the best invitations. I was criticized on every assignment."

"But they were *good*. Whatever Mel might have said about the company's needs, he knew they were good. People change their stories all the time."

"Sure."

"So you're saying you didn't sleep with him."

She sighed. Indignation was probably the appropriate response, but the grass was bedding down her mind, and she would've had to exert herself terrifically to get there. She decided to explain things to him objectively, in as reasonable a tone as possible. "Abe. Professional relationships are complicated enough. They're uncomfortable. You can never say exactly what you think, and one person always has authority over the other. He made my blood boil, but that's not the same thing."

"Maybe it is."

"I loathed Mel—remember? He was like a, like a goddamned lord of the manor. Changing his mind at the last minute, standing in the middle of that shop with his hands on his hips, scowling at me when he was in a bad mood, watching me over my shoulder. He breathed on me. I hated it."

Abe rolled his head to the side, impishly, and exhaled in her direction. "Like that?" She frowned, prompting an instinctive "Sorry."

"No," she said, "he was more like some kind of wild boar sniffing out his lunch. I mean it was just—disgusting." There was no other word to describe him.

"But if he hadn't been so gross, you might've slept with him," Abe mused. He was persistent, but not accusing.

"Why—because of Vince?" She hadn't spoken his name in ages, and to her surprise, it no longer felt sordid. He'd long since moved to Europe, taking his trust fund with him, and relieving her of her most recent punishment of having to make small talk with his girl-ish, airheaded fiancée every time his gallery celebrated another show. "Because I'd worked with him? That was an isolated situation. It really, truly was. You have to accept that at this point." Though she had resumed with him later that year, after Abe was gone, after Eliza-beth was gone, when there was no one left to care. It had been good for a while, a deep exfoliating cleanse, searing her from the inside out. He seemed to want her more than ever, as though her abandonment had left her more naked, expanding her body's terrain, offering him places he hadn't found before. But eventually her finiteness caught up to them, and Cassandra began to approach their assignations in dread, as though visiting an oncologist. She left feeling hopeless, the diagnosis bad every time. In the end, they parted in grim respect, hav-ing done all they could to save her.

"That," Abe said, "and the other one."

She was still thinking about Vince, how he was, in the end, a good kid. For a brief, sweet moment, she didn't understand what Abe meant. Then she remembered.

"And you did say you *wished* you'd had more affairs," he continued.

She snapped her head in his direction, finally indignant. "I never said that."

His voice wafted under the table, bemused but firm. "You did. That day. You said I was acting like you'd had dozens of lovers the way I was punishing you. And then you said, 'God knows I've wanted to. You don't know how much I've wanted to.' Those were your exact words. I've played them over in my head many times."

His quotation took her back to the slick deck of the boat, where most of what had transpired had completely faded from her memory, washed away with the changes that had followed. It was possible she'd said something like that. Anything was possible in the past, before she'd become who she was. "Well, those were the only ones. In twenty years," she added, though it immediately made her feel small.

"How come, though? If you wanted so badly to have others?"

"I guess I must've been chicken. I didn't want to lose you."

Her tone was more abstract than tender, and when she looked over at her ex-husband, he was smiling goofily through the cobwebs, like a kid waiting to be found in a game of hide-and-seek. "A lot of good that did you!" he cried.

"Endless good," she said, and they began to laugh, then laugh further, until they were both unmuzzled and feral, rolling around on their benches and shaking the picnic table with their shuddering spasms, completely uncontrolled and free. They had tears in their red-rimmed eyes, and cracks in their voices. They laughed as though no one had ever died, and the seas had never risen, and they went on, until they had no more breath to continue.

13

In the second year of his residency, he was around even less. His hours were long, and there were additional obligations: dinners he had to attend, often without wives, golf games he had to play.

He said, "If I'm ever going to get this fellowship, I have to do these things." She believed him when he told her where he had to be. It would've been faithless not to believe. She tried to channel all the patient housewives of the movies and television of her youth. She went around twitching her nose for her own entertainment like Samantha on *Bewitched*.

She missed him, but she filled the time. She had started art school. She was taking classes in sculpture, but also drawing and printmaking, and was having some difficulty flattening the world into only two dimensions.

"I feel so stupid," she said, showing him a lithograph she'd done of a female nude, a middle-aged woman with long, supple legs and a mounded pelvis who'd come to sit for her class. She'd done a fine job of rendering the woman's body, but she'd let her feet taper off, her hands meld helplessly into her sides. It was not artful. It was cowardly.

"I just can't do hands," she said.

"Quit saying that," he told her. "Other people will start to believe you."

HER PROFESSOR SAID she had no choice but to practice, so she made a deal with Diane, who she used to sketch carelessly after work and who she missed now that they no longer shared a desk. Diane would come over once a week, and prop her hand up on her elbow for Cassandra to sketch. She had something of the almost-Buddhist in her and she liked practicing being very still. They would often sit like that in silence, Cassandra sketching, Diane absorbing in the pale flank of her forearm the fading shards of light from the windows that looked over the backyard. Those silences were the closest Cassandra had ever come to working continuously in a professional manner, and she found it interesting that Diane should be present for them, as though she needed not just a model, but also a witness, to make her practice real.

Not that the silences lasted long. One of them usually said something after a few minutes, and then the other would respond and soon they'd be chatting, Cassandra still sketching, Diane's arm still unmoving, the pain of her pose becoming heavy and suspenseful, then even heavier and almost exquisite until she couldn't bear it anymore and let go. "Jesus! That one was bad!" she'd cry, shaking out her arm. Diane's limit was Cassandra's, too—this was their understanding— so that when Diane simply had to move on, Cassandra had to quit her current sketch and start a new one.

Of course there was nothing new about drawing hands. Most budding artists did hand studies in school. Leonardo had done hundreds. But Cassandra still felt she was making an important discovery. As she sketched, she looked closely at the hand, and she thought about it. Not Diane's particular hand, though it was lovely—slender and strong—but the human hand in general. It could write great books.

It could play complicated concertos on the piano, an instrument she'd never really mastered despite years of painstaking lessons at the upright in her parents' home. It could make bread and build giant edifices in cities around the world.

It could not, however, hold still for more than several minutes. It was not really, in those minutes, even holding still at all, but rather pulsing, twitching, and fighting passionately against itself. The sketches Cassandra produced of Diane's hand were each of them a little lie: a flat glimpse of something round and mobile, a frozen moment that, in life, cannot exist.

AN OLD COLLEGE classmate moved to the Bay Area that year, a man with whom she'd been friendly. She had dated his roommate briefly, but had always secretly preferred him. His name was Bill, and he was fair-haired and bow-legged, athletic in that vigorous, self-improving manner endemic to small New England towns. Now he was pursuing a doctorate in sociology at Cal.

They met for coffee in the middle of the day, a thing an artist and a graduate student could do.

"Coffee and not much else!" he said, jingling his change. He spoke freely with her, as though they were old friends, former lovers, even.

"You would appreciate this," he said, showing her a cigarette card he kept in his wallet. It featured a blue-and-green butterfly sidling up to a flowering branch. The butterfly had the body of a woman wearing an orange dress and high heels, and when he tilted the card, she flapped her wings, like magic. "Turns out my old man used to collect them." As though she knew his father, too. She liked how familiar he was. It made everything easier.

"I had coffee with an old friend today," she told Abe in bed that night. "Bill Jamison. He's in Berkeley now, so he looked me up."

"Never heard of him," Abe said. "He must be in love with you." He was lying on his stomach, his voice already dropping off, like a sun-battered, overripe fruit finally letting go of its branch.

"I doubt that."

Abe shrugged, pressing himself further into his pillow. He was beginning to remind her of Samantha's husband, Darrin, whose head suddenly got a lot larger in 1969, when Dick Sargent replaced the hobbled Dick York. "Why else would he look you up?"

I don't know, she wanted to say, *because he thinks I'm interesting?* But she didn't. She decided she wouldn't tell Abe anything more about Bill. Which was obviously fine with Abe, because he was already asleep.

IN LINE FOR the next coffee, she stood facing Bill, her back to the cashier. When it was her turn to order, he touched her shoulder and pointed her around.

In the moments that followed, her skin was warm where his finger had been, like a sunburn. She wished he would touch her there again.

After drinking their coffees in the café, they went walking through the city. They stopped at a fancy bakery and peered in the window at all the cakes stacked like sugared hatboxes. In the center was a specialty cake in the shape of a bed on which was drawn a redheaded pinup in a strapless blue one-piece, her legs crossed at the ankles in the air.

Bill looked at the cake, then at her. Strands of hair caught in the corner of his eye.

"Don't you just want to eat her up?" she said nervously, making the obvious joke.

HER PROFESSOR WANTED her to begin a new series of hand studies, this time of a man's hand, now that she'd mastered the woman's.

"Ask your husband," he said.

"He's very busy. He's always going somewhere."

"Then ask someone who has time to sit still."

She tried Abe anyway, because he did have lovely hands, the knuckle bones perfectly domed, the fingers long and ductile.

"Come on, babe," he said. "You don't need me for everything."

She didn't want to be angry with him, but there was a judgment in his voice that wasn't kind. "Of course I don't," she said. "Is that what you think?" As though he were the only one doing anything. As though when he went to the hospital she just sat there where he left her, motionless, until he returned to give her life. Some life. Most nights when he came home he stretched out on the sofa like an automaton. Forget sex. When he reached for her, he made her feel inanimate, like a pillow under his arm while he napped. She used to love to watch him sleep, but now she hated it, felt rejected, unnecessary. Now when he spoke, it was about the hospital, about the significant things that had happened to him.

"Look," he said, sliding his arms into his lusterless white coat. "It's just my schedule. Can't you find another hand?"

"LIKE THIS?" Bill asked her. He propped his elbow on the table and clenched his fingers into a dissident fist.

She licked her lip. "I'm warning you. You're going to get tired."

"Of this? Never. Viva la revolución!"

When his hand began to shake, she laughed. She laughed even more when he collapsed moments later, hanging his head, massaging his fingers and his wrist.

"I told you it wasn't easy," she said, coming over to the table. "Next time you'll have to start with something a little less ambitious."

It was then that he reached for her hand, catching it crisply, like a butterfly in a net.

IT SHOULD'VE FELT WRONG, but it didn't. It felt natural. She had, after all, been sleeping with other men when she'd met Abe. This was the woman she was, and the woman he'd fallen in love with, this woman men wanted, who was unhampered by rules. Why should marriage bury that part of her forever?

She wanted to be loyal to Abe. She had planned to go with him until the end, until their hair lost its color and their hands were so spotted and withered they were indistinguishable when they were clasped. And maybe she still would. Already, they'd been through a lot. But at some point, even grief had to end. Certainly work did. She'd been patient, for a long time she'd been patient, but now her body had grown too insistent. If he no longer needed to touch her, then why shouldn't somebody else? Wouldn't that increase happiness—hers, Bill's, and in some way she was still working on, Abe's?

It was a wonder, really, that no other man had ever recognized her brewing desire. Even she hadn't. But Bill was like an ace detective, zeroing in on all the clues the ordinary cops had missed.

She met him in parks on sunny, beatific afternoons. She stretched out on a sheet and felt decadent, like the pinup on the shop window cake. Bill kissed her neck. She imagined it was made of sugar and creamed butter frosting, smoothed around the edges with a thin metal spatula, a sweetness so splendid he couldn't possibly taste every bite.

"I have to have you," he told her, straining, as though he'd forgotten how to talk and breathe at the same time.

How could she deny him? She gave in again and again.

"Leave him," he said soon after. "You deserve to be happy. I'd do anything to make sure you were happy."

"But I'm happy now," she said.

And she was. Her ego was on a fantastic trip. It was like being in Paris or London and being dazzled by everything—the breakfasts, the cabs, the snap of foreign flags over rooftops—all things she'd only read about in books. San Francisco was a whole new town. Never in her life had she seen such architecture, smelled such flowers, eaten such toothsome foods. People wore fantastic clothing, too: scarves thrown billowing about their necks, dark glasses, pants that hugged their hips. On afternoons when she couldn't concentrate and had no plans with Bill, she went shopping. She brought back treasures: bulbous amber rings, woven hemp belts.

"More shoes?" Abe said when she modeled her new cork wedge heels with orange canvas straps. It was midmorning and he was in bed, having just returned from an overnight shift.

She spun around in front of her full-length mirror, still luxuriating in the glorious vacation she was on. The light rushed through the window, making a perfect square for her to stand in on the floor.

She had forgotten it was possible to feel this way. Did that mean she'd been unhappy before? She looked at Abe under the covers, his body shrinking into the mattress already, his features melting into sleep, where there was nothing to distinguish his face from the face of anyone else. These days it was hard enough when he was awake. He was hardly the man she had married. She saw now how defenseless he was, how easy it would be to leave him.

Bill continued to egg her on. "It's okay to admit you made a mistake," he'd said. "Admit it and start fresh. Why should you have to live your whole life on the basis of one mistake?"

As Abe's breathing shifted into full, faraway sleep, the square of light began to distend itself and drift. In her shoes, she shuffled with it, as though it were a raft, carrying her across a body of water, away from her sober husband, and backward toward the door. Now it was shrinking, as something in the weather interfered. A cloud, probably. Some breath of city fog. She shuffled again, centering herself, but the square, now rectangle, now rhombus, continued to collapse. An instant more and it would be gone. She saw she had no choice. She turned and looked at the open door, gauged the distance, and with a sudden, flying flick of her leg, leapt soundlessly into the hall.

SOME TIME PASSED and she was at last almost ready to do it, to just leave him for good and be through. Bill was waiting for her. Doting Bill, the ace detective. Everywhere she went, people looked at her curiously, wondering why she hadn't done it already.

Soon, she told them wordlessly. *I'll do it very soon.*

But then by chance Abe found them together, picnicking in Golden Gate Park. And to her surprise, that was it. That was all it took.

She sat there in the grass and the look on his face was one of rising dough that had been punched down hard in its bowl. She had done the punching; it had been her body, her fist. Instantly, she was in a panic. She held her finger to her lips as if to shush herself, as if to silence the thing he'd just seen. Not knowing what to do next, she stood and reached out an arm.

She wasn't surprised when he fled. What surprised her was the way his normally shapeless white coat looked where he'd left it, like a man napping, unconcerned, in the grass. The way the sight of his retreating back had awakened a creature in her stomach. Deep inside her it clawed out a message that meant she could not now or ever leave Abe, nor bear for him to leave her. The way Bill had said, "Let me read you something," having somehow missed the whole thing.

14

The high spirits in which Elizabeth and Toby had left the house were in some ways too transcendent to be sustained. The moment the sun hit her skin, she felt herself grow shy, like some kind of nocturnal animal, the Xanax at last wearing off. They would not be shagging in the street after all. But that was fine, and Toby seemed to think so, too. His gait was easy, his attitude "I have all day." It was nice, for a while, just to be outside. They sat together on a bench in front of a public fountain and watched the water exalt and fall back down on itself. They sucked on mints, and when the breeze blew, the smallest sprays of water reached their skin.

The distance between them widened a bit further in the marbled stone plaza, and that was sort of nice, too. Elizabeth didn't need to touch Toby's hand to know he was there, offering her something. Truth be told, she liked this new feeling of uncertainty. It wasn't the sinking doubt she regularly experienced a few days before a big exam, but rather a somewhat pleasurable sensation of suspense. Will we or won't we, she wondered, feeling the excitement tighten up in her thigh.

Eventually he stood. "I'm gonna go to the bathroom in that hotel," he said, and pointed across the plaza. "You want anything?"

She shook her head, happy to wait for whatever. Meaning was everywhere in the wide suburban afternoon. As she watched the fountain plume coyly, catching its reflection in the blue glass windows all around, a strange little memory popped into her head: that of a shiny metal canister with a smooth, mirrored surface and a lid that was being twisted and removed by some unknown person's hand. But what kind of memory was this? She could see it for only an instant before the image fizzled and began to repeat itself, each time less clearly than the last. Utterly mundane, and yet somehow significant. Deeply so. She straightened her back and tried to place it. It seemed like something glimpsed on a billboard in the subway—an ad for moisturizing lotion or a new arthritis pill—ubiquitous, but instantly forgettable, like all the other fragments of suggestion that washed over her each day. But this fragment hadn't disappeared. It had clung to the floor of her memory, biding its time. And now, drawing on some hidden reserve of strength, it had shaken itself free from the seaweed and risen to the top once again, like a body, demanding to be understood.

What was it? The answer gnawed at the edge of her brain. She looked around for billboards, seeing one for *The Washington Post* on a cab and another, on a bus stop, for a fashion designer famous for his handbags. Her eyes came to rest on her own designer purse, which lay beside her on the bench, its mouth falling open like someone asleep. Her phone was inside, her phone with Kyle's text. She could see it there, a little silver sandwich tucked into its pouch. She stared at it; second upon second went by. The canister fled from her mind. She was a coward. Only a coward would contemplate an unread text, go to bed without reading it, and then continue to avoid it for two more days.

At last she reached for the phone. The screen lit up and she pressed the button that led to her in-box of unread messages. She read the oldest one first: Lucie, sending "love and support!" Next was a college friend she hadn't seen in a few years, a guy named Patrick who taught high school in Japan. He was in New York for the night—two nights ago now—and wondered if she was free to meet up. Perversely, it made her feel better to learn that Kyle wasn't the only kind person she'd ignored.

His text was not one, but two.

come home. I love you. I want you to live with me.

I know you're angry with me. You have every right to be. But i got the sense that you needed your space—needed to be with your family not me. When you're ready

The words were disorienting. They were like messages from two different relationships. The first one just beginning, the second about to end. When I'm ready, what? She read them again, searching for the missing word. Then, suddenly, she understood. They were backward. She'd looked at them out of order. First the pseudo-apology, *then* the plea to come home. They were sent at the same time: one extralong message broken in two by the cruel limitations of technology. But why send that last bit at all? Was he really asking her to move in with him? After all their discussions? She saw him nodding, his forehead cleaving in sympathy when she told him, not six months ago in his galley kitchen, that she loved him, but had reason to be cautious. "I just have to take my time," she'd said, tearing involuntarily. "With everything else, I'm fast. But with this, I have to go slow." He'd held her tight to his chest, his heart beating steadily as if to prove he was comfortable with her pace. Had it all been an act, her moment of genuine communication nothing but an improv workshop to him?

I want you to live with me.

Why had he humored her all this time if in the end he still wanted what he wanted? She shuddered, flipped the offending phone shut, and dropped it back into her purse. The front screen flashed 5:59 then softly faded to black.

She looked up to see Toby crossing toward her, a newspaper swinging in his hand. For a moment she was afraid he really was going to make her read about that awful hurricane, pull her even deeper into her well of despair. But when he sat down beside her again and opened the paper to the page he'd been marking with his finger, she saw nothing but ads filled with smiling celebrity faces and giant words in quotes. "How about a movie?" he said, pointing to a timetable that ran underneath. "This thing looks fun. It's outdoors."

WHEN THEY STEPPED off the escalator from the Metro, the setting sun was blazing in the windows of the nearby science institute, making it appear on fire. They paused together at the entrance to the lawn while a formidable woman in uniform peered into Elizabeth's bag. Preteen kids handed out flyers advertising the sponsors, merchants, and remaining films of the weeklong festival. On-screen that night was *Back to the Future*.

Once through, Elizabeth impulsively took Toby's hand and they walked together into the dell where couples, families, and collared dogs had already begun to gather with their well-worn bedsheets and collapsible concert chairs, their thermoses and assorted cheese, all of which had apparently passed the security checkpoint. They wore madras shorts and diamond engagement rings, hemp sundresses and loafers without socks. Music and commercials from the oldies radio station projected from a set of speakers atop a cheerful white promotional van.

Elizabeth and Toby found a spot off to the side, where they weren't as likely to be crowded by others. She'd grabbed one of her grandmother's quilts on the way over, and once they'd gotten themselves situated, she produced two plastic bottles of Diet Coke, one of which she uncapped and handed to him.

He sputtered at the surprise flavor. "What is this?"

"Rum from my grandpa's liquor cabinet," she said, holding her bottle aloft. "To his memory."

"To his memory."

A few feet beyond them was a veritable tailgate, everyone holding a beer.

"I guess I didn't have to smuggle it after all," she said. "But I'm glad I did. Feels like high school again." Under the giant movie screen, which backed up against a slope, a group of actual high-schoolers—boys and girls both—gabbed, slung their bony arms around one another's shoulders, and generally pretended they didn't know or care that everyone could see them.

Toby took another swig from his bottle and rolled onto his stomach next to Elizabeth, his jacket and shirt laid out by his feet. He couldn't believe he'd actually gotten her here. He'd played it cool and then everything had happened so fast. He closed his eyes and let his leg drift so that a tiny spec of it was touching hers, making a bridge between their two bodies. Seconds passed, and he felt her relax into him.

Everyone around them was talking; insects hummed in the air above. Reflexively, he swatted at a spot on the top of his head.

"I have bug spray," she said. "If you need it."

Toby opened his eyes to see her wiping her mouth with the back of her hand after what looked, from the level of liquid in her bottle, like a fairly long drink. He considered the erotic consequences of smelling like deet, and told her, no, he'd be all right; it was probably just the grass.

She shrugged and held her hand out in front of his face. A pink mound the size of a dime stood out near the base of her thumb. He turned on his side, and took her hand, feeling the difference between the swollen and unswollen skin. The bump was warmer to the touch, and textured like a mini rubber ball.

"What does the future dermatologist think?" he asked.

"Looks like your everyday North American mosquito bite."

A lumpy man in a ponytail was now tapping a microphone under the screen, the teenagers having finally taken their seats. There were raffle winners to announce: dinners for two, concert tickets, a Maryland Terrapins T-shirt.

He lifted her hand to his mouth and held it there, tracing the outline of the bite with his tongue, feeling it to be, in his rapture, like an entire island in an ocean far away. He really had to restrain himself now, had to keep himself from chomping off her hand. The tiny, invisible hairs of her skin flicked up against his lips. Lightly pulling them with his teeth, he sucked with his entire mouth: on her skin, her pores, and the flesh that lived below them. He felt her body move even closer as she fed him her thumb, then her forefinger, then her thumb again, and palm.

When he next looked up, he saw that the woman adjacent to them was glaring. She was sitting up high in a rainbow beach chair, and she clearly did not approve of people swallowing fingers in public while there was still light enough for her two Uno-playing children to look their way and see.

Chastened, Toby released Elizabeth's hand. "Let's get out of here," he whispered.

He started to gather their things, but she was already standing. "Leave it," she said, in a tone he knew better than to contradict. They put their heads down and crept away from the quilt. On the aisle that had formed between the moviegoers and the festival booths, they passed people in khaki shorts and striped fabric flip-flops carrying snow cones, tie-dyed T-shirts, and pamphlets about good nutrition. Elizabeth felt the gaze of the crowd on her cheeks, her shoulders, and the backs of her thighs and calves, but each time she looked up, everyone was absorbed in dramas of their own.

They came to the tie-dye booth, where two girls were trying to figure out which was better: an orange-and-pink bandana, or a pair of pink-and-purple shorts. As the merchant bent down to see if she could find some other options, Elizabeth ducked around the booth, pulling Toby by the finger behind her. They emerged in the middle of a sidewalk lined with trees that weren't quite old enough to shelter anyone from the elements. Beyond the trees a drainage slope joined up with an exposed parking lot at the back end of a laboratory building. There were still several cars in the lot, and a woman in hiking sandals walking toward one with a tote bag on each shoulder.

They followed the sidewalk away from the street, farther onto the campus of the sprawling government research center, which seemed to have been built entirely of fences and glass. A guard was visible in the lobby of every building. Their path was flanked with emergency phones and cameras and hissing light from powerful lamps.

"Probably since 9/11," Toby observed, as Elizabeth shielded her face with her hand. She dropped behind him half a step to press her thigh into the back of his. It had grown darker, and she felt almost hidden in the spaces between the lights.

A branching footpath led them away from the lamp lit sidewalk and back down toward the dell with the movie screen. They could hear a voice talking into a microphone and the staticky beeps of the standard countdown that used to signal the beginning of a film. People cheered, and all of a sudden, the opening credits had begun.

As they approached the screen from the rear, they could see members of a tech crew relaxing in the open back of a van. The light from the projector was almost blinding, but when Elizabeth ducked down, she was able to see the silhouettes of people sitting in trees, as well as the earthbound audience, bathed in the soapy beam below. They numbered several hundred at least, so densely packed together that Elizabeth couldn't even tell where she and Toby had been sitting. Cheers rose from the audience at the first appearance of Michael J. Fox, and as her eyes adjusted, Elizabeth was able to make out the faces of the crowd, all of them turned devotionally toward the picture, which flickered back in color across their foreheads. She had never seen a movie audience from quite this angle before. It was like watching a field of strangers sleeping, so private and uninhibited was the expression on every face.

Toby crouched beside her and pointed at a space in the middle of the grass. It was darker than the rest of the night, and it seemed to demarcate some sort of boundary. Bent low, they ran toward it, finding a small, knee-high circle of bushes around a birdbath that had, from where they'd been sitting before, been entirely blocked by the screen. Toby stepped into the circle, surveyed it, and then dropped down out of sight. Elizabeth slipped in after, barely feeling the branches as they dragged across her legs.

She lay down beside him on her back, and became aware as her eyes adjusted that they were fully enclosed and protected. Any noise they made would be drowned out by the film. She placed her palm on the ground and felt it vibrate with the hum of traffic on a nearby road. Even here in her mother's hometown, where nothing was hidden because no one had anything to hide, there was a space for things unseen. It had been nearly a decade since she'd first had sex outdoors—the first time she'd ever done it, when she was seventeen, stringy, and sharp. As she grew up, it seemed more reasonable to keep sex indoors, in private, away from the judgments of others. Its place was in the bedroom, on the sofa, or maybe a kitchen countertop, in a moment of sudden, irresistible passion. But she had fewer rules now. Increasingly, her friends were mellowing out and settling down, while she felt, more insistently than ever, that the things worth exploring were only just becoming known. Things like Ferdinand Toby Steinberg, who hadn't yet turned twenty-three.

She pulled him on top of her, because she wanted to feel the ground beneath her back, the same ground the families with dogs were sitting on, not two hundred feet away. When he pulled down her underpants she already had the condom ready, having tucked it into the pocket of her dress.

The red lights of planes crossed paths overhead, and the glow from the screen seemed to expose her, shoving her up into him for all the moviegoers to see. To her delight, he was a punishing kisser, swallowing her mouth the way he'd earlier swallowed her thumb. "Fuck me," she said, like a woman in a porno. "Fuck my brains out." Like she didn't care who found them; like she wanted to be found. His eyes widened at this, but only for an instant before he was smiling ridiculously, his teeth and the flank of his tongue gleaming, celebrating with each thrust the perfect ugliness of her words. He turned her over and fucked her capably, ground her down into the grass and dirt. This—she thought fleetingly, her face burning with

sweat and glorious shame, her legs practically torn from her hips—
this was how you got on with things, how you cleaned up the mess
you'd made of your life.

THEY HELD ON to the condom until they came across a trash bin
near where they'd left their things. The darkness continued to save
them: no one appeared to notice what it was that Toby had thrown
in. Sex had made them arrogant and lithe, capable of crawling back
into the absorbed and chattering crowd, gathering their blanket and
bag, and escaping, all but unobserved. You could kill a person at
an outdoor film, Elizabeth thought, as they ran along the aisle to
freedom.

They walked back to the Metro, bodies touching at all times. On
the long, vertiginous escalator ride down, she sat on her step, and he
sat down behind her, pulling her body back between his legs. You
were not supposed to do this; you were not supposed to sit on escalators. And yet, they weren't hurting anyone. They kept the quilt and
his jacket away from the moving parts, and they kept their bodies
very calm and still. Sex in public, sitting on escalators. She wanted to
keep tearing down walls.

It would be silly to say that she loved Toby, or was even falling
in love with him. But on the escalator he did things that felt a lot like
love. He brushed her hair away from her face, draped and stroked it
across his knee. He squeezed her, just a little, with the insides of his
bony legs. For a moment she felt this was the purest form of love—
unburdened by time and the complication of knowing a person too
well. Whatever it was, it was better.

At the bottom, they passed the card machines, and took another
short escalator ride to the almost-empty platform. A funereal figure
paced at the end, and closer in, a woman sat on a stone bench, facing
the track that ran away from the city. Elizabeth and Toby found a
space on the other side of the platform, keeping their distance from
the bench, the map, and the garbage—anything that might attract

another soul. She wrapped her arm around his trunk and rested her cheek against his shoulder blade. It was damp and smelled of grass and dirt, though she'd been the one on the ground.

The station was still for a moment, and then the platform lights began to flash. A soft light grew in the mouth of the tunnel until it became two headlamps, and then a train heading in the opposite direction, discharging passengers from downtown. Elizabeth and Toby watched those who'd remained on the train, each one lost in private waiting, their lives a little closer through the idling open doors. A man in headphones and a standard-issue oxford shirt stood just inside the opening closest to them. At the last second, he came to and jumped out, having only just realized he'd arrived. "Doors closing," the automated voice repeated. He barely cleared them, lurching into the path of another man, who was wearing a hat and had been walking quickly down the platform toward the exit.

"Watch it!" he said. The man with headphones shrugged in apology and stepped aside to let him pass. But the other man just stared, his profile tightening into what might have as easily been a smile as a frown. Uncertainly, the first man raised a hand in submission and moved past him for the escalator, taking it two steps at a time.

"I guess he had a bad day," Elizabeth said.

There was something so frank and endearing in these words that Toby couldn't suppress a spastic laugh. His Elizabeth—she was his now—saw the world plainly, in elements that mattered. A day was good or bad. She looked at him quizzically, the whites of her eyes sparking at the corners near her ducts, her nose a proud line from her forehead to her lip. She was adorable, and she didn't even know it. He took her in his arms and pressed her hip bones into his. A continent of warmth spread across his waist.

"You think that's funny?"

Toby released her and turned to see the hatted man behind them. He stood, legs wide and wavering, as though the platform were the subway car and he was riding without holding on. The brim of his fisherman's hat cast a shadow over his eyes but couldn't hide his hanging, unshaven lip or the raw pink of his lower gum. He wore a wrinkled ringer tee and camouflage pants, the kind generally worn by people who'd never served—but in this man's case, Toby couldn't be sure. He was droopy and drunk but also perceptibly strong. He might have been any age between twenty and forty-five, and Toby realized now he was the figure they'd first seen at the end of the platform, moving slowly, methodically, as though counting out his steps.

"Just laughing at something she said," Toby said, taking care not to sound too glib. He was relieved to see the platform lights on their side flashing, announcing an incoming train.

"You think that's *funny*?" the man repeated, more insistently this time.

"Yeah," Toby said, somewhat taken aback. "I mean. What she said was funny."

"Toby." Elizabeth placed her hands on his waist. Her eyes were wary.

"It's cool," he told her.

"What did she say that was so fucking funny?"

"Well, she said . . ." Toby caught himself, not wanting to give him the slightest excuse to go on. "You really had to be there. I'm sorry, man. We were just talking to each other. We didn't mean to bother anybody else."

The train was slowing to a halt, and Elizabeth was tugging at his shirt.

"Have a good one," Toby said as cheerfully as he could manage, before Elizabeth pulled him away. They walked alongside the train until it stopped, and when the doors opened, they kept going, slipping in through the middle doors of the next car up.

"That was a little scary," Elizabeth whispered as they took a pair of orange cushioned seats behind a transparent plastic divider. The car was mostly empty.

Toby looked out the window at the platform, but the glare from the lights inside made it difficult to see anything beyond the fluttering shadows of people moving like moths in a yard. The hairs on Toby's arms stood up and he wasn't sure if it was because the air-conditioned car was so cold or because he'd just narrowly missed being slugged.

And then the man was before him again, glowering by the nearest pole. The smell of whiskey was overpowering. Beside him, Elizabeth sat very still. Toby said nothing, as though silence and stillness would save them.

"Why're you laughing?" he asked Elizabeth through the pitiful plastic divider.

"I'm not," she whispered.

"You're not," he taunted. "You're not." Her words seemed to take on frightening new meanings each time he repeated them back. "What the fuck is good, then? What the *fuck* is good?"

The few nearby passengers had become aware of the confrontation and were moving to the other end of the car.

"It's cool, man," Toby said inanely. "It's cool."

The man kicked an empty seat. "Show me what's cool!" he shouted. "George fucking Bush? Your fucking cop brother, your fucking girl? What the fuck is good, huh? What the *fuck* is good."

Elizabeth knew it was nonsense. The man was raving; he wasn't even talking to them, not really. But it was nonsense of the variety that sometimes made sense. A cylinder rolled around beneath her seat, knocking against her ankles as the train slowed to enter the next station. They had only made it one stop. The doors opened, and everyone else escaped. The man waved his hat and shouted after them. "Get off! Get the fuck off this motherfucking train!" Quickly, Elizabeth ducked down and grasped the cylinder. An empty glass bottle. What luck. She straightened up again, holding it under her legs, then calmly passed it to Toby.

"Only if," she said, barely audible.

The train was moving again and the man whirled around once more. "What's so funny?" he asked again, as fresh passengers scuttled away. "You got something you wanna say to me? You wanna tell me about fucking Afghanistan? Fucking Katrina? My fucking, *fucking* ex-wife?"

He dropped the hat and slammed his hands against the partition. "Don't smile at me!" She bit her lip. "Tell your girl to stop fucking smiling!"

"Just leave us alone, man," Toby said. "We're sorry."

"Damn right you're sorry. Damn *right*." He slammed the partition again.

"Okay!" Toby sat back, hands up, to show he was unarmed. Elizabeth glanced at the ground, where the glass bottle stood upright between his feet. Surely, someone had alerted the Metro police by now. Even so, Elizabeth felt her desperation rise. She wanted Toby to use the bottle. She wanted to see Toby shatter the glass on their aggressor's head, wanted to watch a trickle of blood run down his skull and around his ear before he face-planted, unconscious, before them.

He swooped toward them again, hunching down, like an angry moviegoer ordering tickets. Nothing was stopping him from coming around the partition, and yet, each time, he stopped just short. He hovered there, only inches from her face, his lip curled and his eyes lowered as he prepared himself to speak. Elizabeth sucked in her breath. It was as though he were about to break character and at last say something real—a deep and complicated secret she'd always wanted to know. A drop of spit glistened deliriously on his lip. The truth was in there, she thought, delirious herself, if she could only just wipe it off.

Before he could make another move, Elizabeth got her wish. Toby stood and flung something small and hard into the man's stomach, with the same motion he would've used if he were skipping a stone on a lake. The man doubled over and in that instant, Toby brought the bottle straight down on his skull. Shattered glass landed everywhere. Stupefied, the man staggered backward, holding his head in his hands. He sat down on the floor in front of an empty seat, knees akimbo, spine hunched, looking all too much like a beggar on the street.

Elizabeth rushed to him. "Are you bleeding?" she asked, looking down at the top of his head. There weren't any obvious shards, but a sticky pool was already matting his uncut, gray-streaked hair. Still, it was less blood than she would've expected from a laceration to the head. Toby was next to her, breathing heavily.

"Do you have a handkerchief?" she asked the man, who gave her a bewildered look. She looked around for people carrying shopping bags, or wearing more than one shirt, but Toby was already offering his. It had a design on it, and it seemed too special to be sullied with a stranger's blood.

"It's just a T-shirt!" Toby said, stuffing it into her hand, his shoulder bones holding up the long, flat stretch of his torso. There were his nipples, his coiled stomach, neither of which she'd seen before. He looked like a poster that had just been unrolled.

She put the balled shirt in the man's hand and told him to press down against the wound, then made him watch her finger, look her in the eye, and tell her his name, the day, and location. His pupils were normal, his speech and balance as good as any drunk's. His name, or the name he gave, was James. He gripped her hand like a patient.

"On a scale of one to ten," she asked, "how much does it hurt?"

"A five or six," he told her. "No, seven. I'm gonna have to puke."

Somehow, they got him off at the next stop, where he immediately threw up in a trash can. The Metro police were waiting in a pair to receive them. Walkie-talkies echoed off the barrel-vaulted, honeycombed walls. The cops had cold faces, like pennies, their arms flexed to draw weapons if required.

Instantly, Elizabeth wished she were back on the train. She didn't think she could handle an interview of any kind, certainly not with anyone in uniform. Yet she was soon escorted to an alcove, where a female officer gave her water and prodded her for answers. Elizabeth faltered. The truth was suddenly unspeakable, like some other person's private trouble that it wasn't her place to tell.

"Did this man threaten you?" the cop kept asking.

"We have to get him to the ER" was all Elizabeth could say.

When they were done, she rejoined Toby, who was standing outside the station office and wearing the quilt like a cape over his naked shoulders and back. The dip of his sternum was visible as was the trail of hairs that extended from his belly button and disappeared beneath the waist of his slacks. Elizabeth could see now that his knees were stained with grass and dirt. She combed her hand through the back of her hair, finding it snarled like a nest. A half-dozen tiny red nicks were appearing on her fingertips where she'd inadvertently touched broken glass.

"You told me to," he whispered.

"I know."

"I wouldn't have had the guts otherwise."

Inside the office, they could hear James crying. "They can't keep us here," she said. "He needs stitches."

Toby squeezed her hand, and though it hurt where she'd been nicked, she let him. What a peculiar person he was: a papardelle noodle with unsuspected strength.

"He's a veteran, isn't he?" he said.

"Whatever he is, he's in a lot of pain. And not just because of you." She couldn't help feeling a little angry with him.

He released her hand for a moment, then returned, clasping something into her palm. "Keep this," he said. "It was for you."

She looked down at the smooth striped stone in her hand—an actual skipping stone—and now presumably also a weapon of assault. She dropped it hastily into her bag, unable to recall ever having been given such an incriminating gift.

"We should bury it," she said, knowing even as she spoke that it wouldn't matter either way.

"Like your poem, you mean? Or whatever it was you wrote?"

"I wrote something?" she asked.

"At the grave."

It was hard to get away from that—the event of the week—the shock that had, in fact, allowed her to lose herself for a bit. Toby's hand was back in hers, and he was running his thumb along the ridge of her knuckles. She didn't think anyone had noticed, but as it turned out, he had. She was beginning to realize that there was actually very little he missed.

Grief made people do foolish things. So she had written something—so what? It was just one sentence, an urge to send something human into the ground with her grandpa, one of the best humans she'd ever known. It wasn't a message for the ages, or really even a message for the day, just something she thought he would've liked. Of course Toby wanted to know what it said. But some sentences weren't meant for anyone else to read.

IN THE END, no one pressed charges. The Metro police let them go, without paperwork, without fees, just a stern censure that Elizabeth barely heard. There was no time to question justice, to wonder if their story might've turned out differently had they looked less reputable and good. She was in the glass elevator before she knew it, watching the cables churn them upward toward the sky. Paramedics met them at the surface. She began to tell them what had happened, but like the police, they already knew. Brusquely, they turned to James, who'd grown contrite, a paper tracing of the bully from the train. He still held Toby's T-shirt to his head, his gaze aimed toward the ground. They stood by while the paramedics helped him into the back of the ambulance, then watched it pull away.

A pale blue taxi appeared in front of them, and Toby opened the door for her, the quilt now slung over one shoulder, like a mountain climber carrying his rope. He'd put his dress shirt back on, half-buttoned; his tie hung loosely around his neck.

She hesitated. "Where are we going?"

"It doesn't matter. We're pretty close to my house."

Part of her wanted to go with him, to keep alive whatever they were doing just a little while longer. But equally strong was her instinct to stay on the sidewalk, where she still had control of her life.

When the cab finally pulled away, and she looked back at Toby on the sidewalk, with the gilded logos of designer boutiques hovering bubblelike all around him, she knew she had made the right decision. She'd taken enough risks that day already. She pulled her grandmother's quilt around her shoulders and leaned her forehead against the air-conditioned glass.

15

Abe walked Cassandra back to her parents' house. He'd felt expansive at the picnic table, as though a membrane encasing his head had grown elastic and roomy, a giant bubble inviting everything inside. He found himself willing to listen, even to the heaviest stuff; nothing she said could trouble him. A pleasant echo of that feeling remained with him now as he stood idling by the sauna in the yard.

"Do you want to come inside?" she asked, reaching for the door to the porch.

"Is Elizabeth there?"

"Probably. Want me to get her?"

He nodded and she went in, still holding the newspaper. Though he was sweating, he was enjoying being outside. He looked up at the overflowing brushy treetops painting the deepening, increasingly brilliant evening sky. He had forgotten that there was natural beauty here, but of course there was. He wasn't far from Virginia, its heavy vastness, his old home of long, sleepy mountains floating on an inland ocean of green. If he turned his head he was even able to block out the office tower that rose above the Fabricant roofline. From where he stood it was all trees, as though in this brief corridor, he was still in the wilderness, and civilization hadn't yet arrived.

He heard the screen door again, a springy pastoral sound, and turned back to see Cassandra on the step. "I can't find her. She must've gone out somewhere." In the golden evening light her expression held shadows of concern. She folded her arms across her chest, seemed to shiver in the heat. "I'm worried about her."

"Why?" Though he was, too. He'd always been worried about her. Even as a little girl, her ambition was sealed so tight, it seemed it would shatter at the first knock of disappointment. But time and again she proved him wrong, getting into Harvard, getting into medical school. Even when things didn't go as planned, she'd found a way to explain them for the better.

Cassandra came down a few paces and lowered her voice. "You noticed Kyle wasn't at the funeral."

"What happened?"

"I don't know." She rolled her head around. A light came on in the house upstairs and there was movement in the room behind. "He was here and then he left. I saw him go, and I didn't stop him. That was Tuesday. He wouldn't tell me why, and now she won't talk to me. It's excruciating."

"She knows you—how did you put it?—didn't stop him?" He felt odd asking her this question, as though they were talking about some other man's daughter.

"I just wish she would talk to me about it. I have no idea how she's feeling."

Her face was one giant raw emotion. Perhaps she was the one he ought to worry about, but even seeing her like that felt intrusive, as though he'd barreled carelessly into her room and glimpsed her naked after all these years. He looked at his feet in the grass. "She usually talks to you about this stuff?"

She sucked the hot air through her teeth, as though it were coffee, waking her up to her new reality. "I guess not anymore."

Taking a step closer, he placed a hand on her arm, still looking in the direction of the ground. She flinched at first but then relaxed, her skin warm and a little sticky, her blood pulsing everywhere under his palm. It was the first time they'd really touched.

"I always thought we'd be the best of friends," she said, crying now. "What happened to my little girl?"

"Shh," he said. He pulled her head into his shoulder, and let the tears seep into his shirt. Compared with the air, they were cool.

AFTER SHE WAS done crying, she barely had the strength to stand. She withdrew from his shoulder, and he watched as she tottered across the lawn toward the house.

Back on the main road to his hotel, he passed banks and pizza shops and the occasional yoga studio. Each cross street bore new condos and offices to his left and trim rows of houses to his right. He stayed on the right side of the road. At one corner, a woman in spandex stretched her calves against a brick wall, then took off running. He went over to where she'd been and placed his hands on the wall's hard surface, as though to slough away the feeling of Cassandra's skin, which had lingered, achingly, in his palm.

She was a force, perhaps now more than ever. When she'd collapsed into him in the yard, she'd collapsed like a star, infinitely stronger as a black hole than she'd been as her younger, brighter self. He'd stiffened because he knew he had to be careful. He didn't want to be sucked in by her again.

When he first met her she went around like a giant, crushing by the dozen all the Dianes and Karens and Lindas of the world. Cassandra. He often wondered what her parents had been thinking, and spent many a grating holiday dinner trying to reconcile the name with the namers. But of course they hadn't heard of Priam's Cassandra, as Abe had learned when he asked a drunk Howard that first Christmas, and Howard had leaned forward on the bar, wide of eye, and said that Eunice had always loved the name, ever since a woman in her congregation had gone on a television quiz show and won, and her name had been Cassandra. "Did you know Cassandra was a prophet in Greek mythology?" Abe had said. "Is that right?" Howard asked. "My daughter?" "She was a famous princess of Troy. She knew things no one else knew." "Eunice will love that," Howard had said, failing to swallow a burp. "She always wanted the kids to know things. Hey, Eunice! Listen to this—" By which point Cassandra had interrupted, and was leading her dad away by the arm. "Come on, Abe," she said, her face turning back to him, drained, "you think I haven't told them this before? It doesn't stick with them; it doesn't matter."

Abe remembered being struck by this incredible coincidence— that no one in her family seemed to listen to what she said and, even more boggling, that no one recognized the irony but him. So his myth of Cassandra grew. "You are a whole other person," he'd often told her, amazed, while they lay naked, flank to flank. She was, but she also knew what he meant, and this was even more amazing, that a whole other person could somehow live within his thoughts.

He had to stop; it was too painful. He flexed his right calf as the runner had, then his left, returning to his body. In the distance he heard the tinkling of a dog collar and found himself missing Ferdinand, dead now these past three years. It had been ages since he'd had an evening like this. An evening with nothing to do. At one time, such evenings had exhilarated him. Today, it unsettled him and tugged at the high from which he was already starting to come down. He was reminded of an afternoon years before, in his second year of residency, when he found himself suddenly free.

THERE HAD BEEN a scheduling error and his service was, for the first time ever, overbooked. "Go home," the attending doctor had told him. Sam Upchurch was a stout, grizzled man famous for his diagnostic accuracy. All the residents called him Church, and made regular jokes about worship. Abe didn't care. He admired the man; Church had spoken to Abe about sailing.

"Dinghy, sloop, I don't care. It's worth it to have your own."

"Well, sir, I've always been interested," Abe had said. "It's just the matter of the expense."

Church had exhaled derisively, agitating the outer strands of his vigorous golden bouffant. "That's not something you should worry about." He had a confidence in Abe that was tantalizing, as though he'd been granted a sneak preview of Abe's shining future but had been ordered to keep the details under wraps. In Church's mind, there didn't seem to be much that Abe could do to screw things up. He just had to proceed and take the good things that came to him.

But Abe wasn't built that way. He wanted to relax; he just couldn't. Not anymore. The shadow inside him was too long. So many of the good things that had come to him—his mother, his father, and now his grandmother—had already been ripped away. What if it happened again? What if he lost Cassandra, or even, one day, a child? Worse—what if *he* died? What if he passed on the shadow to them? It was an awful thing to live with, this shadow, a watchman from the ruthless outer world sent to monitor him from within, regulating his hopes and casting his view of human existence in an ever more negative light. The only thing he could regulate for himself was the effort he brought to his work. He was a man now; he had responsibilities, Cassandra's happiness most of all. He couldn't just bail on his shift.

But Church was implacable. "I don't need you, Green," he said, practically shoving him out the door. "I've got too many men on. Go home to that beautiful wife of yours. Enjoy some productive leisure." Abe tried again to protest, but Church was already walking away. Under the buzzing fluorescent lights, he actually looked jaunty, swinging his clipboard under his arm like a surfer on vacation. It was possible, just possible, that Abe could learn more than medicine from this man.

So he was out in the city with nothing to do. Early October and surprisingly warm. The trees that lined Parnassus Avenue fanned upward to shield the concrete medical campus, doing their best to hide its chunkiness, to make it feel better about itself, less like an alien space colony and more like something that actually belonged on Earth. He recalled how many parks there were in San Francisco, normally good as deserts to him, all the time he spent indoors.

He could hardly feel the shadow as he walked to the nearest intersection, which looked downhill in two directions. From there he could see the tops of several parks, lying about the city like the contents of a scattered bag. The city offered itself beneath a gaping blue sky, urging him downhill, past staircases wedged like sandbags against the flood of land, past streetlamps riding high upon the waves. In the sun, every house seemed newly painted in whites whiter than his coat, which he removed and slung over his arm, the other colors—the mints and slates and saffrons and plums—shivering in the light as though they'd just emerged from the surf, salt-washed and freshly wet.

The terrain began to climb, and he climbed with it, then turned at a dead end and descended once more. He let the slope pull his body until he arrived at an extended breach of green—the Panhandle—which, recognizing it, he followed, doubling back toward Golden Gate Park.

He never came up here anymore. He never had the time, or, worse, the inclination. How could he have grown dead to this? It was so abundant, so achingly green. He ambled along the asphalt paths, inhaling eucalyptus, passing densely fisted shrubs and ducking under beckoning branches. Here were parked cars and fellow citizens with time on their hands, women in shorts holding children upright against their knees and men in tennis whites with chummy voices, tossing scorching blurs into the sky. It was as though they'd all been here all along, while he in his space colony had been as good as an alien, so separate from all this leisure and all this life, he might not have existed at all.

Well, he existed now. Church had faith in him. He had a beautiful wife. Maybe the shadow wouldn't rule him after all. Maybe shaking its stranglehold was as simple as charging headfirst into the day. The sky shifted its weight and the treetops threw themselves into motion, clasping and unclasping their branches, throwing their heads back in laughter, like guests at a lavish gala. For a moment, he stood marveling at their easy society, their lively concourse against the blue. Then the breeze that had awakened them made its way to ground level. It caught him, too, and urged him onward, down the path to the botanical gardens.

He found himself a seat under a tree and watched a blond man recline on a patchwork quilt across the meadow, his chesty body propped on an elbow as he read from a black hardbound book. Beside him, a woman lay on her back. Even at that flattened perspective, he could tell that she was beautiful. She was very still and she looked straight up, her thoughts swirling in the suddenly swirling sky, her hair and body cleaving to the ground. He felt dizzy just imagining her divide herself like that.

The man took a bite of a fruit that appeared out of nowhere in his hand. The woman raised a lazy arm as if to examine it, to make sure it really was her arm. They were oblivious to each other, yet together. He thought of Cassandra, and how much he wanted her lying there beside him, just looking up at her arm. He wished he hadn't walked out of the hospital so brainlessly. He wished he'd gone home to get her first. Their wedding anniversary was just a few weeks away.

When the man lowered himself to kiss the woman, it felt so natural and expected, so like a love scene in a movie, that Abe continued, like a filmgoer, to watch.

Even when the woman, having just been happily kissed, sat up and hugged her knees into her chest, and even when she turned her face for some unknown reason toward Abe, and even when he saw that her face—oval, quizzical, and framed with sudden, naked red hair—was not the face of an actress or even a character, but unmistakably the face of his wife, still he watched, as though if he looked away the reel would go on without him, the shadow would return, scornful and taunting, and he himself would disappear.

*   *   *

LATER, IN THEIR HOUSE, Abe held his coat in his hands. She'd gathered it up from where he'd dropped it on the grass, and even though he now hated her, he'd taken it. It had seemed, at that moment, the sturdiest thing in the universe.

The shadow was back, clasping him tighter than ever. Anyone could hurt him. Anyone.

"But don't you see?" she was saying. "It doesn't matter. It doesn't matter, because I love you."

"Never," he said, the word catching on the dry slab of his tongue. Like a block of powder, that tongue. Like something freeze-dried for an astronaut.

She hadn't heard him. She was too absorbed in her defense.

"My mistake was in not telling you. Because I think you would've understood if I could've figured out how to say it. That I have needs that have nothing to do with love, or that do, but not *our* love. At first I didn't tell you because I thought it was over between us, but now I realize that the real reason I didn't tell you was because I love you and I didn't want to hurt you. And actually it's precisely *because* I love you that I was able to do it at all." Here she laughed, a sound like a punch landing clean to the head. "See, I still haven't figured out how to say it. So I didn't even try. I should've tried."

She went on like that, so many words, each one a barb that sliced and nicked at his protective astronaut suit. He'd lose all his oxygen if she kept on this way. Didn't she know she was killing him?

"Stop talking. Just stop."

She jerked toward him suddenly. He took a half-step back.

"But you're my husband," she said. "Don't you know I will *always* love you?" She was crying now. She was scared.

"Never," he tried again, louder than before.

"Always," she repeated at the same time. The word came to a halt on the edge of her lips and bounced there like a diver on a springboard over a suddenly empty pool. She seemed more scared than ever as the word kept bouncing, echoing across the room.

* * *

He took his dinner at the hotel bar, fully surrendering himself to cliché. He sipped a whiskey neat with his burger and thought of all the other men who had ever sipped a whiskey, and what a much harder time most of them had had, dying in gruesome battles and mine shafts. In contrast, he was relatively free: he was going home tomorrow. He was so taken with this idea that he hardly noticed the person who came to stand beside him. First she wasn't there, and then all of a sudden she was, talking to the bartender about sending a bottle of wine up to a room. Feeling suddenly exposed, he stared deeply into the liquid that remained in his glass, and waited for the transaction to end.

"Dr. Green?" she said, just when he thought it had. Her head tilted into his peripheral vision. She was the pretty, cricket-voiced desk attendant from the evening he'd first checked in. "Still with us, I see." She pressed her lips into an encouraging smile, like a teacher before a big test.

"It's only my—" He counted on his hand. "Third night. Jesus, only my third?"

She drummed her fingertips against the bar. "I know how you feel. I'm in a hotel every day of my life."

He looked at her more consciously. She was a dark brunette and her eyes were disproportionately large, like a cartoon's. Yet there was a steadiness and a sense of discretion about her that made her seem mature. She worked in a hotel, after all; she had seen the world in its rooms.

Until that moment, he hadn't understood how men his age could sleep with women their daughters' age. But looking at this gorgeous clerk—for he could see now that her face was actually well beyond pretty—he realized that the daughters had nothing to do with it. They were grown-ups, off living lives of their own. And sometimes grown-ups got lonely.

"I guess you can't have a drink with me," he said, lamely. He'd known it would sound lame, but had chosen to say it anyway. What was he now if he couldn't be honest?

She laughed flirtatiously, acknowledging her power, his weakness. "They do frown on fraternizing with the guests."

"Fraternizing." He repeated her dull, corporate word into his glass. "Of course."

"But if we happened to run into each other at, say, that noodle place across the street, or some other bar not in this hotel, they couldn't exactly stop us."

He looked up in shock. The bartender had reappeared with the wine and the desk attendant was now standing in patient profile as though she hadn't said a word, the consummate hospitality professional. "Thanks," she told the bartender. She exuded nonchalance in her unglamorous blue blazer: a Bond girl in the perfect disguise. With his one question—so pathetic, he almost hadn't asked it—he'd accidentally, unbelievably gained access to her underworld. What incredible luck! It occurred to him that she'd probably done this kind of thing before. Maybe hundreds of times, which only intrigued him more.

"Could you come to my room from there?" he whispered after the bartender had wandered off.

"You know what. Forget the noodle house. I'm about to go on break. I can come in fifteen minutes."

It was extraordinary—no other way to describe it. The kind of thing that never happened in real life. Back in his room, he was relieved to find that his bed had been made. He drew the curtains, which made everything dark, so he turned on the light, and waited.

She arrived exactly on time, absent the blazer, which she explained she had to leave in the staff room whenever she wasn't on duty. Her name was April. She accepted a joint and reclined on the bed closest to the curtained window.

"It was the book that did it," she said. "I wouldn't be up here right now if I hadn't just finished it."

"Which one was that?" he asked from his seat at the little table, the grass already separating his mind once again.

"*Persuasion*, silly," she said, kicking a stockinged foot in his direction. She was, after all, rather young. She reminded him now of one of Elizabeth's childhood friends, the one she did plays with, the little know-it-all one with the eyes. "You had all kinds of things to say about it when you checked in. It was just as beautiful the second time around, in case you were wondering."

"Ahh," he said, remembering. "Of course. So who's the Captain Wentworth in your life, April?"

She stuck out her tongue. "Nobody I know of."

"No? A beautiful woman like you? With all the lonely men who pass through town?"

"Watch yourself. It might turn out to be you."

"Wouldn't that be something . . ." He rolled his head in her direction, taking in the dark curve of her hair, the white drape of her blouse, her length. She was like a mermaid with two legs, washed up on the shore. Behind her on the wall hung her backdrop: a framed watercolor rendering of a beach. He looked for her in the painting, a supple slash of brown somewhere amid the wide umber field of sand.

"Come here," she said. So he went, sitting first on the edge of the bed, then dropping his head back to rest in her lap, which was warm. The overhead light blazed in his brain, forcing him to shut his eyes.

"We don't have to do anything," she said, combing her fingers through his hair. "But I do have to be back in half an hour."

"I have a daughter," he blurted.

"That's wonderful," she said, not even sounding disappointed. She was humoring him. She really was professional. She smelled of almonds and vanilla cream. "How old is she?"

"Don't ask."

"Fair enough." She began stroking his eyebrows, almost maternally. "I bet she's beautiful. I bet that's tough on you."

She *was* beautiful, or at least he thought she was. Not that he was that kind of father—the kind who was obsessed with his daughter's chastity. What was the point? She was probably basically living with Kyle, who wasn't a scholar, but seemed decent and reliable enough when Abe had met him in New York. Whatever had happened between them this week, Kyle was undoubtedly still in love with her. Of course he was. By the time she'd turned thirteen, every male she ever met was at least a little bit in love with her—even, Abe suspected, her teachers. When she was in high school, he always knew the summer was coming to an end when the senior boys on their way to college began coming around the house to say good-bye, as though college were the new Vietnam, and Elizabeth was the girl they hoped to marry. She offered them Cokes and sat with them on the back porch, which he passed through a few times, just to check on a loose step or to let Ferdinand do his business in the yard. Ferdinand greeted each boy with a wet muzzle, wiggling, being generally unsuspicious. Abe was more sedate, a watcher, inspiring a few of the suitors, if that's what they were, to throw in a "sir" when encountering him in the house. "Yes, sir. I'll be going to Cal, sir," they would say, which Abe would sternly pronounce a fine school. They scared easily, those kids, which was disappointing; he was hardly the menacing type. What had happened to the swagger of youth? Well, Elizabeth was too smart for them, anyway, too smart for Kyle, and too smart for the haunted, callow one who kept following her around the reception. Really, she was too smart for every boy, but in this world, what could you do?

"She's going to be a doctor."

"Just like her dad."

He rolled his head back and forth under her hand and squeezed his eyes further shut. "Not really."

"Her mom, then." April was saying, having very generously given up on whatever she'd come to his room to get. He couldn't imagine it was this. "Maybe she takes after her?"

"Maybe," he said, turning the suggestion over in his mind, as though it were something he hadn't considered before. "I guess I'll never know."

"I'm sorry." April's voice softened. "Is she——?"

"Oh no," Abe said. "I left her. But don't worry. I think it was probably the best thing for everyone."

Just like fucking April was now. Her hands were so soft, like felt, and her lap was so warm, and Abe had been punished enough. As he climbed on top of his little hotel nymph, he pictured Cassandra on her blanket in the park. All those years in between and he'd been faithful. Nothing after Hersh even counted as revenge, because by then, their marriage was over. Not the first woman from the yacht club, the frizzy-haired waitress who was probably much younger than she looked. Not Cynthia or Suzanne. Not even Amy. They were just company, and maybe casualties of science—the natural law that man, in the absence of other ideas, will eventually take a woman to bed. But now, seeing Cassandra blaze with helplessness and grief had done something to him, something strange. Far from awakening his compassion or forgiveness, she had awakened in him something scarier, an offspring of that old nasty shadow, a beast he thought he'd put to sleep years before. It was his remorselessness, his own preening vanity and need. This was a creature he'd have to battle to find forgiveness, which was hiding behind it like a scared little rabbit, hoping to survive another day. For now, though, the beast was all. He looked at April's pellucid face, plainly enjoying him. He gripped her cheerful, coltish breast, felt her grip him back with all the athleticism of youth.

This, after all, was why he'd come. Finally, he'd have his revenge.

16

He awoke the next morning aching, as though he'd swum a great distance overnight. April was gone, her break having long since ended. He recalled her stooping to gather her clothes in the light from the bathroom while he pretended to have fallen asleep. He assumed her shift had ended, too, and was grateful she never returned.

He showered and packed his bag, carefully resealing the last of his grass into the still mostly full bottle of suntan lotion. The Lady Liberty M&M, with all her melted, cracked chocolate, still stood in the corner in Cassandra's room, where Eunice would probably find it. The thought pleased him, that she'd hold it in her hand one day, maybe shake it a little, or eat a piece of the chocolate and feel off. He stopped at the breakfast bar with an extra spring in his step. A man in rimless glasses was staffing the concierge. Abe pocketed a bagel and gave him a merry, straight-armed salute as he backed his way out the door.

MARY EXPECTED TO see her brother-in-law again that day, but she did not expect him to look so cheerful. She used to like him, had liked him instantly in fact, from the moment Cassandra brought him through the door that first, revolutionary time, her finger exploding with his mother's diamond ring, improbably banishing all her parents' fears. Whatever his complicated background, this was a man with means. He'd even helped her father carry wood around. A perfect catch. A saint. Though as the years had passed and he began to reveal his true self, she found she liked him considerably less. He was arrogant, for one. For another, he was terrible at small talk. Mary prided herself on her small talk. To most people, it was the only way you really *could* talk, and she didn't want to live without people.

She was standing at the counter organizing a breakfast tray for her kids when he came barreling into the kitchen.

"And what adventures did *you* have last night?"

Her question was met with silence.

"Everything okay?" she tried.

This time he gave a twitch of comprehension. "Fine."

She was tempted to go on asking softball questions, just to see how many more she could toss off before she finally got one in return. But eight years had passed, and whatever her sister had said, it was clearer now than ever that Abe was no more than a visitor in her life. She'd seen them the night before, embracing awkwardly in the yard. These were not people who knew each other anymore. The effort was hardly worth it.

Abe smiled and shoved his hands deep in his pockets, as though waiting for her to continue. Despite his politics (or had they changed?), he reminded Mary now of the president. He had that same self-confident stride, the same trail of destruction in his wake. For a man at a funeral whose family had long since fallen apart, he seemed remarkably undisturbed.

"Elizabeth up?" he finally asked.

"Think so. Check upstairs."

Mary watched him saunter out, and couldn't help pitying her sister a little. She wouldn't have made the same choices. Certainly, she wouldn't have cheated. But it was hard to look at Abe and not appreciate the possibility for distance between two people. The same dreamy eyes he'd once reserved for her sister were now focused on something inside him, and at the same time something much farther off.

In the other room, her children and husband had already begun the week's third game of Scrabble. She set the tray down on a side table and collapsed on the sofa beside Vlad, overjoyed to have made the right choices in her own life, in the parts of it she could control.

Abe didn't even make it upstairs. He found Elizabeth as though she'd been waiting for him, loitering in the hall. She was wearing a tank top and microscopic shorts, and her hair was held back with an elastic that pulled one side flat and pouffed the other like a solar flare. He glanced at his watch: nine o'clock. She had clearly just woken up.

"Drive me to the airport?" he asked her. They'd hardly spoken all week.

Her face fell, nearly breaking his heart. "Oh," she said. "You're leaving?" She slouched against the damask wallpaper. Somewhere along the way, he'd allowed Cassandra and the Fabricants to claim her. As though he'd gotten to keep the dog in exchange for them keeping the daughter. But it didn't work that way. She belonged to him just as much.

"Tonight," he said. "But I thought we could take a detour first. Spend some time in the natural world."

THEY TOOK ABE'S RENTAL, a plastic-scented Ford, Abe at the wheel, Elizabeth watching the storefronts go by, talking little. Before long, the main drag had turned into highway, then river crossing, then science park Virginia suburb, then genuine farm. White three-rail horse fences loped along beside them, and then, startlingly, an actual horse, galloping, with sweat gathering like a stole around its neck. Elizabeth let her window down and the horse turned away, uphill, toward his friends. Flat, warm air and the smell of hay and dried manure filled the car.

As they drove on, the land rose almost unperceivably, while the air seemed striated with different kinds of heat: the heat of rain coming, maybe, the heat of many hot days in a row, the heat of people making decisions they'd never dare make in their right, temperate minds. They were out of horse country now and into woodier terrain. Narrow, windy drives led to houses on higher ground that couldn't be seen from the road. Trees banded closer and closer together until they began to resemble an endless double pipe organ, cresting and falling along the curves of the road, with their car scaling the ridge in between. A blue-bellied bird burst free from the leaves and came to rest on a gatepost on the right. It looked directly at their approaching car, neck pulsing, and an instant later had already darted past Elizabeth's window, wings flapping like a lawn ornament in the wind. She turned around in her seat to watch it dip and veer wildly before shooting back into the trees.

When she faced forward again, Abe was looking at her in that screwy, embarrassing way he had when he wanted to hold on to a moment, his eyes ringed with red and almost watering. Both her parents had taken to doing this. They hoarded time with her, as though it might come in handy in a storm. After years of throwing away plenty of perfectly good moments, whether through absent-mindedness or just plain absence, it was as though they were no longer willing to count on life to give them too many more. They had to store their memories while they could. It was embarrassing, and a bit too little too late, but in a way, it was also sweet. Elizabeth squeezed her father's hand, giving him the moment, if this was one he wanted to save.

Abe pulled the car into a lot, gravel spraying beneath their wheels. They parked near a wooden trail information sign, alongside a few other cars. Abe pressed the button to raise the windows, then surprised Elizabeth by handing her a tube of sunscreen, which he never used. She uncapped it and out of nowhere came the pungent, unmistakable smell of weed. Elizabeth sniffed audibly. Was it on her hands?

"Don't worry about it," Abe said. He was looking at her carefully, his eyes a little bloodshot and pleading.

"Oh my god. *Dad.*"

"It's just for storage. Just in case."

She shook her head. "I guess I don't want to know."

"I don't mind. It's just not very interesting."

"Oh, I'm sure it *is* interesting. But really, whatever." She rubbed a pat of lotion into her cheeks and the bridge of her nose. "Shall we?"

Looking relieved, he got out and took a pamphlet from the dispenser, which he folded and shoved in his pocket. Then they headed for the main trail. It sloped down initially before beginning its slow, steady climb. They walked single file, Abe in front, following the yellow paint that marked tree trunks at regular intervals and was supposed to lead them to an inspiring view. What natural wonders Elizabeth had seen on the East Coast were quaint, majestic only in detail: the wrinkles in a fallen walnut, the gradations of green on a grassy hillside in Massachusetts. Well, there were the leaves in autumn. But this was not that time of year, and this was not that kind of walk. She stepped over a piece of fallen tree that jutted across their path. It was covered in lurid moss and was rotting on its belly like a forgotten cucumber in the fridge.

Ahead of her, Abe walked purposefully in his shorts and New Balances, planting his foot with each step, and visibly swinging his arms. Elizabeth knew she was lucky to have such healthy parents: her father was still pretty strong, with bronze, toned calves, and rarely had a physical complaint. Her hero, the dashing sailor, who all her friends had loved. Nevertheless, he was slower than he used to be, and less certain of his movements. He bent forward at the waist as he walked, looking almost old. After a few turns, he paused at a clearing and looked back, waiting for Elizabeth to join him.

"What's wrong?" Elizabeth asked.

"Just making sure you're still with me," he said, his face shiny, his breath audible and quick.

"All right then, onward."

Abe gulped and gestured that Elizabeth should go first, so they switched places, daughter leading father up the slope. She doubled her pace, almost daring him to keep up. He could do this; it was hardly a hike. She began counting her strides, feeling the stretch of muscle in her hamstrings. The land continued to rise, and soon she could just make out through the trees the blithe light of open space below. Impulsively, she picked up a large stick and began tapping the foliage in time to her count. As the end of the trail approached, she passed more people: bikers in spandex, couples with infants strapped to their chests. Without straining, she could hear the sound of rushing water ahead. The muddy path and trees gave way to a crest of forbidding white stone and then suddenly, at step 822 since she'd overtaken her dad, they were standing together at the edge of a river, looking out across a series of cacophonous rapids several meters below.

"Don't even think about diving into this," Abe said.

Elizabeth pointed to a nearby sign: *DANGER. Deadly Current, Slippery Rocks. Even Wading Can Kill. No Wading. No Swimming.* "I think that just about covers it, don't you?"

"Also no diving," he repeated. He appeared to be only half-kidding. Who was he to talk?

They sat together on a riven chunk of rock and watched the water catapult itself along the gorge. Abe fished the pamphlet from his pocket and read her a few details. In the mile stretch where they were sitting, the river dropped eighty feet. There'd been a canal here once, with five locks. They'd had to blast gunpowder into the stone.

"Built by slaves, of course," he said.

They looked out over the chalky crags at the green shore of Maryland, which sprang like a sudden eden on the other side of the moon.

"Well, here we are in Virginia," he said.

"Now I see. Feel like home?"

He shook his head. "Nah. Gotta get way beyond the Beltway for that." She'd seen his grandmother's home only once, on a visit they'd taken to Richmond when she was a girl. They'd driven down the shaded street lined with saltbox houses and come to a rolling stop in front of one that had a red-capped garden gnome out front. "Of course, that wasn't here then," he'd said, and they'd rolled on. He hadn't even wanted to ring the bell.

"You want to hear a story?" he asked her. He'd rolled up the pamphlet and was holding it now like a remote that would trigger some hidden screen.

"Sure," she said.

"All right, then. Here goes . . ." She crouched forward over her knees, straining to separate his voice from the interference of the falls. "This is a Finland story. Your mother's great-grandfather—Howard's grandfather—was a fisherman there."

"Hold on," she said. These were not the first lines she'd expected. She'd expected something random about Virginia. "Is this a real story? Like, should I make myself more comfortable?"

"Whatever you want."

"Yeah, let me just . . ." She searched the rock for the most natural place to recline, as though there might be a spot that was somehow softer than the rest. Finding none, she finally wedged herself into a grooved recess that resembled a row of tall, tough books.

"So, now," he went on, once she'd signaled that she was ready. "Except for the time he spent at sea, Teemu had lived in the same town his entire life. He married his wife—your great-great-grandmother—when he was about twenty, and had eight children, including Howard's mom. Seven of them lived to be adults."

Already she felt the need to fidget. She arched and cracked her back, wiggled her shoulder blades against the knobby stone, felt a tumorous bulge just under her neck—and found herself longing for her childhood bed, to be tucked into the cotton printed sheets that read *sleep* in dense wavy lines, like some kind of magic command.

The memory sprang out from her, just like that. Like a rubber band she'd forgotten she was wearing until it suddenly gave way in her hair. She hurried to retrieve it. There were books on her bedside table and a soothing fog that hugged the window, blocking everything outside their house. Her father sat by her bed on a stool, with an open book in his hands.

"You used to tell me stories all the time!" she blurted.

"Sure . . ." He seemed not quite to grasp her meaning.

"Every night before I went to sleep." She couldn't believe she'd forgotten. She'd been stuffing her brain with pharmacology and histology. Invisible things that supported life but had nothing to do with living. "We read books together first, and then at some point you just started telling me stories."

He squinted, allowing her adult guise to morph into that of his eagerly listening little girl. It was too painful to see her very often, this pigtailed child he hadn't yet ruined, but here she was practically forcing it on him, and he found himself unable to resist. "That's true," he said. "I did. Did I bore you?"

"Oh my god," she sputtered, "I loved it!"

"Because you took over eventually. I thought maybe you'd gotten sick of it."

"What do you mean?"

"When you were in middle school, probably. I'd pop my head in at the end of the day and you always had a million stories to tell. About your friends, about what you were reading." He'd loved her narratives. They were high-spirited and rambling and packed with information: a pulsing internet of back links that only a parent could follow. But they'd also made him a little sad. From the day she was born and he'd first held her serious little head in his palm, he'd been responsible for her every comfort—her every entertainment, too. If it was hanging a colored mobile when she was still a slug at the bottom of her crib, if it was reading to her fluttering eyelids at night, if it was racing with her latched to his back down the beach, he was there. Or there when he could be. But suddenly she had entertainments of her own, stories he could never have invented. Just another of the many signs that she was fast outgrowing his care.

"Well, I haven't read anything in ages," she said. "Unfortunately." She'd underestimated him. Her father, who seemed to want to forget everything, actually had some memories stored close. "So I guess it's your turn again."

He scanned her face as if it held a sentence he wanted to go back to, to make sure he'd read it right. "I'm warning you, I'm a little rusty."

She swatted the air. "Who cares?"

"I should go on?"

She nodded vigorously.

"So, all right, where was I . . . ?" He turned toward her, creating a little room between them that all but muted the traffic of the falls. He looked at her, tucked away in her crevice once again, received her thumbs-up, took a plentiful breath, and began.

"Okay, your great-great-grandfather. Apparently, he was a pretty aggressive drunk. You know the type: loud, not violent, but a little scary?"

Elizabeth pictured a man with Howard's face in brownish nineteenth-century garb, sitting at a table covered with jugs and fish bones, a busty woman on his knee.

"Anyway, on the whole, he was happy and well liked. So one day, he gets himself into a card game with a couple of gangsters. Or I don't know: maybe they were just rich men who didn't mind sitting down with a fisherman at the pub. It doesn't really matter. The point is, Teemu's betting actual currency with these guys. All in good fun, of course, but he thinks he has a chance to walk away with a lot of money. I mean a lot. His opponents keep betting on bad hands, and he keeps collecting.

"He's generally an easygoing guy, patient. But he also knows luck when he finds it. The night rolls on, and Teemu keeps drinking. And winning. He basically thinks his luck is never going to run out.

"It's unclear what happened next, but there was probably an insult of some kind. Maybe someone accused him of cheating. Regardless, tempers flared, and before it was all over, Teemu had stabbed one of the men in the chest."

"Seriously," Elizabeth said, "he *stabbed* someone? With what? Was it an accident?"

Abe shrugged. "He was a fisherman. They all carried knives. Anyway, somehow he slipped away and hid himself in the woods, living on scraps, until he learned that the man he'd stabbed had died. He was a murderer now, and an outlaw. So he smuggled himself onto a cart bound for Helsinki, where he booked passage on a ship to England, presumably with the cash he'd won in that game.

"People in town had been aware of his situation—some of them must have helped him escape—and word got back to his wife, Anya, that he'd made it to Helsinki and beyond. But Teemu himself never wrote, and days turned into weeks, which turned into months, which turned into years, and by then it was pretty clear that he was never coming back. She had to have been pretty angry, but she came to accept what had happened and went on with her life. She still had a family to raise.

"When her oldest son, Lukas, came of age, he decided to track his father down. Opportunity was disappearing in their town anyway, the richest fisheries having drifted to other waters. England was the place to be, or failing that, America.

"He kept her informed of his travels, sending telegrams from all over the English-speaking world: London, Bristol, Newfoundland, New York. She was about fifty when she got word that Lukas was in San Francisco and had seen a man who looked exactly like his father on the wharf.

"Of course, she had questions. Had Lukas seen Teemu, or just a man who looked like Teemu? Had they spoken? Was it him? How in the world could he write to her so casually?

"'But was it him?' she finally wrote."

"Yes, was it?" Elizabeth broke in.

Abe nodded, pressing his lips together. "Still a fisherman after all those years. So now she had a choice to make: stay near her children, who were grown, and let them take care of her in her old age? Or say to hell with it, she still had time, and track her husband down? I guess you know where this is going.

"When she finally made it to San Francisco, Lukas got her a bed in the house where he boarded. You have to picture her there: lying awake that first night, distracted with thoughts of Teemu's face, so near again after all those years. Of course, it would look different, and he would *be* different, so she would just have to try to content herself with the knowledge that he was still the man she'd once known. If, that is, he wanted to build a life with her again. Lukas had assured her he'd be glad to see her, but what then? Back to their old life—or so long and thanks again for stopping by? She was risking her whole future on an assumption that the past was not really past.

"Finally, she worked up the courage to go down to the wharf. Teemu's boat was late that day, but she didn't mind. She'd waited often enough in Finland, sometimes accompanied by a daughter who'd baked bread or a son who'd just learned to walk. In San Francisco, she was alone and uncertain, with nothing to offer but herself. She'd waited some fifteen years; she could wait a few hours more."

Abe paused. Beneath them the water applauded raucously down the gorge.

Elizabeth's heart was pounding. She felt heady and almost deaf, like at a party. "So—what? Did he show up?"

He jerked at the sound of her voice and their eyes met. "More of their children eventually followed them to the States. Howard's mom, et cetera. They lived together until they died."

She let the clatter of water fill her ears for a moment as she tried to sort out what he'd just said. The story had completely enrapt her, made her proud of her ancestors for living it, of her father for telling it so well. She'd felt her history like a palace inside her, felt herself multiply and disappear in its long, mirrored halls.

"That's a true story?"

"Well," he ran his hand over the top of his hair. "I embellished a little. But the basic outline is true. Knife fight, disappearing husband, San Francisco, the son and wife who tracked him down."

"Does Mom know it?"

"Of course. She's the one who told it to me, long ago. For obvious reasons, I've been thinking about it again."

A woman and child came toward them now, hoping to share their waterside perch, but stopped when the mother sensed the seriousness of their conversation. She placed her hands on the boy's shoulders as though he were a shopping cart and expertly steered him away. He

wore a red T-shirt that was covered front and back with white out-
lines of famous Washington landmarks: the Capitol, the Smithsonian,
the White House, the Pentagon.

"So, wait, do any of their descendants still live in San Francisco?
Do I have relatives there I've never met?"

Abe frowned, considering this. "I don't know. Probably. I don't
think your mom was ever in touch with any of them. But she does
have roots there."

Elizabeth pulled at the dried skin on the tip of her ear. "What must
that woman have been thinking, tracking him down halfway around
the world like that." She let a flake fall from her fingertips and vanish
into the rock. "How devoted was *she*?"

Abe regarded her through a squint. "I guess she probably was.
What I wish I understood is how they had that conversation. What
did she say to him? It's almost impossible to imagine."

"I can imagine," Elizabeth said.

He shook his head. "I guess that's just one of my limits."

He was, she had to remember, a literal person. Good at doctoring, bad at messes. He loved his boat, was decisive in restaurants. He
mistrusted, above all, people who thought they knew more than him.
She clung to his arm, pressed herself against his leg. She wanted to
comfort him, help him remember his strength. "You imagined all the
rest of it, didn't you? You talked to Mom . . ."

She stopped here because the boy in the Washington T-shirt had
run by them once more, this time hollering like a maniac and eliciting
a gasp from the rest of the crowd. Elizabeth gripped her father's arm
more tightly. "Oh my god," she said as the boy approached the edge
of the falls, the white rocks fanning mercilessly about him, the water
trilling its ecstatic siren song. She flashed forward a moment and saw
him tumble, saw his little body flying hopelessly through space. But
then, just at what seemed the decisive moment, when danger could've
too easily and irreversibly become disaster, he stopped, just stopped,
having registered the calm, stern sound of his mother's voice amid
the din. He turned and sulked back to her side, as though he'd merely

been refusing to get into bed, entirely unaware of how close he'd come to oblivion. Soon he was swinging himself back and forth from her arm, receiving her corrective with more affection than resistance.

Elizabeth gave a sigh of relief. How well that woman had handled the situation, and yet how reckless to have let it gone that far. She looked at her father, whose expression was so mixed, it seemed to bear the memory of every emotion he'd ever felt. She let her head fall against his arm.

"I've missed you," she said.

"I've missed you, too, kiddo."

"I mean, I feel like I never see you anymore."

He cleared his throat. "This is a busy period in your life. I understand."

She thought of all the nonsense that filled her free hours: the bars, the restaurants, the TV shows. "I would make time if you came to visit more than once a year. Mom comes a lot. If you lived in New York, I'd see you all the time." But even as she spoke she wondered if she meant it. Did she really want him dropping by on random weeknights? Did she want to know him that well? It was the curse of parents that they were never wholly satisfying. If not tyrannical, then neglectful: imperfect governments every time.

He let her rest against him a moment longer. Then he stretched his legs out and raised his arms to the sky, cracking his back in the way that they shared. When he spoke his voice cracked, too, but in an upbeat sort of way, as though the boy's reprieve had somehow extended his life as well. "Sounds like we need to make better use of the phone. What do you say?"

He stood and put a hand out. She took it tentatively. It felt strange to walk away with the falls still rushing, like leaving a performance before it was done. The sound chased after them, teasing them with fading notes from the first of many songs they would miss.

17

H e'd planned to drive to the airport from there, then give her Metro fare home, but their hike had gone more quickly than he'd anticipated, and he still had several hours to kill.

"Let's just go back," he said. "I really ought to say good-bye to your mom."

She tried to stifle the meek little hope that rose up in her throat that he might've inspired himself with his story. Was he ready to get off his boat at last, and find her mother waiting for him on the dock? She didn't think he'd be that sentimental. She was pretty sure she was the only one of the three of them who entertained any fantasies of remarriage. Even hers were fleeting—her mom and dad walking her down an aisle—and embarrassing to boot.

They drove, and the roads that were relatively empty that morning had by now begun to fill. They rounded a bend to cross back over the Potomac River, and a phalanx of cars descended from Maryland on the other side, as if to meet them for battle on the bridge.

"You doing all right?" Abe asked her. "Your mom's worried."

"Oh." She sank into her seat. "Yeah, I'm fine. You know, considering."

"Everything okay with Kyle?"

She sighed, nearly exasperated, as though he'd been pestering her about it all day. "Honestly, Dad, I don't know."

He nodded. "That has to be tough," he said, making her feel a tiny bit ashamed. "I like him. Assuming you do."

She tried a more contemplative approach. "I just don't know if I see myself with him. That's all."

He took a deep, audible breath, his chest inflating. Even sideways, she saw it. "Well, if you can't see yourself with him now, don't marry him," he said. He struck the wheel with the heel of his hand, suddenly fired up. "Because it's only going to get harder. You have to at least *start off* in the same place."

His words stung, like an accusation. "I don't know, Dad," she said bitterly. "People change. Maybe I ought to marry someone I hate, so I can grow to love him. Since you're apparently obsessed with me getting married."

"That's not fair. I didn't say that."

She puffed at a stray strand of hair. "I know. I'm sorry."

"Hey, you asked."

"No, *you* did. I just told you my reservations."

"Well, maybe you don't want my advice. But here it is." They were merging off the highway now. "I told you my imagination has limits, right? Well, that's no good. You have to be able to imagine yourself changing with a person. You have to be able to see that. Because that's what it's mostly about."

His tone was serious. She felt she was being given an assignment, that she'd be letting him down if she didn't turn in a good draft. She closed her eyes and tried to imagine, tried to build a little fantasy for herself and Kyle. She felt his hand on hers in a cab, the smell of him in her nose. It smelled like air, not like anything special. She tried again, thinking of his armpit, the back of his neck between his shoulder blades, the curving small of his back: all the familiar nooks and shelves of him where she most liked to rest. Suddenly, she felt the absence of his body quite strongly, as though he'd been a battleship in her harbor, too massive to get beyond. Now that he was gone, she had the entire ocean. She was virtually floating in all this new space.

She might see him again a few times in New York, to give him back his things: the undershirts and razor that had lived in her apartment. They might reunite for a brief stint, months later, after crossing paths running in Central Park. They might meet up for a casual dinner and drink too much wine while they talked, falling into bed and, for a time, a familiar domestic pattern of bagels and the newspaper, a regular date to weddings, and his razor once again tucked away in the cabinet over her sink. But however it panned out, they wouldn't last. He had made her world safer and prettier, but he'd also flattened it, made it too simple and therefore less real. It was easy to recognize this now without him there to distract her. Painfully easy. She realized he'd already done the hardest thing: he'd left.

ABE DROPPED ELIZABETH back at the house, claiming a sudden errand, then backed down the driveway into traffic. She looked at him quizzically from the door, her neck long, her hair scorching, in so many ways just like her mother. He circled the neighborhood once, then gave up and came inside.

He found Cassandra on the sunporch, under the ceiling fan, with netted glass fishing floats nailed in chains of three to the walls, totems of Howard's ancestry. Abe had always liked Howard, who shook his hand firmly and clapped him on the back whenever they met. He'd made him feel like one of the men—the dependable guys who lifted heavy things and sweated down the centers of their chests. He'd never minded when his father-in-law conscripted him for some task. Even in his forties, he was flattered. His own father, William, was a first-generation law school graduate, a justice seeker in glasses who taught his son to read. Abe was only ten when an armored truck spun into his parents' car on a rainy highway outside Philadelphia, but he and his father would never have retiled a roof together, even if William had lived.

Cassandra was sitting with her back to him, a glass of iced tea on the floor beside her, condensation shimmering at its base. She didn't appear to hear him coming, which made him pause, as though the universe were giving him one last chance to disappear from her life forever. Looking at the back of her neck, he considered it.

In their house in Berkeley, he'd often checked in on her in the hours after Elizabeth's bedtime, the sound of her wheel spinning too loud for her to hear his weight on the attic steps. He'd loved watching the back of her neck bend down over her work, much as it was doing now, like the stalk of a fibrous plant. In those moments, he'd regretted that she no longer had the opportunity to watch him work—and hadn't for years, since she'd quit the clinic and begun working independently as an artist, devoting herself to her clay. He'd felt that in those glimpses of her private labors—her time spent becoming something, and making something of herself—he was only growing to love her more, while she—who could not witness *him* become, and make something of *him*self—was every day unwittingly risking the possibility of loving him less.

But could he really have been so prophetic? Or was it only in hindsight that explanations came forth, too late to have done any good? As a doctor, it had never been easy for him to say for sure which things he had always known, and which he'd only just learned. Not because he was dishonest, or had anything to hide. It was just the way his mind worked. Knowledge came to him regularly like food, sustaining him in an endless succession of meals that he had, in a sense, been eating all his life.

Suddenly, she became aware of him and swiveled her head around. Her eyes flashed like a living statue's over the rattan back of her chair.

"Taking off?" she asked him.

"Eight o'clock flight."

She smiled inscrutably and tilted her head and there went his chance to elude her. "All right," she said. "If I don't say this now, I'll regret it for the rest of my life."

"So say it." He felt his neck clench in weird anticipation. The red, blue, and green buoys seemed to bob in closer to hear.

"I have to know why you left. Why you just—never came back." Her eyes widened, as though she were a surprise to herself. "Is that silly? Is that a ridiculous question to ask?"

She was so forthright that he didn't even miss a beat. "Because I didn't want to deal with the pain," he said. "It's not a silly question. Why were you unfaithful?"

"Mmm, yes, why was I?" She kicked her leg up over the arm of the chair and seemed to genuinely consider the question. "I have never had a good answer for this. I guess I just wanted to. And I truly didn't believe I could hurt you."

"Please." The word cut through the air with a ferocity he hadn't thought he still had in him. But here it was again, that charge of aggression, a primal sort of intelligence. It felt nice. "You didn't care. For God's sake, will you admit to that at least? You never wanted it to work out."

Of course he was right. If she had cared, really cared, they might have ended up in helpful therapy sessions, where they obviously belonged. But there was something too delicious about not caring, about being reckless with the one thing she ought to have cared about most of all—her own life. She had never admitted it to anyone, not even to the therapist she finally started seeing after the divorce, but the moment when he swam away from her was the most exhilarating moment of her life. *Finally,* she had thought, so privately that she wasn't sure her mind had even grasped its own meaning. *Finally, something has happened.*

"You changed," he said. He gave a bitter, giddy laugh, as though it had exhilarated him as well. "You weren't the person I thought you were."

"I'd say you changed. You were the one who left."

Abe flinched, suppressing whatever he was going to say next. He was choosing his words carefully. "I couldn't look at you after what you did," he said at last. "All of a sudden on that boat, I couldn't even bear to see your face."

She understood what he meant. By the end of their marriage she'd found it difficult to look at him, too. But what he had discovered in an instant, she'd been learning over the course of several years. How you could keep looking at a person when, like some bewitched, befuddled Darrin, he'd been recast so many times? How could she look—Abe didn't even have the same face! Not really. It was bloodless and papery with non-emotion, a surgical mask good for nothing but work and sleep. *Her* Abe had been a young medical student with a healthy face to kiss. He'd run through the rain in North Beach to offer her the only shelter he had: a whole universe in that darkly glowing umbrella. He'd have done anything for her. The man she set sail with that final day did most things in life for himself.

His bloodless chin quivered with the stirring of a long-suppressed feeling, and this was perhaps even worse. "I used to love you so much," he said.

"Don't," she said, embarrassed. "I'll only disappoint you again."

Far off in another room of her parents' house, a clock chimed two. In six hours, Abe would be taking off. They used to eat dinner at eight. In later years he spent the hour reading *Alice in Wonderland* and tucking Elizabeth into her bed. They'd seen plays and movies at eight, fallen asleep jet-lagged in East Coast conference hotels, and taken turns waiting for the other to come home from work. These past eights ran together like scenes on a moving diorama, every one of them as real as the approaching one. This eight was yet another they'd spend apart, though perhaps in some way together, each wondering in violet light just where the day had gone.

She shouldn't have put it like that, in terms of disappointment, even if that was what it was. Thankfully, he was still standing there, waiting for her to go on. "Will you call me later?" she asked. "Back home."

"Do you want me to?"

The diorama moved in only one direction. It advanced, leaving old versions of themselves behind. But they were still there on the scroll, just spooled up tight, out of view. She and Abe had made a child together. They'd advanced the scroll, which was probably all the permanence she could ask. On balance, it was more than fair, and anyway, at this point, it wasn't really permanence she sought, but rather the worldlier, more realistic pace of occasionally, of sometimes, of often. A walk through a park side by side. Here and there a play or a movie and then a drink. A conversation that picks up and drops off and then picks up again, no problem. Forgiveness, really. That was what she wanted. For herself, for him.

"Of course," she said.

He sighed and crouched to retie his sneaker, bending forward so that she could see the creamy curve of his skull beneath his thinning curls. He took his time down there, long enough for her to feel that it would be okay to reach out her hand and place it on his head. He shifted slightly beneath her hand, as though she'd managed to pin him in an uncomfortable position from which he wanted to be released. But she held firm and soon he had reexerted his force upward to meet her in her fingertips and palm. She imagined she was an alien, scanning his brain with her hand. The thoughts she would trap, the motivations she would discover. At long last, she thought, she'd know what was happening inside him when he failed to respond to her questions, when his eyes lost their focus and shrank into tiny black pebbles. Of course it was impossible to really know another person, but even now, he was still the other person she'd known the best.

His hushed answer came swimming toward her like one of those fish that inexplicably travels upstream, flouting reason, refusing every natural advantage. Just two measly syllables—"okay"—but she knew she would save them for the rest of her life. When she finally let go of his head, he shivered, as though she'd somehow been keeping him warm.

Part IV

Part IV

18

Of course, she hadn't known at the time that they'd be the last months of her marriage. At the time they merely felt like life, like something to be taken for granted. Which probably should've been her first clue. With Elizabeth coasting through college applications, and Abe long since commanding his own practice, she felt that they had finally arrived. For years she had yearned for the future: as a child for the glamour of high school, as a teenager for the freedom of college, as an unmarried woman for passion, as a married woman for artistic success. She was still excited for her daughter's future, but her own life—certainly her marriage after that early disturbance—had grown remarkably stable, like the knee-high barrel vase she'd labored over years ago, greedily wetting and rewetting her clay as it grew ever more elegant and impressive, now kiln-fired, cobalt-glazed, and—too dear to part with—fully functional, holding all their umbrellas in the hall.

Stable, but somewhat neglected. Cassandra, Abe, and Elizabeth rarely ate family meals anymore, each of them leaving and coming home at odd hours, especially Elizabeth, who was involved in a different school activity every night. During the week, most conversations seemed to take place in pajamas, in pairs rather than all together, a toothbrush in somebody's mouth, the dog's slumbering paws twitching at the end of the hall. Though she still had her attic studio at the house, in those days, Cassandra did most of her work in a space she rented at a community studio, needing, like her husband and daughter, to have a place she had to go.

Flyers circulated the studio regularly, advertising this exhibition or that lecture, some of which Cassandra attended, many of which she felt sorry to miss, but not sorry enough to have attended in the first place. One day in her box she found a postcard announcing the opening of a new gallery in Oakland. From the card stock alone, it was clear that money had been spent. She hadn't heard of the owner—Vincent Hersh—but savvy colleagues were pretty sure he was a New York transplant, and well connected. Not everyone in the building was invited.

"I was hoping you and I could actually have dinner together Wednesday," she told Abe as she slid into bed that night. "But now there's this opening. It might be a snob scene, but it might not. Regardless, I think I have to go."

"That's a shame," Abe said into his book. Not for the first time, he was stretched out on top of the covers, making it difficult for her to flex her feet underneath. It was one of his many habits—like throwing away her *Artforum*s before she was done with them—that had recently begun to irk her. She had no idea whether he'd always done these things or not.

"Do you mind?" she asked, allowing herself to sound just the slightest bit surly. "I can barely move here." He looked at her as though she'd just asked him his name, and for a moment it seemed possible that he wasn't really her husband. She looked closely at the line of his jaw. She'd once seen a TV special about Capgras syndrome, a rare neurological disorder resulting from severe head injury, that causes the patient to believe a person she loves has been replaced by a perfect impostor. She tried to remember, briefly, if she'd ever been in a devastating accident.

Abe lifted his butt, ceding a few inches of bedclothes. "What's

Elizabeth got that night?" he asked, amiably, as if to prove he'd been listening all along.

She relaxed a little and shuffled her toes around under the slightly roomier covers. Ferdinand, who wasn't allowed on the bed, came and rested his chin by her feet. "Wednesday's cross-country," she said. "A race. I really hate to miss it. But then she goes straight to newspaper. Remember, it's press week? There wouldn't even be time to talk to her."

"When has she ever made a big deal about cross-country? She knows there isn't much to see. I don't even think she likes when we watch her run. It makes her nervous."

Cassandra pictured Elizabeth's pale legs at their steady gait, her determined face flushed and boyish with sweat. "That may be. But I'm still disappointed about dinner. Isn't it your one free night next week?"

"Well, what if I meet you at the gallery? Where is it, Oakland? We can grab a bite somewhere."

Cassandra turned on her side, bending her knees into his hip. "Really? You wouldn't mind?"

He smiled but still did not move under the covers. "Why should I mind?"

THE GALLERY WAS located in a renovated livery that had, in its most recent life, been used as a warehouse for remaindered books. The exterior had been painted a chic blue and the interior still retained its original wood floors and beams, the art displayed throughout on soft white walls and pediments. They were early, but already several dozen people banded together throughout the space. In a corner to the left stood a trio of lifelike animals—a cow, a rabbit, and a sheep— each approximately the size of a basset hound and each bearing sets of painfully tumescent teats. A table piled with berries, figs, prosciutto, and cheese beckoned from in front of the sliding garage door while a bar held down the far end.

Cassandra and Abe took glasses of red wine and stood together in front of the cow, which was made entirely of leather and suede. The artist was a New Yorker in her late twenties and had, according to Cassandra's program, already been included in a few significant group shows. Cassandra was beginning to think she'd actually heard of the woman before, so persuasive was the wording of her bio, and so elegant the slim capital typeface the gallery had chosen to showcase her name.

"They really can get like that," Abe said, indicating the cow's udder. "You'd see it at the Virginia dairies all the time."

"I can't decide if I like it or not," Cassandra said, balancing her wineglass as she bent down to check out the udder from below.

"Well, essentially it's a stuffed animal," Abe said, more diagnostic than dismissive. "*Over*stuffed. What's it made of—suede? Right, exactly. A stuffed animal." He seemed ready to write his report.

"Can I offer anyone a bite?" The voice came from behind them and when they turned they were greeted by a hulking, vaguely goofy man in his thirties clad in the slimmest of black suits, his white shirt unbuttoned a few notches to reveal a wantonly hairy chest. He had the bulging eyes of someone who subsisted on speed, a stretched equine face, full ladyish lips, and mucky black hair that appeared deliberately unbrushed. In each hand, he held a square plate of crostini topped with blue cheese, which he raised in the direction of the sculptures. "Loaded question, I know."

"Cow's milk?" Abe asked.

"Swear to God." The man smiled, revealing bright pink gums.

"Well, as long as we're being honest." Abe reached forward to accept the plate. "Thank you."

"Maybe in a little bit," Cassandra said, holding up her wineglass and program. "I kind of have my hands full at the moment."

"Here," Abe said, balancing his plate and glass in one hand just long enough to pluck the nibble from the second plate onto his own. "We can share."

"Good," the man said, satisfied. "Are you liking the show?" He spoke with a whiff of investment, like a host, not at all like a hired waiter.

"We've only just arrived," Cassandra said, "but we're enjoying ourselves so far. The space is gorgeous."

"You're an artist, right?"

Out of the corner of her eye, Cassandra saw Abe smile. He loved when people in the art world recognized her as one of their own, as though it had something to do with pheromones and intuition and not her immediate surroundings. They were in a gallery; everyone was some kind of artist.

"Yes. Sculpture mostly."

"I *thought* so," the man said mischievously. "Vincent Hersh." He held out his hand, which she shook, flabbergasted, her upper arm still pinning her program to her side.

"Cassandra Green. My husband, Abe. But you're so young!" she blurted. "I'm sorry, you must hate that. I know I would."

He laughed. "Not at all. I take it as a compliment." He rocked forward over his pointy shoes, apparently used to compliments, perhaps even feeling entitled to them. "And anyway, I'm not as young as I look." His voice had the cheerful, stoned inflection of the new straight-acting gay generation. Was he gay? She wasn't certain, but she was fairly certain he was exactly as young as he looked.

"Well, it's a wonderful space you have here. You must be very excited."

"Off the charts. We're going to have some excellent stuff coming through this season." He paused and looked at her searchingly. "You said Green? From Berkeley?"

She pursed her lips, used to the assumption by now. "How'd you guess?"

He snapped his long fingers and pointed. "*The Reaching Man*! Culver Reichman."

"That's right!" Abe exclaimed, his wine sloshing around in his glass.

"But how'd you know that?" Cassandra asked.

"They're my lawyers. I stopped to appreciate it just last week when I was there. Man. It's really something." *The Reaching Man* was one of her commissioned pieces. A resin cast painted bronze, it stood nearly nine feet tall in the lobby of the venerable San Francisco law firm of Culver Reichman Sanders and Schmidt. The man was Greek in musculature, but elongated, arms raised toward some vaunted ambition, which he tilted his head back to see. Her client had been extremely pleased. It was just the sort of neoclassicism the partners had hoped would inspire their associate attorneys on the way to the elevator bank, the sort that makes corporations feel human and thoughtful, not to mention supportive of the arts. Conventional, certainly, but she had to admit, well executed.

"Thank you. One of my bigger projects. I mostly do vases and bowls."

"They're lucky to have it. The distortion is just out of this world." He gave another gummy smile and glanced over his shoulder, having apparently reached his conversational limit. A blonde in a blue Chinese dress took his cue, and waved him over from the center of the room.

"I'm wanted. Great meeting you both—Cassandra, Abe. Stay as long as you want. Eat everything." With that, he sauntered off with the empty plate, bending backward in delight at his next introduction as if inspired by the Reaching Man himself.

"I REALLY THINK you should feel good about tonight," Abe said as he drove them home, gaily palming the wheel. "This is proof, as though you needed it, that people know who you are."

Cassandra pressed herself back into the headrest. She'd had too much wine and her head was beginning to swim. "I told you, it's a coincidence. Trust me, I'm not known. I know who the known people are."

"You got invited to this thing, didn't you?"

"Everyone got invited."

"Ah-ha! Everyone did *not* get invited. You said so yourself."

"I only said that because I thought you weren't listening."

"Liar. You said you didn't know why you'd been chosen. Well, maybe now you know. He put together the guest list, didn't he? Face it: he likes your work. And he's a serious curator, even if he is just a kid." They passed under a series of yellow lights, dancing on their wires in the wind.

"Come on," she said. "You saw the barnyard animals, the industrial installations. He's not *really* interested in tame public art. He's a schmoozer." She couldn't allow herself to let down her guard, but privately, she was grateful for Hersh's praise. Certainly, it was better than the sideways bullying to which she'd grown accustomed in her field, the tough love (more tough than love) she knew all too well from her family, which was supposed to make you stronger or make you quit. Preferably, in the art world, the latter. "He's the kind of person who wants to make everyone feel special so that everyone will keep coming to his shows."

"That may be," Abe said. He barely eased off the accelerator as he spun into their neighborhood. "I'm not saying anything will come of this. A solo show at his gallery or what have you."

"Abe—!" she protested, superstitiously.

"I'm not saying that. Maybe it'll happen, maybe it won't. All right, probably not. But even if it doesn't, you should still feel good about what he said to you tonight." He pulled into the driveway and put the car in park. "Because, after all—it's true." He looked so resolutely into her eyes that she had no choice but to look away, at the grit that had collected around the window buttons in the control panel between their seats.

"Is it?" she asked, hopefully. "You don't know."

"Enough," he said, kissing her. "Enough."

SHE SPENT THE next several weeks working on her most avant-garde piece in recent memory, a three-dimensional resin wall hanging of a woman's body metamorphosing into the trunk of a tree. It was Greek-inspired, too, but she didn't think anyone could accuse it of neoclassicism. Photographs taken near her parents' home of sycamores, which, with their peeling silver bark, seemed to suggest a second body underneath, covered the wall above her desk, and she'd brought in a potted fig tree and a basketful of assorted barks and leaves to give her something useful to touch.

Abe had a new project, too. A sailboat. He eased the word into conversation over coffee one Saturday, as though it were the thing they'd been discussing all along.

"The thing is," he told her, dressed in his windbreaker for an excursion that very morning, "we're doing well. Thanks to Helen's austerity, Lizzie's tuition has long been provided for. You're even bringing in revenue without having to teach. Neither of us wants a second house."

"*I* might want one," she said, stung by the assumptions in that casual "even."

He looked at her skeptically. "Well, then that's something we ought to discuss. You've never mentioned the desire before."

"I didn't realize I had to stake my claim! How could I know you were serious about the boat?" she added, somewhat disingenuously. She knew. He'd sailed every other week for years, returning to the house looking happily electrocuted, his face reddened, his hair puffed outward by the wind. He'd dreamed of buying a boat ever since he was a boy, but she'd always teased the suggestion away, pointing out how expensive it would be to maintain, how much easier it was for him to rent. She herself was prone to seasickness, and feared a wreck every time she'd joined him.

"I am serious. I always have been. We wouldn't be discussing it otherwise." The dog passed through the room on his way to a different perch.

"I don't know." She held her mug in both hands, growing tetchier by the second. "It doesn't feel like a discussion to me. It feels like a plan you've made that you're informing me about."

His mouth tightened, holding words back. He had a knack for giving orders, for speaking in a tone that commanded authority, even to her. Early on, she'd clung to his authority, which had felt so much wiser and more reasonable—certainly more loving—than the kind her parents wielded. She found herself approving of everything he said, found herself defending his views to others. Together, they'd built a fortress of agreements, and for years, it seemed as though this were love, the melding of two into one. He stoked the illusion by listening to her speak and valorizing their "discussions." But what were they really? They were announcements, because he was the one in charge. He had poured the contents of his mind into hers, replacing her intelligence with his, revising her memories, and endowing her with new prejudices she hadn't previously held.

"It isn't fair," she said bitterly.

"Fair? What the hell does fair have to do with it?" He flung his hand at the word, as though it were a housefly buzzing in his face. "Christ, I'm only telling you what I want to do. Would you prefer I just went out and did it?"

"It's no different. Can't you see that? I already know what's going to happen now. You're going to buy the damn boat, and it's not going to matter in the slightest whether you told me about it first or not because it certainly won't matter what I think or feel or want."

He sat fixed to his chair, and spoke in a calm, dark voice that threatened at every syllable to explode. "That's a pretty nasty thing to say to someone who's always talking you up. I'm not going to keep coming to gallery openings and bolstering your self-esteem if you're going to keep throwing my kindness back in my face."

"Well, I'm sorry I made you come. I'm sorry it was *such a sacrifice* for you."

A door opened behind them and Elizabeth appeared, shuffling slipper-footed across the tile, rubbing her eyes awake. "Hey, guys," she said. "*Great* start to the morning." She opened a cabinet and reached for a box of cereal, her tiny cropped T-shirt riding up to expose the full flank of her lower back, her saggy pajama pants slipping down below the lacy purple waistband of her underwear. Who, Cassandra wondered, was she dressing for in her sleep?

Elizabeth brought her corn flakes to the table, challenging them to resume their thorny conversation. She'd heard them go at it many times, but knew they preferred to do it when she was, if not out of earshot, then at least out of sight.

"You don't want any fruit with that?" Cassandra asked.

"I'm good, thanks." She grinned between spoonfuls, savoring her role as antidote.

Abe stood to rinse out his mug in the sink, then grabbed his cap from the rack on the wall. "I'm going to get you out on the water one of these days," he said to Elizabeth as he opened the door to the driveway.

"Aye aye, Captain," she said, saluting him.

"I'm serious, you. You're gonna love it. It's better than running."

"It oughta be. Running kinda blows when you think about it."

"Next time, then, okay?"

"*Maybe*, Dad. We'll see."

He regarded her with eyes half misty, half mystified, then nodded at them both. "Bye, guys," he said, closing the door behind him.

Had Elizabeth not been home, and had Abe not been in such a rush, Cassandra knew she might've really made something of the morning. She'd grown to relish her fights with Abe the way other people relished their sports. The best ones tested her limits, remaking her into an extreme version of herself. They were cleansing, and if they were also a little foolish, they were no more foolish than sailing without a destination or running without being chased. The temptation to laugh was always there, particularly when she stumbled on a piece of unintentional alliteration, calling him a "bloviating bore," or when he got profane and called her a cunt. The absurdity of it—being called a cunt by one's husband of twenty-plus years! But if they could agree on nothing else in the throes of battle, they could at least agree to take it seriously and not ruin the seriousness with laughs.

Of course, there were some humiliations, times when she knew that he was right: when he told her she'd become unhealthily obsessed with critiquing a fellow sculptor's work, when she realized mid-accusation that he hadn't actually thrown out her latest *Artforum* (yet). Even then, the war was worth it. Each showdown left her quaking with the power she wouldn't otherwise have known she possessed. Shouting ripped air holes in the suffocating blanket of everyday life. It was a release, and an enactment of their bond. They were both fully present when they were shouting; they were keeping each other alive and holding each other accountable. Really, she never felt as significant as she did when she stood, exaggerating herself in the bedroom, shaking a pair of mismatched socks in his face and telling him he loved no one but himself. These were great, maybe once-a-year moments, moments of mattering intensely in another person's life.

Cassandra watched Elizabeth play with Ferdinand's ears, a thin moon of milk still shining in her bowl. Their daughter had no interest in boats. What was he doing, investing in an expensive toy that was only fun for him?

"Don't look at me," Elizabeth said, getting up for seconds. "I'm almost out of here. You're the one who'd better learn to sail."

CASSANDRA WAS JUST getting back into rhythm after lunch one day, testing paints on a trial chunk of resin, when her studio phone rang— probably Elizabeth, telling her she'd be home late again.

"Cassandra Green," said a knowing male voice.

"Yes?" she asked, cagily, irritated that anyone other than her daughter or husband should know how to reach her here.

"This is Vincent Hersh. We met at my gallery opening a few weeks back."

It was cute that he felt compelled to remind her of who he was; less cute the way he said *my gallery,* as though it were already some famous place. Still, she was surprised to hear from him, having convinced herself, as she'd told Abe in the car that night, that he wasn't at all interested in her work.

"Of course, hello, Vincent. But how on earth did you get this number? They're not supposed to give it out."

"I have my ways," he said in his vaguely airheaded manner. "I hope you don't mind. I have a proposition for you. I'm in a tight one here, and you'd really be helping me out."

Her heart fluttered so recklessly she actually had to clamp a hand down over her chest to keep her stupid hopes in line. "Don't tell me you need a yacht slip," she said, evading him with the first thought that came to mind.

"A *yacht* slip? That's funny. I don't even know what that means. If I were the type—and *believe* me, I'm not—I hope I'd know better than to bring some good-old-boy request to you." The way he pulled the vowels in "believe," she was suddenly certain he was gay. Arrogant and macho, but gay.

She let her hand drop to her side. "It's just that my husband—anyway, long story, but he's thinking about buying a boat and so he's gone ahead and gotten himself a deal on a spot at the Berkeley Marina, *way* in advance, you understand, because that's the kind of guy he is, and all of a sudden people are coming out of the woodwork at the yacht club because they think he has some kind of in. People we don't even like. You excepted, of course."

She heard him chuckle softly. "Especially since I don't even need a—a slip, or whatever. Really, the Berkeley Yacht Club? I didn't think you'd be the type."

"It's not as stodgy as it sounds. It's still Berkeley. And I'm not the type. My husband is."

"Interesting."

"Not really. I sculpt. He doctors. I cook. He sails." She was surprised to hear herself still talking about herself, even in two-word sentences.

"I'm gonna have to hear more about that," he said. "But seriously, I didn't call about the yacht club. Here's the thing. I have a show. It's going up in a few weeks. It's all local artists, and I just had one of them cancel. Between you and me, I'm kind of relieved to see him go.

He was a total diva about everything, making all kinds of ridiculous demands, each of which I met, until he finally decided I just didn't *understand* the piece and he was going to have to take it elsewhere. It was a total fucking shit show. I mean, I never even *saw* the damn thing. Honestly, the more I think about it, the more I think there wasn't a piece to begin with—just a great big fancy idea."

"I'm sorry," she said, not wanting to believe the direction his logic appeared to be taking. "And this implicates me how?"

"I need a piece!" he exclaimed, his voice suddenly faraway, on the other end of the world. "I need one from you."

"What?" she asked. "Am I on speaker?"

There was a pause and the sound of rapid clicking, and then his voice was up close to her again. "Yeah, sorry 'bout that. Needed my hands for a second. Seriously, whaddaya say? Just one piece."

"Well, I don't know." She had somehow skipped over joy and careened straight into terror. "What's the theme? I'm not sure I have anything appropriate."

"The theme is whatever you want! Sorry—you're on speaker again." His voice retreated to almost nothing beneath the thunderous shuffle of desktop papers, while her mind raced through every piece she'd ever made, including the ones no longer in her possession, trying to decide if any of them were snide or weird enough to hold their own in his trendy space. Not the umbrella barrel, not *The Reaching Man*, not even the series of fetuses that might've sparked some sort of dialogue with the trio of barnyard teats. Not that they'd still be around.

Just as she was about to tell him she'd have to think about it, and could she get back to him, his voice emerged again from under the shuffling papers. "Any style of work, any kind of media," he was saying. "Why don't you bring over whatever you select next Wednesday? Or bring a couple pieces if you need me to help you decide. Say, two o'clock at the gallery. Don't worry if you're running late. I'm here all the time." Dead space suddenly filled her ear. He'd hung up before she had the chance to say no.

She stood there, vibrating, the phone still in her hand. In the quiet, she could see now that a good thing had come her way. Across the studio, her soon-to-be tree sat on its mount, guarded by assorted samples and a set of fresh brushes, patiently awaiting her return. How like Abe, she thought, fondly. How like him to make claims he couldn't defend and then have those claims turn out to be right.

"GUYS?" ELIZABETH stood in the living room door, receiving greetings from a sleepy Ferdinand.

"We're celebrating!" Abe shouted over John Lennon. Ferdinand barked, suddenly alert. Cassandra stopped dancing and raised her wineglass in Elizabeth's direction.

"Shh," Elizabeth said to Ferdinand.

"Your mom just landed her new piece in a group show!" Abe slunk his arm around Cassandra's waist and kissed her, half of his mouth landing on her ear and half of it on her neck.

"Yuck, please." Elizabeth closed her eyes. "But that's great, Mom. I guess this is a big-deal show?"

"Ferd, lie down," Abe said in his growly dog-master voice.

Cassandra danced over to her daughter and hugged her sideways around the shoulder. "I think it will be, sweetheart. The curator has an eye for work that gets national attention. New work. It's like I'm finally getting to sit with the cool kids."

"Bang bang, shoot shoot!" Abe sang.

"Want some wine?" Cassandra asked.

Elizabeth flushed. "Uh, thanks, but uh, no, I'd rather not. I'm really so happy for you, Mom, but you have to admit, *this*"—she pointed at her dad shaking his head by the wall of CDs—"is a little weird."

"Oh, honey, you sure?"

"Yeah, I've got applications to write anyway."

"You get dinner?"

"Yep. Bunch of us went out after practice. It was healthy, don't worry. Sushi." She put out her cheek to be kissed.

"Love you, sweetie."

"Love you, too, Mom."

She watched Elizabeth disappear down the hall then turned back to Abe. "She's in her room," Cassandra said, pulling him toward her by his belt.

"I should've gotten us some dope," he said, reaching back to advance the track. He pressed his forehead into hers, his two eyes momentarily fusing into one. "I'm so proud of you," he said, his breath heavy from the wine and a long day's worth of cannabis-related consultations. The referendum on medical marijuana had just passed and now all of his arthritic patients were entitled to the relief of a second slacker youth. "*I'm soooooo proud,*" he said, this time singing it, more or less with the music, in her ear. "*I'm very proud of you.*"

"Yes," she said. "Get us dope." She began to unbuckle his belt and pants, dragging the tips of her fingers across the familiar plain of skin underneath.

He didn't resist, but he didn't press into her either. "*I'm sooooo tired—*"

"Tired?" she said, coyly, as his pants fell to the floor.

He sighed and hugged her tightly to him, forcing her to slide her hands out from between them and wrap them around his unfettered waist. "I am," he confessed. "I'm exhausted." He cradled her head into his neck and kissed her through her hair, while she waited, in that little burrow he'd made for her, for whatever he planned to do next. They swayed there like that to the White Album, longer than she expected, and gradually, gently, she felt his arms hang down on her more heavily, and more heavily still, until she began to feel her lower back tighten and buckle under the transference of his weight.

"Abe!" she cried, shaking him awake.

He jerked upright, unfazed, his arms twitching but not letting her go. "Because," he said, answering a question she hadn't asked. "They wouldn't take the bait."

* * *

THE PIECE WOULD get its own recess on the main floor, behind an installation of giant pikes sticking straight out from a wall.

"I don't know," she said when Vincent showed her the arrangement. "Doesn't it break the flow to have this one here? You have to walk all the way around it," she said, demonstrating.

"Sure, it's unsettling. But then you have this awesome reward!" he said, extending his arm toward her piece, which was on an easel in the middle of the room. She had done the tree in muted, earthy colors that made it look rather real under soft light, then used a series of glitter paints she hadn't worked with much before to highlight a few of the branches and long streaks of the woman's hair and legs. She'd been at it all week, feverishly, positively diseased with productivity, racked with ideas and coughing them up because she just had to get them out of her body. Twice she slept in her studio, away from Abe and Elizabeth, though neither time for long. There wasn't much use in even trying to rest when her brain was infected like that. She yawned now, more at the thought of sleep than out of need. The whole thing had come together so well that somehow, she wasn't even tired.

Vincent stood back in his jeans and fisherman's sweater to bite his nails over the meaning of the piece. "It's just so fucking good," he finally pronounced, the way another man his age might've appraised a batter's swing. "Because petrified wood really does sparkle." He stabbed his finger through the air along the trunk. "The chase story is right there on her face, asking for a million different reactions. And in the end, it's just about the interplay of light in the natural world. You're doing a little Canova, a little Klimt, a little Koons. It's got it all. I knew I couldn't go wrong with you."

"I'm flattered," Cassandra said. She had feared it was a little too Klimt, but was secretly hoping people would choose to like the connection instead of sneer at it. She liked it. Though she didn't quite see the Koons. "You know, it's unlike anything else I've ever done. I don't know how you knew I had it in me."

He looked at her fiercely. "I would've taken *The Reaching Man*—

seriously!—if you could've pried it away from the esquires. But this one is just lights out. Words cannot express." His pants beeped. "Damn, I've got a call," he said, looking at his phone. He was already scuttling toward the office, pointing a long, Neanderthalish index finger back in her direction. "But I'll be seeing you next week. Don't you dare miss it. *This* opening is gonna take it to the house."

He was her patron, so she tried not to hate his insouciance. It was an art he'd cultivated. She could see that. Cool was his business—most of it at least—and she supposed she ought to appreciate that he didn't condescend to her by affecting some kind of formal voice he only used with grown-ups. She'd just have to take it as a sign of his integrity that he always was who he was. Even if who he was was somewhat noxious and fake.

THE OPENING WAS the first week of December. She wore a simple black dress with a long, clinking necklace of red, orange, and deep pink glass. Abe and Elizabeth humored her the entire night, Elizabeth in one of Cassandra's old patterned minidresses because, at the last minute, none of her own clothes seemed cool enough for a gallery. She wore the dress happily with tights, whispering from time to time with a waiter in the corner. It appeared as though she knew him, though Cassandra was fairly certain she did not. There were cocktails and tiny sandwiches in addition to the wine and cheese, and throughout the evening, various mouthfuls passed by them on sticks. When Vincent Hersh, dressed this time in pinstripes and purple, took the floor to thank the sponsors and artists, he extended a long, flamboyant arm in Cassandra's direction, identifying her piece as a particular standout—or, in his phrase, "an absolute trip." Though her ears warmed and clogged at the sound of her own name, and Abe's arm around her waist and Elizabeth's hand upon her arm were just about all she was capable of sensing, she swore she felt the volume of the room rise ever so slightly, as a few hundred pairs of hands clapped a little louder and a few hundred heads turned to smile in agreement with the compliment the ring master had paid. The piece, which she called *Metamorphosis*, sold that very night.

A FEW DAYS after the opening, she dropped by the gallery at lunch to pick up a duplicate book of prints Vincent wanted her to have. "What am I gonna do with two?" he said, having called, once again, on her studio line. "You gotta take it. It's full of stuff with trees. Your name all over it."

He said he'd leave it for her in the office, that one of his assistants would let her in since he was likely to be out. But when she arrived, he was there alone, flipping through slides at his desk, his shoes kicked off in the corner, revealing a surprisingly dowdy pair of woolen socks. "Always gotta be cooking up the next one," he said. He sounded almost sheepish. They chatted for a few minutes about the opening.

"Elizabeth, right? Your daughter?"

"She's seventeen. Don't get any ideas," she said with mock ferocity, still imagining that he was gay.

He held up his freakishly long hands. "Roger that. She your only?"

"My one and only, poor thing. No one else to share the burden of having me for a mom."

"So sayeth the awesome mom. I see through you. You must've been young."

"Ha! Not that young. What do you take me for?"

He said nothing to this, his eyes drifting back to his open binder, his minuscule attention span having apparently run out.

She couldn't help feeling awkward, standing there with her free conference tote bag. "Well, I guess I'll be heading out, then," she said. "The book?"

"On the table."

She turned to where he was pointing and picked up the square white oversize volume. It was the work of a Danish painter and printmaker and it was filled with images of forests that gave the illusion of three dimensions. They were technically proficient but probably not anything special.

"I guess it's my own fault you associate me with trees," she said. "Though it's funny, because I've never thought of myself as much of a nature person."

Once again he said nothing, so she continued to contemplate the image before her, a dark oblong lake ringed with tall, uneven grass, entrancing perhaps in the right light, over the bed in someone's Palisades home.

He came up behind her so quickly that she couldn't even drop the book, needing its sturdiness to cling to as his hand bypassed two shirts and a bra to her breast. The other hand came close behind and they stood there that way a moment, Cassandra holding the book down over her thighs, Vincent holding her upright against him by the breasts, breathing deep breaths in tandem like skydivers preparing themselves to fall.

Then she was facing him and he was inside her, flinging her open, the rest of him stretched naked as far as she could see, his body large and lean but undefined, like an abstract figure of a man. Even when his head disappeared between her legs, he loomed, consuming her. "Please!" she cried, when she came again this way, the only word either of them had spoken.

THE FIRST TIME, then, was not her fault. He'd come on to her strong, and in a moment of surprise and weakness and, you could argue, powerlessness, she'd let herself get carried away. The same could not be said for the second time, or the third, which was just before Christmas, or any of the times after she stopped counting because the actual number was too humiliating to know.

There was no romance at least, just sex—two bodies working out their frustrations against each other, like a pair of competitive tennis partners meeting up for a game at the club. He continued to talk at her in his dude voice, sometimes of business, sometimes of the stray thoughts that seemed to scroll through his mind like items on a cable news ticker. "One lady at a time," he'd said when, after their second tryst, she asked him if he slept with all his artists. "More than that and shit gets messy." He was careful with himself, socially, retaining control in his many interactions, always the one to walk away or end the call, so she was tempted to believe him. Even so, she brought a condom the third time, an act of premeditation that sealed her betrayal, though in her foolish heart, she'd convinced herself that she was bringing it to protect Abe.

Vince, as he now insisted she call him, turned out to be the passionate sort of man she might've expected to want her at twenty-two. Why he'd chosen her now remained a mystery. He was charismatic, of an age and position at which he should've been dating squeaky models and jewel-encrusted socialites barely old enough to drink. She was, she soon discovered from his driver's license, a full fourteen years his senior. Yet in the heat of sex, she never doubted him. He was ravenous for her, unfailingly generous, and eager to show off the pleasure she gave him. A maker of bodies, she didn't find his terribly beautiful. It was exaggerated and, like his face and hair, vaguely comic: his bones large, his flesh lean, so that without the cover of his crisp modern fashions, he resembled an earlier species of man, the hairy kind that hunted with spears and crouched around fire pits in caves. But he also had the energy of a caveman, never less ardent than he'd been the first time, with the strength and cunning to hold her looser, older body at many ecstatic angles when they fucked. It was this, above all, that kept her coming back—to his office, to a glamorously kitschy hotel room he often arranged in downtown Oakland, where they made good use of the mirrors she now understood were meant for sex—once or twice a week throughout the winter.

It wasn't until the third time, the time she brought the condom, that she realized she'd been here before. *Never*, Abe had said. *Never never again*. She was tugging her underwear back on in Vince's office when the memory hit her. That had been ages ago. She'd been another person then, or so she thought. She'd forgotten she was capable of this, forgotten she needed to be on guard. Yet here she was, carrying on an affair. Another one. Apparently, she was a person who carried on affairs. If only she'd remembered, she might've seen the whole thing coming.

"What?" Vince asked when he saw her face. He was still completely naked, sacked out across a Barcelona chair.

"This is so bad" was all she could manage.

"Don't think of it that way."

"But I made a promise."

His eyes drooped. He looked genuinely mournful. "Shit. I know. I'm sorry."

She rushed from his office to the grocery store and filled a basket with Abe's favorite things. Christmas carols shoveled her down the aisles and she felt a bunched-up sensation between her legs, as though she'd put herself back together too hastily, and not everything had settled into place. At the end of one aisle was a giant holiday-themed cathedral of Hershey Bars and Hershey cocoa powder. She stopped before it, wanting it. The very word, so like his name, licked her all over with warmth.

Why? she wondered. Why was her body responding like this? She supposed it had something to do with loving herself, either too much or not quite enough, but the distinction there was too frightening to explore. After so many years of partnership and motherhood, could she really be this self-involved? She hurried to the checkout lane and drove home under an invisible sunset, shrouded by the thick winter sky.

She knew it was perverse that she grew to admire Abe more during that time. She'd been irritated with him before Vince appeared, but now she could find no fault. He was devoted to his patients. He was well-read and wise. He would certainly never cheat. They made conjugal love every other week or so, and each time, she followed his lead, striving to be the exact woman she thought he loved. She quickly gave in on the boat.

Rainy winter became rainy spring, and though she continued

to look forward to her afternoons with Vince, she began to tire of putting on her clothes again when they were done. Everything had stretched in the rush to undress, and she went back to her studio feeling balloony and unaligned, a constant warning of the physical evidence against her. The days had lengthened, too. Now, when she left him, a sturdy, elastic light looked on. It had gone on long enough. Any longer and she was asking to get caught.

"I think this has to be the last time," she told Vince one hotel date in March, after he'd overwhelmed her so totally that his scent—an even but heady herbal cologne—seemed to have carried beyond the walls, rendering the sky through their bay-view window a felted and streaky sage.

He sat up on his sturdy elbows, spread naked on the wine-red coverlet like a game hunter's shaggy bear rug. He nodded studiously. "Sure, yeah, I can see why you'd say that."

She slipped her wedding and engagement rings back on, as she always did once she sensed their encounter was complete. She hated taking them off, but hated even more the idea of them pressing into his skin, fearing they might somehow pick up his scent. "You don't mind?"

"Hey, no better time to walk away than when we're still having fun. We ran a perfect course. No bad aftertaste, no regrets."

His relentless cheer was no surprise, but his failure to protest was. "Jeez, I'll miss you, too," she said, realizing she'd been expecting—even wishing—he'd try to talk her into carrying on.

He laughed. "Are you kidding?" He sprang from the bed and enveloped her with his body. She held her left hand slightly away from him, relieved she was still naked, too. "Look," he said, pulling back to see her face. "I knew this day would come. What can I do?"

"You'll miss me?" She was being pathetic, but at least she knew it.

"Hell, yeah. I'm gonna be stroking it to you for a long time. I'll miss you like crazy."

He *was* peculiar: his intimacy so casual and uncomplicated, his amorality so oddly kindhearted. She inhaled, soaking up his musk and as much of his adulation as she could bear. Any more and she might have been in love. She was dangerously close as it was. "You'll find someone else," she finally managed to say. "Someone barely legal."

"True. And you've got your someone else already."

She wished he hadn't said it, but she couldn't hold it against him. Her real life wasn't the secret.

They buttoned their shirts on opposite ends of the room, surrounded by carnival-striped wallpaper and fleur-de-lis throw pillows they themselves had thrown to the floor. There was a question that had dogged her since that first afternoon in his office—or really, if she was being honest with herself, since he first called her up in her studio. Only fear had kept the question unasked, boxed up in the back of her mind. But what the hell, she thought.

"I have to know. Did you ask me for a piece because you wanted to sleep with me?"

He puffed out his lower lip, reminding her, not for the first time, of the wealthy students she used to teach. "Ignoring the awesome double meaning of that question, no. I wanted to sleep with you because of your piece. *And* your piece."

She still couldn't quite believe him, but she'd been wrong about him in so many ways that at this point, it was probably best to finally take him at his word.

"Just don't be a stranger," he said. Her hand was already on the door handle as he pulled on his boots at the desk. "There's nothing I hate more than burning a good-looking bridge." She envisioned the next time she'd see him in public, amid a crush of well-dressed, track-lit bodies holding wine at some occasion. There'd be a broad smile and a friendly word, perhaps a European kiss on the cheek. He tilted his head now, awaiting her assent. In that throne of an armchair, with the herbal sky steeping behind him, he looked every inch the lucky conqueror, the heir to a decadent continent he would rule for decades to come. In another life, she might've ruled with him, and it might've been a good life, too. She was sorry to go, but she pulled herself together and pulled the door tight behind her.

* * *

A FAITHFUL WOMAN AGAIN, Cassandra focused her energies on being a supportive partner to Abe. She did every extra errand she could think of, relieving him of any responsibility around the house. She went out of her way to seduce him, wearing cleavage-bearing shirts, sidling up behind him at the mail table, where he stood, contemplating winches and life jackets in glossy sailing-gear catalogs. She licked him behind the ear and went down on him unbidden, and told him she'd do whatever he asked. He responded to this with great enthusiasm, his eyes sparking, his breath heavy. He grinned at her mid-thrust, almost boyishly, as though he couldn't believe his good luck. Yet somehow, for all that, he seemed less real to her than ever. When she rode him, she felt detached, as though she'd somehow divided in two, and all the cells that were capable of sensation had gone off with her other self. She had to rely on fantasy, or fantasy-memory. Young Abe lifting her onto the desk at the clinic where they met, a chorus of ailing immigrants watching curiously. Vince turning her inside out in the middle of the gallery floor. Only then could she muster the intensity to come. Try as she might to look forward, her past stayed with her. The Abe she married hovered alongside Vince like an ex, each of them suggesting an alternate life, a life without her current husband. She'd broken it off with Vince, but she hadn't walked away unchanged.

In April, Elizabeth got into Harvard. She had rushed home from school to find the large white-and-crimson packet waiting for her behind the door, calling Cassandra shrieking before she'd even read the cover letter in full. Ferdinand was barking in the background and Cassandra had to hold the studio phone away from her ear to make out what Elizabeth was saying. It was the most excited she'd heard her daughter sound in a long time, and Cassandra grasped only then how badly Elizabeth had wanted to go.

They celebrated as a family with repeated dinners out—Harvard was their excuse for sushi, then for pizza, then for fancy meals in San Francisco. Less than a month later, Abe had signed the papers on the sailboat, a year-old sloop he bought secondhand from a venture capitalist who was relocating to Vail. Abe spent his first few weeks of ownership washing it, purging it of all traces of its original name and having its new name emblazoned on the transom: *Cassandra,* in a slanted purple hand she wouldn't have expected him to choose.

When she saw it, she wanted to cry. "Oh, baby," she said, slipping her arm through his on the dock. "You didn't have to name it after me."

"No other name would do." He had driven her out to the marina to see it in what he believed were the best conditions, in the pale yellow of early morning, under the meshy veil of fog. "This is the start of something new for us," he said. "Empty nesters on a boat."

"I almost can't believe it," she said, thinking of Elizabeth, still tangled in her covers at home, not likely to stir much before eleven. She would graduate in June.

They stood watching the boat dip back and forth on the current, its body groaning against the dock whenever it was nudged too close. The water beyond was all but hidden by the fog, though they could feel it dissipating, even then, through the tiniest of perforations.

"You've been happier," he said toward the water they couldn't see.

She pulled her cable-knit cardigan more tightly around her body, looking where he looked, and leaned into him, not fully comprehending. "When?"

"No, you have," he insisted. "Ever since that Oakland show."

"Oh. Well. It was a big moment for me."

"And you deserved it. I just wish you could get that feeling from sculpting alone."

"What do you mean?"

"I mean you made the work. Even if no one ever praised or bought it, you made it. You make art every day and that's what should matter. It's all that's ever mattered to me."

She pursed her lips as the urge to cry returned. How could she tell him it wasn't enough just to make it? She knew what a fine thing he thought that was—maybe the finest in the world. He wouldn't understand how insignificant it made her feel. She imagined explaining it in terms of medicine. Could a person legitimately and happily be a doctor without ever having helped a patient? Of course not; it was a ludicrous idea. You had to confirm your talents. You had to have success. Though it wasn't a perfect parallel. She knew he'd have something to say to that. He had something to say to everything when he was arguing her into happiness.

"I've got some champagne in there," he said now. "Two bottles, actually. One for the christening, and one good one for us."

She watched a shadowy form come into focus through the fog screen. There was a plaintive horn and then a peal of wings as several white gulls flapped into sight from above. Farther on, down low against the increasingly visible surface of the water, a blazing red prow advanced into view. A lone tugboat, making its passage up the bay to escort tankers in and out of busy harbors. She thought of Vince's buoyancy, his comfort in a crowd, and wondered, with a pang of regret, if she was truly done with him.

"Come on, Cass. What do you say?"

"Do you think we'll have time? Elizabeth's going to wake up eventually."

"Which is why we left her a note. Come on."

Abe stepped aboard and helped her after him, directing her to sit in the stern while he ducked into the kitchen for the pair of plastic flutes and the two bottles he'd stashed in the refrigerator. "You're supposed to do this in front of everyone you know," he said when he emerged. "But I say screw it. This is about the two of us."

With an uncharacteristically exuberant yelp, he fired the cork of the first bottle into the water. She looked around to see if his outburst had alarmed anyone, but there was no one in sight but an older man in nautical stripes, walking away from them on the dock.

"We're not actually taking it out, are we?" she asked him when she turned back. "You would've warned me if we were going to do that."

Abe shook his head and handed her a flute and a folded slip of paper. "These are your lines," he said, growing more animated with each instruction. "Now, I'll give the three toasts and after each one, we'll say these choruses together in unison. In this order here. Got it?"

"Got it."

"Now, raise your glass." She complied, no longer able to resist his infectious energy.

He stood by the mast and began to speak in his best showman voice. "*Hear hear! For thousands of years, we have gone to sea. We have crafted vessels to carry us and we have called them by name. These ships care for us through perilous waters, and so we affectionately call them 'she.' To them we toast, and ask to celebrate* Cassandra." He paused to give her the cue.

It had startled her at first, hearing him hurl her name to the sky. She had to remind herself that she wasn't being scolded, or mocked, or called upon to speak before a crowd. It was just the two of them there with their future, aboard the vessel he'd wanted the most. The vessel she'd finally been able to give him.

"TO THE SAILORS OF OLD . . . TO *CASSANDRA*!" she cried along with him. They clinked their plastics and drank, the breakfast bubbles tickling her nose.

"*The moods of the sea are many,*" he went on, "*from tranquil to play-ful to violent. We ask that this ship be given the strength to carry on. May her keel be strong against the hazards of the sea.*"

"TO THE SAILORS OF OLD . . . TO THE SEA!"

"*Today we come to name this lady* Cassandra. *We send her to sea to be cared for, and to care for the Green family aboard. We ask the sailors of old and the god of the sea to accept* Cassandra *as her name, to help her through her passages, and to allow her to return safely to this shore with her crew.*"

"TO THE SEA . . . TO THE SAILORS BEFORE US . . . TO *CASSANDRA*!"

Sipping once more and feeling the rush of alcohol in her chest, she was grateful to have had her morning grapefruit. She opened her ears to the sound of her name, which still knocked about in her head.

The more it had been repeated, the more comforting it had come to sound and the more genuine her wish for safe passage and protection—for herself, yes, but also for all of them, for the whole Green family aboard.

Abe refilled their glasses and then opened the second, cheaper bottle, which he poured out in doses around the perimeter of the vessel, chanting nonsense syllables as he went. She sipped again, watching him through the curved plastic of her flute, his steady, contained body rippling and doubling like a swimmer's, somersaulting through a current in the sea.

They'd be back here again all summer. She would have to prepare herself for that. She'd discovered, in her life, that she had to prepare herself for many things to which others gave no second thought. Doctor's appointments and all the questions she needed to ask. The packing required for simple overnight trips. Not to mention pregnancy and parenthood: the body that had formed inside her, the stranger she had somehow made.

Even marriage had become a preparation. She was only twenty-two when she'd met Abe. Back then, she'd had no problem plunging right into things. It was only now that she'd known him so long that she had to prepare herself, each day, to be his wife.

He stood at the opposite end of the boat. The morning fog had all but parted, leaving a sandy blue sky washed with a thin, bumpy layer of cloud. A low-tide sky, from which it could sometimes be difficult to tell if it was early morning or late afternoon. Beneath it, he seemed like the tide himself, retreating somewhere alone, leaving her an uncertain beach, strewn with cryptic shells and exposed, wondering who she was without him. Perhaps he'd always been this way; perhaps she was the one who'd changed. She stretched her legs and tried to take comfort in the tides: the low waters, the medium waters, the high waters. The eventual inevitable return.

19

It was nearly dark when Abe's flight took off, and it would be fully dark by the time he landed in San Francisco. Even so, he would come out ahead, something he'd always loved about returning home from the east. Three extra hours. He clicked himself into his seat and looked down the aisle toward the cockpit, where the crew was busying itself with controls. A book on Thomas Jefferson sat open in his lap. He was still a little wired from the week, but he intended to make good use of his time.

He put the book aside on takeoff, and once they were airborne and climbing, he leaned over the shoulder of the woman next to him to look out the window. They tilted over green Virginia countryside scattered with blocky shopping centers, gray cul-de-sacs and highway cloverleafs, and thousands of roving, insectile cars trundling along to their hives. The land rose and fell beneath a gathering breath of cloud, and soon they were clear above the world, every bit of it out of view while they sat suspended on a shelf of sturdy, well-worn white, the sun setting for hours straight ahead.

His seatmate, who'd been watching the ascent as well, turned to him now and smiled. "Do you want to switch?" she asked him.

He leaned back into his own seat. "No, sorry. I didn't mean to hover."

"It's no trouble. I always request a window because I like to watch, but I really shouldn't have this time." She patted her belly, and he saw that she was pregnant. "I'm going to be getting up a lot."

"Boy or girl?" he found himself asking.

"Girl."

She was young, maybe even Elizabeth's age, Elizabeth who was still tumbling, still shifting into the person she'd become. This woman wore a plain gold band on her ring finger and her hair in a large, curly knot. Because he'd just met her, she seemed already to be the person that she was. He wondered if Elizabeth appeared that way to strangers, too. Or if he did, for that matter. Or Cassandra. She had at one time to him.

He switched seats with the pregnant woman, chatted briefly about raising daughters, and eventually turned to watch the cloud face below, now unobstructed. It stretched like an endless mattress. He leaned his head against the cabin wall.

When Cassandra announced she was pregnant, they were living in their second apartment. She had by then begun art school, and he was a third-year resident. Their troubles, it seemed, were behind them. He remembered thinking how he'd once been a guy with friends, and what a comparatively small existence that was once he became a man with a wife.

He recalled her standing in their bathroom doorway and waving the beige e.p.t. box at the bed. She spoke with cautious pride and put a hand on her belly to make sure he understood. Tightly tucked under the covers and exhausted from another marathon shift, he had the sensation that he was an old man, and for a moment he envied the effortless athleticism of her body. He had never seen her exercise, and now here she was, lean, powerful, and invisibly replicating. He would've taken the time to really appreciate his own strength had he realized how quickly it would fade.

"Who are you?" he asked her, making a great effort to point his toes.

"Silly," she said. "Do you think it'll be a girl or a boy?"

"Come here," he said. He stretched out his arms and she dove into his chest, evidently unaware of his infirmity. He rocked her and kissed her head.

"What do you think?" she said. "I bet you want a boy so you can play catch with him. Of course, you'd love a girl just the same—or maybe even more, the way some dads do."

He was spent—how could he ever become a father? It was too late for him; he had no idea what to do. He tried to picture himself chasing after a small person, the back of a little red head bobbing and weaving through some yard. He saw himself reaching, missing, grasping air. An old man left behind. The truth was he'd never really been comfortable among people, never quite understood where they were going. And for a parent that was quite a liability. After his grandmother, who knew something about not belonging, only Cassandra had been able to tolerate his alienness. Cassandra and his patients, because they were uncomfortable, too.

"Oh, sweetie," she said. "Are you crying?"

Of course he wasn't. He wiped the very notion from his face. He slowed his breathing and tried again to point his toes. With a great effort, he brought up his knees, and along with them all the covers she'd carefully tucked.

He cradled himself around Cassandra's body and squeezed, remembering that he was, after all, rather young. He was twenty-eight. He could bench-press his weight and run a seven-minute mile. He could surely catch up with a child. And his wife—his wife was even younger than he was. When she looked at him her face was the world, her eyes as deep and boundless as the sea.

"If it's a girl," he said, "I hope she's just like you."

20

Valeria Gonzalez arrived on a gurney at close to ten that evening. The undertaker who brought her smoked a cigarette in the drive while his guys carried her inside. He was Alvin's friend and colleague: thin and pucker-lipped, like most undertakers, who were ultracareful with their own lives but couldn't survive them without smoking. Nothing kept depression at bay like nicotine, and nothing covered a death stench like the familiar fog of tobacco. It was a necessary evil, an occupational hazard. He maintained a wide stance beside his hearse, waiting patiently while Cassandra shook her pen to sign the forms.

When Alvin Dao called about Valeria, Eunice was already in bed. Howie had answered the wall phone in the kitchen and, not knowing what to do, had walked as far into the dining room as the cord would allow to call for his sisters' advice. Cassandra and Mary came in to listen while Howie repeated the information he was receiving from Alvin on the line.

"He says not to wake Mom, but that someone has to be here to receive the body," Howie said, the curly beige phone cord wrapped loosely around his midsection. "There was some kind of mix-up. An arrangement they'd had with another funeral home fell through, and they need to have her ready tomorrow so they can fly her to Mexico for burial. Even without that, Alvin wouldn't want to waste any time because this kind of heat really accelerates decomposition."

Cassandra squeezed a grotesque vision from her mind. "Tomorrow?" she asked.

"That's what he says." Alvin could be heard insisting on something through the receiver. "He says you never turn a family down," Howie repeated, "even on short notice. He's doing this as a favor to an undertaker in Fredericksburg—" Alvin's voice issued a corrective "—sorry, *Gaithersburg*."

"Well, what do we have to do?" Mary asked. "Open the door?"

Howie nodded. "He'll be here as soon as he can. His friend's coming ahead with the corpse. I mean decedent. Sorry." It was a more respectful word than *corpse*, and all three had known it as long as they'd known words like *senator* and *broadcast*.

"It's going to be a rush job," Alvin said, loud and clear. Cassandra couldn't tell if he sounded irritated or excited at the prospect of such a grueling assignment.

"So you've got this one, then?" Mary asked when Howie hung up—Mary, who was usually the martyr.

He looked at her. "Just because I happened to answer the phone?"

"You know I hate seeing the decedents when they first come in."

"Come on, Mary, no one *likes* it," he said, stretching the gnarled phone cord away from his hip so that he could step over and out of its loop.

"But it'll be easy," Mary said. "Cassandra and I have the kids to worry about." She looked at her sister hopefully. Cassandra had used the excuse before, in various selfish ways. She'd canceled professional appointments to chaperone Elizabeth's field trips. She'd dodged chatterbox colleagues with the claim that her daughter was supposed to call at any minute. But this time, it seemed unfair. Why use Elizabeth against her brother, who didn't have any kids, and—who knew?— might have wanted them once, very much.

"I don't even know where Elizabeth is," Cassandra said. Mary's hopeful look eroded into desperation. A lock of hair fell in her face, making a slash between her eyes.

"Please," she said, heavily, not even bothering to brush the lock away. "I don't think I can look at another corpse this week."

"Again," Howie said, indignant now, "*none* of us—"

"It's fine," Cassandra said. "I'll do it."

They blinked at her. "You?" Mary asked, bitterly. "You wouldn't even look at Dad."

Cassandra winced at this reminder of her reputation: the family wimp. "How hard can it be? It's just opening a door. I'll look away if I have to." The more she thought about it, the better she felt about the decision. She was the oldest. Every now and then the oldest had to take on the burden of everyone else's pain. She felt her chest rise and float a little, like a tablecloth outdoors. It was an unmistakably nice sensation: the levity of goodness. She understood why Mary was so often a willing martyr. It felt good, sometimes, to do the hard thing, and it felt even better when no one else would.

"She's young, but she had cancer," Howie warned. "She's not going to look very pretty."

AFTER CASSANDRA saw off the Gaithersburg undertaker, whose name she immediately forgot, she went into the embalming room where his crew had left the body supine on the porcelain table, still dressed in the rosebud-patterned pajamas she'd died in. Her head sat upon its block like a melon on a stick, her skin a pale, sea-foam green. She was bald, of course, like a wigless department store mannequin. Her toes and fingers were swollen and curled under and her mouth was slightly open, as though she had one last thing to say. Valeria Gonzalez looked old, and at the same time, no more than thirty-five.

Inappropriate though it might have been, Cassandra was taken now with the thought of how unfair it was that Valeria, like Howard, had died the same week that a major catastrophe had seized the nation's attention. Compared with drowning in your home with a thousand other Americans, succumbing to cancer wasn't so bad. Neither was breaking your neck at age seventy-nine. At least Valeria had had time to say good-bye. At least Howard had lived a long life. Neither of them were casualties of government negligence. She thought of how much worse it must have been to have died, coincidentally, on September 11, 2001—in New York City, even. An old lady in a nursing home in Queens expiring peacefully in her sleep, as oblivious to international events as she was to the oatmeal growing cold in her bowl. A drunk man plowing his car into a sound barrier on the West Side Highway in the wee hours of the morning while the towers still stood, and no one but the terrorists and a few befuddled intelligence officers had ever dreamed that they could come down. Could you even mourn such banal deaths in the midst of national tragedy? It had to take a lot of determination to reserve a funeral parlor for a drunk driver when there were martyred firefighters and financial analysts waiting in the queue. But tragic deaths were always more important. One only had to read about the latest plane crash to understand this. The grainy faces of the victims would stare heroically from the newspaper page, as though they'd known all along that this would be their fate. Their career in product management, their recent engagement, their devotion to the Knicks—all mere preludes to this single, defining fact of their lives. You couldn't help feeling guilty you'd survived when you read such coverage. You couldn't help feeling guilty that your dead loved ones had avoided the panic of plunging altitude, shearing metal, and the acrid, unjust smell of fuel igniting into flames. If they'd been aware of how much worse the crash victims had had it, the assumption was, they'd feel pretty guilty, too.

Valeria lay on the table now guilt-free and, if not serene, then at least aloof. Alvin's colleague had closed her eyes, but it would be up to Alvin to wire her mouth shut and relax her shoulders, which were narrow and had tightened upward.

Cassandra stepped closer and leaned over the body, holding her breath more tightly with every inch. Then, as if remembering a trick, she lifted the back of her left hand to her nose and exhaled, feeling the warm, bacterial swampiness of life. Tentatively, she held her right hand in front of Valeria's face, lowering it with care toward her nostrils. Nothing. Another millimeter closer. Nothing still. Any closer and she'd be picking Valeria's nose. Her dead nose.

Cassandra withdrew her hand. She felt brave and in tune with the life cycle. She would be lying there herself one day.

"Boo!" she shouted.

The corpse's right pinky finger moved, making a small brushing sound against the table. A postmortem spasm. To imagine anything else would be insanity.

"Gotcha!" Cassandra shouted, nervously.

Valeria's left eye opened. She was looking at an empty spot on the wall near the ceiling, and she seemed no longer on the verge of speaking. Her mouth had shifted position so that she was now practically grinning at Cassandra, who backed away, all the while telling herself that rictus was just a part of death, and if she couldn't accept that then she really was as weak as everyone had said. She retreated until her elbow touched the doorframe and she was halfway into the hall. The next thing she heard was the mannered tread of Alvin's shoes coming down the basement stairs.

"You didn't have to stand watch," he said when he arrived. He was dressed like a golfer—khaki slacks, polo shirt, cotton sweater vest—and holding a brown briefcase.

"She's moving a little," Cassandra confessed.

"Well, she wasn't about to get up and walk out, was she?" Alvin said, more loudly than she'd ever heard him speak. He brushed past her to get a look. "Aw, she's winking at you!" It came out flat, like an impersonation of banter. He was not the sort of person for whom teasing or sweetness came naturally.

"This won't be hard," he said, after peering down her throat. "I'll be right back." He went off humming in the direction of his office. He swung his briefcase as he walked.

Cassandra looked back at Valeria, who was still winking, her mouth even more open than before, and oblong. She looked almost, but not quite, like an opera character on her deathbed, summoning the breath to form the final note to her final aria. At the same time, it was clear that no breath would ever come.

Alvin returned wearing a monogrammed lab coat, and goggles on the top of his head. He moved with a physician's sense of purpose, picking up where the actual doctors had left off. The words had changed—the woman who was once a patient was now a decedent, and wasn't really even a woman anymore—but otherwise it was the same. A body with organs, just a little bit further along: yesterday dying, today dead. Alvin took a pair of latex surgical gloves from the box on the counter and snapped them onto his hands. He clearly had everything under control. Finally, Cassandra could leave. When she got upstairs, she was going to stick her face in the tin of coffee beans and take a long, deep equatorial breath. If that didn't work, she'd fry a whole head of garlic in a pan.

"Yours are in the cabinet," Alvin said.

"My what?" she asked. He gestured at his head. "You don't mean goggles?"

"Goggles and lab coat, yes."

"Oh no, I'm going upstairs."

"I told Howie my guy's on vacation. One of you has to help." He was busy opening drawers and placing various metal tools on the counter. His voice was even and unconcerned; he expected her acquiescence.

"Well, he didn't mention it to me."

Alvin shrugged. "Regardless."

"But my dad . . . this week . . ."

His eyes were sympathetic but no less relentless. "I know. It's been very hard."

"I've never done this before," she pleaded. "I'm not even licensed! My parents never made me do anything more than keep accounts and answer the phone."

"And that was very kind of them. But you're an adult now, and this is an emergency."

She couldn't believe she was being spoken to this way, as though she really had no choice in the matter. Of course she had a choice. She didn't work for Alvin. She didn't even work for her family. She was an adult.

"It's illegal for me to assist with an embalming."

"Right, because you've never done anything illegal. Spare me. All you have to do is hand me these tools when I ask for them and follow simple instructions. You can't mess this up."

"What's that supposed to mean?"

"If that's what you're afraid of." He blinked at her pointedly. Everything he did, it seemed, he did to make a point.

Cassandra shook her head. She wasn't afraid of messing up. The only thing she was afraid of was Valeria. She didn't want to touch her, or watch Alvin touch her, or look at her any longer than she already had. There might be slime, or dismemberment, or the sudden discovery of rot on the chest—things once seen, she could never unsee. She wished she had a cigarette, or better yet, a joint.

Alvin was now holding out the coat and goggles.

"I'm afraid of her," she said, feeling instantly foolish. Alvin's expression remained blank. He had no sympathy for cosmic anxiety in the workroom. She looked up at the place where the ceiling met the wall and tried very hard not to cry.

"I'm going to start on Mrs. Gonzalez's paperwork now," he said at last, his tone measured, if not tender. "That's a one-person job. You have about ten minutes to find someone to fill in for you. Otherwise, I'll see you right back here."

"Okay," she said, her mind already racing through her options in relief. "I will, I will."

ELIZABETH WAS WATCHING Katrina coverage on mute when Cassandra popped her head into the den.

"Have you seen your aunt and uncle? Either? I have to find one of them for Alvin. He's downstairs."

Elizabeth glanced at her watch.

"I know, I know," Cassandra yammered on. "It's an emergency and I'm just not as strong as I thought I was . . . and well, I won't bore you, but it's a *very* long story."

Elizabeth was still thinking of Teemu and Anya on the San Francisco wharf. She wondered if she should try to call Toby when she got back to New York. Even just to say she was sorry. "Remind me to ask you something later."

"Okay, what?" Cassandra panted.

"Later. Have you been moving boxes? You seem out of breath."

"I am!" Cassandra laughed. "I am out of breath! You couldn't have said it better."

Elizabeth didn't quite get the joke. "Well, anyway," she said, "Dad left."

"I know. We've been talking, actually. I'm sure you've noticed."

"I have." She always noticed. She watched people, and the people she'd watched most were her parents. "I'd been trying not to get excited."

"That's good." The words came reflexively, but Cassandra was saddened to hear herself say them. When Elizabeth was a little girl and still discovering her abilities, Cassandra would never have dreamed of encouraging emotional restraint. Everything was worthy of excitement. It was the same way she'd felt when she first moved to California, when she was really just a child herself. Elizabeth was not much older now than Cassandra had been then, and yet her eyes were already weighted with experience, her attitude resigned. She knew what everyone eventually learns: that it's better not to get your hopes up, not to want or expect too much. She'd learned it from her parents, but unlike swimming or a love of modern art, it wasn't something Cassandra was proud to have taught.

Sprawled on her grandfather's gray sofa, Elizabeth's color stood out more boldly than ever. There weren't many true greens in the world. Cassandra had been looking at people long enough to know. Most were light or dark—pastel yellows and pinks for the happy, easy people; blackish purples and reds for the wicked or sick at heart. You had to possess a special kind of variety to claim a whole spectrum of any shade, let alone one as living as green. But Elizabeth had it. She really did. She was at once fresh and spoiled: a new head of broccoli and a bag of last week's wilted romaine, sharing quarters in the refrigerator drawer.

Cassandra sat beside her and grasped her daughter's hand, wanting to meld it into her own.

Elizabeth's fingers squeezed back, lively as ever. "Just tell me what you need, Mom. I've been a bitch. Just tell me what you need me to do."

As A CHILD, Elizabeth had envisioned time as a never-ending staircase: straight and ascending with a landing here and there. And maybe it was a staircase, if you wanted to see it that way, but it was obvious now that it was also a Tilt-a-Whirl, revolving upon itself so fast that it was all you could do not to puke. Just like light was a particle and also a wave.

For here they were again, in her grandparents' home, and here she was again in a standard white lab coat, just like the kind she wore at the hospital, and once again she was bending over a cadaver, learning something new. With both hands, she kneaded the woman's right leg, imitating Alvin's rapid motions on the arms and neck. Under her thumbs, the muscles relaxed inch by inch, as though finally accepting that they were dead.

Cassandra stood across from her at the preparation table, her hands gently working the woman's other leg, her forehead illuminated by the work lamp, which made her look rather young. Elizabeth worked her way from thigh to calf, glimpsing her white lapel every time she glanced down. The coat reminded her it was time for seriousness, and time to grow up, though she didn't quite know what that meant. When she was a girl, she'd pictured herself somehow catching up with her mom.

When they were done with the postmortem massage, Alvin tucked a piece of cotton under each of the woman's eyelids. "You wear contacts, right?" he said to Elizabeth. He handed her two small round disks. They were opaque and egg-toned, with a bristle of tiny spikes on the top side, and much larger than anything Elizabeth would ever dare put in her eye.

"Same principle," he continued. "Just slide it onto the eyeball, put a dab of this cream on top, and close the eyelid over it—firmly, so it holds. Couldn't be simpler."

Elizabeth followed these instructions while Alvin set about threading a long, curved needle with string from a wall-mounted spool. It all felt very normal. Surgery was like this, though the dead seemed to have it even better. No surgery she'd scrubbed in on had ever begun with a six-hand massage.

"She's a natural!" Alvin said after he'd examined her work.

"She *is* practically a physician," Cassandra said. She was standing back against the counter, holding one hand over her heart.

"Transferrable skills. You could come work for me if your doctor plans don't work out. I'm not saying they won't. Only if."

"God forbid," Cassandra exclaimed encouragingly.

Elizabeth blushed. She was surprised to find herself feeling rather proud to have earned Alvin's esteem. She wasn't sure she'd ever performed a new medical procedure without first seeing it done by someone else. Even then, she often stumbled. For however close she was to becoming a physician, she was still unqualified for everything. It was the nature of medical training that for years, moments of real proficiency were rare—the opposite of her educational experience up until then, which was marked by one inevitable success after another. She'd forgotten how wonderful it felt to demonstrate a skill without much effort or study. For a brief but passionate instant, she wished she'd offered to help her grandfather with his work while he was alive, so that he could've witnessed a triumph like the one she'd just performed.

Alvin sutured the woman's mouth shut with his needle, piercing her first between the lip and gum, then securing the jaw through her nostrils. Before Elizabeth knew it, he was tying off the knot with as much flair as a master costumer securing a bodice backstage. Alvin nodded at Elizabeth, and as directed, she followed up with the mouth former, another perforated piece of plastic, this one resembling the apparatus her dentist had commissioned to stop her from grinding her teeth in her sleep. She slid it into place, topped it off with a dab of cream, and pressed the woman's lips down over it until she was certain she felt them catch. It was somewhat gruesome, but she'd seen worse.

Alvin glanced over his shoulder. He was mixing a chemical cocktail in a contraption that, aside from the giant orange biohazard sticker, looked very much like an old-fashioned kitchen blender. "Right common carotid artery," he said. "Right internal jugular vein. Know where they are, Elizabeth?"

Of course she did. They were right next to each other—neighbors in the neck.

"I need you to access them both for me," he said. "Scalpel and hook are on the counter."

He was as presumptuous as the most arrogant attending doctor she'd ever assisted. But he was right to presume. She knew just what to do. She used the scalpel to make an incision that cut through the skin and no farther. Then, with the aneurysm hook, she pulled back the tissue above the artery and vein, taking great care not to pierce either one.

"Ready," she said.

Alvin came over with a rolling cart that held two tubes and two lengths of clear hose. With the scalpel and more suture string, he fed one tube into the artery, while Elizabeth continued to hold the tissue aside with the hook. He did the same with the vein.

When the fluid began to flow, the corpse perked up, as though coming alive once again. Her veins bulged visibly above the skin and the color returned to her cheeks. She almost seemed to be enjoying herself as preservatives, dyes, and perfume traded places with her blood, which Alvin drained away in regulated pulses from the tube attached at the vein.

"So long, blood," Elizabeth said. She had to admit she was enjoying herself, too.

"She's looking good," Cassandra said, in the supportive but semi-condescending tone Elizabeth and her colleagues often adopted in the hospital. It was the signature tone of the funeral business, too—a wry appreciation for procedure in the face of human suffering. Elizabeth was filled with admiration, hearing her mother speak this way. Her mother, who hated everything to do with death and funerals, was now bravely placing her finger on the corpse's wrist to feel the chemicals flow. *You can do this,* she seemed to be saying to herself, the way she might have encouraged Elizabeth when she was young.

The arterial embalming done, Elizabeth sutured her incision closed, while Alvin instructed Cassandra to remove the paper gown. She did, tearing it into two pieces that she used to cover the breasts and groin, revealing a stony white torso in between. Armed now with a new length of tube, an aspirator, and a trocar, Alvin pierced the abdomen and suctioned off the remaining liquids, this time from the body's cavities. These, too, he refilled with chemicals, releasing into the room a scent of gum like the kind Elizabeth chewed in high school when she was preparing to make out with a boy.

Hours had passed, but no one seemed tired. Alvin screwed a plastic button into the puncture he'd made in the corpse's stomach, plugging her up for all eternity. Cassandra removed the paper censor panels altogether, and the three of them began to wash the body, as if performing a religious bath, then clothed her in the dress provided.

"Now for restoration. Normally, we wait several hours. But time is of the essence tonight."

"He means makeup," Cassandra said.

"Our resident artist." Alvin bowed. "I leave it to you. Cosmetics are in the far cabinet. Remember: always subtle, never dramatic. Just knock on my door when you're done."

He left them there with a snapshot of the deceased and an arsenal of powders, lipsticks, and creams. They looked at the photo, which showed a laughing petite woman posing in front of the U.S. Capitol. Her infinite teeth flashed between red lips and her black, lustrous hair waved in the wind. So she'd been pretty. It was their job now to restore her, make her pretty one last time.

"Always, never," Cassandra said, holding up two bottles of liquid foundation. "That was Grandpa's mantra. I got to be his assistant a few times when I was young. Too young, actually."

"Did Howie ever help him?" Elizabeth asked. "Howie or Mary?"

"Mary . . ." Cassandra said as though trying to recall who she was. "I *think* she did. . . . I don't know. We'd have to ask her." She looked at the bottles in her hands. "Nude or Buff?"

They looked the same to Elizabeth. "Mmm, Buff?"

Cassandra frowned and held the two choices at eye level. "Really, you think? I don't know. I think it might be Nude." She tested a drop on the back of Valeria's hand.

"Wow, you're right," Elizabeth admitted. "Perfect match."

They rubbed moisturizing cream into Valeria's face, neck and hands, then with long, slender brushes, began applying the chosen shade. Cassandra painted the face in quick, crosshatch motions, working the color into something beyond pigment. On the hands, Elizabeth employed longer, smoother strokes, taking care to spread the foundation fully and evenly across the knuckles. She paused several times to wipe excess smudges from the nails, and at one point glanced up to observe her mother's progress.

With the makeup in hand, Cassandra was at home as she hadn't appeared all week—in a genuine state of flow, totally oblivious to how she might look to others. She bent close over the body, her chin doubled, eyes dim and posture slackened in concentration, as though she were transferring her own liveliness directly onto the corpse. Sure enough, as she worked, Valeria's previously strewn features regained their proper positions. Nose and cheek were merging back together; a chin was coming out of the dark. Liner and shadow brought out the eyes, closed and rested. The lips budded with a trace of reddish gloss.

Dustings of blush added an air of amusement, and Elizabeth sensed for the first time the sort of person Valeria Gonzalez might have been: a mischief maker and free spirit who talked too much to strangers, loved helplessly by all. Elizabeth wanted to cry. Nobody made a face like her mother.

Cassandra brushed a final daub of powder onto Valeria's neck and stepped back, regaining her own expression. "What do you think?"

"I wish I'd known her."

Her mother nodded, liking this, spinning the shaft of the brush in her hand. "I have to admit this is probably the best work I've done all year."

"Mom," Elizabeth protested, only to be seized by a sneeze.

"Bless you. I'd never say it to anyone else, but I'm serious! Better than most corpses you see." She set the brush down on the counter, where it rolled, fanlike, until it struck the cotton ball jar. Wasn't it true, she thought, that the body knows from birth that one day it will cave in and die? And so couldn't it be said that every action outward was an effort to leave a piece of itself behind? Every sneeze, every child, every love affair? Every work of art. Every dive into water from a boat.

They topped Valeria with her sleek black wig then peeled off their surgical gloves and took turns washing the chalky dross from their hands. Cassandra had put her hair in a ponytail before they began, and after drying her hands, she shook it down. She combed her fingers through it, feeling the hump that remained where the elastic had been. Strands came out in her hand, as they had since she was a teenager. They curled like broken violin strings and, under the fluorescent work light, appeared red only in painted segments.

She recalled afternoons with her father in this very room, before she'd grown afraid. Much of the equipment had changed from those days, but the cotton ball jar, sitting flush against the wall on the countertop, was the same one he'd always used. It was a stable, fairly girthy cylinder, stainless steel and shiny, having apparently been polished rather recently. There was a lid that clicked free when twisted just so, and the inside was filled more than halfway up with enormous frothy cotton balls.

She looped the hairs around her index finger and waited until Elizabeth had turned her head. Any normal person—and her daughter, God bless her, was normal—would have put the hairs in the trash. But in this moment, Cassandra didn't want to be normal. She wanted to leave her mark. She removed the silver canister's lid and tucked the strands inside.

Shifting her hand back to her pocket, she caught Elizabeth's untroubled glance. Perhaps all daughters were sphinxes, but hers was particularly metamorphic: half recognizable, half not. "You're just like me," she'd blurted countless times, to Elizabeth's great joy as a child, to her great chagrin ever since. But the older Elizabeth got, the more evident their resemblance became, and the more difficult it became to remain silent. Even when Elizabeth disapproved of something her mother did—as she surely would've of this—she did it in a way that Cassandra might've done. Which was not to say that Elizabeth was not her own woman. To the contrary. For all their similarities she lived by a modern clock Cassandra wasn't sure she'd ever understand. She brushed her empty hand against her leg, grateful, at least, that Elizabeth hadn't seen what she'd done.

But Elizabeth had seen. As she glimpsed her mother's hand withdrawing from the jar, she knew that she had tucked something private inside, and she experienced a feeling of acceleration, like coming around the bend of a forgotten favorite song as it swells into the familiar refrain. She had seen her do this before, back when she was a child visiting her grandparents—before anyone had died or divorced or even broken up, in the days in which time alone with her mother was just one of many possible ways to pass a late summer night.

They went upstairs to check on Eunice, another version of themselves. Old as she'd always seemed, Elizabeth knew she'd been young once, too. Twenty-one when she met Howard at that dance, a government secretary living in a boardinghouse not far from Capitol Hill. Though he'd always claimed he was completely intimidated by her, something in him had compelled him to down his drink and cross the floor. And something in her was impressed. Elizabeth pictured them moving together for the first time, he in his suit, she in her gloves, tightly trying out the roles they would play for the rest of their lives.

Now she snored under her bedcovers, mooing faintly, but somehow sweetly. More resilient than either of them, she was already moving on in her dreams. Cassandra switched off the nightstand lamp and closed the door behind her.

Still unready to sleep themselves, they went down to the kitchen to load the dishwasher with all the plates and drinking glasses that had been piling up in the sink all day. After the last of Eunice's prize tumblers had been stationed in the top rack and a shower of snowy detergent mounded up in the plastic dispenser, they sat awhile at the kitchen table with a bottle of red wine Cassandra had stashed away earlier in the week. Elizabeth accepted a glass, but hardly drank from it, while Cassandra leaned forward on her elbow, her cheek resting lightly on her hand.

"Is it over then?" she asked. "Between you and Kyle?" As though Elizabeth had brought up the subject.

The question tired her, but she couldn't blame her mother for asking. She'd seen how desperately she'd wanted to know these past few days, how urgently she'd been restraining herself.

"I don't know. I spoke to him this afternoon." He'd been walking when he answered, and he sounded faraway in her ear, as though a cascading river gorge ran between them. He was on his way to the cop show audition, they'd moved up his time, and the relief in his voice at hearing hers made her want to leap into the river, haul herself across the bony crags and up onto the other side. He was not even angry it had taken her so long to call. He just wanted to see her. She wanted to see him, too, she said, tentatively. Though she knew there were things she had to tell him, things that wouldn't offer much relief.

"So I don't know," she said again. "We'll see."

"Good," Cassandra said, and raised her glass to her lips. The wine caught a strip of light from the fixture over their heads, which cast a rosy wave across her cheek, illuminating the few dilated capillaries that had in recent years become visible. A dryish rim ringed her mouth and her jawline sagged a bit. In general, though, she'd taken good care of herself, and it showed. She wore sunscreen daily, and more of it when she spent time outdoors. She reminded Elizabeth to wear it too, as though she, and not Elizabeth, were the future dermatologist, preparing to devote herself to the surfaces of life.

Stay young, Elizabeth begged her mother to herself, and it was almost as if she'd heard. Cassandra cocked her head like a woman on the prow of a ship, shaking her hair off her shoulder the way a changing sea wind might've done. It wasn't fair that Elizabeth would never get to be young with her mother, or her grandmother, that the three of them would never sit together at a table like this one and conspire to take over the world, each of them hungry and fast, with indefinite time ahead. Elizabeth sipped her wine and let the bitterness of this reality soak into her tongue with the tannins. Well, if they couldn't share time, they could at least share this moment of resignation.

But Cassandra, it seemed, was of a completely different mind. Her eyes were blue-green and open wide, as if taking in an ocean, her hair a red flag of victory, somewhat tattered perhaps, but whole, forever unfurling itself over the waves. Why lament what they could not change? Elizabeth's mother was still as beautiful as a Disney mermaid, which seemed to mean that somehow, it was not already too late.

Acknowledgments

I am deeply grateful to my heroic agent, Jim Rutman, and to my editors, Nan Graham and Mary Mount, for their abiding faith and wisdom. Thanks also to everyone at Scribner, especially my life-lines Kelsey Smith and Daniel Burgess, and to Ulrike Ostermeyer, Szilvia Molnar, Dwight Curtis, and Kelly Farber. Thanks to Allison Lorentzen and Gail Winston, for their indispensable guidance; to the Virginia Center for the Creative Arts, for precious time and space; to my former colleagues at the University of Pennsylvania, especially Lois Chiang and Marcia Longworth, for supporting my double life; to Commander Bob, for his christening ceremony; to the faculty of the Bennington Writing Seminars, especially Lynne Sharon Schwartz, Alice Mattison, and Martha Cooley, who encouraged this book in its rawest form; to my readers Kirk Michael, Jenn Scheck-Kahn, Dave Scrivner, Ross Simonini, Elizabeth Farren, and Kate Marshall, who gave me excellent advice; to Freddi Karp, whose wings are always flapping; to the irreplaceable Barbara and John Hill, who bought me books and taught me to learn and who never, ever doubted; and to all the other outlandishly generous people who have cared and rooted for me over the years, answered my questions, and turned up at my door with dessert. Above all, to Matt Karp, my partner in everything, my constant friend.

He just wanted a decent book to read ...

Not too much to ask, is it? It was in 1935 when Allen Lane, Managing
Director of Bodley Head Publishers, stood on a platform at Exeter railway
station looking for something good to read on his journey back to London.
His choice was limited to popular magazines and poor-quality paperbacks –
the same choice faced every day by the vast majority of readers, few of
whom could afford hardbacks. Lane's disappointment and subsequent anger
at the range of books generally available led him to found a company – and
change the world.

*'We believed in the existence in this country of a vast reading public for intelligent
books at a low price, and staked everything on it'*
Sir Allen Lane, 1902–1970, founder of Penguin Books

The quality paperback had arrived – and not just in bookshops. Lane was
adamant that his Penguins should appear in chain stores and tobacconists,
and should cost no more than a packet of cigarettes.

Reading habits (and cigarette prices) have changed since 1935, but
Penguin still believes in publishing the best books for everybody to
enjoy. We still believe that good design costs no more than bad design,
and we still believe that quality books published passionately and responsibly
make the world a better place.

So wherever you see the little bird – whether it's on a piece of
prize-winning literary fiction or a celebrity autobiography, political tour
de force or historical masterpiece, a serial-killer thriller, reference book,
world classic or a piece of pure escapism – you can bet that it represents
the very best that the genre has to offer.

Whatever you like to read – trust Penguin.